A SLANT OF LIGHT

A SLANT OF LIGHT

Jeffrey Lent

B L O O M S B U R Y   C I R C U S

LONDON • OXFORD • NEW YORK • NEW DELHI • SYDNEY

Bloomsbury Circus
An imprint of Bloomsbury Publishing Plc

50 Bedford Square
London
WC1B 3DP
UK

1385 Broadway
New York
NY 10018
USA

www.bloomsbury.com

British Library Cataloguing-in-Publication Data
A catalogue record for this book is available from the British Library.

ISBN: HB: 978-1-4088-6898-0
ePub: 978-1-4088-6727-3

2 4 6 8 10 9 7 5 3 1

Typeset by Hewer Text UK Ltd, Edinburgh
Printed and bound in Great Britain by CPI Group (UK) Ltd, Croydon CR0 4YY

MIX
Paper from
responsible sources
FSC® C020471

Marion

ONE

THE BOIL OF dust rose from the road still hidden below the curve where the land fell away toward the lake, hidden also by the green stand of Fulton's cornfield between his own dooryard and the curve, but somehow he knew what was coming, could picture the flashy two-wheeled gig he'd not yet seen but had heard more of than he wished. He turned to where his younger hired man stood between the team of mules, holding each by the bridle, and the mules seemed to know what was coming also, both shifting foot to foot, the lines still looped around the near mule's outside hame. They were setting out to make hay.

Malcolm Hopeton spoke to the hired boy, Harlan Davis. "Get me something."

"What? Get you what?"

He'd turned back, could hear the rattle of gravel under the wheels and the snapping trot of a fast horse and the gig came into view, leaping in the heat mirage of the road. Amos Wheeler in a slick suit, hatless, his hair the color of wet clay plastered back with the wind, reining up a blood-bay gelding. Beside him on the narrow seat, squeezed tight, one arm around Wheeler's waist as an anchor against

1

the day, sat Hopeton's own wife. Until this moment he hadn't laid eyes upon her in four years come September.

Later he'd say he couldn't remember what happened next, as if he were back in the worst of the war but in fact he recalled every moment of it. Much like the war itself.

Bethany's black mass of curls was pinned under an oversized hat but wild as ever, matching the glisten in her eye, her lips improbable as a small split plum barely traced with road dust. She called Malcolm's name as Wheeler brought the gig to a stop in the yard. Wheeler wrapped the lines around the whip socket and young and unburdened by any hardships of the past years, came out of the gig with both feet in fancy patent boots and an outstretched hand. Grinning. Only the slip of fear in his eye. Malcolm had seen that countless times in all fashions but it always meant the same thing.

"We done our best to hold things together, Mr. Hopeton."

"You sorry sum of a bitch." Then he was moving fast to the pile of gear next to the empty waiting hay wagon, where he snatched up a neck-yoke evener and came back around swinging it, flailing right through Wheeler's upraised arm and shattering his jaw and the side of his head and popping one eye from its socket.

The mules broke free of Harlan, snorting and farting as they fled for the safety of the barn. Wheeler was dead on the ground, or nearly so, one leg kicking like a dying dog trying to right itself, one hand scrabbling against gravel. Hopeton stepped forward, straddled the man and lifted the evener. There was a cry from behind as Harlan tackled Hopeton, trying to get both arms around his chest, and even in the moment Hopeton knew the boy was trying to save Hopeton from himself. He had the evener in his strong left hand and so drove his right elbow back into the boy's ribs, knocking the wind from him and causing him to stumble back. Hopeton followed and knocked the boy a tap the side of his head and laid him down in the yard. Harlan groaned twice and slipped into a semblance of sleep.

"Oh my Lord in Christ, Malcolm, you've killed them dead," Bethany cried, her voice trailing breath.

She was down out of the gig, the horse tossing his head against the taut-wrapped reins. Someone had trained it well, most likely Amos Wheeler.

"Bethany," he said. "Oh Bet, you ruined yourself and done your best upon me as well."

Even wrapped in the white linen duster and sun hat, she was lovely as ever. Blooming cheeks made more so by the pallor welling over her. Her wide frighted eyes. For a moment he was dulled, the brackish taste back in his mouth, limbs heavy and he dropped the evener. Just so she brought out from under the duster a two-barreled derringer and pointed it at him, the bores alarmingly large in her small clenched hand. Then came the crack and a fire-sear and smack against his right ribcage, the scar tissue there hard as leather from when he'd been pinned against the already trodden bodies with a bayonet two and a half years earlier, his right thumb shot off moments before that. He threw himself upon her, his size and strength all within muscle memory of the countless ways toward survival as he caught her around her waist, pulled the gun from her hand even as he spun in a circle like a dervish, hurling her down near the haying gear, where she landed with a thump and snap as her head struck against the ground.

Amos Wheeler was hitching his way toward the stack of gear, seeking a weapon of some sort. Hopeton jumped forward and snatched up a three-tined hay fork and stabbed Wheeler in the chest over and over until his palms burned from the sliding fork handle.

He stopped. Cupped his hands over the end of the handle and leaned, breathing. The tines in the dirt. He looked over at Bethany.

There was blood coming from her mouth and nose. The duster had come open, revealing a yellow dress with white lace trim over the tight bodice, high-button boots under the long skirts. How small her feet were. Her eyes were open, void, the long gaze of the dead he knew so well.

Sometime during all this the fancy horse had bolted, running itself and the gig against the side of the hay wagon where both were tangled in the side slats.

Hopeton looked up and down the road, to the curve, the one way where all this had come from, to the long flat stretching away in the slow swell of land toward the east where some few miles away it turned down toward the next lake. There was no one in sight. He expected no one. Everyone else would be out doing what he should have been. It could be evening before anyone happened along. He went to work with a heightened crisp efficiency. The task of the moment at hand.

He wrapped the duster back around her, then lifted and carried her around the barn where he laid her on the grassy berm one side of the ramp that led into the upper reach of the barn, the ramp where he'd hoped to unload wagons late that afternoon. Back around to the front where he took Wheeler's legs by the boots and hauled him to the same place but with no care or dignity in placement. He'd taken Wheeler on when he was still a boy, against better judgment and was thus rewarded.

Finally he rolled Harlan Davis over. The boy was breathing but insensible. He carried him into the stable end of the barn and laid him upon a heap of barley straw yellow as sunlight. He went to the stone trough with its steady-dripping pipe from the rainwater cistern, took up the battered tin cup, dipped and drank, then refilled the cup and teased a small amount of water down the boy's throat. A blue and purple clump the size of a walnut stood out from his head over his right ear where Malcolm had clouted him.

Hopeton went back to the yard. He had no plan, as would later be claimed. He untangled the fancy horse from the wagon, led it to his own carriage shed where he stripped the horse out of the gig

4

and harness and left them there, taking the horse to the stable, pulled the headstall off and tied it in a straight stall strung with cobwebs. He hung a bucket of water from a hook and attended to his mules, which were at work eating hay forked down just hours before through the trapdoor in the stable ceiling. With their bits in their mouths they were making a mess of it, long wet strands of half-chewed hay twined with ropey green strings of slobber hung from their lips. He left them at this while he pulled off their harnesses and hung them on pegs high on the wall, then took the Bart mule to the pen, pulled off the bridle, and shut the gate. He turned the Bill mule about and tied a loop of hemp rope over his withers, bit-ring to bit-ring, to function as reins. He left him in the pen also and went to the house.

He didn't know to what purpose but still he went. It was much as he'd found it almost two months ago. The parlor furniture and what she called the dining room mahogany pedestal table and matching chairs gone. Much the same upstairs with only the old shuck and cotton mattresses remaining. The kitchen still held the large range, he'd guessed because either it was too cumbersome to move or as likely no one had the ready cash for such a luxury. The old pine drop-leaf table and ladder-back chairs he and his grandfather had carried into this country were in place. He got his purse with the slender sheaf of weathered bills from the drawer, put his town jacket on over his work shirt and lifted his summer straw from the peg. He left the house with no idea but to get Harlan Davis to Doctor Ogden in the town.

In the stable he took down a sheepskin with the wool still on, outfitted with a rude girth strap and put it on Bill, wool side down, and cinched tight the girth, all the while talking to the mule in the way of a man to which such nonsense words of soothe were second nature. The mule had been ridden many times but that didn't mean he liked it.

Harlan seemed to be breathing easier, eyes still closed but for occasional fluttering lids. Hopeton prayed the boy would stay so for the five miles to town. After some thought he determined the best method was to hold the boy upright before him, fearful if he tried to strap the boy over the mule's back neither mule nor boy would benefit.

It took some doing, Bill backing and forthing as Hopeton got the nigh-deadweight of the boy slung legs down either side and leaned forward with his chest and face in the cropped roach of the mule's mane, but finally it was done, as all things are with mules, knowing beyond a certain level of protest, the man will prevail. Off they went, Malcolm's strong left arm holding Harlan upright tight against him, pressing with his thighs to keep the boy's legs in place, his right hand holding the loop of rope. Once out on the road and turned toward town, Bill settled into an easy long stride.

Harlan fell off the hay wagon and struck his head on a stone. Malcolm's story for the doctor and any passersby met upon the road. Accidents happened all the time. And Malcolm Hopeton knew that any he might meet, known or unknown to him, would know the story of his disgrace, his scandal, his near-ruin, some perhaps in greater detail than even himself. He'd managed to rectify some but far from all since he'd walked up this same road in mid-May. But it did not occur to him that he'd moved beyond rectification of any sort or kind until he stood in the doctor's office after delivering Harlan and the story and proffered bills from his purse—which Doctor Ogden refused, instead looking Hopeton up and down—and Hopeton briefly studied his own blood-smattered clothes not well hidden by the coat open to the summer heat.

He remounted Bill and made his way through the backstreets of town to come out on a westward course where he cut crosslots and along smaller backroads toward Jerusalem, where Bethany and her kind had settled and lived, then northward into the wildlands of the Italy Hills. His destination not vague but precise. To hide.

By late afternoon he was not as close as he'd expected, having made detour onto lesser lanes that wended more than the straighter, more traveled pikes, spooked early on by the stares and gapes of a passing buggy of women headed to town, again by a pair of boys set at gigging frogs in the creek running down the valley to the head of the west branch of the lake. Journeying toward the crossroads scant miles from the farm of David and Iris Schofield. His in-laws, and as such he would be recognized by any passing. Now he was up in the edges of the hills, moving slowly along little better than a path, seven or eight miles from his destination. The mule was lathered from the climb and the heat, the day grown sullen and dense, the bright high clouds of morning changed to a dull leaden sheet toward the northwest, faint rumbling thunder. His side ached where the bullet had nicked him, his missing thumb throbbed and a red scrim edged his vision. Twice he paused at small streams tumbling down through clefts in the woods to allow Bill to drink, sliding off to cup his own hands full as well. It was mostly rough woods here, a tangled mixture of oak and ash, wild cherry, black locust and scrawling nets of wild grapevine with main stems the thickness of a man's forearm, then spongy marshland where the path threaded past beds of cattails, small ponds green with scum and dotted with beaver lodges and muskrat burrows. Deerflies swarmed his neck and the neck and ears of the quickly bilious mule. Hopeton swatted and crushed as he could, the mule assuming this to be only more offense directed its way. And so onward through the long high-summer evening.

The storm came just as dusk fell and also as they came into an older, greater woods, the land more rough with upthrusts of ledge but a more visible path. Thunder and lightning snapped and crashed just above the crowns of the trees and water fell in lashing sheets. Wet dark shot through with slashing moments of green and purple illumination. Bill was restive, throwing his neck about and crow-hopping whatever direction suited him with the lightning, each time almost casting Hopeton off, the sheepskin grown greasy with the wet, the roached mane offering no handhold, nothing for purchase but to clamp his legs hard and stretch his hands as far down the rope reins as he could and haul back the mule's head. Hopeton had spent many a night afield in storms with mule or horse teams, but hitched to heavy wagons mired in mud and slung out for miles with countless like teams and wagons ahead and behind. Such conditions made it more difficult though not impossible for a team to bolt, which was clearly Bill's desire. Hopeton slipped off and led the mule, if the continuous struggle for forward motion could be termed such; nevertheless he kept his grip on the rope and together they weathered the storm. Nearly as sudden as it was upon them it passed off eastward, leaving only water splattering down as it drained from the trees.

Hopeton turned and faced the mule, gripped hard where the reins met beneath his jaw, and said, "Now, you nutless, gutless wonder, we're going to ride again."

Much later they passed through a patch of woods reeking of skunk cabbage and lit here and there with bits of foxfire. As another deluge began Bill came upon a steep bank so abruptly he had no choice but to slide down the wet clay and slippery broken shale, pitched back on his haunches, Hopeton rearing backward as well, losing his fine straw hat but otherwise as smooth a descent as either could hope for. At the bottom was a stream, rushing and churning from the rain. The smell of wood smoke hung low from the weather and on the far side, in an opening in the trees, stood a small dwelling with attached shed. The single window of four panes showed a timid flicker. He jabbed his boot heels over and again into the mule's sides before Bill would tackle the stream, which was finally done with great thrashing and snorting. "As if you ain't already wet," Hopeton told him, sliding down for the final time that night.

Bill allowed Hopeton to lead him partway into the shed, which held a deathly ripeness made more so from the damp, years of winter fur–stripped carcasses and stretched flensed pelts, the summer racks of smoked fish, big lake trouts, pike and pickerel brought up the trails out of the westward-lying Canandaigua Lake. Hopeton still had the rope in hand but had unknotted one side of the bit, intending to tie the mule in the shed, so when Bill threw his all into exiting rather than entering, the rope burned through Hopeton's hand and the mule vanished into the night. He swore like a quartermaster, then made his way out of the shed and alongside the house, feeling the squared logs fitted tight. The window was the far side of the door and he'd not peek anyway. A man could get killed that way. He knocked once out of habit, then found the latchstring out, tugged it, and the door swung open. He stepped inside.

The dwelling was a single low-ceilinged room with a fireplace of blackened stones, a crude table with two sawn rounds of logs for seats, two shelves of cooking and eating mess, a wide rope-slung bed covered with neat folds of layered blankets and bundles of nets and coiled lines hung on the far wall. On the seat between the fire and table sat a well-muscled man wearing deerskin trousers smeared with fish scales that appeared to dance as the firelight rose and fell, a finely napped black wool vest over his naked torso, his head shaved but for a tied-up topknot and long slender mustachios dangling either side of his mouth. He wore a beaten copper bracelet tight on one wrist and was mending a net draped in his lap with a spool of heavy waxed thread and a large needle. A coffeepot of blackened tin sat in the hearth, an empty but greasy spider over dying coals raked also onto the hearthstone.

"Malcolm Hopeton."

"I've lost my mule," he offered.

"And trailed him here, this sort of night?"

"Not as simple as that."

"Coffee?"

"By god, yes."

9

The man made gesture toward the shelf where tin mugs stood. Hopeton helped himself, using a rag hung on a nail hammered between the fireplace stones to lift the hot coffeepot and pour. Steam rose up so sweet and sudden tears came to his eyes. The man remained intent on his repair until Hopeton settled on the upright log the other side of the table, hitching it a bit closer to the fire. He blew on the coffee, burned his mouth with a swallow and set the mug on the table. Only then did the man look up again.

He was a woods-colt son of Gaiänt'wake, the Cornplanter, and a rumored Canadian woman known as Frances Goulet or Golt, both long since departed although Cornplanter, following the destruction of his people's nation, had remained some years in a small hidden village to the south and west, becoming a farmer alongside women, when not engaged in debates of land policy in New York or Philadelphia, or theology with the Public Friend closer to home in Jerusalem. This one alone of his several sons made his own version of his father's life, hermitlike in the woods. John Crow. If he had another name none in the white communities knew it.

John Crow said, "I was out on the water this morning and there was high clouds burned away when sun came over the hills so I pulled my set lines and nets, good hauls anyways and got back to my camp at Rock Glen, set to gutting and cutting out those side-slabs, had my salting racks set and ready when a little wind come from somewhere behind me, from east of there and went out over the water, made a bit of frothy chop and come back to blow cold over me. Maybe nine of the clock." He paused with eyes set on Hopeton.

Who said, "Don't play magic with me."

John Crow resumed mending net. "I like to be where it's warm and dry, comes a heavy rain. That coffee all right? I brewed it for supper but the beans is from last winter."

"I learned in the war to take what comes and be glad when it does."

"And you have lost a mule."

"Just recent."

John Crow nodded. Set his net and mending gear upon the table and said, "The rain has not washed you clean as you might hope. Your war is not ended, is what I think."

Hopeton said, "You have heard what everyone else has. I can't say I came from bad to worst, but more like worst to more worst." He fell silent a moment pondering all John Crow had said. Then continued, "I didn't come seeking you but to find a place to rest quiet. I thought you was at the lake."

"Did you kill the man stole your woman?"

Hopeton paused. Then said, "I did what had to be."

"If a woman is so easily stole . . . Or was she?"

"She'll trouble me no more." Hopeton took up his coffee, his body suddenly thick-limbed and leaden.

"You think not?"

Hopeton shook his head, not to deny the possibility but against his sluggish mind. He said, "It's a cursed day." Then added, "Those people she come from, followers of that Friend person. Her father is a lunatic, the mother little better."

John Crow said, "My father told me the Public Friend was the only white person he ever met, wasn't crazy."

Hopeton shook his head. "I'd not know. Bethany, I knew her better than any other could, I surely thought. Twas Wheeler I miscalculated and that's a fact. I'm in a terrible agony of mind, trying to figure it. Since the war, little in the world makes sense and once you see part of it that way, all else follows."

"It's rest you need. Take the bed. I'll finish my mending work silent as a footstep."

Hopeton stood. He was both rattled and about to fall down. "I thank you for the refuge. And the coffee and offer of a bed. But before I lay my head, I'd step outside to try and spy my mule."

John Crow nodded. "I think you should."

Hours later, Malcolm Hopeton woke to sunlight splintered by the summer leaves but casting through the open door and over the blankets under which he lay in a sweaty knot. Dredged from deep sleep, for moments he did not know where or why he was, thinking it only another bivouac in some abandoned house, slave quarters, the like. Then as quickly the prior day and night returned upon him and he touched fingers to the welt on the scars of his side and groaned, fresh images flickering behind his eyes to join the trove already there. When he moved a deer mouse rose from its nest far down the bed, gazing at him. He made to sit up and the deer mouse fled toward a crack where the wall met the floor and was gone. He stepped from the bed and rocked unsteadily upright. He still wore his trousers and the work shirt, thought then of how he might have made hay and felt the sharp pang—why had they chosen that day to return? Why not one or the other of them, alone? Wheeler he'd have dealt with the same, given the chance; but Bethany . . . ah, Bet. Why'd you not return on your own? Hard questions he'd have had but, he knew from Harlan Davis, harder answers from her. How it all had changed. By riding in together. From fear of him, he guessed and rightly so. He'd answered that question.

His boots were beside a fresh fire in the hearth and a new pot of coffee stood beside them, his empty tin cup as well. He sat and laced his hard-used feet into the boots and filled the mug. This time when he did, he stood more easily, and took himself outside.

John Crow was sitting on a plank bench under the shingle overhang, dressed in the same deerskins but in place of the vest wore a balloon-sleeved bright green open-necked shirt and wound round his head was a turban of faded scarlet.

John Crow said, "A fresh morning."

"Have you seen my mule?"

"First light he was rubbing his head against the door. I tried to catch him but he'd have none of me. I got hold of your rope he was trailing and we danced about the yard a turn or two but I was no match for him."

Hopeton looked, then back at the man. "What direction did he go?"

"Off into the trees, downhill along the stream."

"I'll walk him down."

John Crow stood, put his hands into the small of his back, and stretched. "I think, friend, you should sit here and drink your coffee. I'll walk up the stream to the waterfall and watch out for what happens."

"No, no," Hopeton said. "I'll need my mule."

"He's of no help to you now. Sit and rest. Refill your tin. But it's time I leave, now."

"I don't understand."

"Take what peace the morning offers, friend," John Crow said. "Can't you hear the hounds?"

TWO

AUGUST SWARTOUT WAS not yet thirty years old and stood just under six feet with the muscled body of a man who worked a daily round. Both hair and beard he trimmed short, himself. His features had grown composed through the years of his grief and waiting, alert, sometimes inward-looking but not weighted or grim.

He had all his teeth save for one rear molar that had fallen apart in the starkly dark year after Narcissa died, until the night, his jaw swollen as if he had an apple cupped within his cheek, he drank half a pint of whiskey and stood in his kitchen and used horseshoe nail pullers to clamp the remains of the tooth and pull free the roots from his inflamed jaw. The next morning his head throbbed and his eyes ached as he stood under the risen sun grown huge, worse for the whiskey than the missing tooth, his body chittering with cold from the gusting northwest wind, squalls of snow whirling around his farmyard. It wouldn't be until the following spring when he'd hitch one of the horses to the jog-cart and ride to the Four Corners and hire the girl he knew of to keep house, in the way that he needed. It was not a mystery to him, but rather a fact of life, of how things worked, that the girl was not only known to him but connected in ways to his farm and land, and so to his life.

On the late June morning after he'd delivered his butter to the steamboat and heard the news, he'd slapped the lines against the horse hauling the cart to get them more quickly home, and coming in at a high stepping trot he called out for Becca Davis to tell her the news of her brother, Harlan, already understanding that another unexpected change was entering his life.

He lost his wheat to blight in 1857 but finished building the yellow-block stone farmhouse he'd promised his new wife, Narcissa, who was also his first cousin. They were natural together nearly as brother and sister since they grew up not a mile distant, born the same year. The wheat crop was cash money but otherwise they were not poor that winter, with oats and corn and ample hay to feed the livestock, the growing herd of blooded Ayrshire cattle for milk, butter and cream, the dry new cellar with racks of shelves for jams and jellies from fruit picked wild or the apple and cherry orchard, crocks of pickled vegetables and brined meats. From what he read in *The Progressive Stockman* there should be no fear of the blight returning the following year. So it was a matter of caching money for new seed, which was done by bits weekly as the butter was shipped by steamboat at the Four Corners, where it traveled around the Bluff and then down the Outlet Canal to Seneca Lake and the railhead at Dresden, then south to the Elmira market or north and then east on its journey to New York City. The Dresden broker made the decision based upon reports delivered by telegraph from further brokers in both places. Elmira had the advantage of proximity, New York of premium price. The sacks of wheat seed grew in August's mind as the winter progressed.

Following the Christmas Day meeting in the grand hall of the long-departed Public Friend's manse, a meeting in silence save for when the attorney Enoch Stone stepped to the landing midway between the first and second floors and delivered a homily as muted and brief as the occasion called for, back at their new home with fires burning in the parlor stove and also in the kitchen's great fireplace that would hold logs three and four feet in length, eating a simple supper of bread, cheese and cold ham, she'd turned her round sweet beloved face toward him and informed him that come July they would welcome a new soul into Time. The ideas behind the wording were familiar as her bright countenance, perhaps more so, yet it took a blank moment before he understood the news. That night in bed she told him he'd been drop-jawed as an old woman. He responded by kissing her until she roused toward him, when he stopped.

"What's wrong?" she'd asked.

"The baby," he replied.

"Don't be silly. There's no harm can come to it."

Still he insisted.

He loved her so, and always had. And she loved him, both knowing they were intended for each other by Providence even before the summer they were eleven and were down in the gully between the farms belonging to their brother fathers, grown weary of filling baskets with the wild blackcap raspberries they'd been sent after, and so were on hands and knees making tunnels through the canes, close to the earth so most thorns and the spread of leaves and fruit were above them when they met face to face. Lips, cheeks and chins smeared with juice and she leaned the final inch and kissed him, then both pulled back and studied each other until he pressed forward and kissed her back. They did this for a while and never really stopped, only paused, interrupted by the other demands of day, life, school, season, all those only tipped toward the next hidden encounter, sledding the blizzard-drifted slopes of winter, feeding calves in one or the other barn, finding refuge in the woods or atop the great mounds of hay reached by ladders in the lofts, their breaths commingling and smoking with cold. A hasty snatch behind a door when both families joined for common meals. Until the September afternoon both were fourteen and walking home from the dame school of their people and hand in hand veered wordless from the road where it crossed the Kedron Brook, down among the high sycamores where the mottled trunks reared against the clear cloudless sky, the ground littered with shards of shed bark and yellow leaves, the yellow leaves overhead making a glowing golden world where after kissing she'd unbuttoned his trousers and tugged them down before lifting her dress and pulling off her knickers, then pulling him down and fumbling him into her with her hand. They lay clenched, newly made, mouths hungry. Only when the first swirl of cool air came over them did she speak words.

"We're not celibate now."

"I don't think we ever were," he said.

"You'll have to marry me."

"I think we already are."

Children of the Light of Christ, but also farm children, they knew full well what they were capable of but luck held and they were more cautious, discovering pleasures not possible to the creatures of the field. No one had told them of such things and so they owned no guilt beyond the shared good sense to remain concealed. In not so many years he would wonder just how concealed they were. And they were filled with light, all ways.

Three years later they stood in meeting, from opposite sides of the hall, and announced their intentions. The slender handful of ancient celibates, women all, aligned like so many doves in gray skirts, cloaks and bonnets on the front-most bench nodded almost in unison; celibacy being the preference of the Public Friend but even that personage had not required it of followers, while others spoke of blessings, of new-made lambs of Christ. Finally both sets of parents stood and

17

offered their own blessings upon the union, and in the eyes of the community and by the words of their charter, the two were married. It was less pleasant when they traveled with their fathers to stand before a clerk of the county court for the State of New York, who peered at them with a contempt disguised as curiosity.

"How convenient. You both already bear the same surname."

August's father, Samuel Swartout, said, "There's none to be inconvenienced."

"You and the bride's father, Emmanuel Swartout, you are cousins, perhaps? Of the same extended family?"

Narcissa spoke up. "Sir. We are all brothers and sisters in Christ."

The man worked his lower lip against the inside of his upper teeth swiftly and said, "So my wife reminds me, although I see much to suggest otherwise."

Narcissa had been studying the printed slip with the vows of the state. "This bit here?" she said. "Till death do us part? Can we omit that?"

"Why ever for? It's been used forever."

"Death, one day, shall part us briefly. Our union is eternal."

"No, we'll have the vows recited as the State demands. I leave eternal unions to the hereafter. Beyond that, if your children sprout tails, it's naught to me."

The two brothers bought the farm of the widow Phoebe Davis, which adjoined their own holdings and which they'd already been farming by shares in the years since her husband died and she struggled to raise her own two children. The house was a ruin by then but the barn and outbuildings sound, the pastures fine, mature orchards, fields of rich mellow soil already known to them by hedgerow, fox den, wet spots, the obstinate boulder; which best suited to grains, which to grasses for hay, as well as their own history of rotation, of failure and success. Years earlier, Phoebe Davis had moved down to the valley with her children and rented rooms from an old man who'd lived alone all of his life, eschewing the celibates' rooms and cabins about the manse of The Friend, a man both ferocious in zealotry and pacific in nature who only wanted to live as he believed the Lord intended him, who found solace in the words and wisdom of The Friend but went his own way nonetheless. Albert Ruddle. He'd known The Friend well, sought counsel and doubtless offered his own with the cautious challenge of one sure of his own wits but also not lacking in veneration. As he aged he knew it would be a question if he would be smothered by the collapse of a house he could no longer maintain. Too proud to shed himself of it, too sensible to allow pride to overrun him after a lifetime holding it at bay. He did not take boarders but opened his home to this family in need: He kept them and they kept him.

Up the hill, August's new house rose. Blocks of stone were brought by sledges hauled by four- and six-ox teams from the single quarry that yielded this hard yellow stone a dozen miles away in the still unsettled land south and west, a rough timbered country with no promises of good farmland. During the first explorations of the area some forgotten soul had found the outcrop and a pair of grand homes had been raised from it; August Swartout had admired them since he was a boy on those rare trips to town and when the farm was bestowed he presented well-executed plans for the new home, impressive in detail, and so his insistence upon the building material was accepted. Even those most given to the life of the spirit may indulge their children, perhaps more so when closely twained—not only the children but the builders. And from first vision on paper to the rising courses, knowing they were making a fine thing, pride moderated by knowledge it would withstand fire, great storms, piercing bitter winter winds, any manner of calamity. It would outlast them all. And so August and his father and uncle and male cousins and other men from up and down the valley gave their time that spring, fall, and winter and the next spring, as each of them could, to raise the house that August built for Narcissa.

The spring and summer of 1858 the entire world, at least what small section of it was their domain, seemed given over entirely to fecundity, to increase and gain. Mild weather first came in March, allowing August easy access to pruning the orchards, also getting up the firewood for the next year. The cows bred for summer milking freshened with ease, the calves sturdy and bolting about the new grass come April, which brought enough steady rains to enrich what the March winds off Ontario had dried, then sunlit days with high sailing clouds, if any clouds at all. What plowing he'd not accomplished the previous fall he did now, long days on the new sulky plow with twin moldboards, which allowed him not only to ride, but at the end of the furrow, rather than traveling the length of the headland, to simply lift the one moldboard with its lever, swing the team about, drop the other, and start again on their way. The days were lengthening and he worked them, usually with one of Narcissa's younger brothers sent with a second team to drag the harrows hitched in gangs over the freshly turned ground, breaking the clods and smoothing the surface for planting. By the end of May his wheat, oats and finally the last of the corn was in. And still the weather gave what was needed, stretches of warm sunny days broken by slow soaking rains, the rare passing shower that might send the men to the barns to sharpen plow coulters and harrow teeth, before going out again. They cut hay in the well-drained south-sloping meadow below the orchard the first week of June, the earliest any could remember making hay.

Narcissa grew large in her eighth month, a great mound of belly that she seemed to walk around even as she pushed it forward, her chestnut hair parted in the middle and pulled back into a tight bun to keep her ears and neck open to the cooling air. Her skin had always had an olive cast and took sun easily so by midsummer ever since she was a girl she'd been brown as a hickory nut, this year only changed by her own glow underneath that of the sun, as if she'd captured something of that light and infused her skin with it. She kept great meals on the table at breakfast, dinner and supper for the famished men, mid-morning and afternoon carried a pail and dipper to the fields, the chill well water infused with honey, cider vinegar and spices for vigor. There was no younger sister to help but her mother and his came alternating most days to manage the garden, to launder, to do the few tasks she could not. Only at evening, when August was finally in from the barn and fields, both fed and exhausted, would she sit on the wide porch that stretched along the back of the house, overlooking the gardens and orchard and soak her swollen feet in a tin basin of cold water.

The Fourth of July they traveled to the Four Corners in the high wheeled cart drawn by one of the silver-dappled Percherons, the tail tied up in a bob, fly-netting over the harness against the several hours the horse would stand while they listened to the oratory and the brass band, ate freshly cranked ice cream flavored with crushed vanilla beans and studded with pitted halves of oxheart cherries. It was their sole secular holiday, but for them it had a spiritual side: Otherwise only Christmas Day and Easter were observed as having signal significance. And while the Fourth did not match those two solemn days, August each year pointed out, as if the thought came fresh to him, it was only after the new nation had formed that those such as themselves gained freedom to worship, to gather in praise and contemplation of the Lord and his Given Son, each as they chose.

She had charted her date as falling in the third week of July. Beside their bed was a cradle he'd built from cherrywood in February, long hours in the barn sawing pieces, cutting the fine joints, assembling, and then with hand planes smoothing it to a satin finish, rubbing oil into the wood, then hiding it in the corner of the workshop where he stored odds and ends. In the second week of May she'd been folding washed squares of newly made swaddling cloths when she'd turned to him and said, "You'll have to go to Mother and ask to borrow my old cradle. Unless you'd rather find yours." He'd only nodded and agreed, his manner when facing any minor crisis, but that evening brought the beautiful thing in from the barn. Narcissa had smiled, not surprised although she hadn't guessed, only knowing this was the man she loved, and this forethought of his but a small part of the whole.

The corn was high, pressing toward the roadsides, the oats nearly ripe, the slender stalks with their fragile seed casings bending with the slightest of breezes, the fields the color and tone of doeskin, the wheat sturdier, a sharper yellow, the tight hard bundles of seed topping the stalks like many-sided arrowheads. The fear now was a thunderstorm with winds and hard rain, perhaps hail, that could flatten entire sections of the grain fields. The McCormick Reaper had been oiled and greased, the threshing mill readied on the floor of the barn between the twin tiered stacks of rising hay. Except for all daily chores, there came a small pause.

At breakfast she was pale, a little moist, but it had been a warm night with no breeze pushing through the open windows, where she'd turned in no more discomfort than other recent nights. But he came in for noon-dinner and found her in bed and insensible with skin alarmingly hot to his touch. Both mothers were summoned, other women with age and experience, finally Doctor Ogden was brought out from town. She was bathed with cool water, regained consciousness long enough to swallow tonics of infused herbs, cried out for August then slipped away again, her body convulsing with both labor and wracking spasms of fever. Two days later in a great wash of blood she delivered stillborn conjoined twins and was dead herself by nightfall.

August Swartout did not speak a word for three months. At Christmas of that year when he resumed attending meeting, and most

Sundays after that, he sat silently, his face a dark inward-turned study as if he was asking a question over and over and listening hard for some distant answer to come.

Becca Davis had been keeping house for August Swartout four years when she received word that her brother Harlan had been bludgeoned by the murderer Malcolm Hopeton. August brought the news back from the Four Corners, where, after delivering his butter, he'd posted a notice seeking a man of reliable character to work through the fall with all aspects of the harvest. Wages paid weekly. He always found help this way, more than once young men who'd worked for him years previous, but he preferred keeping his obligations short. The board was the three meals she served up and the bed a small platform with a sleeping pallet above his woodshed, separate from both the house and the barns. Narrow stairs led down for the outhouse, the yard pump. It was six days a week with no certain promise of Sunday off, conditions and needs determining.

The exception was herself, who each day walked up from her room above Malin's store at first light and back down at dusk, in winter the trip both ways made in darkness. Every day except Christmas and Easter, but each of those days she labored beforehand to ensure he'd have whatever might please him. He liked fruit pies but ate whatever she prepared with diligence, thanking her for the food after each meal. Christmas and Easter he ate simply, bread, cheese, a bit of smoked sausage or ham, dried fruit. At threshing time, summer and again in winter, he expected her to feed the crews, and travel with him the following days to neighboring farms with her baskets of breads, stewed meats, pies, jars of pickle and relish. She beat rugs and did laundry. Used a slurry of ash and water to polish the four silver candlesticks, and kept the lamps filled with oil, wicks trimmed, chimneys clean. He called her Becca and she addressed him as Mr. Swartout. And on the last Friday of each month an envelope with her name in neat but crabbed script waited on the cold breakfast table with a sheaf of bills inside, not so few that she felt taken for granted; nor so many as to pop ideas into her head.

Of course like every other person in the county she'd heard the story of what the wife and senior hired man had got up to after Mr. Hopeton had gone off to war. She figured Harlan could hold his own and also assumed the tales were embellished and overwrought. Her own life had informed her so.

So when August Swartout swept into the yard calling her name, causing her to drop a washbasin of water which splashed up onto her skirts, stubbing a toe as she ran outside, she was stunned by his news but more so how he followed it.

He said, "Climb up in here. I'll drive you to town to see your brother."

"You will?"

"There's no one else to look after him, is there?"

"There's not."

"Climb up here," he said again. He extended a hand to help her and said, "And I might stop in at the sheriff or a lawyer to see what I can learn. I know your brother held what was left of that farm together after Bethany Schofield ran off with that other feller. So it might be I'd carry him back there, perhaps leave you with him for a few days—"

She interrupted. "I won't abandon you to fend for yourself."

"Will you get in or shall we discuss the possibilities here, and arrive after decisions have been made?" He gripped her hand and she steadied herself and came up into the cart. She realized they'd never touched, hand to hand. August clicked the horse up and started out of the yard and said, "I can take care of myself for a week or two, if that's what's needed."

The horse moved in a limber downhill trot, holding the cart back, wheels rolling smoothly on the baked road. Corn and grain fields lined the road, stretched away over the curving bowl of land and the glimpse of Crooked Lake south of the Four Corners, the Bluff rising across the water. They passed fields where men they knew were haying. Some looked after them, puzzled by their passing, raising hands in greeting before returning to work. Some few faces here and there followed them long and August knew the word of the tragedy was spreading.

Becca said, "What did he do to Harlan? And how were the others killed?"

"I don't know," he lied. "We'll learn more once we get there."

They passed through the wooded shade onto the bridge over Kedron Brook. Red-winged blackbirds rose from cattails along the brook, mothers above nests in loud alarm. Then turned onto the valley road, not south toward the Corners and the long road around the base of the Bluff but north toward the County House road that was a more direct route to town. They rode without speaking. August Swartout admired Becca Davis and guessed she had no idea he did so. Another girl in her place would've chattered with worry, or pestered him with questions he could not or would not answer. Becca merely watched the day around her, her concern only betrayed by the firm clench of her jaw. The summer after Narcissa died, he'd realized he might make do with part-time help around the farm, but he couldn't do so and keep house for himself without falling into a mild degeneracy, and once he recognized this he knew his wife would not want him to live so. Although after his long silence—which was a meditation not about God, as he knew some believed, but rather how he might live out his span without her, that woman at once forever beside him and yet also a ghost of his blood, an ever more distant sound perhaps but the peal within his ear, always, and knew he would live in the company of others but never not alone. This, he understood, was part and parcel of what The Friend had taught: We exist but briefly in the human form of Time, and then throughout eternity with Christ, and, it followed, he and Narcissa had entered Time together and she would be his bride forever, merely waiting what for her would be a blink, before he joined her. So he brought Becca Davis home, wondering if she might find it odd to be back in the distant memory that was the house she'd left, and that he'd replaced. If so, she never showed it, never spoke of it, never did anything but what he expected of her, not as if she'd been humbled by life but as if walking one foot before the other and doing this well was all life required of her. After her mother died, Becca and Harlan had attended Meeting with Albert Ruddle; but once she came to work for August her attendance was more sporadic. He suspected what mattered for himself also held for Becca Davis. Which was living life by the simple guidelines The Friend offered. That Christ offered. Quietly then he admired Becca Davis. And was grateful for her. This he hoped she knew.

They rose up the eastern side of the Jerusalem Valley and proceeded over the height of land the few miles to town. Here were farms of later settlers out of New England, Pennsylvania, some youngest sons of old Dutch families from the Hudson Valley. There remained the massive home of a sort not otherwise known in the country, three stories high with wide veranda porches and Greek columns rising to the roof overhang, ornate porticoes and huge windows built by a man from South Carolina who had ventured north with a wagonload of slaves to make a new empire in the early decades of the century, an effort short-lived as the slaves melted away to the fastness of nearby Canada. It now stood empty, a reliquary of dreams broken, of other dreams realized. Another southerner of more recent years, a family man from the Tidewater of North Carolina, who'd lost three children to malaria in those swamps, had removed to the town with the remains of his family and built a fine home from the same yellow stone August had used for his own new house those short endless years ago—his inspiration. No small matter that the builder of that house had hired local men, had brought no slaves into the country but for an elderly pair who kept kitchen and grounds and were soon manumitted, resettled to a property along the Outlet Canal with deed in hand, a lifetime annuity administered through the bank. That builder's oldest son fought for the Union until he was discharged after losing a leg from the knee down at Vicksburg and now was reported to spend his days in a backroom of the Elmwood Hotel, playing cards and nipping from flasks with other veterans.

Briefly they could see far down the eastern branch of Crooked Lake, as well as the smudge of Seneca to the east, the land plaited with the green rectangles of fields bordered by darker hedgerows, farm buildings, the barns red and the houses mostly white, then they dropped down into the town at the head of the lake. They passed through a shade-dappled residential section, stopping short as a pair of boys worked head and tail to move a reluctant cow across the street, then onward into the intersecting four commercial blocks. The upper two stories held offices or warrens of cheap boardinghouses, while boardwalks stood between the storefronts and the churned dust and offal of the street, littered with hawking bills, sheets of newsprint, a stove-in derby hat. Storefront windows held dresses on wooden forms, layers of dry goods, a rack of shoe lasts and a pair of finished boots, hanging carcasses of beef, swine, fowl of all sorts. Placards in restaurant windows held scrawled offerings, one had a chalkboard on an easel before the open door. Smells braided throughout the air: leather, sawdust, roasting meats, raw fish, tobacco smoke, stale beer, horse sweat and piss, the sweetness of new hay from a loaded wagon moving along ahead of them. And throughout the movement of people, men in suits or rough clothes, workmen with leather aprons, a printer's devil rushing by clutching a ream of freshly inked advertisement bills, boys with hoops and whips, leather balls, idlers in straw hats, women and girls plucking their way with their shopping bundles wrapped in brown paper. Overhead the nest of telegraph wires, the gaslight lamp posts, swallows cutting the air, pigeons fluttering up from a rooftop to settle again.

"Do you hanker after it?"

"After what?"

"The wonders of town."

"I see all I need of it, visiting the shops, the mercantile. Upon my errands."

They'd come upon the main intersection and he threaded the horse carefully through the knot of traffic, then headed up Elm Street. He said, "Look there. That's the new opera house. Have you heard? Thirty rows of seating, a balcony and boxes around the sides."

She said, "Perhaps. But there are more pressing matters at hand, aren't there?"

"I've not forgotten your brother."

They passed the fire station with the two wagons out front, rigged with ladders, water tanks, pumps and coiled canvas hoses with brass nozzles, the teams in harness but unbridled, bored and switching tails against flies, hot in the sun, the men within the opened doors, sitting in the shade of stifled hot air, smoking, playing cards, reading a newspaper, all passing time. Ahead was the yellow stone mansion set back on a broad lawn; beyond it and over a high privet hedge rose the steeple of the Baptist church, lofty elms hugging the street sides, casting cooling shade, slight air moving, while on the other side ran the iron-railed fence and deep lot surrounding the red-brick two-story courthouse.

He reached to tip down the brim of his hat against the slant of sun in his eyes when she spoke, her voice pitched up. "What's this?"

Around the courthouse was a large cluster of men and horses, a rock-thrown bee's nest of activity about the scene. Farmers and townsmen and a handful of men in dark suits with brass badges on their lapels rushing back and forth in the throng. Off to one side beside a farm wagon stood two men restraining three large dogs on short leashes. From under the large maples surrounding the courthouse and

28

the spread of sparse lawn and gravel that led to the iron fence there drifted a babble of angry voices, demanding and seething.

"What's all this?" Becca asked again

"Hush," August said, and flicked the reins against the Percheron's back. The horse surged into a high trot and they went up the street. Becca remained silent but leaned around to peer back as the courthouse fell from sight. She stayed that way until he made the turn onto a cross street and then slowly righted herself, face forward. Her shoulder brushed his as she did so.

She said, "That was about the business with Harlan, wasn't it?"

He turned the horse once again and the street narrowed, all houses here, with carriage sheds or small barns, gardens behind.

"I'd guess so. Look, there." He held the reins in one hand and pointed ahead.

"What?"

"That white house. That's Doctor Ogden's."

Harlan was resting on a daybed, his head wrapped in white bandages, one eye puffed and bruised the color of old ham. The doctor remembered August and, once satisfied that Becca was Harlan's sister, he offered a short version of events: Malcolm Hopeton bringing Harlan here, the trembling distress of the man and his abrupt departure. While the doctor was still treating Harlan, the sheriff had arrived accompanied by Judge Gordon and they set to questioning Harlan until the doctor put a stop to it.

"They'd learned what they needed. The young man was greatly disturbed by his recollections. I administered drops of laudanum and he's been sleeping ever since. I'd keep him here for the night, though. It was a mighty blow to the head; his brain was rattled and I'd want to see how he is when he wakes, not only later this afternoon or evening, but again in the morning. Then you may take him home with you, if he appears able."

Becca said, "What if they were to come back and arrest him?"

"Dear girl, he was clearly a victim and nothing more. By his own account he sustained his injuries attempting to restrain Hopeton from further violence."

"What did happen?"

The doctor glanced at August, then said, "I suspect the story, truth or not, will be fully out and about the town soon. If it's not already."

August spoke up. "Might it be all right if I were to leave the young woman to sit with her brother an hour or so? If he were to waken it would hearten him to see her, and I doubt she'd interfere with your duties."

Becca quickly said, "I'd be a fly on the wall, it comes to that."

Ogden smiled briefly. "I'm sure, my dear. Of course, August. You have other business to attend to?"

"I do."

"If all were as tight-lipped as you."

August nodded but turned his attention to Becca. "It's best this way. I wasn't thinking, bringing the cart. In the morning we can bring the democrat wagon, with a mattress in the bed for him to rest upon."

She studied him. "But the haying."

He nodded. "It's only getting under way. This evening I'll see if one of my cousins can be spared tomorrow. He could start my mowing, or drive you himself. I'll know better which by afternoon's end. Now, sit and hold your brother's hand. Speak to him. Even with the brain battered, no one can know what the soul can hear and know." Glancing once at Ogden as he said this, and then placing his hat back upon his head, August bid them farewell and went back out into the day.

In the cart he kept the horse to a walk, digging into his coat's inner pocket and drawing out a half cheroot and a kitchen match. He struck the match off the metal strap around the whip socket and drew fire. He smoked and went along. The group surrounding the courthouse had clearly been setting out, not returning. Hopeton could be anywhere, at least by muleback. A four- or five-hour lead was a great distance in all directions, unless someone else had spotted him and come forward with the news. August guessed he'd find the courthouse empty, at least the sheriff's office that occupied the first floor; no doubt all the able-bodied men would be out on the manhunt but perhaps there would be someone about, a janitor or the county clerk. August knew little of the workings of the court other than what he read of court cases in the weekly newspaper. He'd been within the building exactly twice, for the transfer of the deed to his farm and for his marriage license from the state. And what he read of court cases in the weekly newspaper. Yet it seemed the place to start. His instinct of men informed him that Doctor Ogden had divulged all he would. Perhaps it was not within his office to do more.

He turned the horse up the drive and circled behind the building to the horse sheds that lay under the shade of maples old enough to have been left standing when the bricks were fired and the building made. As expected, with court not in session and a manhunt under way, the sheds were empty but for a pair of fancy blue-roan geldings with black manes and tails, working at a pile of hay, tails flagging flies. Next to them, in its own bay, sat a fancy carriage appointed with brass and silver fittings. August pulled up and considered this and then climbed down to tie his own horse in the shed, the horse left standing hitched to the cart. The owner of the fancy team was clearly there for the day. And August knew who that was and guessed he was the man to speak to.

Judge Ansel Gordon wore his hair long, tucked behind his ears and spilling over his shoulders, a neat mustache and chin whiskers adding to his bearing while hiding his tight, thin lips. As with the buggy, he favored displays of his wealth. He indulged in lengthy written decisions and concurring opinions, and was most famous for his declamations when passing sentence.

He was also pragmatic. He could cut a deal against long odds and appear to most all that he'd enacted wisdom and avoided prolonged suffering for the beleaguered. All in all, formidable but human.

August pulled a final long draw on his cheroot and ground it into the gravel. The judge might see easy political hay to be made. Perhaps. But this was not August's concern. For the moment, some questions about Harlan Davis, the plight of Malcolm Hopeton. The parents of the murdered girl were members of his community, not quite neighbors and, truth be told, not but glimpsed for years. But nevertheless.

He walked the long way around to the broad front where a flight of ten granite steps led up to a deep porch fronted by four Doric columns and the high double entry doors. August climbed the steps and turned his eyes to the figure of a man seated in one of a pair of high-backed rocking chairs far down one side, almost hidden in the shade.

Judge Gordon wore a crisp black suit over a boiled shirt and four-in-hand, the pants with knife-edge creases leading to black patent boots, and was bare-headed, his brushed-beaver felt bowler upon one knee. Between his legs rested a walking stick with a brass lion's-head knobbed top, held in place by long, almost dainty fingers on the shaft below the knob, which he twirled in place. He watched August with the curious open stare of one who'd witnessed all manner of men, and the doings of men, and knew no surprises.

Hat in hand, August introduced himself and waited.

"Despite appearances," the judge said, "I'm a busy man today. What's your business?"

"I'm here in the matter of Malcolm Hopeton."

He blinked but otherwise didn't move. "How so?"

"I have interests. And questions."

"Why don't you inform me of your interests and then we'll see if I have answers of any sort."

"The young woman murdered this morning was the daughter of neighbors of mine."

Ansel Gordon studied him a long moment. "Do you represent them in a legal sense?"

"No."

"That's probably best for them. But I have nothing to say about the matter, relevant to them, to you. And I'd guess Esquire Stone will assist them. Isn't he also a friend and neighbor, as you put it?"

"He is."

"There then. Let him see to this business. As for yourself and the Scovalls—"

"The name is Schofield. David and Iris. She—Bethany was their only child."

"The Schofields. I suggest your wife cook them some food. You might organize a work party to attend to their farming duties. The usual fellowship, yes?"

August offered no corrections but said, "The second issue is more complicated."

"Ah." The judge left his hat perched on his knee and cupped both palms atop the walking stick. "Do tell."

"When Hopeton murdered his wife he also, or first, killed Amos Wheeler, who had been a hired man of his for some years. Also injured in the attack was a younger hired man, Harlan Davis."

"The precise chain of events has not been firmly established in the eyes of the law."

"Of course not, sir. But it's commonly said that while Hopeton was off in the war, most or all of his livestock disappeared. I choose my words carefully, since Wheeler's extended family has a certain reputation. There also are rumors that Wheeler, either acting alone or with Bethany's assistance, ran through whatever fortune and other assets Malcolm Hopeton had amassed."

"Mr. Swartout, I've heard all these rumors and more. Where the truth lies is uncertain, which is now the purview of the court. I fail to understand your interest."

"I have a young woman in my employ who is the sister of Harlan Davis. Once he's able to travel I'd bring him to my farm in Jerusalem, so she may nurse him and aid in his recovery. They are orphans; he has no other family."

"There may be a question of the young man's liability, at the least, as the sole witness. However, if Doctor Ogden is satisfied with his condition, I see no reason not to release the boy to your custody. Until the sheriff might inform me otherwise. He makes those decisions; I merely sign warrants."

"I may attend to my affairs by other lights, but I'm not ignorant of the law. If the sheriff had reason or intention to arrest Harlan Davis he'd already have done so, regardless of his injuries. My questions are more practical."

"Would you get to them, then?"

"I'm trying to determine if there are livestock of any sort on Hopeton's farm. One such as Harlan Davis would feel obligation to care for them, regardless of the actions or consequences for his employer."

"The loyal worker."

August only looked at the man and waited. The judge took the gaze, shot his eyebrows and placed his hat upon his head and stood. Briefly he twirled the walking stick and said, "I've no idea of the conditions at Malcolm Hopeton's farmstead. But I'd imagine the boy you seek to champion does. Why don't you ask him? As for Hopeton, we first must find him. Then see if he's brought in alive. I'd think he'd be a most desperate man at this point. By all accounts the story is complicated but the fact remains there are two people killed. I imagine livestock is the last thing on his mind just now. Wouldn't you? Good day, sir."

The judge strolled down the floorboards of the porch and entered the courthouse. The doors boomed shut after him.

★   ★   ★

Out on the gravel drive again August halted and considered the day: the sky still open but the light thinned by a skim of high cloud and the air about him more dense, hotter. Rain moving in. He stood a moment, blinking and feeling dulled, slightly abraded. He was not unaware of the doings of the world but his daily round of work and life occupied most of his mind and much of his spirit, save for such times when the world reminded him of the relentless turmoil of humanity. Such as the quarter hour just passed. He mounted his cart and wished he'd not squandered the half-cheroot earlier; its bracing and clarifying effect would be welcome. He pulled his hat snug on his forehead and chirped up the horse.

He collected Becca. There seemed no change in her brother but Doctor Ogden assured them his pulse was strengthening. He gave August a questioning look, curious about what he'd learned; but when August looked away, Ogden didn't pursue, believing the farmer held a mixture of anger and dismissal of his skills in an equation Ogden had no interest in discovering. Country people, farmers, and other unskilled laborers forgot all else when the doctor failed, however hopeless the situation.

August interrupted this contemplation. "We'll fetch him first thing in the morning. If he wakes please tell him so. And unless his pain is terrible hold back the opium; I'd as soon have him sensible." August already had a hand on the girl's shoulder, steering her toward the door.

Ogden said, "It's not opium."

August glanced back. "Is it not?" Then stepped out and was gone.

The doctor stood a moment, the slap of the door high against his eardrums. That was the problem with the war, and the newspaper hacks; all manner of things were written up but in half-measure, true but not truth, but allowing any skimmer of newsprint the sense they held knowledge. It was a sad world, to work and live in. He walked over and placed his own warm hand on the cool brow of Harlan Davis. Yes, the boy was stable. Ogden made a note in his mind to make

35

sure his wife sent out to the hotel for a pot of chicken broth, then went to the glass shelves, plucked down the little brown stoppered bottle. Rolled it in his palm. Most people were idiots. He'd read parts of *The Voyage of the Beagle*. Now, there was a man.

August lay awake, the night crashing, splintering, rending itself in slabs of swift blanching light. Water poured off the roof, too much for the downspouts to accommodate. At one point he must've slept as he lurched awake when balls of fire raced blue and sparking about his room. Or had in his dream; he could not say. Aware of the girl sleeping for the first time ever under his roof, two doors down and across the hall, he could calculate the cumulative inches of horsehair, blood and sand-plaster walls that lay between them. It had been his idea and now he wondered if the storm kept her awake in her room also. He'd felt none of this unease when, hours earlier, he'd stopped the cart at Malin's store, where she'd collected those things she had to have, bringing them out in a cardboard suitcase strapped together with an old belt and butcher's twine.

The rain fell to constant patters that lulled him down. Beyond a sense of the storm he'd recall none of this in the morning. Except to know no hay would be cut that day.

He was milking in the gray light of dawn when she came into the barn in her best dress of dark navy with white piping at the neck and wrists, hair arrayed atop her head, hooked boots with a high polish. She carried a platter of browned sausages and hunks of bread and a steaming metal can of coffee.

He rested his head against the warm soft-haired flank, his hands pumping in slow alternation. Turned his face slightly to look up at her and the cow lifted one hind foot, then settled it.

She took up a piece of sausage and one of bread, folded them together, and reached it toward him. She said, "I had dreams. Terrible dreams. We have to go soon as we're able."

"I've had my share of those dreams. Not one came true. Mostly, they were after the fact."

"I'm telling you. We have to get going."

He understood and was about to tell her so, opened his mouth to speak and she stuffed in the food. She set the platter up on the open window ledge behind the cow and walked away as she said, "I already hauled a mattress to the wagon. I'll harness the team while you finish up. Mr. Swartout, I'm sorry but I have a bad feeling about all this."

And she was gone. The cow slapped her urine-soaked tail against the side of his head. He resumed milking and started to chew the mouthful of food. It was just what he needed.

With both big horses clipping smartly and the democrat wagon rolling light as air behind, they were approaching town less than an hour later. The sky shimmered like new-washed glass and it was already hot. She was quiet all the way but it was not the contained quiet of the day before. Her eyes roved over the land, not as if she was looking for something but as if she must keep her eyes in motion to avoid whatever thoughts were lying behind them. She kept her hands in her lap, holding a handkerchief she worked through her fingers like a rope, to one end and then back again. After setting out he'd remarked once upon the day but she'd only glanced at him, then away with no response. So he drove the team and waited. She looked fresh, not like someone who has been awake much of the night, so he guessed the dreams had come late and roused her from sleep, leaving a vivid imprint.

As they crested the hill that led down into the town they heard the tolling of bells.

"What's that?" Her voice strung high as if any moment she might jump from the wagon and run on ahead. Or flee backward. "It's not Sunday."

"No."

37

"They've caught Hopeton, is what it is," she said. "Some fool announcing it by swinging on a rope." The words were barely out before she swatted a hand against her mouth.

"I expect we'll see. But Becca, we're here to fetch your brother home. That's our job. The rest is beyond us."

They were headed into the downtown blocks, the horse's shoes kicking up hard swats of mud drying from the rain. The street ahead was mostly empty. She said, "What's beyond us depends a great deal upon what's before us, isn't that so, August."

Not a question. And she'd used his Christian name. He imagined it to be a slip of the tongue, a moment of excitement. He wondered if privately she thought of him so, or as Mr. Swartout. It wasn't important to him either way, except there seemed no method to learn the truth. Time, he reminded himself.

As they came into the center of town there was a flow of traffic, all headed up the street, and they merged with it and were carried along. A clot of people on foot, others in buggies, wagons, on horseback, all crowded the street and overflowed onto the board-walks. Mostly men but a few women, many children, boys racing and weaving their way ahead. Together as a tide they made the turn and carried along past the opera house, August no longer driving so much as holding his reins tight and letting his horses pick the way.

In the street before the courthouse the crowd milled, spreading wide and deep. August's team, eyes walled and necks arched, had come well up and halted.

A procession was advancing down the street. They waited and watched. There was a vanguard of mounted men, three abreast, then came a vehicle, then another, followed by an array of men on foot. From that group the steady clomp of horses and booted men walking. The waiting crowd went silent, ahush and atremble as they knew what was coming.

Becca elbowed August, pointed toward the courthouse lawn. Where a raw-timbered gallows stood unsteady in appearance, the wood white as a skinned apple.

"Will they kill him so easy?"

"I'd think not. My guess is that contraption was built overnight without authority."

The horseback men spread as they advanced and so split the crowd back to a peeled opening. Into which the buggy and following wagon came. The judge rode in the buggy, the sheriff on horseback alongside him. The wagon was driven by a deputy, his hat pulled low. In the bed of the wagon Malcolm Hopeton lay propped against a heap of straw, wrapped in chains, his face bloodied, his arms and upper body mottled with bruises. Once the wagon was stopped, the group of men behind surrounded it, a protective guard. August saw all this and also waited.

It was then he spotted the sorrel mule tied to the back of the wagon.

The buggy had stopped and the judge stepped down, raised a hand and waited for the crowd to quiet for him to speak.

When the hush was sufficient Judge Gordon waved toward the scaffolding. "Whatever that damned thing is supposed to be, it wouldn't stand to gut rabbits from." He pulled a watch from his vest pocket and announced, "It's quarter past nine. It will be gone by ten. If a single nail or splinter remains I'll have the sheriff find out who built it, and throw every law I can find at em. It's an abomination to civilized society. If, time comes, there's any hanging to be done, it will be at Auburn or Ossining. Am I clear?"

He glowered about, not expecting an answer. Then he said, "As you can see we have Malcolm Hopeton in custody. You may go home and rest in peace, by which I mean I want all of you the hell out of here. This is not a circus or spectacle of amusement."

The crowd pushed back a bit, making a larger circle and clearing away from the courthouse steps but not more. No one was willing to miss the chance to see the murderer and none believed the judge had either the right or the authority to enforce his proclamation. Ansel Gordon seemed to expect this as he waved at the sheriff, Byron Taylor, and called, "Bring him in."

Taylor sat on a heavy bay, the horse antsying sideways though he paid it no mind. He said, "You six, get him out. Albright, you ride the other side of them from me."

The elect six moved toward the rear of the wagon, as a man on a white mare made her sidestep closer to them, on the side opposite of the sheriff, who had not yet moved. Two of the six pulled the pins and let the tailgate of the wagon down and then all worked together to lift and drag Hopeton out, holding him upright on his shackled feet. Hopeton resisted, slumping backward and twisting in his chains. Hands were readjusted and then they had him firmly and began to walk him forward, Hopeton in an awkward duck-step. They moved passed the judge's buggy, then came abreast of the judge himself, who stood planted on the courthouse lawn, having ceded authority to the sheriff but not willing to abandon overseeing the operation.

As Hopeton came nearest the judge, he suddenly thrust his head between two of the men and cried, "Make judgment of me, will you? It's a half a man does so and not walked in my boots. Fuck yourselves, all of you."

There was a suck of silence but for the blows the deputies pummeled upon Hopeton, and Becca said in a low voice, "That's an awful thing." Before August could respond, someone jeered, then others shouted curses, taunts and a sewage of obscenities, causing the sheriff to wheel his big horse about in a circle as he drew his pistol from his belt and discharged it in the air. Silence fell once more and the crowd began to fall away as the clump of men worked their charge up toward the courthouse.

August sat a moment longer, looking at the judge, who stood unmoved, smiling after Hopeton, his eyes dark and bright as stones of night. Then August flicked the reins and the team moved forward. They passed the wagon, the old hay fouled with blood. He studied the mule, which stood with its head up, ears pricked high, seeming to also watch as his master was hauled up the steps and then went out of sight in the dark behind the doors.

"Let's see how your brother is." He clucked the horses up into the still-bright morning.

THREE

HARLAN SLEPT THE whole ride home and much of the afternoon. August guessed Dr. Ogden had drugged him and decided that wasn't a bad thing. By the time Becca and August got the boy into bed and settled, August's cousin Marsh was already out mowing the first of his hayfields with his sickle-bar mower. August hitched his own and by milking time they had that field and half of another down in broad swathes. Marsh rode home, leaving August to clatter into his own yard to find Harlan Davis sitting in a straight-back chair on the porch. Harlan made his way down into the yard, where he helped unhook the team. The bruise around his eye was even darker but the eye was clear and the lump above his ear stood through his hair.

August called, from the near side of the team, "Don't you be doing that."

"I reckon I can. I got a bump on the head is all."

"Don't rush things. You've been through a rough patch."

"I'm not the only one. Is there any news of Mr. Hopeton?"

"Your sister and I saw him brought in this morning, on our way to get you."

42

"You did?"

"Indeed. It was not a pretty sight but he appeared hale enough. You go back up to the house now and let me get my work done. There's time to talk this evening."

The team was free of the machine and August drove them off to the barn, where he had to feed and milk. He felt Harlan's eyes upon him but did not look back.

Later they sat together and ate supper: an old hen Becca had quartered, battered and fried in lard, along with shelled peas and yellow snap beans, radishes and scallions dipped in salt, red chard boiled with salt pork, lettuces drizzled with sour cream and cider vinegar, and beaten biscuits pulled hot from the oven, with butter and honey. After, with coffee, a strawberry pie. He admired her industry after such a day, knew she was not only reminding him she was capable but also feeding her brother.

Once the plates were cleared and all were sipping coffee, Harlan said, "Mr. Swartout, I'm awful grateful for what you done for my sister here, these years. And also for taking me in, in my hour of need. I'll make it worth your while and be out of your hair first chance I get."

August rose and went to the high shelf over the mantle where he kept the tin box, took out a new cheroot, struck fire to it and blew smoke into the late light of the day, and said, "You landed here for reasons beyond your sister working for me. I can't tell what those are because I don't know em yet, anymore than you do. But they will come clear. Patience, is what I'm saying, Harlan Davis. Patience and welcome."

Harlan said, "Seems the first thing is to learn what to do for Mr. Hopeton. His farm."

"I'd guess nothing at the moment. The law will be all wrapped up with that place. I'd hazard a lawyer will be along to speak with you at some point. Perhaps the judge. I don't know."

43

"Amos Wheeler was a evil man. People need to know that much." Then he said, "I'm not in any trouble, am I?"

"I'd think not, otherwise you wouldn't be where you are. There will be questions about why you stuck it out so long at Hopeton's, though."

"I had my reasons."

"I'm certain you did."

Harlan stood and went to the Dutch door and looked out upon the falling dusk of the yard. Then turned and said, "I believe I need to try and see Mr. Hopeton. If they'll let me. I'll talk to the judge, if that's what it takes."

August considered this, all the way around. Then said, "I take my butter to the landing at the Four Corners the morning after next. You could catch that boat to town and the mail boat or the noon boat back. I'd go along if I could, to sit with you and the judge, to help remember what was said. But I can't. I got hay down."

Harlan said, "I know you do. And I'll get back quick as I can to help with it. I will."

August said, wanting to lessen the weight upon the boy, "You're in a good place to get healed best you can and should get on to bed and do that. The morrow will bring what it brings, and the day after also. Becca, can you light him a candle for the stairs?"

Late the next morning August and Marsh were back in the fields, Marsh raking with his team and August on foot, pulling stray bits of hay to the windrows with a bull rake. He looked up from his work to watch his dappled team hitched to a wagon coming down the field with Harlan driving and beside him, hay fork in hand, Becca Davis. He frowned and leaned on his rake and waited.

She had a basket of cold dinner and a pair of sweating tin cans of water. As they came upon him, she called out, "You dawdling? Let's make hay." And so they did, working through the afternoon and long evening, Becca holding the reins as the team made their known way alongside the rake-rolled hay, August forking it up and Harlan building the loads upon the wagon. Then up to the barn and unloading, and back out again. Finally, late in the day, the last load forked upon the growing stacks, all three sitting reeking, too tired to move, August comprehended something of Becca Davis: Because life had upended her so young, she knew everything was uphill from where she stood but had the innate grace to know when and how to step herself forward. And he knew, swinging his tired legs, his face and arms itching, all was bequeathed of the Public Friend, passed down in words from their mother, or not that—perhaps in their poverty, the greatest bestowing were the teachings of life passed from mother to children. None of it simple to an adult but to a child, as Christ and The Friend understood, the whole wide truth of the world made clear.

Just then the team swung both their heads sideways where they stood in the open door and one whickered a greeting. August walked out from the dense still heat of the barn into the bright sunlight and Harlan went with him. Becca remained behind, happy to sit resting on the empty wagon bed, drinking lukewarm water from one of the tin buckets.

A towhead boy of nine or ten in worn trousers held over a ragged shirt by a single suspender, hatless and sunburnt, sat astride one of Malcolm Hopeton's mules in its work harness, an old rein cut to make riding reins for the boy. The other mule was alongside its mate and tied to a hame ring was a dun-colored horse. All the creatures were dark with sweat, soapy yellow lather gathered along the bands and straps of harness, and the boy kneed the mule forward a last step and, keeping hold of his rein, lifted his leg clear of the inside of the mule team, then vaulted away, landing in the hard packed dirt a couple of yards away from the mules and darting fast to snug the rein around a hook set into a block of stone at the base of the ramp. All this in the time it took August and Harlan to walk out of the barn and down the ramp.

45

August said, "You're Benny Fulton's boy, aren't you?"

Harlan said, "Howdy, Calvin."

The Fulton boy looked to Harlan. "I known they worked good for you and Bloody Hopeton but Papa got em on the dump rake when one or both spied somethin and shot into a dead run like hellhounds and went right around that field and were coming up toward where the crick runs along the end, faster all the way. I was standin there watching Papa look over his shoulder trying to figger if he jumped could he miss the rake tines, when them mules smelt the water and stopped dead and Papa flew off the seat and landed on the ass-end of one of em. I thought he was gonna get kicked to death but both mules turned their heads back and watched while he got hisself freed. He left em standing there and walked out into the field and fired his pipe and stood there, smokin and lookin up at the sky. He called me and we unhitched them buggers right where they stood. Then we got em geared together like they is and it took some tries but here I is. And now will get on that brown mare which has more sense than them two together and less than a stone, and ride it home."

"Hold on," said August. "Why'd you bring them here?"

"Him." The boy pointed at Harlan. "When the deputy brought the mule Bloody Hopeton tried to escape on, Papa asked where you was. After they started tearing things up he recalled you worked em just fine and their goose was cooked."

Harlan said, "Well, they ain't horses. Here, let me help get your ride home freed up. You want some water afore you go?"

"No sir. I just want daylight tween me and them ornery bastards, the more the faster the better is how I see it. I'd take that hand, though, freeing my horse. She don't like em any better than Papa or me. You shoulda seen us tryin to set out. No, I'm only wanting a peaceable trot home."

Harlan turned to August. "Give me a minute to sort this out," he said with a calm certitude that left August with no choice. Both mules were watching Harlan now, ears pricked high like two sets of bows.

Harlan let the mules be and set about getting the horse untied, then walked around in a circle away from the mules and cupped a hand to let Calvin step up onto his horse. The boy gathered his reins and looked down at Harlan.

"You goin to watch Bloody Hopeton swing?"

"They ain't tried him yet, Calvin."

"Papa says he'll swing all right. I plan to be there, myself."

"Why?"

The boy reared back on his horse and studied Harlan, as if wondering if some good bit more than mules had rubbed from Hopeton to Harlan. He sat straight and turned his horse, looked over his shoulder, and said, "To see it, a course." Then kicked his horn-hard heels into the mare and trotted fast out the drive, his body tight and smooth with the horse's gait.

At some point Becca had emerged from the barn to watch all this. Together she and August stood silent as Harlan stripped the harnesses from the mules, which both stood trembling a bit but otherwise steady as he did so. August and Becca could not hear words but while he worked Harlan spoke to the mules in a steady, low sing-song, as if he were reciting songs or psalms toward natal mule memory. When the harness and bridles were laid on the side of the ramp, Harlan stepped between the two and, still talking, reached a hand up to gently cup the underjaws and then walked off, the mules stepping easily alongside him. He took them down the lane, their backsides now diminishing, powerful legs and hindquarters ambling, ragged tails in futile swish against flies, until he came to the gate of the pasture where the milk cows were settled around two big beech trees, and turned the mules in with them. He didn't bother to watch how the cows or mules might react but turned and walked back. When he approached his sister and August Swartout the edge of his mouth, his eyes, might've held the smallest of grins. But when he spoke it was gone.

"Should we pick up here and get set to milk?"

After supper they were all three sitting together on the porch, looking out over the night pasture where the red and white Ayrshire cattle worked their way along, tearing up mouthfuls of high clover and timothy, the mules some distance off, grazing but sporadic, lifting their heads to look around them both at once or turn by turn as if scouting danger.

The porch looked east, so they sat in shade, the house behind, the barn downhill from them and the road a step up the ridge westward, a track parallel both to the ridgetop and the valley below. The sun was burning huge into the ridgetop trees and above a small string of clouds held motionless with red bellies, darkening above. To the east but high overhead a gibbous moon loomed. Past that the evening star, a hole poked toward heaven.

Two meadows remained for the first cutting of the year, the hay already mowed this afternoon by Marsh. Even with Harlan gone for at least the following morning, they'd have the hay in the barn by the next evening. Following that, August was thinking, would be a good time to run cultivators through the fields of corn, the plants still young enough so the teams could traverse the rows as the narrow spades of the cultivators not only tore free weeds between the rows but also turned small heaps against the young stalks of corn, giving them a more sturdy base, as well as loosening the soil a final time before the corn grew too tall, this loosening making it easier for the earth to absorb water from rainstorms, in general aerating the soil, to also inhibit the varied blights, rusts, and corn-borer worms, any or all of which could diminish the crop. Beside him on the porch both brother and sister sat quietly in their own contemplations. You don't always have to know all the ways a thing is right to do, it's enough to know it must be done, August understood, still thinking of the corn.

He was also thinking that the garden was beginning its first heavy overflow and soon days would be given over to canning and pickling. Becca would be back in the kitchen, which he felt some relief over: a small step back to the normalcy of the life he'd established four years earlier when he'd hired her, but also thinking, It won't be just for me this year. The notion of a household ongoing, not just a needed convenience, intrigued him. Perhaps these unlucky orphans were part of that larger design set in motion beyond ken and so now only revealing this small particle, to him and to them. Perhaps a regrouping all three needed and not any accident at all. He knew Narcissa would smile and nod, as if they were the children he might've had with her, or, in fact, were the children he'd had with her. That he'd been appointed to oversee and guide, and they, in their turn, would oversee and guide him.

Out in the meadow in the slow dusk one of the mules brayed and the other answered, and both went silent. On the porch or in the tiger lilies tall against the railings a cricket started up, paused and waited, tried again; and then first one and then others joined in. A spare handful of stars studded the vault of approaching night.

"Your mules seem to be settling in nice and easy," August said.

"They're not my mules. But they'll work for me, you got work for two teams."

"There's most always work for two teams. Except when there's work for none. You still wanting to go see Malcolm Hopeton in the morning?"

"Yes sir. I'd be lying if I said I wasn't nervous about it, though."

August was quiet a moment and then said, "I'd expect the sheriff or the judge will ask you some questions. You want to be polite but you don't have to tell them anything you don't want to. If you're uncomfortable, I mean. The judge didn't say it in so many words but you can tell him I understand myself appointed guardian of you and if there's questions you'd rather not answer you can say you want to wait until I'm along."

Harlan looked away. He said, "That business Amos Wheeler got up to with Missus Hopeton, I wasn't any part of that. Not the first bit."

"I don't believe there's anyone thinks you were. But the law is a strange stew. Keep in mind all you're after is to see if Malcolm Hopeton requires anything of you, as a hired man. Stay that course and you should be fine. Just don't be thinking you can help him by telling too much. At least not yet. He doesn't even have a lawyer, that I know of. There'll come a time for you to tell all you want, or all he needs. But right now you can't be sure if those are the same thing, is all I'm saying."

"He and I sorta spoke about that."

"You did?"

"We had right much to talk about, that seven weeks."

"I imagine you did. Some of what you talked about, maybe some of that's changed, that's what I'm trying to say."

"Not so much, I don't think. But I'll keep quiet as I can. What you says makes sense."

"Lord," Becca said. "I was just setting here thinking I'd never felt such a peaceful ease. Now I'm nervous as a cat."

Harlan said, "There's nothing for you to be nervous about."

"How can you say that?"

"Because you're not the one going to town, that's how." His grin turned toward her in the dusk.

Becca scraped her chair forward and took her bare feet off the rail, ready to stand, but August was ahead of her. He struck fire and knew both were watching as he inhaled and the small flare lit his face. He held the cheroot out to his side and exhaled. "It's a fine evening, isn't it? I'm going to walk a last check of the barn. Why don't the two of you get on to bed? Busy day tomorrow."

50

He stepped down off the porch and into the gathering dark. There was a lantern hung on a peg inside the dairy door he could light. There was a heifer might freshen anytime the next two weeks. There was also a spotted sow with a new litter could stand looking at, a big litter with not one but two runts. In his experience a good runt, nursed through, could turn out to be the stoutest sow or boar of them all. The root of another stronger tree.

He could also walk up to the night pasture and stand and look at mules.

Curious if they'd even notice him. Or care to walk over and touch a nose to his extended hand, palm open and up.

FOUR

At the Four Corners landing Harlan stood off to the side while August conducted his business and a worker from the steamboat loaded the four crates of butter, stamped with numbers in sequence to mark them as belonging to August, aboard the *Catawba* alongside other crates from other farmers. There was an orderly milling of wagons about the landing; all the farmers were in haste, all, like August making hay, caught in the heady turmoil of summer heightening. And, it being summer, all of August's butter would be making the shorter trip to Elmira rather than to New York City: The premium market was best served in the cooler months. Then Harlan paid his fare out of the dollar August had palmed him as they'd approached the landing, stilling protest with the flat statement that it was an advance against wages. When Harlan protested the amount August reminded him it was not just the fare and back but also against possible unforeseen expenses.

"Such as what?"

"I don't know. Neither do you. But it's in your pocket if you need it, it comes to that. Could be as simple as needing to buy dinner in town, things don't work quick as you hope."

The boy nodded and then they'd arrived. August wondered if Hopeton had paid the boy or simply offered room and board. Or if the promised funds had been used up some other way, by other people. He wanted to know but also knew this was not the time to ask. So he gave Harlan the money in such a way that it could not be turned down. And noted that Harlan didn't protest or offer proof of his own ready funds.

Just as he was about to leave with his wagon and his returned empty crates from his last shipment, a more distant neighbor but a steady man approached August and told him, "The only thing I know about mules is, unlike horses, they get loose from their stalls and get into the oats, the mule will eat only enough to fill hisself, while a horse will eat to founder." August had wanted to respond that he'd never had a horse get loose, let alone founder, but he only looked down upon the man and smiled and said, "That so?," before turning his team toward the road home.

But not before looking back a final time toward the laden boat, the engine thumping now as the drivers gained their head of steam to turn the side-wheel, dark jets of coal smoke emitting periodic and rhythmic from the short stack. And seeing Harlan Davis working alongside the sparse crew, shifting sacks and crates to correct the boat's balance. The sort of boy he was. August chirped up the horse to roll the wagon home, intent on the work before him but also more comfortable sending the boy off, thinking he was only beginning to know him. And thinking also that Malcolm Hopeton had not made such a bad choice. At least that one time.

A pair of long, narrow windows was set into one wall high up near the ceiling, obscured by a film of dust and some sort of foliage growth beyond the thick, wavy panes; but nevertheless he'd noted that they faced west, given the low light they emitted until end of day when broad rectangles slowly spread across the basement floor until they finally rose high enough to spread a pale yellow light upon him in his cage. Where, when this happened, he turned away from the light, seeing his own monstrous shadow waver and glide upon the bricks of the foundation, the shadow overlaid by those of the bars of hard steel that surrounded him in this otherwise empty fastness, constructed he could only guess to hold such as himself. The three common cells one floor up where men came and went, some few no doubt spending greater amounts of time than others but alongside other men, those miscreants and swindlers, drunks and thieves, liars and fools, all certain of their innocence. Proclaiming it loud enough time to time so he heard garbled self-witness echo down through the oaken floors that formed above his iron-strapped ceiling.

It was not that he was grateful for his entombed solitude but only that he'd have murdered those fools if he'd been among them. Idiots so smitten with the base fact of their own existence they'd lie and believe their own truth so told, if it might restore them to their old lives beyond those cages that held them now. As if it, whatever it was, was only a grand misunderstanding, a mistake to be put right if only the right man would hear them. If said enough, surely must be true.

He was not among them.

This is how it ends, Malcolm thought. Crouched on a slab of bunk, his chest a great welter of pain, his head throbbing with the pulse of his own lifeblood, eyes unable to focus but all vision rimmed with a scrim of black and red and yet he sat upright, that wretched hard gaze that vibrated throughout him held steady as if upon a far horizon it was his last duty to reach. He did not eat; the plates of food, tin cups of water or bitter coffee, the bowls of morning boiled mush were carried away intact only when some man or another brought the next meal. Even the chamber bucket stood empty. He would void his shit and urine only when they took him forth and stood him upon that peeled raw-wood platform and fitted the rope and sprang the trap to dangle him, feet kicking for the earth he'd finally left forever and then, only then, his body would purge itself, smearing himself with the shit and piss withheld as a debt finally paid.

The foul man, witnessed.

He longed for that raw wood, the rope. He twisted upon his finger the slim band of precious metal as he had so many countless days and nights those long months and years of war as if his touch could be felt upon the ring's twin those hundreds of miles north. Some talisman flowing through the air to the life he'd thought he'd left only behind, thought he'd return to. All ways he'd failed. More than a fool.

The rope a pale substitute for that ring. His final—no, his only act of contrition. And that a meager one.

How he'd failed her. How he'd killed her, countless times. And the only one he'd known was that last heedless and irrevocable action of hurling her hard upon the ground.

He could not claim he did not know what he was doing. These last days he of a sudden started as if from sleep, wet with sweat and stink, his arms sore from that action replayed. Then the freeze over him and his skin goosefleshed and cold. Her dead on the ground.

The blood flowing from her nose, her mouth. Slow threads, turning black even as he'd watched in the morning sun. Nothing he'd not seen before, countless ways.

Nothing he'd ever seen.

He knew what he could have done that morning. But he had not.

He yearned for the ring of rope.

There was a scrape upon his forehead that he lifted his hand to time to time. If the crust was hard he'd slide down from the bunk upon his knees and again batter his head against the rough brick flooring. As if scrubbing. Except when he was doing this he otherwise had no memory of this urgency.

In the upper corner of one of the windows lay a smear of dust-laden webs, new overlaid upon the old. The spider, of medium size, brown-speckled with gray legs, hid in the shadow of the frame until a blue-bottle or smaller fly sought the light late of day and tried to fly through the glass and was ensnared. Then the spider darted out upon its own spun strands and wrapped the fly and retreated with it to the corner. Then edged back out to repair the torn web and wait anew. To eat the fly later. After dark. Malcolm would kill Amos Wheeler a thousand times each day if he only could.

He waited for, wanted only, oblivion. They had taken his braces, his bootlaces, the bunk was bare of all bedding but for a thin pallet of sailcloth canvas stuffed with cornhusks. To deprive him of his own opportunity, as if he would take it. If he so wanted he could shred his shirt to strips and make do. But he would not. For her. She deserved to have the multitude stand witness to his end. A small offering compared to what failures he'd meted upon her. His own foul mind, his thoughtless mind. What greater crime than thoughtlessness?

Truly. Do tell.

None.

Ever.

"Mr. Hopeton? Mr. Hopeton, it's me. Harlan Davis? I come to see you, see what I might do to help."

He swung his head low as a bull challenged and saw nothing, the dim cellar a swarm of shadows and speckled bright lights darting to and fro, and, as a bull will, shook his head against uncertainty, swarmed vision, the scent of something known but not certain. His bare feet smacking the floor and then he saw the cringing, frightened boy standing without the cage, the boy's hands caught before him and wringing them over and together as if he'd wash them clean of what he stood before.

56

Malcolm Hopeton stepped and took upright bars of his cell in each hand and roared forth. He made mighty effort to shake the unshakeable steel bars and did not care that only his own body sagged and rose against them, feeling himself moving was enough, that and his voice sounding forth. For sound he did. His eyes upon the pale window far above the boy, he spoke everything he knew, everything he might say and everything he needed to say. There was a great booming within the basement room and some far distant part of him knew it to be his own voice and that same small part took a strange pleasure in that voice of a sudden loosed. His voice rose and fell but mostly he studied the window as he railed and spoke the truth none had sought, not even himself until this moment and he knew as he was doing so this would be the last time on this earth he might speak such truth and so a great and terrible agitation filled him as he spent himself.

Sometime during this the boy fled up the stairs.

The spider had not moved.

Harlan forked up hay to August, who built the load, the team walking unguided along the windrow of cured hay, the lines looped over one of the front uprights of the wagon. By the time he'd ridden the mail boat back around to the Four Corners the worst shock of Malcolm Hopeton had subsided, at least enough so he stepped off the boat with wits enough to stop at Malin's store and buy a handful of soda crackers and wedge of cheese to eat as he loped along up the lanes toward August's farm; once there, the last thing he wanted was his sister quizzing him. The gentle upward climb along with the food helped still his mind. He paused where the bridge crossed Kedron Brook and knelt to drink and went on, then cut off the road before the house and into the young corn. He already knew his way over the land and so came out into the meadow where August was walking alone, pitching up hay and then whoaing his team to jump aboard and lay his pitches to swathes along the bed—slow work, but a man could make a load in this fashion. An extra fork was twined into the rear uprights and Harlan snatched it free while August had his back turned and called up with his first forkful already in the air, set to land right where it should.

"I'm back. Let's make this hay."

August turned down a long glance but Harlan was at work and so they went along to the end of the row where the team turned out on the headland and stopped.

"Were you able to see him?"

"When I asked, the sheriff only looked at me and told me to go ahead down. He's in a separate cell alone in the basement."

August nodded and said, "How'd that go?"

Harlan looked up at him then and August saw the stricken eyes of a boy unsure of all the world. Harlan said, "Not so good. Tell you what. Could we just go along here and do this job?"

August almost told the boy he'd be glad to be an ear, perhaps two minds were better than one alone, and then was wise and simply said, "Why, sure. The load gets high and you want to trade places just say so."

"I can pitch it up."

"I know it." He chirped up the team.

They'd made a full round of the meadow and were most of the way through the next when Harlan, without pause in his labor, spoke.

"I recall that day in May he walked back upon the farm. I didn't see him come in; I was out with the mules turning ground but I was expecting him. A telegraph had come the week before and Amos Wheeler went into a panic and within the day they were off—I don't know where to, maybe Utica. But I knew he was coming and I was doing my best to do what he'd charged me with almost four years before: to look after things. There wasn't so much to look after then but that wasn't my fault. Amos had not sold the mules, though I'd guess he'd tried. I'd fall plowed the previous October and so was

58

running a harrow gang over that land, trying to smooth out the furrows to make ready for spring planting. The Bill mule swung his head and I looked and seen Mr. Hopeton walking out from the farmstead toward me. I knew what he'd seen there, what he'd found. And all what was gone. I'd pictured that moment in my mind over and again that last week and was more than a bit frightened but it wasn't anything like I'd thought. He stood at the end of the field and watched me and waited.

"Maybe I was a coward, but at the time I felt I was only doing what he'd told me to do and I wanted him to see that. I wanted him to see that at least *one thing* was as he expected it to be. So I didn't cut across the field to meet him but kept making my rounds and quartering crossways, doing the job as it was meant to be done, and only pulled up to a stop when the work finally brought me close to him.

"I set to fix one of the harrow teeth that had got catty-corner while he walked out and stood before the mules and fussed over them. As I worked I tipped my head to look at him and he was the same man had hired me and not the same man at all. Hard and muscled tight from the war and sunburnt dark as if it was July but also faded and shrunk down and he waited until I met his eye.

"His face was so confused, his voice all broken-up, I just dropped the lines and fell to my knees in the dirt and started to cry. It just came over me and there was no stopping it. And he walked out there and lifted me up and held my elbows and told me it was all right, that he knew none of it was my fault. Then he unhitched the team from the harrow and told me to come along and he drove his mules down to the barn and put em in their pen and we went to the house and there we set and talked. He talked near as much as me, at least it felt that way although once I got going I poured out most everything I'd been holding those last couple a years. Since it was only those years things went so wrong. And he was kind to me, even when he asked about this thing or that thing and even things I'd forgotten until he asked, as

59

if he held a greater inventory after those years away. And I answered best I could even as I saw how it pained him. But like I said, all the time he was kind to me.

"Which was how it went along, those weeks. Oh, there was times he'd go quiet and gaze off toward nothing I could see, other times he'd set after a day of work and tell me things about the war, and there was times he'd stop whatever job we were doing of a sudden and turn to ask a question. Well, I had to search a moment to understand and then do my best to answer or tell him I just plain did not know but he kept that gentleness all the way along. He never once blamed me for anything or asked why I'd not done anything different or nothing like that. As we went along I got the sense he was pulling a truth out of me, a truth I only barely knew I had. And I guess he certainly was.

"For the next six weeks we was rebuilding what had been lost, what had been taken. He in his own way, which was his job to do, and me in mine, which was mostly just to help him, be it answering questions or getting seed into the ground. I'd say we was best when we were about the work at hand but I'd have to say there was plenty of evenings sitting and talking when I thought I was helping with that work as well. More than once, end of day as we were headed off to bed he pause me with a hand to my shoulder and thank me. Truth is, I'd been holding my breath a long time until he got home and once he was there I felt I could walk and breathe and work like a normal person once more. It was a blessing, pure and simple, to have him home."

When Harlan went silent August looked down and saw the boy standing with his hay fork held sideways in both hands against his thighs. August then looked up and around and saw that they were at the end of the meadow, the load made, the work done. He'd had no idea of how they'd progressed, listening and stacking the load. But the work was done.

He coughed a hack of chaff and dust, spat it free, and said, "He sounds like a good man."

Harlan looked up. He said, "I don't know. I didn't know him, today." He looked away at the raw green stubble of the cut field, at the curve of land below, the slender finger of lake and the rise of the Bluff. At the sky. He said, "He wants to die."

He looked then at August as if to confirm he'd been heard.

August stood upon the load and looked down and waited.

Harlan said, "I asked him what I could do to help him and he stood hollering at me like a crazy man. It wasn't nothing like I'd seen from him ever. I didn't know him."

August frowned in thought. Then he said, "Sounds to me perhaps the man doesn't know himself just now either. I guess I could understand that."

Harlan looked off and back again and said, "Let's get this hay in the barn."

Becca Davis had a bounty of garden vegetables laid out on the table with sliced hard sausage and a kettle of freshly boiled small new potatoes, split open and slathered with butter and salt. She also had a hot fire burning in the brick oven set hip-high within the great hearth, and on the drainboard beside the sink she was punching down a bowl of risen bread dough.

She said, "I don't know how I did it but we run right out of bread so I'm baking this evening. I know it's hot in here and sorry for it." She glanced over her shoulder at August and said, "I been more distracted by my brother being here than I thought I was. I'm sorry; it won't happen again."

Mildly August responded, "It's early still, a warm heel of bread fresh from the oven just before bedtime is a good thought. Are those beets, there?"

"Boiled to only tender and the best of the cider vinegar over em."

"Lord knows, I love a beet. And the cucumbers are plumping up also. I do say, I think we're well served, here."

"You're kind," Becca said.

"He's honest, is what I think," Harlan said.

"You two eat," she said. And pulled the cracked-open door of the oven and added more wood, which snapped and crackled. "This bread's rising even as I talk."

August was filling his plate and Harlan sat beside him, doing the same, both of them on the far side of the table from the fire, not that it changed a thing: The room was steaming. August said, "I thought if that team of mules can pull I'd borrow a cultivator from my cousin in the morning and Harlan and I could cultivate the young corn. About the last chance, and it'd be a good thing to do."

Harlan said, "Those mules work steady. And happy to do so." Both men eating as if they'd not seen food in days.

"It's what I've heard. My, Becca. It is hot in here."

She looked up and wiped a wet strand from her forehead, a small bead formed on the tip of her nose about to drop into the bowl of dough. She said, "You'll want bread come the morrow."

"I will. And thank you for it." Then he stood and tipped his cleaned plate into the washbasin set into the sink, pumped water and filled a tin cup and turned back to the room. He looked at Harlan, still eating, and said, "When you finish up, come join me on the porch. Might not be so much cooler but at least the chance for a breath of air to come upon us there. And leave your sister to her work."

The early evening sunlight ribboned across the orchard pasture, making bands of light and dark where the cows grazed and the mules also. On the trees where the light struck, small globes glowed almost yellow, the young apples now visible. Swallows wafted above and then swiftly darted among the trees and up again and gone toward the barn and the nests that lined the rafters of the dairy, the mud-and-daub

structures where the small speckled eggs were hatching and the young
naked birds gaped and cried during afternoon chores. The same birds,
adult and young, awake and striving at first light. Life ferocious and
yearning.

Harlan carried his own tin cup of water when he joined August,
who was tipped back in his rocker, his cup untouched resting upon
his crossed knee, his right arm lifted into the air, holding the cheroot,
smoking. August remained silent as Harlan pulled another rocker up
and sat, drinking a bit from his cup and then leaning to set it upon
the boards and after a moment of lifting first one foot then the other
lifted both and propped them against the porch rail and settled back
into his chair.

August said, "I don't know much about any of this business. The
rumors and gossip, somewhat, but I discount them mostly."

He felt the boy stiffen, come to a halt from his already mild rocking.
Harlan said, "I'm sorry. I never meant to bring it upon you."

"No, no. You misunderstand. I told you once and will once more
but please don't have me do it again: You're most welcome here,
Harlan Davis. And besides that, I'd do whatever I can to assist you."

"It's Mr. Hopeton needs assistance. And I can't see how to do it, the
state he's in."

August blew a smoke ring that floated perfect and he blew another
he watched go through the first, not proud but thoughtful as if direct-
ing his gaze thus allowed his mind greater play. He said, "As The
Friend taught, we are caught in Time, but time also catches and holds
us. I'm thinking of this man I never knew, at least not yet. And how all
of this with him came to pass. He went away to war, for, as most men
do, a host of reasons. And he stuck that war out. This county is filled
up with men who did the same but also those who went and fulfilled
their obligation and came home. But he stayed. Now, I'm a peaceable
man myself. War is not for me, sanctioned murder is how I see it, even
if, and I do double back upon myself here, I recognized it was a great

and necessary evil. To halt the traitors that would rend the country asunder, all in the name of a most terrible estate—that of keeping other souls in bondage. For that matter I did my part. Paid my forfeit and shipped my grain and butter to the effort. And made my prayers, daily. Other words, I did what I knew to do."

August still looked off away, smoking. The smell of heated working yeast came down the hall and out upon the porch. Bread in the oven or bread on the final rise—at a small remove could be either one. The high eastern clouds belly-lit by the slow falling sun but the land all now shades of blue and charcoal, pigeon breast feathers, small orbs as if caught daylight in the flowers against the porch. Even shades of winter gloaming hiding twixt the heat of day and falling night. Harlan was sitting quiet, lost in worry, lost in his own thought. Perhaps even wondering what August was saying. Or asking. For August himself was suddenly unsure.

"I wish he had come home. He could've. Even before his enlistment was over, he had the chance. And if he'd took it, none of this ever would've happened. But he didn't."

A mournful, sad boy.

Gently August said, "Why didn't he?"

Harlan now also gazed off toward the slow-falling night. He made fists of his hands and lifted them and rubbed his eyes. August was about to speak, to say never mind, it can wait, when Harlan dropped his hands into his lap and worked his fingers over and around each other, as if rubbing worry or soreness from them.

"He found me, I still don't know how, after he'd signed on with the Keuka Rifles the summer of sixty-one; they was set to march off that fall. He hired me and we had some months together all four of us before he went. And it seemed clear: Missus Hopeton and Amos Wheeler was to do the job of running the farm and I was to be the hired man that Amos had been. It wasn't that simple but that was the general idea. And late September, just before he went off on the train, he took me aside and told me he counted on me, counted on me to do my part and also to keep a eye on things. The very words he used. They stuck hard in my head but I have to tell you I don't know if he meant em the way I came to understand or was just trying to make sure I knew I was important to keeping things going. Eighteen months. That's what he signed on for. If he'd done that and walked home it would've never come to what it did. Those first couple a years we all three of us worked that farm mostly the way it needed to be done. Looking back there was small things I understand different now but it was mostly all on the up and up.

"What turned things was Hopeton himself. Or more true to say he made a opportunity without knowing he was doing such. He thought he was doing another thing altogether. Thought he was doing the right thing. See, a year into his enlistment he was wounded. September of eighteen and sixty-two. The battle of Antietam."

Harlan paused and looked at August and asked, "You know about that one?"

"I might not've been a soldier but I followed the war. Close. Not just *The Chronicle* but also *Frank Leslie's Illustrated, Harper's Magazine.* I read them all. That was a terrible battle, one of the worst, early on. What many of the rest looked like as time went by."

"I guess. I didn't read so much as you, just know what I heard. And what he told me these last couple months. I guess I learned the most during that time, though it's all mixed up in my head now. But this is what I do know. Because it didn't just happen to him but happened to me also.

"At Antietam he was wounded. He told me the whole story, how he and a mess of Union boys was up on a hill and there was a road at the base of the hill and across the road some woods where the Rebs was dug in. And those Union boys went down that hill to attack the Rebs. But what no one knew until it was too late was there was a big cut in the base of the hill above the road. And the

Rebs just started cutting em down and the Union men was stumbling and falling as they went, being killed also but many of em falling down into the road still alive but carried along with it all. And Malcolm Hopeton was among that first wave of men but back enough so he didn't know what was happening until he tumbled into that mess of dead and dying men on the road. Where the Rebs had come out of the woods and was killing men, sticking them like frogs with their bayonets and long knives and clubbing em with their rifle stocks, all which was quicker than reloading. Anyway, there he come down the hill all in a jumble but with his rifle up ready to shoot when he felt a burn like a bee-sting on his right thumb and looked down and seen that thumb had been shot right off, where it was propped up ready to pull the trigger, and then down he went, tumbled down that bank. Said he looked up and a Reb was standing over him and stabbed him with his bayonet and it hit a rib and the Reb pulled it out and heaved up ready to do it again when a pair of Union boys fell dead across Mr. Hopeton and that was all he knew until long after that morning.

"He woke sometime in the night and was laid out on the ground with other wounded men outside a big tent glowing like a lantern. He had a bandage over his right hand and was wrapped all around his middle with more bandages soaked right through so they looked black in that pale light. Said he lay there listening to the screams from within the tent and the scrape and rasp of saws as the surgeons done their work. The other men around him groaning with pain or crying out for help, water, Mother, all such things. And he told me he turned his head sideways and seen a pile looked in the shadows like a mighty heap of cordwood thrown all which ways and realized it was parts of men, arms and feet, legs, a great many legs, at least good pieces of em. And how he then recalled the face of the Reb that tried to stick him all those hours before—said he'd recognize that man anywhere and everywhere.

"About that time one of the sawbones came along that row of men and was stopping to check on each one. He come to Malcolm and changed the dressing on his hand and he said the doctor was kind and tired as he ever seen a man but still the doctor finished his work and looked Malcolm in the eye and told him, 'Your war is done.'

"As if delivering good news. But he, Mr. Hopeton, lay there thinking about that and also thinking about the face of the Reb who'd undone him so. And made up his mind he'd find that man one way or another, or enough like him, and see that *their* war was done. Said he felt that and felt it also as a great sadness in him.

"After that night he was taken to a hospital in Maryland where he spent a month recovering all the way. Which I gather was tougher than he told, that his wounds to his belly was more considerable, since it took so long. And let those people keep telling him how he was going home. He didn't argue with none of them but only waited. Then one day when he knew he was able he slipped out of there and hiked until he found what he was looking for, which for a hospital was not that far. He was looking for a quartermaster of one of the wagon trains that run a army, you get down to it. Not a bit of army is any good without a train. And he told the man he was about to be cashiered from the infantry but wanted to sign on as a teamster. Said you might need a thumb to fire a rifle but any fool with horse sense could manage a team. All of which is true.

"But the quartermaster looked him up and down and asked something like did he know horses, teams and hauling.

"And Malcolm spoke back and said I know horses and hauling but if you've got em, I prefer mules. And that was that. He was in until the end of the war."

A silence grew out between them now sitting in the full charcoal throat of dusk, the night air not cooled yet, the smell of bread upon them and fireflies winking off in the orchard. August's cheroot had long died and he'd held it dead in his hand throughout this telling.

Now he flicked it into the flowers against the porch and hitched upright in his chair, feeling the work of the day stiffening within his shoulder and arms, his thighs.

He spoke, quietly. "So was it revenge upon that one fellow that drove him? Blood lust?"

"No," Harlan said. "I misstated. He said it was when he saw the fury in that man's face that he understood truly what the war was about. Before it had been simple, to keep the United States together, to end slavery if that could be done. But he said it was in that man's face he understood it was a war against evil, pure and simple and as wretched as evil can be. How evil rises up and distorts men's vision, their understanding. How that fellow and all his other Reb soldiers and their armies and the states and the Confederate government, the whole of it, was saddled by evil and driven by it. He told me this one evening; we'd planted what seed corn he'd been able to buy since there wasn't none held back from last fall and we was beat but happy, the way you and I felt this afternoon, getting that hay in the barn. We'd drunk water from the trough and were spraddle-legged against the side of the barn in that good May sunlight when he told me all this.

"He told me it was thinking about that man, lying on the ground outside the hospital tent, when it came to him: What if the war was lost. If the Rebs won. What sort of world it would be, what sort of country we'd live in, forever. And then how he wondered if it might be—and he leaned over and pushed my shoulder with his stunt hand as he said it—what if by some action of fate, the war was lost because he was not there, that he was not doing his part. Because he understood however big wars and armies are it also comes down to what each man does. And could he let that evil flourish and walk the earth? So he signed up and stuck it to the end."

After a long moment, a thoughtful and respectful one, August said, "My Lord. That's some kind of a man. To order things such a way. I see why you stuck by him."

Harlan turned then and August saw a faint quick grin in the dark. The boy said, "I guess. But what he also told me?"

"What's that?"

"That he struggled all through that war, doing his best and never sure how it would come out, though he knew how it must and knew none of them would quit until it did. And then it did. And he said, 'So I rode the rails home ready for my old life again and also, small patch of pride, feeling I'd done my part and had vanquished evil.' Even those bastards killing Lincoln, that was what he called a last desperate flourish of evil. So he come on home. And what he found."

"I see."

"Do you?"

"Tell me."

"Four long years and then some, he'd thought he'd spent to drain the evil out of this land and he come home and found evil was alive and well. Had snuck in behind him and worked at him and done its best. Which was not some great war but a smaller war as if evil had a head that could be severed but would slither fast and reconnect to whatever was closest and dearest. He told me that and I didn't say a word but I knew he was right. Because I'd seen what he was talking about."

August said, "It seems you have."

"I'm sticking by him. Even if he says he don't want it."

August stood. He stepped to the edge of the porch and peered into the dark and said, "I'm thinking he doesn't know what he wants just now. It's a bad place to be, where he is, what he's done. I can't imagine, myself. But I also think you're right to stick by him, that he'll need you if he knows it or not. I'd say he's a lucky man to have taken you on. Or perhaps smart, even if he didn't know how smart he was at the time."

"I'm dearly frightened for him."

"Of course you are. But patience, boy. Sometimes life feels endless and grinding. Other times it changes in a day."

"I surely seen that."

August said, "Those mules will truly work for you?"

"Like magic."

"I guess we'll see about that in the morning. As to Malcolm Hopeton, trust I stand behind you."

Harlan was quiet.

August turned and said, "I stand with you. Is that clear?"

"Yes sir."

"Good. Now let's get on to bed. But first, I'd have a hunk of the fresh bread we're smelling. With butter. You?"

The boy smiled in the dark, the stripe of lamplight down the hall and out the open door. He said, "I feel I could eat a loaf."

"That could make your sister testy but if you can you shall. It's been a long day."

FIVE

THE NEXT AFTERNOON the wind sprang up from the west, by midnight was in the west-southwest and it was raining, a gentle, steady, soaking rain. Not all the corn had been cultivated but he'd borrowed a sulky rig from his cousin Marsh and so Harlan with his mules and August on his own rig had made considerable headway: The cultivators were light, with little drag, and once the teams found their stride the workday had been pleasant and easily long. All a man had to do was ride with the soft rasping swish of the longer leaves brushing the cultivator arms and to look about; killdeer running down the rows ahead, bobolinks and meadowlarks and butterflies in all hues lofting along, birdsong from the hedgerows floating over them, a small gathering of crows in the clump of big oaks at the edge of the stream's ravine barked and circled and circled again. The pair of red-tails that lived in the ravine and that had followed the haying intently, watching and diving for fleeing mice and voles, drifted above, patient, too high for the crows to plague. The trace-chains jingled and tails swished against flies.

When August felt the breeze he pulled onto the headland and instead of turning south went north to meet Harlan, who was quartering the western half of the field, and Harlan saw him coming and drew up the mules and waited. Going toward him a woodchuck, grown fat from the headland grass and the clover and timothy of the hayfield on the far side of the hedge, trundled fast toward the protection of her burrow. Some farmers shot woodchucks, others dropped poison baits into the burrows, the argument not being the damage of crops—which none but a fool could put forth—but rather that cattle or other livestock might break a leg stepping into those burrows that dotted pastures, meadows and hayfields. August practiced none of these exterminations, calculating that he'd never once seen or heard of such actual damage, considering also that while woodchucks might not be under man's dominion in the sense of livestock and husbandry, they were nevertheless beasts of the fields. He held that interpretation more broadly than others but was content with it. The exception being his house-gardens, which he fenced with high plank stockades, trenched three feet down to keep out the burrowing chucks but also rising six feet above ground to hold the deer at bay. Though there were fewer deer than when he'd been a boy.

The teams came abreast of each other and stopped nose to nose, leaving the men a dozen feet apart. August drew slightly on his reins and his team held while Harlan chirped up the mules, which advanced, stately, their tight sorrel coats hardly showing sweat. Harlan turned his curled fists down slightly and stopped his team, looked at August, and grinned. "If it was all like this."

August said, "You smell that air?"

"Rain?"

"I'd welcome it. You get to the end of your row, trot your mules back to the house and tell your sister you and I will be at this until dark. We'll milk after. She could carry some supper out here when it suits her and otherwise carry her bushels out to the gardens and start picking everything nigh ready; my guess is we'll be canning tomorrow."

"I ain't never canned."

"I'm curious what in the world you lived on winters at Hopeton's. No. Don't start. Get on with your message and get back. But, Harlan?"

"What is it?"

"You said 'If it was all like this.'"

Harlan had a stalk of grass tucked one corner of his mouth. With just-parted lips he used his tongue to roll it to the other corner. "We'd think it was hard work. Mr. Swartout, I damn well know hard work and the difference."

"I was jesting you, son. Now get on."

"I know you was." Then he hauled back on his reins and backed the mules around and went on. But going away he gripped the reins in one hand and raised the other in a flat salute. A proud boy, stoic and strong.

August turned his own team and headed back to work. The hawks were gone and the air was just enough to flip young beech and mulberry leaves to show their undersides, the silvery sheen of coming rain.

The next afternoon they were all in the kitchen, with a good fire going, rain against the windows but the upper half of the Dutch door open for relief against the heat; the overhang of the entry porch kept the rain from the door. Lined up on the hearth were half a dozen plain pottery crocks, filled with beans—green, yellow wax, and purple runner—also small whole cucumbers, sliced beets and cut-up cauliflower. Becca had filled the washtub with cider vinegar and mace, nutmeg, black peppercorns, cloves and allspice and was stirring this to cover the vegetables, while on the crane over the fire a large kettle heated water and sugar and lemon peel, a smaller one melted beeswax. These for the rows of brown glass jars on the table that would soon be packed with pitted cherries, filled with the syrup and sealed tight with hot wax.

73

August was tending the fire, squatting to push and prod the flames to keep even heat under the two kettles. Harlan sat at the table, milk pails of cherries on the floor to his right, a single pail to his left for pits and a bowl before him as he used his pocketknife to slice round the cherries, pop the pit into the pail, then the halves into the bowl. The mound of ready fruit was growing, slowly.

He said, "This is a job."

August said, "You'll be happy, come a January day. Maybe eating the pudding or pie, whatever gets made that cold day, you'll also recall the heat of summer and get warmed twice that way."

"At Hopeton's there was some of this. Wheeler would make biscuits sometimes and we spread jelly or fruit on em. After that it was taters, parsnips, carrots and squashes that come fall I'd haul down to the root cellar for the winter."

Mildly and without looking up from his fire duty, August said, "Mrs. Hopeton did not cook?"

Harlan paused before answering. Then he said, "When Mr. Hopeton first took me on she set a good table. Hearty and plenty of it. She was a hand with pies and baking also. Mr. Hopeton always had a compliment for her, saying he didn't know how he'd survived himself until he found her, words like that. There was a fancy iron stove in the kitchen and she worked it like a wizard. She kept it up when he went off to the war, for Wheeler and me. But there was a slow change there, I seen looking back. Amos Wheeler lived in a shack he'd built in the woods; well, it was a snug-enough-looking place the couple times I seen it. And he liked his food too, I can tell you. But he had a taste for wild food, squirrel stew or a mess of sunfish fillets floured and fried, things his brothers or cousins brought him. They were some bunch. And Amos, he sort of elbowed Mrs. Hopeton aside, there. In her kitchen I mean. There was something strange about how he done that, as if it was only natural for him to do so but also I got the idea she was a little afraid of him. Then quick as a flash he'd have her laughing at his jokes; he was quick with words and sometimes I wasn't sure what he was saying but she'd get all red-faced. The second Christmas he tried to roast a haunch of a young beef he slaughtered just for the occasion but I guess he had the oven too hot; it was crusted black but raw inside. When he sawed into that meat and the juice shot out she got up and walked out of the room and upstairs. A hour later they drove off, to the Elmwood Hotel I heard, where they sat to roast goose and what not. Which was the beginning of all that. At the time all I did was jimmy around with that stove a bit and got a skillet hot and sliced those slabs of raw meat into bacon grease and ate good. If I'd had any sense I'd of sliced the rest of that beef thin and laid it in the oven and had meat for a while. But I didn't have that sort of sense yet; I was most caught up with worry over Wheeler killing that young steer before his prime. As if Mr. Hopeton would somehow learn of that. Well, I was a fool and remained one."

Becca said, "This syrup's about ready. How many jars of cherries you have?"

"I don't have the first idea. Some."

"You could work more and talk less. None of us are the least bit interested in what happened with Hopeton's wife and that man. August, I'm ready to turn the pickle brine into the crocks. It's heavy, can you help?"

August rose up from the fire and glanced at the boy as he said, "Of course." Harlan's face was stricken, as if his feet had broken through ice and dropped him into frigid water. And August recalled the vague movements overheard the past nights, when all should've been exhausted to sleep, quiet footsteps as she left her own new room and went down the hall to her brother's, then sometime later back again. He'd thought she was only checking on him, making sure he was comfortable, perhaps reassuring him about this new place he had landed in. Now he was wondering if it was she who had been listening. And to what. And why had he not made some greater effort himself? Thinking he was not so very much ready to be any sort of father to the boy. But he must and so he would.

"I'm ready. Just steady the crocks," Becca said as she turned with the big tub held tight to her chest. She went on, "Pack those cherries into the jars but not too tight and leave a good two inches. Here we go, now."

Just then at the Dutch door a man spoke. "Ah, industry! my brothers and sister. May I intrude?" He unlatched the door and stepped in.

August nodded greeting, slightly guarded, wondering what this was all about. He said, "Let yourself in, Attorney, and welcome. A wet day to travel."

Enoch Stone's grandfather had been one of the trusted scouts sent into what then was the Phelps and Gorham Tract, to look it over and, if the rumors of the land's plenty were borne out, then purchase sufficient acreage for the Public Friend and the close to two hundred souls dedicated to a community built upon the teachings and tenets of The Friend. Enoch had barely been in his teens when The Friend died, but it was said that The Friend had seen something in him, at the least had singled him out and urged him to step away from the agrarian life, saying that the community would need someone more versed in the workings of the larger world. At fourteen he had begun to read law with Ansel Gordon, not yet a judge but clearly an up and comer. At sixteen Stone had been admitted to the bar and the next year Gordon had been appointed judge of the newly minted county of Yates, carved off with others from the unmanageably huge Ontario County. For another year Enoch Stone clerked for the judge, and then left his work with the county, married, and settled in a pleasant, well-appointed cottage just beyond the crossroad hamlet of Jerusalem, eight miles up from the Four Corners. He had declared himself a simple country lawyer, intent on serving the members of his community as they navigated the legal waters of deeds, land transfers, wills, property

76

disputes and such. By all lights fulfilling the burden The Friend had placed upon him.

A dozen years older than August, with two children, the daughter married and the son yet single, Stone had prematurely gray hair, which he lightly oiled and swept back from his forehead down to his shoulders, the glowing complexion of a man freshly shaven, and all of his teeth in milk-white rows that he displayed in wide smiles between thin lips. This day, as most days, he wore a collarless white shirt and a black vest under a charcoal swallowtail coat, having already removed his overcoat of waxed linen on the stoop; the coat was folded over his free arm, and he was holding his broad-brimmed felt hat, both these items dripping from the rain.

The hat resembled those favored in all seasons by the Public Friend—appearing plain, as was the rest of his wardrobe. Near-ordinary clothes that one such as he would be expected to wear. The almost miniscule golden links that crossed the front of his vest from fob to watch pocket were but a thread—what a man who must know the time of day would resort to. As was the neatly pressed and folded linen handkerchief poking its snout from the breast pocket of his coat. Ready to be offered if needed.

Enoch Stone seemed to be smoothly moving several directions all at once as he stepped and hung his wet overcoat and hat on pegs beside the hearth and greeted August by name, leaning to shake his hand, then turned and caught up the fingertips of Becca's free hand as he spoke her name also and kissed her cheek before kneeling beside Harlan's chair, and placed an arm about Harlan's shoulders and said, "Lad, I beg your forgiveness; I can't help but feel if I'd only come to visit you when the stories first began to circulate much of this tragedy might've been averted. And ignorance is no excuse, although it's true I can't swear I heard your name spoken. And might've not thought of you as the man you've become, recalling only the small boy at your mother's side or later years with your lovely sister, here, and Albert Ruddle."

77

Harlan hitched his chair back and said, "If you or anybody else had come out there'd only have been trouble made. I did all right keeping my head low, the best I could. I forget your name."

Stone had both hands swiftly joined in his lap but did not otherwise move. He said, "Forgive me, I overstepped. I hold no presumption any of us could've altered the course of events, once set in motion. Such is the hand of the Lord." He made a small smile and went on. "My name's Enoch Stone, some call me Attorney, others simply Brother, while in truth I'm both of those. And forgive me also my trespass upon your peace as well as your daily efforts. My own wife has been steaming up the house with a great array of the same work, surprised I don't reek of sweet berries. I'll be brief as I can but I'm Malcolm Hopeton's attorney and would ask a few questions, if you'd be so kind."

Harlan said, "Mr. Hopeton does not have an attorney. I know that for a fact. Ever since he walked back in from the end of the war he and I were working to get his farm back in shape. He claimed aloud he didn't need a lawyer because he said it was only a matter of time before Missus Hopeton come to her senses and came home. That was what he was waiting for. He was certain of her."

"I suppose he was," Stone said. "But with the events of this week the situation came clear to me and I spoke with the judge, who agreed to let me take on the role of representing Malcolm Hopeton. To speak bluntly, there's little to keep Hopeton from hanging save Christian intervention. Which is what I believe I'll help provide. The Lord willing but also the truth of the matter, best I can see. So I came to talk, knowing you can shed light, Harlan Davis. Will you do so?"

As he spoke he'd slowly eased upright, his knees cracking, and he pressed a hand into the small of his back against the effort but stood looking down at Harlan.

"I don't understand much of what you're saying," Harlan said.

"It's mostly simple enough. For instance as I stood at the door I overheard you speaking of Amos Wheeler. He's of great interest to me. Will you tell me what you know of him?"

"Well, it wasn't only him. There was a mess of em. Times they came and went and other times I'd not see much of em. But they were always around. And Amos, he was the king, least how he showed it to me and he did that plenty. I don't know how I can help you." As he finished speaking, Harlan looked to August.

Who said, "Please sit, Enoch. Becca, is there coffee left from dinner?"

Stone took the chair next to Harlan. "No coffee, thank you. It overstimulates my mind." He sat with his feet apart, hands on his knees. He said to Harlan, "What can you tell me about Wheeler's people?"

"He called em his brothers and cousins. Except for maybe two there wasn't much family resemblance except for the one name of Ellis, who had a gimp leg. There was a woman he called his sister but when she was around and Missus Hopeton wasn't, she didn't act much like a sister. Say, I'd rather not be thinking those folks know I'm talking about em."

"I'd not worry about that. The day after Hopeton was brought in, the judge sent the sheriff and his men down there along the Outlet Canal where they had their shacks. There wasn't anybody there but an old woman and a one-eyed dog."

"That news don't reassure me much. They're all good at melting away and know every swamp and bed of reeds for thirty miles or so. And every bit of woods along the ravines and creeks. They could be anywhere. And I know that dog, too. He might have only one eye but he's got a set a jaws on him. Surprised he didn't get a chunk of that sheriff."

"I believe they did have to shoot the dog. Edward and Ellis are Amos Wheeler's brothers. Ellis got his bad leg by shooting himself with an eight-gauge goose gun strapped to the front of a floating blind some years back while he was towing the blind around Reed's Point, trying to sneak up on a raft of ducks. The woman you mentioned is one Alice Ann Labidee, who hails from Utica and has been arrested there on morals and other criminal charges. Fortunately for her, none of those charges ever landed her anywhere but back on the street."

"You said Utica?"

"That's right."

"Wheeler and Mrs. Hopeton traveled there often enough. Mostly, when they returned she was in low spirits and he was best avoided for a couple of days. He never was in a good humor, lest he wanted something done, but those times he was foul. I seen him beat on a cow just because it was there when his temper went."

"So those trips, those occurred when there was still livestock on the place?"

"That time, yes."

"Did you ever get an idea of what those trips were for?"

"Over and again he talked about a horse." Harlan frowned as if deciding something. He said, "You know how people, when they think they're more clever, will let on when they're trying to hide something?"

Now Stone paused. Finally he simply said, "I do."

Harlan nodded. "That's how Amos Wheeler talked about the horse. Like it weren't a horse at all. And like he didn't care if I figured that out. As long as I didn't understand what he truly meant."

"And you did?"

"Not at first. But it came clear bit by bit, you might say."

"I hate to interrupt," Becca said. "But this syrup's going to candy if I don't get it jarred."

August took away the bowl of cherries and began to ladle them into the jars. "You and I can get this done, Becca. Let them talk."

80

Harlan said, "It was clear some of em wanted to hang about, as if Wheeler had got a grand new headquarters for em. But he wouldn't have it. At the time I thought he just didn't really care for their company. Later I guessed he was afraid Missus Hopeton might figure some things out he might not want her to."

Stone removed a pencil from his inner vest pocket and began to turn it slowly about with his fingers, as if sighting different angles along it.

Stone said, "You're a thoughtful young man, Harlan."

"I had a lot to think about," he said. "Especially the last year."

Stone bowed his head a bit and lifted his hands so the pencil lay along one side of his nose, almost a gesture of prayer. Or holding back the itch to employ the pencil, to make notes. Becca had sealed the jars and turned the crane out from the dying fire. She announced, "I'll just carry the pickle crocks down cellar and the jars, too, when they cool."

"Thank you, Becca," August said.

"With all this, the work still has to get done," she said, but without heat. She set a lid on a crock and went through the open cellar door and down the steps. It was quiet for a moment in the kitchen, save her thumped treads on the stairs, the hiss and snap of the coals, drops heavy off the overhang plashing down into muddy puddles; and beyond that the steady curtain of falling rain, less a sound than a muffle, as if the air had been sucked out of the day and distance had been collapsed, the world grown close.

Stone tapped the pencil on the table, peering at it as if it held the answers he sought. Still tapping but a slower and lesser tattoo and without looking at Harlan, said, "So Wheeler had his people up some to the farm?"

Harlan also had regathered. He said, "There was work needed to be done. More than I could do, or he wanted to."

"Can you elaborate?"

Harlan looked at Stone. He said, "You ever worked at farming?"

Good for you, thought August. Then, because he had a moment where he feared he'd said this aloud, he busied himself moving the freshly sealed jars to the counter beside the pump and sink. He lifted the kettles from the crane and placed them on the hearth to cool, pumped a new kettle of water, and swung the crane in and pokered up the fire, settling a tripod of dry sticks over the coals. Thinking a pot of mint tea might not be a bad idea.

Stone said, "Many hands are needed to do the work at certain times. Is that what you're saying?"

"It is. From the fall when Mr. Hopeton went away to the war until a year ago, whenever there was hay or grain to be got in, there was a plenty of help to do it."

"That sounds neighborly."

"That's how I saw it, too. At first. But there was another part to it, also."

"Which was?"

Becca came and went with another crock. August had crumpled leaves out of a tin and dropped the handful into the teapot with its cracked and ancient glaze that Narcissa's maternal grandparents had carried into the country. The kettle was close to a boil; the rain had been backed by a fresh wind and was beating against the north windows. The storm had almost worn itself out.

Harlan said, "The first I noticed was, a week, a handful of days, after that help was given, a cow or heifer, a few calves, some shoats, even chickens, disappeared. It was real slow at first but toward the end was like pulling the drain on a sink."

"I see," Stone said. He waited a moment, during which August set cups of tea swirled with honey down before both of them. Stone took his up, inclined his nose toward the steam, smiled and blew, then sipped. Harlan left his on the table, waiting.

Stone sipped again and looked off toward the ceiling plaster. Then he said, "Anything else? That you noticed?"

"What they helped with," Harlan said. "Was meant for the farm. But was also cash crops. You know what I mean?"

"I believe I do."

"Now the first couple years—"

"You're speaking of sixty-one?"

"Yes. That fall, the harvest made enough grain and hay to feed the stock, enough seed grain for the next year also. What surplus there was, I figured Wheeler and Missus Hopeton had been instructed to sell off. Also," he paused.

"Go on."

"That first year things was mostly normal. We all thought the war would be over quick. And it seemed to me she was happy I was there. For Wheeler, I was just a hand to put to work. For a good while I thought that was all there was to it."

"What changed your mind?"

Harlan drank some of his tea. He took a cautious pause, glancing at the window to look upon the rain. Then finally he spoke. "This and that. Things I'd overhear. And on from there, if you take my meaning. That last year everything that could walk itself or be carried by others, left the farm. And Wheeler and Missus Hopeton was gone near as much as they was there."

Stone now paused. He rolled his tea cup and peered in, as if he'd read the leaves matted at the bottom.

August asked, "More tea, Enoch?"

He was rewarded with a broad smile. "No, August. Thank you. I feel I've taken up too much of your afternoon already. I'll say, Malcolm Hopeton chose well when he hired this boy on. Sharp eyes and mind, also." He turned to Harlan. "Can you stand a couple more questions?"

"I'll talk all day and night if it'll help Mr. Hopeton."

Stone smiled.

"You've been a great help," he said. "And I'd caution that in the weeks ahead there may be others asking these questions of you. You're an honorable young man, Harlan Davis, but you must understand that those other lawyers, it's their job to prove Malcolm Hopeton murdered his wife and Amos Wheeler, and to see him hang."

Harlan was in a sudden red sweat. He said, "But he did!"

Stone reached and laid his hand upon the boy's shoulder. In a calming voice he said, "It's my understanding you saw nothing. As to the murders, no one doubts he killed Amos Wheeler. In a blind rage is my thinking. As for Mrs. Hopeton, there's evidence to suggest he didn't intend her death, that it may have been accidental. The truth of this will come clear. That's what's important, in the end. Don't you agree?"

Harlan was quiet a long while, staring off again at the window over the sink, where the rain had fallen off to dripping eave streaks and where, beyond that, there was sunlight diffused among the treetops, the tip of the barn peak lit visible. He said, "I guess I do."

Stone said, "My work in this life is about Truth, not about what the law says, or can do. Because there is a higher law than we make as men. If truth is allowed to come out stark-faced, there is no one who can deny it. The laws of men can be turned upon themselves, as men can be. But truth is a light that streams over men, leaving laws but pebbles in the dirt we must step over."

He stood then, and looked at August first and then Becca. As if he'd forgotten they were in the room. He said, "The rain has quit?"

August said, "Seems it has."

Stone nodded and turned back toward the table. "I have one last question today, Harlan. You can manage that, can't you, son?"

"Yes sir, I can."

"I know it." He addressed August and Becca. "Perhaps, would you be so kind as to bring up my horse and buggy, hitched in your barn in the downpour? I'd be so grateful."

Becca said, "I'll go."

"Thank you," Stone said. "But I was thinking, the both of you? It's a delicate question."

84

August watched Harlan's face swing up as if tied to a wire pulled taut. He reached into his trouser pocket, found nothing, and walked to the shelf above the fireplace, opened the box, and lifted a fresh cheroot, turning it over in his fingers while eying it. While he did this he said, "Becca, give Mr. Stone his hat and cloak, please, then bring his horse up to the house." He rolled the wrinkled black-leafed cylinder again, slowly, until she was gone. Then clamped it between his teeth, leaned down, and pressed a kindling splinter into the coals, then lifted it slowly and dabbed the end of the cheroot as he inhaled. Once it was going he turned and settled again into his chair.

Stone said, "You should've gone with the girl."

"P'raps. What do you think, Harlan?"

"I'm as glad you're here."

August asked Enoch Stone, "Is that what you were after?"

Stone said, "It's how it has to be." He swiveled on his boot heels and dropped to his haunches close to Harlan, one arm again over the boy's shoulders. He said, "It's concerning Mrs. Hopeton. You knew her first name, didn't you? Bethany?" He paused, letting the word hang in the air. Then said, "It's a pretty name. And she was a pretty woman. Most say more than pretty. Did she ever show herself to you? By accident, out of her bath? Or was there more? Did she come to you in the night? Tell the truth, Harlan. What happened in that house, all those years? Harlan?"

Harlan jerked upright from his chair and Enoch Stone lost his balance and fell back onto his buttocks. Harlan grabbed his teacup by the rim and threw it down to splinter to fragments on the floorboards.

"No!" he cried. "It was none of that, none at all." Then was gone, running out the door and off into the muddy yard, where he slipped and fell and rose up again plastered brown and slopping, not seeing his sister as he dodged hard through the orchard and cut behind the barn and was running toward the woods and out of sight, his voice trailing

85

high diminishing cries that rose and held as smoke rings drifting upward and then finally gone. Into the world freshly green and wet.

Becca flew in just as August had helped Enoch Stone to his feet and brushed him off. He was in a quandary, needing to talk to Stone but not willing to send Becca after her brother, not wanting her to find him, to hear what he might say.

Becca, a red fury, bit her words, "Where's my brother run off to? What'd you do?"

August took the moment. "Give me a second to send this lawyer on his way. Then we'll find your brother. Listen to me: Down cellar, behind the crocks of pork there's a corked quart bottle snugged down against the wall. Find that."

She paused. Stone was turning to leave. August said, "Becca, please."

"I know the one you mean." Her voice hard as starch, a way he'd never heard her.

He caught up with Stone in the yard. He said, "That was a terrible thing to do to a boy who was trusting you."

Stone shook off August's hand from his arm and climbed into his buggy and took up the lines. For a moment August thought the man would just drive away. Instead, the lawyer looked down and said, "Do you doubt it? After how he reacted?"

"I'm speaking of what he's lived through the last week, the past almost four years. Not to mention his life before that. Do you know he only turns sixteen come November? He's no child but he's had more piled on him than many a man twice his age. Did you need that last, today? Couldn't you've waited?"

Stone said, "I spoke with David and Iris Schofield day before yesterday, then David took me aside. He gives an account of his daughter that's most disturbing. I needed to answer what I suspected. And asking Harlan cold would not have worked. I'm sorry, August. I blindsided him and am leaving you with that to mend the best you can.

And I pray you will. I need, we all need, Harlan Davis. For many reasons. First among them being to save Malcolm Hopeton from hanging. New York State law is barbaric, Old Testamential, the tribal laws of the ancient Jews. You know of what I speak?"

"An eye for an eye."

"And Christ taught?"

"I know well as you what Christ taught."

"Ah, August, you're angry with me. And you don't have the time this afternoon for me to salve that anger and explain. You'll be distracted until you find the boy and calm him. Some days this is the best we can do. As you said, he's lived through more than he should've. Which is not the same as what he can endure and rise above. I think he's already shown that to be so, even if he doesn't fully know it yet. You did know Bethany Schofield was buried quietly three days ago, with no meeting or gathering, in the pauper's ground?"

"I heard as much. I know some wanted a meeting to mark her passage. Better than most, I think I can understand why that didn't happen."

Enoch Stone adjusted his hat and spread open his waxed coat against the sudden sunlight. He said, "Your devotion over grief serves as a steady reminder to us all, August. But you doubt me, you always have. I take it as a compliment. Now consider this: As soon as possible, prior to the arraignment, I'll be calling upon Judge Gordon to ask for clemency in this case. David Schofield has made clear his desire to speak at the formal proceedings as well. I'm hoping to humbly demonstrate Christian virtue. If upsetting Harlan Davis provided me the assurance I need to follow this course I call it a small cost."

August had a headache clamping his mind. Past his left shoulder outside the entryway Becca stood, the bottle he'd asked for in one hand held away from her side, and Stone waited, paused. All of the moment put August in mind of swarming bees who've lost their queen. The rest of him ached toward wherever Harlan might be.

He shook his head without knowing he was doing so and looked at Enoch Stone and said, "Explain yourself as you will. It means little at the moment." He tugged the horse's bridle and turned it sideways to him, causing Stone to switch sides to look down upon him, and August swatted the horse as Stone heard him and in a spurt they went up toward the road, the wheels sucking in the wet gravel and clay.

He went to Becca and took the bottle from her hand.

She said, "I know what that is."

"Good," he said. "Then you don't have to ask questions about it."

She said, "Where's Harlan? What happened here?"

He said, "I don't know the half of it. But I'm going to find him. A day like this, might take a bit if he run far but won't be that hard. Then he and I might sit and talk a bit. Or not. What I need from you is to get a good sturdy supper ready. Pull some pork or beef from the brine and get it going. Just have food ready. It might be a hour from now or three. I don't know."

She said, "Just the hired girl, then? Now as always?"

"By God, girl, you are! Can you do your job? While I track your brother and do the best I can?" He turned, stepping off in slow, boot-sucking steps. It was suddenly hot and sunlight beat down upon him as deerflies and green-backed flies rose out of the dooryard muck and swirled about him. He jammed the bottle down in his rear pocket and headed for the wet grass and firmer ground of the orchard.

Behind him Becca called his name. He slogged on but lifted one hand and waved without looking back. If she thought he was angry the better chance she'd get done what he'd asked her to do, and nothing was gained by letting her know of his own uncertainty.

He had an idea where Harlan might be. It wasn't so hard. He circled the barn, saw the path through the wet grass toward the woods over the narrow ravine, also saw how the path looped out away and back. To and fro. He turned and went into the barn, entering the empty tie-up, the young calves in their gate-folds, and the pen where the mules were stabled and on through the connecting door where the horses stood in their stalls, big curious heads tipped back against shoulders to watch him, the bulks of muscle all craned and curious. Against the wall hung the harnesses slung from hooks, the workbench area where he made repairs, the bench and foot vise, leatherworking tools of all sorts. Beyond that, through another door, was the dung shed, with high arched openings to the south free of doors where in winter he wheelbarrowed horse and cow manure until the weather broke enough to haul it out by sledge or wagon and spread by forkfuls on his fields.

From the horse barn he climbed the ladder through the floor of the high vaulted loft and stood there, between the tiers of hay, listening. He heard nothing. He thought to say a name, plain and calm, to rise around him but did not. There were ladders rising left and right, east and west; he must pick and hope he picked correctly.

When the wheat died from blight, Narcissa had said, "You have to trust and if you're wrong you must trust the failure will lead you closer to the answer. In Time we're crushed by the gears or learn how to drive the machine. And the machine always breaks down, doesn't it? Oh, how you worry."

Touched his forehead.

He went up a ladder and found Harlan. The boy sat deep in on the hard-packed hay, knees up to his chin and arms wrapped around his knees, behind him the peaks of new hay, overhead the shingled roofing shot through with beads of light, mud-daubers and paper wasps drifting from their rafter nests.

August stepped from the ladder and the boy didn't seem to hear him, didn't look back. August found his own perch in the tiers of hay and settled down. Harlan, in his canvas trousers and worn blue serge shirt, barefoot and hatless, a shrunken but muscled boy with ears like dried apples clumped back against his head, hair the color of the mules he loved, cut rough with sheep-shears or somesuch, perhaps only his pocketknife before a crackled mirror-glass. Ill-mended was what he was, shrunken, looking no more than twelve years old but for the weary old-man sag of his shoulders. And whatever clots of worry buzzed between his ears.

So August sat hushed. The bottle wedged in his hip pocket felt a foolish thing. As did the words he carried, had imagined himself saying. He studied his hay and once deftly and silently swatted away a yellow jacket droning fast from the rafter nest. And waited.

After a time Harlan did not turn but said, "Mr. Swartout?"

"I'm right here."

"It's near time to milk. If we did that, you reckon we could not talk about any of all this mess?"

"I think that would be a good plan."

SIX

MALCOLM HOPETON WAS seventeen years old in 1844 when he came west from Vermont and spent the summer and early autumn traipsing by foot the new county of Yates, quiet enough so most thought him a raw country boy with small prospects; but he was wise in the ways of men, cattle, horses, and mules, wisdom he held close. When he found the farm in Milo between the lakes, the land agents all but laughed at him until he drew his purse from his pocket and offered cash money less fifty dollars toward the asking price.

He didn't mention it but beyond the fertility of the farm the deal-clincher was the orchard of a dozen old peach trees, mere saplings not discovered when Sullivan's army had swept through the Iroquois lands burning villages, fields and orchards with great thoroughness, missing only a handful of small outlying settlements, one of which had been here. Malcolm Hopeton had only once in his life eaten a fresh peach but had never forgotten it. And so with a mild face, he sharped the land agent into including every last tool and item, including the pruning saw and hooks, by withdrawing the offer three minutes later. He spent a week itemizing all of these goods and storing them in the root cellar that he then strapped with metal bands, a heavy clasp, chain and lock.

He departed the country until the following spring, when he reappeared at the very end of March while the drifts from the blizzards were still rotting on northern slopes or lees of buildings, driving a team of big bay mules hauling a canvas-covered wagon of household goods, a string of three Jersey cows tied behind and one side of the wagon a cage strapped on holding a spotted sow heavy with young. On the seat beside him, his grandfather, Cyrus Hopeton, twisted sideways from a poorly healed hip shattered by a horse kick years before. Once they were settled the old man became as a shade, a spectral being, to the curious neighbors. He hobbled about using a pair of ash-wood livestock canes but mostly remained in the house, where evenings they ate the food he'd prepared and discussed the business of the day. In mild weather he'd make his way to the barn to sit on a stool during evening chores, and on certain days in the spring or fall there was a sheltered corner that faced south behind the barn where Malcolm fashioned a bench for him, where he'd sit to let the sun soak heat into his old bones, the spot looking over the grove of now reclaimed peach trees. His mind was sharp as ever but he trusted his grandson to be their public face; he was done with the world of men, and for good reason: He'd lost his family to the apocalyptic teachings of William Miller. It was not only Miller's extreme vision and calculations of the world coming to end, but his followers' determination to ascend from their hilltop unencumbered by material goods on that golden morn, and so Cyrus had watched his son sell his farm outside of Poultney and take rooms with his wife and daughters in a cramped house with other Millerites; but when Cyrus's own wife entreated him to do the same he'd taken pause, consulted with his grandson, and sent the boy west. When Malcolm returned with his news, Cyrus had summarily sold off his holdings and sent his wife to live with the Millerites, and had ridden west with a stony face that softened as they came down the west shore of Seneca Lake and he saw the land his grandson had described. Malcolm thought at the time that he knew very well what old Cyrus was leaving behind; but it would be many years before, standing alone with his own mind crumbling, he'd truly understand how he and his grandfather had been a team in harness, pulling their slow steps away from a world lost.

Malcolm offered nothing of their past to the usual prodding queries, and such interest faded as it became clear he would prosper. A couple of years in and all anyone spoke of was his corn, his grain, the sleek hardy cattle that turned out butter like bejesus, and the mules. Not a few girls cast eyes his way but saw only a gritted determination toward his work and despite threshing bees and harvest suppers were unable to impress themselves upon him and so looked elsewhere. As the years rolled over, his neighbors decided he was a solitary man and forgot that he was still young. And so left him to his work and counted on him when he was a needed hand and returned the effort. They thought they knew him, and he was happy enough with that.

Their seventh winter was mild, with meager snow, a few cold barren stretches, days warming above freezing even in the short light of January. Rain fell, and often toward dawn turned to ice. The ice would melt to slush and freeze again at night, then more sunny days revealed bare brown grass, bare brown earth. People spoke of an open winter. In early February there were five days in a row when it was warm enough to work in shirtsleeves and the ground remained soft overnight. On the fifth day Cyrus had made his way to the barn to sit and watch a first-calf heifer a week overdue while Malcolm worked in the woodlot. Around noon a light rain blew in and a couple hours later the sky suddenly swam to a foreboding indigo and within twenty minutes the air was cold as an anvil, every limb, twig, stem and blade of grass sheathed in hard ice. The sledge was frozen into the mud. The steaming mules were encased and brittle, the harness leather stiff, buckles frozen. Malcolm tore free a beech limb from the brush pile to beat the ice from the mules and climbed on and rode the team home, a slow journey as neither mule wanted to do anything but stand stock still and wait for a thaw, clearly seeing all about a land designed to break their legs and smash their jaws. He pressed them on. It was late dusk, twilight, near the dropping swift dark of night when they eased into the farmyard, where the ice was even thicker. He pulled them up short and jumped down to go toward the body he'd seen tumbled and sprawled only feet outside the barn door. His feet shot away and he bruised his tailbone and was breathless, scared for a bad moment as he tried to get to his feet and could not, then slowed himself and studied the situation. He might not walk but he could crawl, except when a hand or foot shot away and he smashed his chin down on the ice. Cyrus had not moved at all and Malcolm was certain he was dead. He knew if he could reach his grandfather it was only feet more to the barn and up close among the cows, warmth. He eased himself down flat on the ice and rolled himself over. And did that again. He slipped back a bit with each roll but was gaining, then of a sudden was up against something cold but soft. He reached and his crimped stubbed fingers held cloth.

Cyrus Hopeton spoke. "My hip's broke again. Help me to the house?"

Malcolm said, "We'll do something here."

"That cold come down like the wrath of God."

"It did. Can you hold on a bit more?" The barn wasn't more than ten feet away.

"I willed myself to fly but it didn't take."

"I'll be right back." Without waiting for a response he commenced rolling again until he hit up against the siding, reached until he felt the give of the door, gained purchase and pulled himself upright, just catching the latch as his feet began to slide away. Once inside the barn he found the lantern and lighted it, took down a coil of rope and tied

94

one end to an upright post, set the lantern on a stool so the lantern threw light sideways out the door. He wrapped the rope once around his waist and on his knees paid out rope until he was beside his grandfather again, all the time waving his free arm above his head to keep the mules spooked and from charging the door. They loomed at the edge of the faint sprawl of light. He worked more rope free and looped it under the old man's arms, about his chest. Cyrus was silent throughout but for his ragged rasp of breath.

Malcolm said, as much for himself as the old man, "I'm going to haul us both inside, a hitch at a time. Can you stand that?"

"It kills me, I'll die happier than I expected a bit ago."

"Don't get maudlin on me. I'm the one doing the work."

"Go on and do it then. Christ, I'm busted like a rag doll." He hacked out a cough that trailed to the slightest whimper of pain.

It rained again, then snowed four inches overnight, and Malcolm was able to carry Cyrus from the nest of hay between two cows where they'd spent the night to the house and settled him into bed. It was the same hip broken again but the old man refused a doctor or any attention at all but spent the remaining winter and spring mostly in bed. He'd hobble down in the late afternoon and eat supper, sit in a padded horsehair-stuffed chair and talk of the day, reading the newspapers and weeklies before being helped back to bed. Once spring came and his windows could be opened he seemed to revive but only to the point of lying propped on pillows, watching what he could of the world outside of his room, in all ways. With summer Cyrus was not better but no worse, easier perhaps for the warm weather. Shrunken from his months mostly abed.

It was this way the morning Malcolm walked out into the peach orchard and saw the peach stones on the grass. Several times that week he'd strolled through to lift one of the first ripe fruits and stand and eat it and so knew soon would begin the cascade; but that morning he studied the stones in the grass and knew he'd just missed it. But someone else had not. He leaned and picked up one of the stones. Clean as a whistle. These peaches were best stewed or dried, the old Indian fruit that would begin to rot before it lifted easily away from the hard knotted stones. Something had been working, stealing his own pleasure.

He ate a peach, pocketed three more, and went on to cut his oats. Mid-morning, his hair slicked with sweat, eating a peach, juice running down his chin and a forearm also, he almost laughed. Coons, was what he thought. They'd been stripping the sweet corn not yet ripe and so moved on and found the peaches. He gnawed the stone clean, tossed it off into the creamy tan stand of oats, and clucked up the team. The binder teeth chattering. It was later in the morning when he'd stopped to let the team cool in the shade and prized another peach from his pocket, was eating it when he paused.

He could see a coon or two climbing a tree and sitting on branches to eat the fruit. Dropping the cleaned stones. Perhaps they even had the nose and knowledge to tell ripe fruit from hard or perhaps they'd eat a hard peach happily as a soft one. But could it be possible they were so sure-handed to never drop one as they plucked it free? Or partly eat a hard peach, drop it and seek a better sweeter one? It was not dead of winter and he knew with sweet corn that coons would be picky, leaving half-gnawed cobs dangling or down in the dirt between the rows.

Coons had never got into his peaches before. Or if they had they'd gathered drops and carried them off to eat elsewhere.

He tossed the stone and went back to work. He'd thresh his way until the binding platform was half full, halt the team, and step around behind to tie up the stalks in a bundle, stand it upright behind the machine and go on. He knew it was slow for want of a hired man but was delighted with growing oats and wheat and barley and having the machine do work that as a boy he recalled being done on a scant acre of thin oats by his father and grandfather and himself, with hand sickles, each man slowly working to make a small bundle and passing it to the boy to tie with braided oat-straws. Three days, maybe four to gain scant ration for a single horse over the winter. When there was prosperity they bought wheat flour from the merchant overstreet; when not, and most of the winter anyway, they ate griddle cakes and dodgers made from coarsely ground flint corn. So he went on, hot as blazes, sweated through his trousers and shirt, wishing he knew how to flatten wheat straw and braid a hat as some men he'd known could; but he worked on, bareheaded. He wouldn't spend the money yet to buy such a thing in town.

By the end of day he had four acres of oats cut and bundled and those bundles stacked neatly on the threshing floor in the barn. Another day and four more acres of oats, then on to the barley. The wheat still ten days or two weeks away. Just when he'd be starting his second cutting of hay, but he was young and game and looked forward to the challenge of reading which to do on what day, portioning his days and time, each to the next.

Which he as all men already did.

Still thinking about peaches, he milked and fed up, made up a supper from the garden and slabs cut from brined pork and fried in bacon drippings, ate with his grandfather and left the old man propped abed in the summer evening heat with the most recent *American Agriculturalist* and the local weekly *Chronicle*, then went off downstairs to his own long, late summer twilight. He puttered about intent on his regular routine, not wanting to alert his grandfather to any change, knowing the old man heard everything and knew every pattern of life about him.

There was a crescent moon just risen and a wash of stars when an hour before midnight he stepped off the front stoop with the smooth-bore shotgun loaded with a charge of number-eight birdshot, and keeping to the house shadow the moon cast, made his way until he could dart to the shadow of the barn, hugged that tight and went around the end to sit on the bench that overlooked the peach trees. He took a great amount of time doing so, silent all the way but for the faint slur of dew against his bare feet. Barely seated he made out a dark form up in the blanket of leaves in the third tree down. He almost raised the gun but reconsidered and slow as he could he set the shotgun aside, upright against the bench. He heard the phewt and then the spit stone plop into the grass beneath the tree. He laid both hands flat on the bench and launched himself.

The boy saw him and dropped out of the tree and took off running. Malcolm charged hard and scooped the boy up, arms locked around his chest, and the boy kicked wildly, striking Malcolm in the groin, and both together hit the ground and rolled over, Malcolm not letting go. Then the boy started using elbows, knees, feet and hands to hit whatever he could hit that held him, writhing and striking all at once, a gritty earth-bound determination to get free.

One elbow caught Malcolm against his nose and he huffed a cough and gripped the boy tight and rolled over, pinning the boy between his much larger self and the ground. The boy could squirm but only.

Malcolm said, "Quit. I got you."

"You ain't."

"I'm flat on top of you. Now quit."

The boy twisted his head and bit Malcolm's hand hard, and he reared back. The boy began to squirm out from under him and Malcolm jumped to his feet, twisting the boy around so he had one arm levered up against the boy's back. As he was doing this he stripped off his suspenders and quickly lashed one end around the jerked-high wrist, so the boy grunted with pain even as he was tied tight. Because his hand hurt, and to show the boy he was truly caught, Malcolm booted him in the butt, sending him reeling forward before the suspender snapped him back, upright.

"Now," Malcolm said. "We can have us a talk."

The boy shrugged and turned sideways as if he was done fighting it, then slapped his free hand down against his trouser pocket and snapped out and open a jackknife, was slashing toward the suspender when Malcolm realized what it was and jerked the boy off balance as he also kicked him hard in the groin. The knife flew into the dark as the boy sagged and Malcolm jerked again, causing the boy to stumble forward, and caught him with both arms, spun him around away from where the knife had gone, and sucker-punched him in the stomach.

Finally he had the boy subdued on the ground. Malcolm squatted some feet away, close enough to loom and pounce, far enough to see the need coming. The boy was sucking to get his wind back.

"I'm half of a mind to lock you in the smokehouse."

"That's kidnapping. I'd have the law on you."

"No. Come morning, I'd truss you like a roasting hen and haul you to town and show the sheriff the knife you pulled on me and explain how you was stealing my peaches and I'd guess he'd see it my way."

After a moment the boy said, "You can't eat em all anyway."

He considered this and then said, "It's not about what I eat or store for winter. It's that they belong to me. Every winter I prune the trees, so they bear best. If I had extra, I'd likely give em to a neighbor who helped me out some way."

"You do that?"

"That's not the point. There's a value to em. When you slink in at night and eat your belly full, you're cutting into my value. It's mine, see. To do with as I want. If I didn't care for peaches at all and let em rot on the ground, that'd be my choice. It still would not excuse you eating em."

"That's flat stupid. If you was to let em all rot, you'd never known I was here."

"You'd come and asked me, I might've said, fine, take some. Maybe even loaned you a basket if you hadn't thought to bring one."

"There's something wrong with your head. Do you know that?"

"There's no talking to you. I'm thinking the smokehouse is best."

"It'd just be trouble for you in the morning. Ain't you got work to do?"

"What's your name?"

"I ain't saying."

Malcolm sighed. He said, "Best I figure you ate a bushel, maybe closer to two. So far."

"I never."

"So it's between seventy-five cents and two dollars you owe me. Since we never will agree, let's call it a dollar on the slim side. Do you know what a dollar means?"

"Nothing. My count is three peaches tonight, less the half a one I dropped when you come running after me."

Malcolm said, "So call it a dollar. That's two day's wages for a hand. You being but a scrap of a man, I make it four days work you owe me. You shoot bluster but you don't want the law in this, so let's make it easy. Starting first light you'll work those four days dawn to dusk and I'll feed you breakfast, dinner and supper to boot. How's that sound?"

"It's awful late, to put in that sort of day come dawn."

"For me as well. And though I'll work you hard, I'll put in the bulk of it."

The boy was quiet a while. Then he said, "All right."

"All right what?"

"You leave the law out of it and I'll give you four days."

"We're agreed, then? You'll be here first light?"

"As soon as I can."

"Oh, I know that. Look, walk along with me a bit and I'll show you a shortcut."

"A shortcut? Mister, you don't even know where I live."

Malcolm snorted and stepped off toward the bulk of barns before the night sky. The moon was low. The forgotten suspender jerked tight and Malcolm slowed to let the boy come even with him, as if they weren't tied together. So they went around the barn and into the farmyard, up toward the icehouse and buttery, the other outbuildings between the house and the barns. Malcolm paused then and looked up at the stars, twisting his neck a bit and reached in his pocket and pulled out the last peach picked that morning. He held it out and said, "You want this?"

The boy was nerved right up. He said, "I don't reckon. You said there was a shortcut."

"I also asked your name."

"Yer fucking me, ain't you?" And swung a wild, desperate roundhouse.

Malcolm stepped under it and popped a fist to the lower jaw, the other into the boy's midsection. And once more watched the boy go down. He hauled him a dozen feet to the pump and ran cold water onto his upright gaped face until the boy came up stuttering and spluttering.

Malcolm Hopeton said, "There's a dozen ways to skin a cat. But only one right one. We'll be talking about that, the days to come. Don't never ask me why I chose you; you needed choosing and that's all I know. Now, get on to bed."

He walk-stepped the boy the short distance and pulled back the door of the smokehouse and kicked the boy inside. It being summer there wasn't any fire, just the tight confines and the high peak where hams and sides of bacon, beef brisket, a venison ham were shelved, and rows of dangling hard sausages rested. With no ladder, far from the reach of even the most intent and practiced thief. The boy landed on his side, hawked a gob from his lungs and spat it into the small circle of dead fire.

Malcolm said, "You're the Wheeler boy, ain't you?"

"Fuck you."

"I was only thinking you know my name and if I knew yours maybe we could get on faster to a better place. But that ain't my call."

He shut the door and latched it and turned toward the house. He was terribly tired and more so because he knew he'd just taken on something he didn't want or truly need. He hated this part of himself but also knew he couldn't live without it. Life had informed him against trusting other men, a message reinforced by the old man laid up until death in the home neither would have if not for both of them; and yet Malcolm knew hope in his heart for the business of life. How to sum that equation, beyond countless ways? And why should it be otherwise?

Then, walking away from the smokehouse, the voice came over him, frightened, plaintive.

"It's only Amos, here. That's all. Just Amos."

Amos Wheeler looked fully small as possible for a ten-year-old, not five hours later when Malcolm unbarred the smokehouse door. Skinny as a starved rat, trousers and rough linen blouse rotting off of him, sunken eyes encircled with bruises not made by man but most of all trembling with a terror of where he was. First thought Malcolm had was, I should send him on his way. But he needs meat on his bones and peaches won't do that. When he reached in through the pale light as the sun crested over the eastern edge of the world, the boy shrank away.

Malcolm said, "If I was of a mind to kill you, last night would've been the time. What there is right now is a pot of coffee and a table of eggs and ham, dodgers and molasses. After that oats to harvest. It's not terrible work and easier with two than one. So follow on and learn something or cut and run, I don't care. But if I ever see you again I'll fill you full of buckshot and know I did a good thing." He walked away, hungry himself and tired but already stepped into the day. As if he had a choice. And was almost surprised when Amos Wheeler pattered after him. Malcolm Hopeton had never been hungry for food, but had been for much else, and could only guess where belly-hunger would take a person.

102

By noon Amos had got the hang of bundling the oats, riding on the platform of the thresher. Behind them stretched a line of sheaves that wobbled and then straightened. In the long evening after milking and supper they'd returned to the shorn oat field with the wagon and brought the sheaves to the cover of the barn. Beyond questions and directions they'd not uttered a dozen words all day. Walking out of the barn into twilight, Malcolm picked up an old horse blanket.

Amos said, "You going to lock me in the smokehouse again?"

"Aren't they going to miss you at home?"

"No."

"I've got no other place for you."

There was a silence. Then the boy said, "It weren't so bad."

"The smokehouse or the work?"

"None of it. The food weren't half-bad, neither."

"It's a clear sky and warm night. Tomorrow we get into the barley. Early as we can. You want to snag a couple peaches if you wake famished the middle of the night?"

"Mister, I am done with peaches."

"Saying that doesn't change the deal you struck."

"All I said was I'm done with peaches."

"You might change your mind. No harm with that."

"I'll never eat a peach again, my whole life."

They were at the smokehouse. The boy had tugged the door open but stood, waiting.

Malcolm said, "That's a big presumption, against a small thing."

Amos Wheeler said, "You don't know the first thing about me. But you will."

At noon dinner on the fourth day Amos excused himself to use the outhouse. He and Malcolm had rinsed their heads under the yard pump before coming to the table, so their hair was plastered cool and wet, their faces clean and hands also, otherwise they were grimed with sweat-caked dust, chaff, hulls, dirt tossed up by the cutting bar. They were still at the barley but that morning as they climbed the swell at the end of the field, Malcolm had been eyeing his wheat, washed pale gold, heads tight and high, the field alive as swirls of breeze moved through it, wondering if he might hire the boy at a better wage to stay on for that harvest, also. Amos wasn't a talker but had been quick to learn and was steady at his job.

At the end of the first day when Malcolm had placed food before the boy and then carried supper up to his grandfather, he saw that Cyrus Hopeton had clearly been watching best he could these new doings from his perch on high. He'd listened to the story of the capture and the deal made and how it was working out. When he finished gnawing the ham hock stewed with red chard and speckled beans, he'd only said, "You took it on. But tomorrow noon and supper I want to eat in the kitchen with the both of you. There's that horse-hair-padded chair can be pulled to table. I can gimp about enough with both canes to fill out meals; you see there's all I need on the table to do it with. From the garden or cellar."

After ducking his head at first introduction, if Amos Wheeler thought a thing about the old man across from him, there was no telling, as his sole interest in the kitchen was the food laid upon the table and how much he could consume before the platters were empty and Malcolm would rise and stretch and say, as if addressing some obscure corner of the room, "Let's get back to it."

Malcolm knew his grandfather was making a thorough study of the boy and guessed they'd discuss this when the four days ended. An evening conversation, at the table, perhaps on the small porch, Cyrus aided by Malcolm—perhaps even farther, to the barn or the bench before the peach trees, which were now drooping heavy, ripe. The next pressing job to be done mornings before the dew was off the wheat.

Then Amos went to shit and did not return. After a bit this was clear to both men.

Malcolm said, "He wants to impress upon me that his calculations and mine differ, and that he sticks by his. I guess we've seen the last of Amos Wheeler."

"You can be a fool," Cyrus said. "Every minute he was here, even locked in the smokehouse, he was looking about and calculating what you had and how he could make use of it. Oh, he'll be back all right but likely you'll never lay eyes upon him."

"I might never see him again but I believe I gave him something to think about, to consider how to live his life. And I think in his way that was what he was after, even if he couldn't have said it, when he came filching fruit. There's a smartness to that boy that wants well beyond what's been offered him so far. I think he might just reach for it."

"Be careful of what you wish for, as has been said. If nothing else, you fed him, and he knows he can always find food here. Lock the smokehouse is what I say."

"Now then. Hear yourself. You're up and down stairs, moving about these past days, after months of lying in the bed. I'd say he was good for you, also."

"It was the urgency," Cyrus said. "Malcolm, you're a fine young man. You show promise. You need a wife."

"I thought you and me were doing just fine."

"I won't be here forever."

"It didn't work out so good for you, did it?"

"You've every right to think that. But you're wrong. Your grandmother was the best thing ever happened in my life. I couldn't have done what I did without Leona beside me. Not the first bit of it. It was a grand life. All I'm saying is, you need a wife. If she won't put up with me, tell me. We'll work it out."

"But you left her. And Mother and the rest."

"What happened was some strong notion of God caught them up and all of them became people I no longer knew. For you, as well. The most terrible thing that can happen to a man. I could've gone along with it all. But what would I have been, then? A liar to myself. God is God and whatever he does, he does not jump down and bestow a man with special knowledge held back from the rest of us. At least not more than once. Once is enough for God. Understand, I think of your grandmother, my son and his wife, your sisters, every minute of every day. And if even one of em was to show up knocking at the door this afternoon I'd open it wide and welcome them in. But they won't. And I won't."

"You wouldn't if one did?"

"I'm saying they won't. Because they can't admit God fooled em. They can't think it was the preacher that did that; he was just the chosen voice. So it comes back to God. And if God fools you, well, what do you have then?"

Malcolm drummed his fingers on the table. Of a sudden he was dumped into the questions that had been stirring him for a dozen years, and getting glimpses of answers and wanted only to sit and talk on through however many hours, the afternoon, night, the following day and days falling after that until he knew all he could learn.

He also wanted to finish his barley and look again at the wheat. Once again, he was on his own.

He said, "Maybe God fools all of us, all of the time."

Cyrus planted his palms on the table and pressed himself up, then reached for one cane and then the other. Once he had them he stood no higher, wavering side to side, almost shimmering. He said, "It's possible I suppose, but I couldn't see the point in it. Go on, get out, I know you want to get back to work."

"There's work to be done."

Cyrus nodded. "There always is. Get to it. Have I ever told you how thankful I am for you?"

106

Malcolm was half-turned, stopped and looked back at the fierce old man. He smiled. "Can I get on, now?"

Cyrus said, "Yes. Find yourself a wife."

"In the barley?"

Cyrus did not smile. "I've seen the girls looking at you. The Miller girl is comely. So's Mina White. Others, also. And some of those have younger sisters. But they all stopped. Looking at you in that way, I mean. Mina got married, didn't she?"

"She did. A great strapping fellow from Dresden, works the steamboats."

"I'm saying there's plenty and some. Best is a farm girl herself, already knows the work and the life. Good bones help. Picking a wife's not like picking a heifer but you want to look at the mother, how many siblings. Of course you have to feel some attraction. Discover it's there, between the two of you. But like anything that grows good and strong, you need to cultivate it. Nurse it along, allow it to bloom."

Malcolm shook his head. "It just hasn't happened. I'm not dead, yet."

"I've known my share of bachelors. You recall old Humphrey down the road in Poultney?"

"He was a hand to hay."

"Most end up sad. Alone, and then all alone, and then on the Poor Farm. Tell me, you like girls well enough? Speaking broadly."

Malcolm smiled. "Granddad? When I find the right girl she and I will rattle the rafters all night over your head and you'll wish I'd waited just a while more."

Cyrus grinned back. Most of his teeth were down to yellowed stubs, his gums white and pink. "Most nights I don't sleep more than two, maybe three hours. I'd welcome the diversion. The worst part of getting old is not how your body breaks down and your mind frets over it; the worst part is when your mind forgets how old all else has got, and sees the world as if all of you was twenty-five. You'd be

107

surprised how often that happens. Now there, you. Get on to work. And don't worry about me."

"You'd quit jawing, I would."

"Go on," Cyrus said. "And keep a sharp eye peeled against the Wheeler boy."

"Now, I can't do it all. How about I do the farming and the wife hunting and you keep on the lookout for the mighty outlaw?"

His voice rasped high, a scythe into the pliant warm love between them, Cyrus said, "No. You have to do all three. It's your job, your time. Now get out of here and let me settle down. I'll have supper, you work long enough."

Malcolm swayed with arrested motion, then came and kissed his grandfather's cheek. He said, "I love you, old man."

"Get along," Cyrus said. And the young man went down out of the house back into the day. The old man stood held up by his two tree-limbs planted from his hands to the ground. As if he was pressing down to the earth he knew in his heart he'd come from, and to which he was returning. He was passing blood in his stools and urine; he had not told his grandson that he was dying, and it would be soon.

Amos Wheeler did not take long to reappear. Less than a month had passed following his abrupt departure, and Malcolm was cutting his wheat when he looked up squinting with the heat shimmers over the grain and saw the figure crossing from the woods and even with the sweat and dust in his eyes, knew who it was. His first thought: It's not an hour until dinner. Then considered the hike the boy must've made from his family compound in the Outlet gorge and grew more gracious. Hoping the boy wanted work, welcoming the idea of help. He pulled the mules to a stop and tied up his sheaves and waited.

Amos wore a new pair of serge overalls, cut down to fit him, and a woven straw hat Malcolm briefly coveted.

Amos said, "I know you think I welshed on our deal, but I was due late that afternoon to do a job of work with my brothers and Pop."

"I'm not so unreasonable, if you'd cared to explain instead of just slipping off."

"I asked around. Seventy-five cents for a bushel of peaches is a mite high."

"Did you tramp all this way to discuss the past?"

"You need a hand. I can do the work. I ain't a man but am tough as spit and shoe leather. You seen that. You took a measure of me. I ask you do that again. And pay me a fair wage for a day's work. That sound like something?"

"I don't need a full-time hand the year around."

Amos spat. "You think I don't know that? There's plenty else I can do, when you're not needing me."

"I imagine there is. I don't know. I could use some help. And would pay a fair wage. You'd want room and board, as well?"

Amos shook his head. "Mister, I am done with that smokehouse. I don't need no bed. You should feed me while I'm working, that's all."

"It's long days this time of year, most any time I'd need you. Making that hike home and back, that would cut into your sleep, not your work, is that clear?"

The boy looked off toward a pair of high smudged eastern clouds. Then he said, "The way I see it, that's my worry and none of yours. Is this oats or barley you're trying to get up? You want to get on with it?"

"It's wheat. And nearly noon-dinner time."

"I recall how to bundle, whatever the grain. I could work a hour, even two before I needed a bite. We going to work or did I just waste my time?"

"You're some kind of wonder, aren't you, Amos Wheeler?"

"No sir. I'm just looking to get things done."

★   ★   ★

109

He was there at first light and worked until the work was done, which those days was in broad sun-stroked evening or twilight. Ate what was offered at all three meals and in between and walked off into the bat- and swallow-riven dusk. Strode in mornings soaked with dew, the same swallows out as the sun broke fresh over the land. There wasn't much to him but bone wrapped with hard thin muscle, a sharp face with eyes the shade of river ice, lank, dull brown hair grimed with sweat and grease. Not quite handsome but striking, a feral man-boy quality about him, supple in his movements but with a coiled tension. Malcolm guessed the boy was used to quick words and a quicker retribution, most likely for infractions both real and imagined. But he was impressed with the boy's steadiness in those very long days. As he was also impressed, and upon reflection, chastened, by the thoughtful, deliberate, and unremitting consumption of food at breakfast, dinner and supper. Mostly, though, he was glad of the help and glad to share his food with a hungry boy. Despite, perhaps because of, the wreckage that the Lord, one way or another, had wrought upon his family, Malcolm held a strong if mostly untouched streak of believing it was up to him to do his share and then some. To provide aid and assistance when and where it was needed, and that determining those degrees was an especial burden gifted upon him. And upon those like him who did not look to God.

Early August holds high summer's most brutal blistering heat, the days as long as July, the wheel not yet turned but crimped like a storm across a far plain lay the end of the month when nights were cool, goldenrod and purple asters bloomed, long shadows draped both dawn and dusk longer. So, for the man working those long, hot days, a breath of cool tongue strokes toward him, unfelt yet but there, certain as the first glimpses, late of night, of Orion and the Sisters. Winter rising.

With all of this, in the hours just past midnight after the fourth day of Amos Wheeler's return, Malcolm woke knowing he'd missed something. They had finished with the wheat early afternoon and had managed to cut a small field of hay late in the hot afternoon and through the open windows with no air moving the sweet smell of laid-over swathes of long grass just beginning to cure filled the room. Likewise, floating downward from the trays in the attic overhead came the pungency of sliced peaches in their third week of drying. A vinegar tang in the house from the night before when he'd chopped and put up two crocks of pickled cabbage. From outside the window he heard a fox bark, calling kits or just signaling itself. Moments later and fainter he heard a return bark, from over the lake and high on the Bluff. He thought, He's not going home at night. He can't be. There's not anywhere near the time.

They worked right through the next day, Malcolm pushing hard. They cut more hay in the morning, raked the ready hay before dinner, and got it up by mid-afternoon. Then for the first time Malcolm took Amos into the buttery and they churned and paddled salt in and buttermilk out, and filled tubs to be settled back into the cooling well. Done with that, they returned to the barn, where he left the boy sweeping the cobwebs, dust and chaff from the granaries, readying them for the threshing.

He killed and set a chicken to roast, dug new potatoes, sliced tomatoes, shucked sweet corn to boil in the kettle atop the potatoes and dropped corn dodgers into a spider of bubbling lard as he stepped to the door to call the boy in to eat. He wanted him worked out and filled up when he walked away into the early evening. He had a bowl of wild plums sliced and stirred with sugar and clotted cream.

Cyrus watched, a shipwreck of a man in the horsehair chair. Malcolm dropped a handful of ground coffee beans and half a crushed eggshell into the small kettle, stirred it once with a knife blade, and then covered it as he pulled the crane back a bit from the heat. Cyrus said, "What's this, you're up to?"

"It's been long days, is all. I thought we'd make a short one of this."

Cyrus said, "You're aiming to trail after him, find out where he's nested?"

Malcolm paused, then said, "You've already figured it out."

"He sure wasn't hiking all the way to the Outlet and back, the hours you two have been putting in. And get any sleep at all."

"When did this occur to you?"

Cyrus made a wry mouth, as if he was sucking alum. "Bout the second morning. Don't be hard on yourself; you're out there thinking one step to the next. All I got is my mind and it wanders all over creation."

"Plus you mistrust him."

"I mistrust everybody, mostly. But you gotta ask yourself, if he's not doing what he leads you to believe, what else is he up to. Or will get up to."

"I think he's a clever boy figured out a way to not make a long walk for scant sleep. Now, with all your rumination and cogitation, did you figure out where he's made his camp?"

"In the woods, surely. And yours, no doubt, so he can't be rousted by anyone but you. I seen him out my window twice, once of a dawn and once at sunset. Stepping on the road or off it. He's cutting crosslots through the flint corn and the lower meadow to the ravine and wood-lot. My guess is that old tree you told me about."

"The chestnut grove."

"If I was a boy, that's where I'd hole up."

Motion caught Malcolm's eye. Amos Wheeler was coming across the yard. He looked again at his grandfather and said, "Amos recalls yourself to you, doesn't he?"

"Not one lick."

"You say. I'll stand my ground on that one and time will tell. You ready for a nice supper?"

Cyrus shook his head. "I don't know how it is I can still eat like I'm working first light to last, but my belly takes it. I should be sipping tea and choking down dry toast once a day. I imagine it's just a bad habit."

"Or a good one."

"What's good?" Amos Wheeler asked, stepping in the door.

The three chestnuts stood deep in the woodlot near the ravine that the stream had carved throughout all of time, to its bedrock of stone, small pools, chutes, waterfalls, all starting in a small marsh farther east and flowing west and slowly downhill to where it ran into the Crooked Lake. The chestnuts also ancient, so much so that they had formed their own clearing in the smaller, younger growth of shagbarks, oaks, locust, cedars and pine. The chestnut trunks were a three-man span at chest height, great loopy roots worn smooth as kneecaps above ground, a high, dense canopy and the glade within large enough to shelter a horse and rider from a storm.

Malcolm walked the direct route, skirting his corn and then crossing the meadow before entering the woods, and so stood watching, unexpected and hidden in the long dusk. Amos Wheeler had kindled a small cautious fire, for cheer, not heat. He'd gathered a considerable stack of deadwood across from the fire-ring of blackening stones. There was a crude lean-to constructed with the opening facing the fire, three feet high at the peak-pole that sloped back five feet, where it hit the ground. The sides snapped branches and brush laid up against the pole. Not much more than a hole to hide in, a burrow barely above ground. He had a tin pail of water with a dipper gourd tied to the handle at his feet and was smoking a cob pipe.

"Don't jump," Malcolm said, as he stepped around the chestnut and into the fire-glow.

"You think I didn't hear you coming? Crashing around like you was a lickered bear."

"No doubt you've seen such a thing."

Amos Wheeler blew expert smoke rings toward the few uplifting sparks. "Mister, I seen more than you might think." He sighed, a small roll of his shoulders. It struck Malcolm the boy was unaware of doing so, a natural wearied physical release or reaction. Amos went on. "You come to kick me out?"

"You might've asked."

"It's just a mite of firewood would rot anyway. But I'll go, you want."

"You're a hardworking boy. Could make a fine hand all around, one day."

"I earned my way since I was five years old. You tell me what I got to do, to earn this spot, I'll take it on. Walk in when the first bird sings, split wood, help in the barn. Show me and I'll do it." He paused and said, "I'm awake anyway."

Malcolm took a stick from the pile and pushed the fire around, added the stick and then two more. "I expect you are."

"Then I can stay here?"

Carefully, thinking he was being careful, Malcolm said, "It won't be so long and the nights'll get crisp."

Amos spat to the other side of the fire, lifted the dipper from the pail and drank. Water pilled on his chin and dropped. "I thought, we get a wet day or some other reason, you was to go to town I'd catch a ride. I seen them wool blankets they sell at Earley's. And them checked shirts. I got a pair of them, I'd be good until snow fell."

"I see. Boots? Socks?"

"Like I said, I'd be good until snow fell. There's those lace-up boots felted inside. You seen them? I bet they're some kind of warm. Time comes I needed such, maybe I'd have earned up enough." For only the second time that evening he looked at Malcolm. "That'd be some nice."

"You go barefoot until hard winter, is what you're telling me?"

"You did the same you'd know it was a waste of shoe leather to do otherwise."

114

"I guess I would. But you want those boots you've glimpsed."

Amos shook his head and spit again. His pipe had gone cold and he lifted a splinter and stirred the bowl, then held the splinter down into the coals until it caught, brought it up and sucked new fire into his cob. He said, "I do."

Malcolm stood abruptly; the boy reared back on his stone and then steadied as Malcolm helped himself to the dipper. As he settled himself back on his tired haunches he looked up at the spark-trail reaching up until it winked out, leaving only the low heavy spread of the star field above the opening of the ancient trees.

As if he were speaking to that opening, he said, "Does your father know where you are?"

Amos leaned and set his pipe on the ground. Then rubbed his hands on his knees as he studied the fire, his face cut in planes of dark and red by the light, his eyes hidden, sloped away. Finally he said, "Mr. Hopeton. He run me off."

Malcolm sat a long moment, considering this. What sort of man would send a ten-year-old boy off to fend for himself? He started then, cautiously. "Was this before the peaches?"

"No. That was all my doing."

"Was it after? As a result of being gone and unexplained?"

"No. He thought it funny, cuffed my ears."

"So what happened?"

Amos took another drink of water. Now it was his turn to tilt his head back to watch as the sparks swarmed. Eyes heavenward, he spoke. "Pap has a hand in a great big pile of things. He runs traps in the winter, pays boys to do the same. Pays a penny for what he can get a nickel for. Them boarding houses and railroad hotels, from Watkins to Geneva, Dresden to Dundee and up to Canandaigua, he keeps in geese and ducks, venison, coons and chucks, the year around. Time to time he has fresh beeves or pork. But he's most a wizard with critters on the hoof. He'll buy spavined horses or heifers that won't take, why, not six months pass and they're spry and ready for the bit or fresh with a first calf. Ma says he must have some gyp blood to him but he says all he knows is what he learned from his own pa. But that talk also rips him some; he'll kick his own chair to flinders cros't the room and stomp out the house. He gets that way, no chap wants to be in his way. Yes sir, there's a scurry when he riles."

Amos punctuated this last by looking at Malcolm and touching two fingers to his brow in a salute. Then dug into his pocket for a pouch and went to work refilling his pipe, head bent over his task.

"And you riled him?"

"I'm here, ain't I?"

Malcolm waited.

Amos bent and plucked a twig from the pile, held it in the fire until it caught, and lifted it to place the flame against his cob, sucked and blew smoke, sucked again.

He tossed the twig into the fire and said, "I wouldn't do the horse trick. He had it all set up and I said No. The last time I almost got caught and so I said No, he could do it hisself. Although he couldn't and we both knew that. It lathered him right up. He'd made his money a dozen times over on that horse and once more, to boot. It was crowding up on us, folks was talking and he was lucky to sell that horse one more time. That was how I seen it, and I told him so. He took down the strop and set into me. I don't know if it was me saying no or telling him why, but he was whaling away on my backside, had my head pinned between his knees. That's when I seen the poker. I've had a smart bit of time to think on this and wonder if it was just a accident or Ma left it so."

"I see."

"I twisted my head enough so I caught a good mouthful of his leg and bit down like to tear it out. He hollered and pushed me off him cros't the floor and I come up with that poker red hot at the tip, waving it toward him. He was bent, one hand clenching where I'd bit

116

him. And that was when he commenced yelling at me to get out, to get out and not come back. The door was right behind me. I throwed that poker tip-first into the wood box where it could set the whole place afire in a heartbeat. He let out a whoop and dove toward it and I jerked up the latch and hightailed it outta there."

"And came back here."

"I did."

"What makes you think he won't come after you?"

"He won't."

"I'm listening."

"When Pa says something, he don't turn away from it. He said Go; I went. He's got my brothers coming on, and other boys, his trappers and such, will do what he wants. He seen I wasn't cut out for it, didn't want it. That's that."

"So that's your story?"

Amos reached a long, skinny, hard arm like a snake and dragged three pieces from the pile and tipped them onto the fire and used his foot to nudge them into place and said, "You wanted to know about the horse."

"Horse-doctoring is what you're talking about."

"The only hard part was figuring out how long to wait once we got Pete back, and where to go next. Sometimes it would be five-six months, other times just a week. It was nose to the ground. Some fellers would holler loud and wide and cut out thirty miles in a circle around. Most times though it was the lay of the land. We sold Pete in Himrod, didn't mean the folks down Chubb Hollow had heard a word; and so Lamoka was the next best place. A course, that was Pa's job and he done that fine. He never jumped on a guess, it was all thought out. He stuck a wet finger to the wind, every day."

"I'm pressed to wonder, your pa is such a wizard, why'd he need you in the first place."

"I could slip in and blow the cone of powders up Pete's nose easy as could be. So in the morning he was staggering and foaming. The feller would claim we'd sold him a bad horse; Pap would argue the horse was sound when the feller bought him and so it had to be wet oats or moldy hay that brought it on. Pap would end up buying Pete back for half what was paid. There's not a farmer wants a horse with the founder or staggers. Most times the horse ups and dies. Now, Pete, he didn't care for that cone of powders but he stood for it because he was my pet. Yes sir, I loved that fool horse. Enough so I ended up freeing him from all that mess. Last time he was sold, Pap made to send me in. And I wouldn't go. Simple as that. So the man had hisself a sound horse and Pap had none."

"You know this is a bad business you're speaking off?"

"Pete's happy with it," Amos said. "But best I know, it's what makes the world turn. From horseflesh up to judges and presidents and such."

"It could be argued, I suppose. Although plenty of folks live otherwise."

"I thought I told you. That's why I'm here."

The crude shelter grew into a substantial lean-to shed within a few short years, tall enough for a sprouting boy to move about inside, with a wide bunk built into a wall, a stick-and-daub chimney above a rough stone hearth, a wide door on the front and chinked-log openings in the side walls for ventilation, or a breeze in the milder months. Summers Amos Wheeler slept outside beside his fire pit. Beyond his newly purchased garments, odd bits of cookware and tools accumulated: an ax, a crosscut saw, a froe and wooden wedges. Malcolm visited a few times those first years, with the growing sense that he was intruding, once coming upon the boy naked as a skinned squirrel, his creek-laundered clothing hung over branches and limbs to dry. There were times he'd disappear for a day, a night, several days in a row. Malcolm didn't ask where he'd been and Amos Wheeler offered nothing, even if he'd missed work he'd been expected for; but those absences were brief and upon return Amos set at the job before him with grim ferocity, equal part trying to help catch up what had been missed on his account and fury at whatever had drawn him away. Malcolm assumed, despite the bold brash talk, there were family obligations Amos could not refuse.

The winter after his grandfather died there were certain days when Malcolm walked to the high point in the yard to scan the woodlot horizon for a hint of movement, even if there was no work. But that winter Amos was gone much, there when they'd agreed beforehand but otherwise taken up with other things. Malcolm guessed he was trapping, or in some position of authority more active and lucrative than the slowed work of the farm. Once on a bitter January dawn, the sky a pewter plate with the least daub of red to the east, screels of snow over the rock-froze ground ahead of a northwest stinging breeze, Malcolm had stood overlong, gazing at the smudge of woodlot, hoping hard to see a curl of smoke, deciding he needed help to clear the buildup of manure from the swine pen. He dipped his head, a bead of cold snot fell from his nose, and the red smear of hopeful day shut down as the sky descended and it began to snow, stinging pellets driven by the wind. By nightfall there was a foot of snow on the open flats and high broad drifts in the lee of any building or fence or least sapling, leaving an altered land of shadows and ridges, dunes and drifts, hard crusts and hard going one place to another about the yard, the late sky suddenly clear, the starlight a dazzle that made the altered ground all the harder to read. When he fell on skim ice and his lantern went out, he didn't try to light it once he made his way upright again, but went on for the barn. Two days later the wind at dawn had swung to the south and Amos came sloughing in on Iroquois snowshoes strapped to his feet, throwing up chunks of softened snow behind him, waving and laughing as he called out, "Hell of a snow, weren't it? Hell of a snow!" They made butter from the stored milk through the morning, ate a big dinner, and by afternoon the mules were able to haul the sledge through the sinking drifts and got the butter to town, whooping in the warm sunlight as they plowed along. Though Amos disdained the mules, made no secret he preferred horses even as he grudged that the mules would do.

In this way the young man and growing boy formed a team, pulling together most times, enough so Malcolm lost any doubts he might've held about Amos Wheeler. Those few occurrences when Amos failed him, he chalked up to the basic nature of their agreement. Mostly, and greatly, he was happy with the arrangement and Amos seemed to be also. Amos was quick and clever and paid attention. So when Malcolm Hopeton married, he thought of nothing except that he and his new wife had a solid hired man. It did not shine with promise, but outright beamed. More so because Amos was ever-more right where he needed to be, doing what needed doing, and then, not needed or wanted, gone like a blink.

What more could a man ask for?

He was almost thirty and about given up hope, when he met Bethany Schofield. Not for the first time in his life and certainly not for the last, meeting Bethany was a vast connection of so many moments, as if time were simply waiting for him to work himself out to certain correlations and then what came to pass spun elaborate webs backward, to show how exactly he'd arrived at each joining point along the way.

At his grandfather's funeral he'd been approached by a merchant of the town among the others offering condolences for a man they'd never known. But Harold Pinnieo had come with a different message. He'd heard of Hopeton's peaches. If Hopeton was interested and had enough fruit to spare from his own use to make it worth their while, he would buy, for resale, all Hopeton could bring him. That following winter when Hopeton was in town he'd gone by the Italian's store, which sold all manner of foodstuffs, from coffee beans to whole nutmegs, hard and soft cheeses, olives and a variety of peppers in brine, bottles of unfamiliar oils, dried egg noodles in fantastic shapes—none of which Malcolm Hopeton had the first idea how to use. He was a simple but efficient cook for himself. Still, the next summer he loaded careful baskets with his best peaches and drove to town one early morning. Pinnieo lifted peaches from half a dozen baskets and smiled, then nodded.

"They're good."

"I wouldn't have brought em if they weren't."

"Eight cents a pound?"

"I measure by the bushel."

"I sell by the pound."

"Well, I don't know by the pound. So take em and sell em and we'll see how it pays out. How's that?"

"I'm a honest man."

"Never doubted it."

Two summers later she was there before the store on the boardwalk when he brought his peaches to town. An idling town girl, was what he thought, in her neat white dress with navy piping on the long, tight sleeves and edging the bodice top above her soft gray apron, high-button boots peeking, a frilled scullery cap failing to hold the bounty of thick dark curls where sunlight burrowed and refracted back, proliferated. Then she'd turned to him, eyes dark-shining, cheeks full and bright, her lips peeled open laughing and then swiftly serious, her voice caught back in her throat, as she said, "Oh. There you are. The peach man, finally come. I've been waiting for you. I think you want to meet me."

In his stunned moment he managed this: She was no town girl, not only a farm girl, either, but some other creature altogether. What he'd been waiting for. Just like that.

SEVEN

It was a Wednesday morning that Enoch Stone met in chambers with Judge Ansel Gordon; in the afternoon they convened again, this time with the county prosecutor present as well.

By Thursday word had spread from those paired meetings of a presumed substance, scattered details, lies and ugly rumors. Enough reached August Swartout to cause him a rough sleep-tossed night and the resolution to pay a visit come morning upon David and Iris Schofield. They weren't close neighbors and he'd not known Bethany well but with Harlan under his roof, as well as his own particular turn of mind, he felt compelled to the undertaking. Fueled further by the news that Enoch Stone intended to address the subject at Sunday Meeting.

Friday morning found August and Harlan in the buttery, August turning the barrel churn and listening to the splash grow heavier as the solids separated from the buttermilk, Harlan using paddles to spread the ready butter into the wooden trays. It was pleasant within the structure with the deep cooling wells, the high stone foundation holding the cool against the day; the same foundation

122

that kept the winter freeze at bay, also the steady circulating water from the uphill well and the gravity-feed wooden pipe that ran year-round. The previous day all three had finished jarring the ripe cherries and the remainder of the early-season garden produce, although August had been preoccupied after his morning trip to the Four Corners. He had spoken briefly of the news of Enoch Stone and then with uncharacteristic sternness made clear he didn't wish to discuss the issue further. An hour later Becca had burned the last batch of black raspberry preserve and Harlan had carried the kettle to scrape off best he could into the hog-trough, then returned to the house where Becca scalded and scoured the kettle. August had sat on the small front stoop, smoking and looking off at the drying world.

Now he looked up from his work and said to Harlan, "I'll be gone today. Most of it, anyway. I'm overdue paying a call upon David and Iris Schofield."

When there was no response other than downcast eyes from Harlan, August elaborated. "The parents of Bethany Hopeton."

"I know who they are." The boy paused, then looked up and said, "Would you have me come with you?"

"Why no, I hadn't thought so. Unless you wish to."

"I druther not. I can't see any reason they'd welcome me."

"Whatever Lawyer Stone thinks, whatever he said, I wouldn't assume David and Iris would think ill of you. Among much else, you were not responsible for what happened to Malcolm Hopeton's farm. And should not feel you have to answer to those events. But, that said, I was intending to go alone, for my own reasons."

"What would you have me do?"

"I can't say. There's always work to be done, as I'm sure you know. But nothing pressing. Perhaps you might like to walk down and loll by the lakeside, take the plunge into the cool waters there? Something of that sort? A bit of rest is what I'm saying. You've earned it."

Harlan was quiet a moment, then said, "I want to go visit Mister Hopeton again. That first time, I ain't never ever even imagined him that way. I need to make sure he knows I'm ready to help. However he needs."

August regarded the boy. "What if there's no change?"

"I'd take that as I find it."

August was quiet a moment, then said, "One of those mules rides, is that not so? We know Malcolm rode off on one. Do you know which one?"

"He always rode Bill. But while he was gone to the war I messed around with both of em and maybe it's only me, but Bart's a better fit for the road."

August stood then and pulled his purse from his trouser pocket. He reached within and dug and lifted out a bright, thick coin and held it out. He said, "Take that."

"You keep giving me money I ain't earned."

"By my lights you've earned it and then some. Now listen, that last time you went, that bit of money made a difference, didn't it?"

Harlan said, "Paid my fare, but I ain't taking any boats if I ride the mule. And while it was nice to have, I'd not've perished if I hadn't been able to buy some food on my way back. I'm all right."

August said, "The point is once you step off into the unknown you never truly can guess what you might need."

"But that's a double eagle."

"It is. And this evening, or whenever it may be, you hand it back to me, we'll both be happy. But between now and then both you and I'll know you're well set against what they call contingencies. You know what that is?"

"I think Bart is all the help I need against contingencies. But I'll slip that beauty down into my boot just so I can walk around on it. That way, anyone asks my age I can tell em, Well, I'm over twenty. And I won't be lying." Harlan let a grin slip over his face and August did likewise as the boy pocketed the coin.

Then both stood awkward a moment. Both ready to step into an unknown day, both unsure. August was again grim, Harlan in a surging confusion. So he spoke first.

"You see a way, let her folks know how sorry I am."

August said, "You go on and see if you can help Malcolm Hopeton. Not a one of us can fix all that's wrong in the world."

He stepped around Harlan and went down the yard to the house and came out almost immediately with his jacket and straw hat on and went to the barn to hitch a horse to the cart. Harlan watched until August drove out, then cleaned up around the buttery and closed it tight. He'd have changed his shirt but not so much as to have his sister question him and so went on to the day pasture and led the mules to their pen in the barn and separated them, which was a job until it was not. He brushed down Bart and fitted him with a bridle and rope reins and the mule understood the boy was about to torment him once again and grew still and watchful. Harlan unlaced his right brogan to tuck the heavy coin within and the mule took this moment to swipe its head about to clamp teeth to the upturned bottom presented and Harlan turned and swatted the mule on the nose. Bart rose up and settled again with his legs spraddled and his neck strung high, nostrils blowing.

Harlan gathered up the reins and tugged the mule toward the rear door of the barn, intending to cut crosslots toward the road and walking along but not looking back as they exited the barn, said, "Don't have a hissy. You bite my ass, I'll clobber your nose. You should know that. There now. You ready to ride along a bit?"

It was a fine morning and despite some nervousness about what he might find in town, Harlan found himself riding along in high spirits, hard not to be with the easy stride of the mule, the light clear and the roadside swarming with orioles, brown thrashers, cowbirds, a flutter of a half-dozen or so goldfinches. A myriad of small blue and black butterflies rose off the road surface around him and his passing mule, then were gone. Why they chose that spot? The wonders of the Lord. As he came down into the valley above the Four Corners and crossed the brook, a red-winged blackbird rose up from the reeds along the water, fussing and crying at him, protecting her nest down in the reeds. A pair of crows rose and fell as they rowed the air above the fields of young corn, oats, wheat and barley that spread upon the valley floor. Men at work making hay. The hay fields already cut bare had lost the blond stubble after the rain and glowed a luminescent green. But it was only passing Albert Ruddle's old house, now abandoned and used to store hay from the neighboring fields that Harlan fully understood that he was, in most all ways, back at home—his not-quite-four years up in Milo at Malcolm Hopeton's farm not so bleak and dire, so endless, as they'd seemed at the time. He knew a comfort and ease he'd not felt during those four years—not even at the early start of them when it seemed he'd lighted in a good place; and not now, when, he knew, should fortune turn so, he'd be back up there on the farm and happy to be there. Greatly so, he thought, as he spit down into the dust, ruminating. But this was home, the land he'd come out of. For the first time in his young life he understood that it always would be.

A heron lifted out of the stream and flapped off and away, legs stretched behind like the sticks of a broken kite. He rode on, the mule happy also it seemed to him, at least happy with the job. Easy for a mule. They climbed up the valley toward the County Farm road and there over his right shoulder he saw the bulk of the Bluff splitting the Crooked Lake, the long high massif of land looking in the gathering heat haze as some huge creature crouched forever, caught before a pounce. Below on the waters he watched the white skiffle of wavelets turned by a breeze he didn't feel up here, also the sails of boats plying up and down the lake, the larger, more squat side-wheeler and its trail of coal smoke from the stack. The same boat he'd ridden just days before, or one of the fleet of three, all identical unless you knew the schedule, which he did not, or were close enough to read the painted legend of name: *Catawba, Keuka, Seneca*. It was a busy land, busy water, too. All a-churn with life.

He came down into the town and let the Bart mule snort and toss his head as they made way through the press of crowds upon the streets and on toward the courthouse. Some few looked up and let their eyes follow after him; never before had he been a known figure, and it caused a strange discomfort within. At the courthouse there was much milling and men striding about compared to the first time he was there but he only kicked up the fractious mule and passed around the building to the back side, where the horse sheds stood. These too were mostly full and he felt a twitch of panic, wondering if all this activity was related to Malcolm Hopeton, if he was someway too late. Court was in session, this much was clear. When he found a space in the sheds for the mule, there stood a pair of men outside the shed, holding forth in argument—the one stating he'd spill blood or die before accepting such a decision and the other allowing how it might be so and the better for those left living.

Harlan tied the mule and fetched an armful of hay from the common rick midway of the sheds and walked around to the grand front entry, where he paused again and took breath and lifted himself on tiptoe to settle back down and feel the weight of the double-eagle coin under his foot, giving him the final courage and he walked up the broad granite steps and then through the double doors, propped open to the day.

Where he stopped and watched. Within as without, all was a great hive of busyness. None looked at him at all. He passed through the entry and was in the sheriff's office proper and here it was much the same or more so. All a-bursting with furious business, all engaged. He looked over at the door that led down to the basement and there was not a soul near it or paying attention. He ambled slowly back and

127

forth again, sidling sideways, until he was leaned back against that very door, his arms crossed over his chest and one foot kicked before him, the other crossed over it and still it seemed no one in the room paid him notice.

So after a long moment he finally turned and tried the door, which opened silent and easy upon him. So much that he paused one last time to glance over his shoulder but there was not a man watching and he stepped through and pulled the door just-to behind him, not wanting to hear the click of a lock.

There, then, he stood in sudden near-dark, pausing a moment for the outcry without. When it did not come and his eyes had made out the stairs before him, he walked down, his brogans clapping upon the raw old planks but otherwise silent. And this way he came into the basement and found Malcolm Hopeton in his cage.

Hopeton sat on his bunk. He wore new black trousers and a new collarless white shirt, but despite these garments his appearance had worsened. He was barefooted and had not shaved, his hair sprang about his head, dull brown shot through with white, and his short beard was also stippled. In his days in the cell his skin had lost its color and was a dirty parchment gray. His eyes were sunken and dark-rimmed and his great farmer's hands lay in his lap as if they were separate from him. His head had been turned to watch Harlan descend the stairs and he kept those eyes upon the boy but was silent, making no sign of recognition or even acknowledgment.

Also now there was a three-legged stool half a dozen feet from the cage. Harlan sat upon it and studied the man before him, who endured this as if he'd done so before and would again and cared nothing for such appraisal. Harlan met and held the man's eyes and thought again of fish, the dead eyes of a fish pulled from the depths of a lake, eyes glazed open as if behind those eyes lay worlds forever frozen and lost, worlds not seen by man.

"Howdy, Malcolm," Harlan said. He'd never addressed the man by his Christian name but did so now as if the man had no other. "I wanted to come by and see you. I rode that Bart mule to town. At least for me, he rides better than Bill. Until this business gets cleared up I'm staying on the farm of a good man name of August Swartout out near Jerusalem. My sister keeps house for him, is how I ended up there. And the team of mules was brought to me to tend also. They're good mules, settled in and working as they need to. I'm not telling you anything you don't know about em. But I wanted you to know how I'm situated for the moment. Until we get this business cleared up. Which is also why I come back to see you. There's been a lawyer come to see me and while I don't care for him someways, I do believe he means you well. What I'm saying is that there stands a chance that the truth of Amos Wheeler and everything else might come out. You and I know what that truth is. And, well, I want you to know I'm ready to stand in a courtroom and swear to what I seen Amos do. How it was."

He then sat silent and silence greeted him and held within the room. The eyes of the man through the bars gazed toward him. In this silence he smelled the room, the reek of human waste, mold upon the rafters, some other dank effluvium seeping up from whatever chambers or tunnels lay beneath this basement.

Malcolm Hopeton looking through him where he sat on the stool as if beyond the sunken stone foundation into some far distant clear day never to be seen again.

Harlan said, "I seen it all, you know I did. I was there. You know it yourself; fact is, you knew it enough someway to ask me to be there. I'm here of a purpose, Mr. Hopeton. I always was. Can you see that?"

After the boy had come the first time and run away, the sheriff and two of his deputies had come down and beaten him to silence. The one man was named Smith. A lineage of men made to smite, and he and his helper had. The sheriff had stood back and watched and all three left together. Malcolm had known a man named Smith in the war and had watched him die. Listened to him die. Crying and gasping in pain-streaked moans and calling upon God to save him. As with most such entreaties overheard during the course of those years, God had failed to intervene as if He were not there at all. Some men survived; but Malcolm deemed those holding luck, proximity to surgeons, luck again, the minor severity of wounds, even a man of unusual strength with wounds of such outrage that those likewise afflicted were already dead but that man survived. He never once believed God had a hand as to intervene in such matters. So life had informed him, from when he was but a boy not so different from this eager, earnest boy before him, when his family, parents both and siblings and those of wider reach—uncles and aunts, cousins and his own grandmother—had fallen to the sway of a prophet, or not a prophet, but simply and deeply and with great conviction a man deranged by his particular absorption and also perhaps by his own great need to be anointed by the Lord, and had thus made ill testimony. Then, too, thirty and more years ago the Lord had deigned to answer those calls upon Him. Had left bereft and impoverished fools upon the top of a high hill, gathered there to be closer to heaven as the Kingdom of the Lord was to be offered to them. Except it had not been offered. The Lord had ignored those who would love Him most.

The Lord either was not such a thing or did not care. For all of his life this formula amounted to the same thing. Trust to nothing but what you are able to make.

All this he'd done with Bethany. He'd staggered the war through, always this hope to return to love, his own love, the one who also had known the fury of men wrought by the Lord. And the one with whom he'd made a new life, not so much disregarding God as both having learned that if there was any God, He made himself manifest in simple marvelous works of creation all around them, the beasts and grasses and trees, the sun, which made life quick, and the distant stars, mystery enough to ponder right there, far overhead but within sight. Most all of wonder could be touched; and if not touched then seen, witnessed. Also the wonder of the countless ways man and woman joined together. In daily rounds of work, shared or divided; in words of conversation, discussion, argument, passion. In the bed, that joining seeming at times to be the creation of a single creature from halves, other times both each yearning ever deeper toward the other, those times also more brute but not brutal. And the slender handful of failures, or hopes advanced and then crushed by a flush of blood and even then, when they well might've, never once did one turn to the other and wonder if this was a divine condemnation upon the two of them; for it was not the Lord at all but the hands and hearts of men that made destruction and both also knew some creatures breed with ease and humans not always so. What worries they held private concerned awful practicalities. Was his seed thin or lacking someway? Was her womb barren of eggs, or were those eggs that caused her monthly flow deformed someway? They knew such tragedy had fallen upon others. And possible as well, some combination of strain upon both but with time and effort would meet and match. A child would issue.

Meanwhile the country seethed and boiled and then sundered and he knew it must not be allowed to remain so. This division was not hope for two to be made of one but a great hope destroyed. And so he went to war. She'd begged him not to go.

She'd stood in their kitchen once the day's work was done and the hired man fed and gone off to his abode in the woods and had begged him not to go, to pay for a substitute as so many others had done. She'd dropped to her knees and entreated him. And all he'd seen was any wife faced with such a prospect and had assured her, had finally left the kitchen and her sobbing to walk out alone into the summer night and stand upon the rise of land beyond his peach orchard facing south and studying the stars hanging down to that horizon. And a pale shadow of thought came to him and he misunderstood it or perhaps did not, but in the weeks ahead he queried about and then one day had driven most of the way across the country to find the young man he'd heard word of and had hired him and brought him home. Because his wife had told him that she and the one hired man could not do it. Could not hold it all together, the two of them alone. He thought he'd seen the truth in her words.

He thought as much throughout the war. He had no reason not to and many reasons to hold tight his vision of his home, steady and strong. Intact and merely awaiting his return.

Then he walked back in, his brain thick and red-rimmed with the vestiges of his years away but also with the traitorous, foul killing of the president. That great man undone by desperate fools. The war done but most clearly not done. And so he walked back into his own promise of peace, hope and desire. And none of any of it was there. Stolen and swept away. His own life assassinated.

Things fell apart.

The blood from her nose and mouth where she lay cast upon the ground. By his own hands.

His grandfather had told him, "The Lord had nothing to do with it. It was people, and what they will get up to."

"I wish you'd talk to me. Not just set there staring. I'd help you, I told you that. I seen what Amos done, I seen it all. Like I said, I'll tell any man that needs to know."

"Harlan Davis," he said and stopped. His words came at great cost and he measured them through his breathing, feeling his chest heave and fall. He'd not spoken to anyone since his arrival in this cage, not to any living person and certainly not aloud. Otherwise he'd been in a flurry of communication. So he breathed and pulled words forth between breaths.

"Yes? Yes sir. Mr. Hopeton?"

"You say you're in a good place? That the man is good and you're welcome there?"

"He is and I am."

"You're working for him?"

"I'm there. And I'm working."

"He has need of you? Or is he accommodating you?"

"What I seen, he has need of me. My sister, Becca, she told me he usually hires a man for the summer, in fact was looking to do so when—well, when the news come. And he and she went to the doctor and fetched me back. And I been helping right on along. We got his first cut of hay in and Calvin Fulton showed up with the mules and I used em just a couple of days ago to ride a cultivator through his corn. And . . ."

Harlan went silent and held it and Malcolm breathed and waited.

Finally Harlan said, "It's a good enough place for the time being and I'm grateful for it. But you're the man I work for. And there's work needs to be done. You and me, we both know I'm the only one can stand and tell how it was. What happened after you left. What sort a man Amos Wheeler was. And I'll do it. I'm here to tell you that. And there's that lawyer—"

"He has been to see me." Malcolm went silent.

Harlan said, "Then you know—"

Malcolm said, "I have no interest in what he said. I want you to go back to where you now are and work like the dickens for that man. Make him proud to have you there and let him see just how worthy you are. Perhaps he will take you on year-round. You say your sister is already there? That's good; she may be able to sway him if he holds any doubts of you, although I'd say after a few more weeks he'll want you as a full-time hand. And this, also: I give you the mules. If they help secure a position there, so much the better. But if they seem a liability, if the man does not have enough use for them or doesn't want to feed them through the winter, you may dispose of them and pocket the cash money. Perhaps, if the farm is lean of work during the winter months, such money might allow you to board through those times. It sounds the right place for you, now."

Harlan sat on the stool, tipped a bit sideways, his face in a quizzed pinch. Finally he said, "I'm not understanding you."

Malcolm breathed. His vision had cleared and the basement was brilliant as if flooded by some light carried in upon the shoulders of the boy. He said, "You know why I'm here?"

Harlan said, "I know what brung you here."

"No. You do not. You may think so but you don't. I murdered a man and I murdered my wife. That is what I did. Cast the story any way you want but the end remains the same. Now, go. Make that home it sounds you already have. But leave me, Harlan. Leave me to what is mine."

The mute boy on the stool did not comprehend what was being said.

Malcolm stood from his hard platform bunk, his knees cracking and threatening weakness as he rose. He stepped to the bars of the cage and the boy also rose up from his stool and stood, his face drained.

Gently as he could, Malcolm said, "The state will hang me for what I did. As they should. Truth is I'll welcome it. I'd not want life after what I did. You go on, you're but a boy and can't understand. One day you might, but I hope dearly you won't. Go. Now. I'm done with talk. I'm done with it all."

He then turned and walked to the back of his cage and placed his hands upon the bars and stood upright. Dreading that the boy might speak, that he would not understand. It was very quiet in the basement, quiet enough so Malcolm heard the faint whir of a fly striking the window glass, heard the scrape of the stool legs pushed back, shoe-soles gaining purchase as the boy stood. Heard the boy draw breath as if he would speak again. That breath held a great time and no words came but finally an exhalation as a burst upon the room and then the rush of feet up the stairs and the hidden door snapping to.

Malcolm Hopeton turned and lifted his hands to hold his head and staggered to the bunk and sank swift and hard upon it. Still holding his head.

Harlan was in the horse sheds behind the courthouse, breathless and crimped, with no sense or memory of how he'd gotten there, no memory of anything he'd seen or heard or if anyone had spoken to him or even noticed him as he exited the building, unsure if he'd run the whole way or strolled out seemingly cool. He lay up against the side of Bart, who was, unaccountably, still working at the small pile of hay Harlan had fetched some very long time ago, leaned against the mule and buried his face in the sweet, dusty hide and got his breath back. Then finally thought to look back outside the sheds to see if anyone had followed him.

He was alone, but for the mule.

Ways, this most recent vision of Malcolm Hopeton was even more terrible than the lunatic seen days before, Hopeton so cool and lacking all passion as he'd stood and proclaimed his fate and acceptance, even his embrace of that fate. A man otherwise brave and strong wanting to die. As if he'd forgotten all Harlan and he'd discussed those weeks after his walking back in from the war.

And Harlan then understood that Hopeton had not so much forgotten as he was grief-maddened and, though appearing calm, was out of his mind. There was no other explanation possible.

Which meant he'd forgotten all he'd learned about Amos Wheeler; and that was wrong. Harlan Davis, collapsed against a mule for comfort, knew it to be wrong. And because it was wrong, knew he could not let it stand so.

He pushed off the mule and stood upright. In that moment he knew he was alone and also knew that alone he was not enough.

He'd be seen as a boy willing to say anything to save a man he'd worked for, a man he'd come to admire. Most importantly a man who had killed another man and his own wife in a terrible moment and Harlan the sole witness, if only a partial witness. And thought of Enoch Stone and how that man had ambushed him and saw how he could be so easily torn all those ways if he alone tried to stand in a courtroom and tell how it had been. Not that terrible day, not the weeks after Malcolm returned from the war. But the years before that. For only by understanding those years could people make judgment on the rage of that day.

He needed someone else. Some other person who could also tell how it had been.

Bart lifted his head and stamped, flicked his tail at flies and shook his head and neck and dropped down to eat again. And it came to Harlan who he needed. In the whole wide living world there was only one other person who could tell the sort of man Amos Wheeler had been. Could also, perhaps, tell a bit about the mess Bethany Hopeton had found herself caught up in. Though he was less sure about that last part.

He didn't have the first idea about where to start. But a tickle at the back of his mind told him he did. He walked out of the shed and went to the privy and sitting there in the high stink of a hot day, took off his brogan and pulled out the twenty-dollar gold piece and stuck it in his trouser pocket. And perhaps it was the stink or some other clarity against the risk of memory but it came to him. The day the winter before when he'd left the house to go to Hopeton's barn, sent by Mrs. Hopeton to seek eggs so she could bake a cake, and been stopped short, hearing Amos talking and the girl talking back and he'd stood silent as a post hidden in the passage between the chicken coop and the horse barn as he listened.

It was a slender thread but all he had and so within minutes had led Bart out of the shed and mounted the mule and gone down through the streets of the town to the landing of the Outlet Canal. From there he turned east along the towpath through the gorge toward Dresden, it being the shortest route he knew to travel the five miles. He'd pass by the wide meadow in the gorge where the Wheeler family had their camp but he was emboldened by the report from Enoch Stone that all were gone from there save perhaps Amos Wheeler's mother, who, even if she were still there, would not know Harlan from Adam. And though he'd never been there he guessed, it being the nature of the Wheelers, that the camp was not right up against the canal and towpath. And he intended to kick up Bart and pass through there fast as he could. All he wanted was to get to Dresden fast as he could, hoping to find Alice Ann Labidee.

When he arrived at Dresden he rode up from the landing to higher ground above the village and on to the hotel, a square, red-painted structure with a modest signboard on the entrance porch above the steps. As he tied Bart to the simple rail under a butternut tree for shade, he heard the snuffling gulps and nipped squeals of hungry swine and followed toward the source, around to the back of the building. Jutting behind was an unpainted weathered cookhouse with a rear door, three rough steps, a thick stovepipe rising from the wood-shingled roof, with a pale steady stream of smoke rising. The yard was packed earth, and twenty feet from the bottom of the steps was the drop-off into the Outlet gorge. Against that was a fenced enclosure holding a dozen or so shoats trundling about an empty trough. The smell was high and the pigs watched Harlan. Inside the pen there was a cut-down barrel for water and in one corner a few planks cobbled together to make a rough shelter from sun or rain.

The slap of the kitchen door roused him from this standing slumber. A large woman with pinned hair under a cap, clad in a washed-thin dress with a heavy splotched apron, feet stuffed into laceless men's boots, came out hugging a steaming tub against her chest. She maneuvered the steps downward with a certain caution; then, her feet hard upon the ground, her eyes came up from the job and she saw Harlan.

"Stand back," she cried out. "I can't stop."

She swaggered along with the tub. It looked like hard going to Harlan.

He said, "Do you need a hand with that?"

She went on, spitting behind her, but not at him. At the hog pen she lifted the tub a bit and dumped the contents into the trough. The pigs strove and dove, flailing corked tails.

The woman turned and dropped the tub and reached up to press her cheeks with her hands. "What are you lurking after, pie-eye?" she asked, without much heat to the question.

"You must be the cook," he said. "I was hoping to buy a cup of coffee."

"I'm Bertha Pinckney, the owner of this sweet honey-pot since my husband run off to get rich in Kansas ten years ago and I ain't seen nor heard from him since. I got a pot a coffee on the back of the stove, made strong for me. The drummers and flimflams get it watered down."

"I could use a cup of strong coffee. Cash money."

"Um-hmm," she said. "And hungry, too. Get up the stairs, I'll be right behind you."

The room was vast, steaming hot. Bertha Pinckney poured coffee from an oversized pot into a cup pulled from a shelf of them, curiosity bright in her eyes. She said, "Take that stool at the table. No, not that one, the one the other side of the range, next to the larder. This stool's mine, so's I can perch and watch the stove."

The stove was a wide-topped iron giant with double ovens, a five-gallon pot steaming at the rear, oversized skillets filled with chopped onions and potatoes browning, one of calf's liver, one of brown gravy speckled with coarse black pepper. She bent and opened an oven and basted a pan of trussed roasting chickens. On the table before him was a baked ham sweating juice and a platter stacked with tiers of biscuits, corn dodgers and sliced rounds of steamed molasses bread.

Harlan took the coffee and moved to the appointed stool, unsure how to proceed. So he plunged.

He said, "Can I confide in you?"

She spread wide over the opposite stool and held her coffee between both hands, the enameled cup disappeared.

"A course you can."

He nodded and said, "My name's Harlan Davis and—"

"Oh!" she said and looked away. Then, "I heard your name. You were up to your knees in that mess in Milo, weren't you." And swiftly added, "What the papers said, anyway."

"I was more at the edge of it, though I did get clouted on the head, sorta by accident. It was a terrible business all right, but not what most people think."

Now her brow was furrowed by thought or worry and Harlan guessed if Alice Ann Labidee wasn't here she had been recently. So he waited and sipped the strong coffee that had the vague taste of licorice root.

She couldn't help curiosity. "How so was it different?"

He shrugged. "Simple. All the talk for years was how Missus Hopeton and Amos Wheeler was paired up, stealing money and such grain and livestock as they could turn into cash. But it was Amos Wheeler all along; I was there. I seen it. Missus Hopeton didn't have no say once Wheeler took charge."

She said, "I seen them in here a few times. I ain't so sure of what you say about her, but that Wheeler, he was a nasty piece of work."

"That is the Lord's truth, ever it was spoke."

"You're a godly boy."

"I am. I was raised as such. I only stuck it those last years cause I'd promised Mr. Hopeton. And I felt bad for Missus Hopeton, though I couldn't see a thing to do about it. There wasn't no one to listen to me."

She nodded and then heaved off her stool and poured more coffee for the both of them, then took up a knife and sliced slabs of ham onto a plate set before him, added a half-dozen biscuits and pushed a crock of dark honey across toward him, another of butter. "Them biscuits won't be good cold. You eat up."

He looked at the food, looked back at her and said, "I appreciate it." And went to working on the food. Bertha Pinckney stood spraddle-legged and forked biscuits, molasses bread, more ham onto his plate as quickly as he cleaned it. All the while the both of them hedged and hunkered, both knowing the question nudging for entry into the room.

Harlan finished up slowly and, without standing, dug in his pocket and pulled forth the double eagle and set it beside his plate. "My goodness," he said. "That was a feast and badly needed."

She eyed the coin and filled his coffee again. She said, "I was raised New Light Baptist myself but have mostly fell away as life will do to you. What is it you're after, here?"

"I'm looking for Miss Alice Ann Labidee."

"I never heard that name."

"There's a man's life hangs in the balance."

"I can't help you."

"She was done wrong by Amos Wheeler, that's common knowledge. All I want is to talk to her. Nothing more."

Bertha Pinckney again raised her bulk, this time effortless as breathing and turned to the stove. She pushed pans back and forth, turned slabs of beef liver, stirred the contents of the big pot. Then reached up to the shelf above the stove and brought down a stoppered bottle lost in her large hand. She turned and pulled the cork with her teeth and poured a thin short stream into her own cup. Placed the bottle back on the shelf and again filled her cup with coffee and then Harlan's.

She put the big blackened tin pot back on the stove and stood at the table and sipped from her cup, taking a pause, waiting for the coffee and infusion to strike within her. All that time studying Harlan with wide blue eyes frank and true upon him before she set her cup down and looked up to the smoke-strewn rafters and daubed plaster.

She looked back to Harlan and said, "I won't see her come to harm. She's a good girl and ain't got a friend in this world."

"I'm only looking to talk to her. And, I beg your pardon, but you're wrong on that account."

"How's that?"

"I'd say she has a friend and a good one. That, or she pays you right well."

Bertha flushed red and said, "Oh my Lord, child, she ain't got a dime to her name, not these days."

"Can I ask how she landed here? And how she's keeping herself?"

Bertha paused then and set her chins upon the knuckles of one hand and pursed her eyes into a soft distance. Finally she said, "She does the best she can. The answer to your first question, you'll have to get from her, if she's willing to share it."

Harlan understood he'd just made the first hurdle. Or second or third; he was unable to parse the moment to make a count. He said, "She came to you and you took her in, in her hour of need. Much the same has happened to me. You're a kind soul and true, I can say that freely. I'll also promise you her whereabouts is hidden with me, unless she allows otherwise. Swear my solemn heart."

Bertha Pinckney heaved herself upright from her stool again and walked around the table, pausing by the range to rearrange the assembly of skillets from hot to cool in an order known only to herself, then went on to a wire-caged pantry where she lifted down a brown clay bottle with a wax-sealed cap and locked back the pantry before setting the bottle before Harlan. Still wordless, she took down a tin tea canister and filled it with coffee, milk and a

141

prodigious amount of sugar. Thought a moment with her hands on her hips, then pointed at the door leading to the interior of the hotel and spoke.

"Carry this up to her. She's not a drinking girl like some but will likely welcome the beer with you surprising her such a way. Once you pass through that door, another opens onto the back stairs. Take them all the way to the top and you'll find yourself under the eaves. Up there, there ain't but the one door what opens onto my cramped quarters. She's camped with me. If she don't want to see you, you respect that and leave her be. I hear her make a sound I'll be up those stairs in a fury. You doubt me?"

Harlan had stood. "No, Ma'am, not for a second."

She studied him again hard and reached and pushed the gold piece across the table. She said, "Some people can't purchase a thing from me, try as they might."

He stood and stuck the coin in his pocket and took up the bottle of beer in one hand, the canister of hot coffee in the other and said, "I thank you."

The rear stairs were narrow and lit only by transom windows set high in the landings, the walls unpainted beadboard. Harlan climbed quietly, slowly. He came to the door at the top of the stairs, paused, and listened; but all was silent except for the faintest creaking where the heat of the day worked against contracting clapboarding. Still he doubted she was the sort to sleep in until almost noon. Even Amos Wheeler had not done that. Not much. Bethany had, upon occasion. Or at least hid out in her bedroom. Harlan had never been able to decide which it was, the times he put his mind to the question. Much the same as he never knew what corner he'd turn, what door open, or shadow in the barn move to reveal Wheeler when least expected. The oily mirthless laugh when Harlan took fright. It all felt like long ago, and only yesterday.

He rapped on the door. Waited and rapped again. Heard footsteps come close and pause.

"What is it?"

He'd anticipated the question. "It's me." With as much quiet certitude and familiarity as he could muster, soft enough to be heard and still indistinct.

A long silence. He was about to speak again when the bolt was pulled and snapped, and the door opened. Not a slender gap but open wide. Alice Ann Labidee was wearing a yellow robe belted tight but showing the lace top of a nightgown. The robe was heavy, more suited to winter, though it showed her bare feet. Her honey-colored hair was loose upon her shoulders and her mouth was open in surprise. Her eyes the green of bottle glass.

"I hate if I woke you, Alice Ann, but I needed to see you," he said.

She reached quickly as if to shut the door, then dropped her arm.

She sucked her lower lip into her mouth, thinking, and revealing her upper front teeth. Her right canine jutted slightly, a slight signal toward him. Doing this allowed her to draw a deep and calming breath.

She said, "I know you. You was at the farm. You're Harold."

This error pained him more than he'd thought possible. He said, "I brought you up a bottle of beer. And Missus Pinckney thought you might want some coffee."

She made no effort to take either offering but said, "So Bertha sent you up. I figured someone was likely to track me down. Maybe best it was you."

She plucked up the tea can of sugared coffee and walked away toward the set of beds under the low angled roof, itself made of beadboard, and stood, sipping slowly. Harlan stepped all the way in and set the beer on a low table that otherwise held a potted fern as brown as it was green; and while she held herself in pause, savoring the coffee, her back to him, he surveyed the room.

143

Besides the two beds strung with ropes and holding mounded feather mattresses there was a settee daybed pushed under the short wall under the eaves, a large chest of drawers overflowing, an pigeon-hole desk also overflowing with papers, a slurry of smeared inks and scrawls. A portmanteau sat in a bare spot on the floor with both sides let down and heaped with clothing which he guessed belonged to Alice Ann. The room ran the length of the building, the flat ceiling a long, low narrow span and then tapering to elbows either side as roof became walls and joined the attic to the building below. The quarters of a woman who utilized all other space for paying guests, cold in winter and hot in summer; even as he stood in heat of day he heard nail heads lift in the cedar shingles from the roof.

She turned back, glancing at him over her coffee before she shot her eyes away, gazing out a window. He thought, What in the world is she doing here? Maybe learning that was all there would be to this job.

"It's Harlan," he said. "There's no Harold to me."

"Harlan," she turned, flagging her free hand in greeting or brushing away a fly. "No one ever showed up afore noon trying to tempt me with cheap beer. What do you want, Harlan? What're you bothering me for?"

He said, "I'm here on account of a good man, one you witnessed most of the best efforts to ruin."

She lifted the canister and sighted across the top at him, one eye squinting as if aiming a gun. "You're talking about the husband of that slut who stole my Amos?"

"Whatever stealing was done, was Amos's doing. He was the one who deceived Mr. Hopeton every way he could think to." He paused and said, "Seems he deceived you, too."

"Amos Wheeler would kiss you like it was the last kiss on earth at the same time he was picking your pocket." She eyed him carefully as she said this. "I believe you know something like that about him, yourself."

144

He nodded but looked away, then back upon her. She lifted the coffee and drank as she considered him. Then she crossed the room and set the tea canister on the platter and prized the cork from the beer and settled on the settee.

She said, "Come and set, Harlan."

"I'm fine right here."

"No," she said. "You came to see me because you want something. It's a funny place to be in. Now come set. Come over here."

He crossed the floor and eased down on the settee, a few inches from the end but otherwise as far from her as possible. She pursed her mouth as if swallowing something distasteful and said, "Tell me what you want. Don't think for a minute I'll be of any help, but I'll listen, you made all this effort."

Brief as he could, thinking less was better and keeping in mind the notion of keeping her curious, he told her of Malcolm Hopeton's situation. When he finished she held her silence and so he went on a bit, adding, as cautiously as he could, "What you said earlier about Amos picking your pocket: There's truth to that and then some. What you didn't say was he'd be looking at you as he done all those things and the look in his eye was enough to keep you from saying a word, isn't that so?"

She remained silent, but her face had gone thoughtful and she eased back, drank off a good part of the beer and gazed off. Finally she spoke.

"You're asking me to come into court and testify against Amos? Is that what you're thinking?"

"It might not come to that. It might be enough if the lawyers, the judge, knew you were willing to do so." He doubted this but also knew he had no idea what he was speaking about.

Alice Ann went on. "I can't do that. None of those men, not a one of em, would believe me. They'd think they already know the sort of woman I am, even if they're dead wrong. There ain't a soul alive knows me, anymore. I never thought it would go so bad when Amos come back; I thought it was the last chance for him to see the wrong of his ways. But that don't change what happened and never can."

Harlan took pause. He shifted slightly, pushing back into the corner of the daybed and turning his knees toward her, making a greater wedge of space between them. He said, "You knew they was coming in that day?"

She stood off the daybed with a forward hitch. Walked down the room as she said, "Lord, that coffee woke me right up, atop the shock of you banging on my door first thing." She turned and said, "Let's say I had a inkling."

He took the opportunity to stand. Last thing he wanted was to be sitting on the daybed with her again. Since coming up the stairs he'd felt off-kilter, as if he could not keep up with her. She sent his mind darting one way one moment, another the next.

He said, "Are you saying he was keeping in touch with you? Letters? Or telegraphs sent here? After he ran off with Bethany Hopeton when they got word Malcolm Hopeton was on his way home?"

A snorted laugh broke from her and she choked it back, her face turning serious. She said, "No, no. Nothing of the kind. I never heard a word from Amos those last months." She glanced off toward the low western windows in thought and said, "Pity your Mr. Hopeton didn't take the time to walk down to the woods and talk with me once he got back." Then swung her eyes back to Harlan. "Not that it would've done a bit of good. I couldn't help him, any more than I could help myself. And that's your answer: I wasn't no use to him then and I'm not any now. It's all done."

"But you as much as said you knew Amos was coming in that day it all went wrong. Isn't that so?"

"I never said such a thing. And not a living soul can prove I did. I think you need to get along, Harlan."

"You're not making sense to me. Not one bit."

146

"You don't know a thing about women, do you?"

"What I seen so far is a mystery I'm not sure I want to study further." He moved toward her, toward the door. "I got to get on; there's a afternoon of work ahead of me."

She stepped close of a sudden, her breath sweet of coffee, sour of beer. "I'm half of a mind to show you the reasons you'll want to study that mystery—why you'll be up to it all your life long." She reached and pressed a finger into his skin below his throat and he felt his trousers jump. As if she knew this, she took her finger away and said, "But we're both better off if you just go on along."

His face was hot as sunburn. "I'm sorry to bother you. Maybe we should just forget I was ever here."

She studied him a long beat and said, "I don't think either one of us could forget it if we wanted, could we, Harlan?" Then she lifted her hand and pushed her loose hair from her face. "Get out of here," she said. "I'm tired."

He went down the stairs and paused behind the first-floor door, heard nothing and let himself out quiet as he could and then walked down the main hall, past the dining room filled with people eating and on out the front and down the steps to where Bart waited at the rail under the butternut tree. He mounted up and remade his way down to the Outlet and paused there just past the eastern landing where the canal-side was almost at bank level, letting Bart drink and sliding off to kneel just upstream from the mule and cup water one-handed to drink himself. Not letting go of the rope reins. He knew his mule. Then remounted and turned west.

The sun was just past noon and it was very hot. He'd trotted and even loped much of the morning's journey; but while he knew the mule was rugged, he also knew mules remembered ill treatment, and so settled into the long ride back to Jerusalem at a walking pace. Any guilt he felt about missing work was overshadowed by his care of the mule, his knowledge that August was also out making what could be a lengthy and difficult call, and, finally, the chance to absorb and consider all that had passed thus far this day. So boy and mule wended their way along, twice pulling off the towpath into the brush to let teams hauling barges make their way along the path. One barge-master smiled and waved, the other scowled and shook a fist in the air as if Harlan was someway impeding passage.

He went on. As he did he realized he was flustered by Alice Ann Labidee and wondered had she intended him to be so affected. And concluded that while she might not be of use in his quest, she'd not ruled that out altogether. The mule sawed the air against a plague of deerflies and Harlan thought, If she was so afraid of someone chasing her down, then why had she remained so close? And then guessed he was reading too much into her poor hiding place; she might simply not have the means to get farther away. All in all, a parcel of thought not to be pressed for a conclusion. His head felt to be swarmed much as the deerflies upon Bart and sweat dripped into his eyes and burned, and he wished he'd thought to wear his hat and went along, studying the flowing water beside him and thinking of stopping and stripping down and cooling off but did not.

He came into the town and stuck to the back side of the Burkett brothers' mill that adjoined low ground along the canal and he paused there, studying the huge mill and the sprawl of sheds that stretched around, all attached, one way or another. The mill was a three-story mass of yellow brick that held steam-powered grinding wheels as well as vast storage vaults for oats, wheat, barley, buckwheat. Dried shell and seed corn. Farmers brought their grains here to be sold, processed and shipped east or south. Or milled on shares and returned to them for livestock feed through the winter. And the steam-power plant that drew in water from the lake also sent power to the lathes and riveters of the buggy-works that filled one of the adjoining sheds and to the tannery close down by the canal where green hides were cured and shipped or trundled by carts to be made into harness or shoe leather in another of the sheds.

Not a month earlier Harlan had sat in the wagon bed when Hopeton had gone to town to buy seed corn from the Burketts, there being none in the web- and dust-strewn empty granaries of Hopeton's own loft. And Malcolm Hopeton had left Harlan waiting while he went inside to conduct his business, then came out pushing a dolly with the sacks of seed corn, heaved them down into the bed of the wagon from the high dock, settled himself, and turned the team toward home. Malcolm told Harlan the Burkett brothers had first been lucky by securing the location for their mill, though it had been their father who'd done that, and the canals had come and they had begun to make money and then the railroads made them rich. But, he'd said, looking straight ahead as they rode up the grade out of town, it was the war that had made the Burketts wealthy.

He'd said it as if stating a simple fact of day: My, it's warm. That mule look a bit gimpy his near front hoof to you? A stone lodged. I reckon we should check. Those fellows made a bundle and a bundle again. Not a trace of irony or bitterness, only a comment upon human affairs.

Up there in Milo there was uncut hay gone to seed and grown tough. Young corn with dusty leaves and weeds coming up, no one to run a cultivator through it—although there was no cultivator in the shed anymore. Not even a man and a boy to arm themselves with hoes and go out and do that work until their fingers and palms scraped off the calluses there and so raised new blisters, which would break and wither down to raw skin, smearing blood onto the handles of the hoes.

Boy and mule slowly plodded through those lower reaches and then the back side of the town until he was finally out on open ground again, the waters of the east branch of the Crooked Lake falling away to the south, the Bluff that split the branches rising and shimmering in the heat of mid–afternoon. A couple, maybe three more hours and he would be back in Jerusalem with August Swartout and his own sister, Becca.

Behind him, underground in a cell in the town, was the man he not only owed loyalty to but the only man on earth that needed him. That truly needed him. He pushed the mule on almost to a trot, a long extended stride of a walk.

EIGHT

AUGUST DROVE OUT in the jog-cart intent on the four miles uphill
into the rougher land atop the ridge at the south end of the Italy Hill
wilderness. Sunlight falling through the trees, dew drying off the
roadside grasses and flowers. Brown thrashers, cowbirds, meadowlarks
and bobolinks rising up chattering and chiding his passage. The horse
prancing a side-stepping trot in a morning frisk, the iron bands
around the wide wheels crunching the packed roadway, small scrapes
of higher pitch as they rolled over rough gravel, not yet kicking up
dust but the dark clots tossed by churning hooves.

He soon turned uphill on a lesser track, the horse still jogging but
working now, moving through fields and woodlots, making for the
top of the long north–south–running ridge that separated the water-
sheds of the Crooked Lake to the east and Canandaigua Lake westward,
up here a rougher, less fertile land, still south of the Italy Hills but
running out of Jerusalem. The farms were smaller, with fields of corn
but lesser cereals, small plots only of oats and hard rye, pastures dotted
with rock outcrops half-protruding like vertebrae of ancient giant
beasts, scraggly pines or a clump of hickories making shade for the

herds of mixed cattle. Larger woodlots lay between the farms and swamps ringed with cattails and coated with green slime. A wood-duck drake broke from a drowned tree, a wild flare of color in the morning sun.

There were members of his community he knew less well than the Schofields, but not many. David raised hogs, turkeys and chickens for the local markets and spent his winters in the woods cutting cord-wood to sell to village residents or those without woodlots of their own. He was a man of hard, wiry build with thin sandy hair and a ruddy chapped complexion year-round. August had difficulty conjur-ing an image of Iris; and, for that matter, his memory of Bethany was of a younger girl. During the time she was grown and meeting Malcolm Hopeton and then marrying him, August had been building his house and settling into his small known world of Narcissa. He recalled only a girl with a mass of dark curls and bright blue eyes, quick to blush.

He smelled the hog lots before the farm came into view around a curve of road and down a small hill. The place struck him as hard-used and sad, the house of unpainted clapboards darkening toward the color of light molasses, the barns low and with uneven ridgelines. The yard before the house was packed earth with only a sparse flower garden of hollyhocks and dahlias either side of the small front porch offering some attempt at brightness. Several dozen mixed red or black-and-white hens worked the edges of the yard or lay dusting themselves.

He slowed the horse to a walk to allow the hens to scatter and also to announce his arrival as he saw a woman sitting in the shade of the porch, working from a basket beside her to shell peas into a wooden bowl on her lap.

His own peas had been done a month now. It was colder here, spring slower to come and the soil less willing to give. Even with the rich hog and poultry manure.

He drew up by the wooden post and as he stepped down to tie his horse to the ring the woman spoke.

"August Swartout. Of all souls to grace my yard and day. Shall I be cheered or is it ill news you bring me? Ill news has been too plentiful of late but we can't pick our days, can we?"

He smiled, not from her words but the tone of delivery and also the woman herself; once before her, he wondered how he could've forgotten her so easily. A bright face with the same curls her daughter had carried but these a salt-and-pepper spray pressed forth from a simple day cap, her form not plump but not wizened and dried as he might've imagined or expected. Most striking was the uplift in her voice, almost a singing clarity and while not jovial still lacking in grief or the presumption she was to be an object of pity. Perhaps stalwart also against such expectations carried toward her. He said, "I carry no news but only goodwill and cheer."

"Yes," she said. "Pleasantries. It's few that can look such a mother in the eye. Or is it David you're after?" Now within the pitch of her voice he heard the jittery anger hidden in her greeting. He stepped onto the porch and took the empty chair that had the rush seat broken and mended with heavy twine. He leaned forward slightly with his hands on his knees.

"Iris," he said. "Nobody but those who were there know the circumstances and I have only sympathy for Bethany, no judgment. The Kingdom of the Lord is hers now, and that alone is all we know."

She blinked, her eyes lit bright but if with held-back tears, anger or some other condition of her mind he could not say. She said, "Surely she's with Christ now, but I fear the devil walks upon the earth striving to snatch her soul back. Could be he was always after her. David's about somewhere. I'd guess you came to see him, as the others have. But just where I don't know. He walks out of the house at first light and spends his days as he can. This time of the morning he's likely candling and crating his eggs. Or he could be rambling in the woods. I don't know his mind anymore and wonder if I ever did."

153

While speaking, she kept her eyes upon his even as she continued shelling peas.

Gently August said, "I was not myself for some months after my wife died." And never again what I was before, he thought but did not say.

Iris Schofield looked off across the yard to some indeterminate spot and in a sudden small voice said, "In most all ways Bethany left us years ago anyway. When she married that man. What he drove her to, I can't say." She looked back upon him.

"My understanding was they made a good match. The troubles began after he left for the war, and it's not clear Bethany had much say in any of what happened."

"You did not know Bethany, did you?"

"No, not beyond at Meeting years ago or saying hello in town."

"That's right. You did not. Bethany Schofield always had a say, even if it hurt her. That's half of my grief or more, and all of hers, now. She always had fire in her, grit, I thought, when she was a girl. Strong-willed, free-spirited; I don't know what to call it. She'd argue The Friend showed that a woman was more than a helpmate but didn't have the courage to speak so. She had a quick tongue and would not hold it; after she was twelve or thereabout she and her father had got to the place where they'd not speak but for the necessaries of day-to-day living. Malcolm Hopeton was cut from the same cloth, best I could gather. Their only marriage was at the courthouse, you know, and after that I did not see her more than half a dozen times until I washed her body for her burial. If it's David you want he's likely about somewheres, you walk out around past the barns and call for him. He'll show up or not I can't help you there. Lawyer Stone found him easily enough the times he's come by. It's David you're after, isn't it?"

Midway through this she'd stopped shelling the peas but her hands were still working, breaking the pods in half and dropping both the loosed peas and casings into the bowl in her lap and he realized she thought she was working snap beans. And with a low dull headache blooming, realized he could not simply leave her now to look for David but must sit gently as possible and tease out what he could of her troubled mind. Even as he considered her comments about her husband and wondered what torments the man might be living within. And again his thoughts were turned to Enoch Stone.

"I called upon you both and if he doesn't turn up I'll amble out after a while and look for him. But for now I'd sit and keep company with you, Iris. I didn't come to intrude or upset you, but I must confess there's some in what you said I can't make sense of, perhaps none but a mother could. May I help shell your peas?"

She looked down at the bowl in her lap with the handful of broken pods atop the mound of smooth green peas. "Oh dear, look at this." She plucked out the pods and dropped them on the heap beside her. A red hen had come up on the porch and was stabbing at the empty pods. Iris said, "My mind seems all akilter with no more sense half the time than that hen. No, no, it's my job to do but I'd welcome the company. Tell me how your life is, August. I know you're rare to go to Meeting and don't blame you for that."

Again she stopped and looked off and continued, "David goes each week but it's been difficult for me these last years and now not at all. I can't face people, what they're thinking if not saying. That's small of me, I know." She looked back to him.

"It's understandable. Meeting is meant to succor and offer fellowship but if we don't feel it within . . ." He let his voice trail.

Her fingers were back at proper work. "I feel little within. Anger, but toward whom or what I'm often at a loss. As tumultuous as my household was all those years it seemed nothing more than what we're called for, to struggle as much as we must to understand how Christ moves in each of us, in those we love. Few souls come easily into Time and fewer dwell there in peace. That was always how I saw it."

His thoughtfulness was deliberate. "And those that do shall be tested, it would seem."

"Or we order our lives in hindsight to make it seem so. Perhaps peace never exists in this vale but only strife and meanness and we fool ourselves by painting it as the toil demanded of us toward that peace, a notion that blankets our eyes and hearts, that allows false peace only."

He reached and touched her hand, took his away. "I once wondered much the same."

Her chin lifted. "You're a young man, even younger when you lost your wife and babies. Of course you found your way back to a sensible life."

"I was guided. Not to the peace you speak of but to a purposeful life, one not without a measure of serenity and solace."

She ignored this and simply said, "I can't see how to live in any of the worlds before me. I want none of them." And then as if it naturally followed, "Did Enoch Stone send you?"

"No," he was able to truthfully answer. As swiftly he decided he didn't want to discuss Stone with her and so said, "Iris, may I impose for a cup of water? There was much dust off the road this morning-"

"There!" she said, rising quickly but holding onto her bowl of peas. "You see how it is with me? All at sixes and sevens. There's coffee still warm. Or I'd make tea?" And again he saw within her fluster the beauty faded but peeping forth, the bright rise in her cheeks, the bow of her lips; and a wrench turned within him, that she had come to the distress she inhabited.

He stood also. "Water would be the best. Cool water. Truly."

While she was inside, he waited standing at the edge of the porch overlooking the barns and the stockaded hog pens and poultry runs, the earth between them torn and mired as a single sow and her brood of a dozen or more piglets worked their way snuffling alongside the turkey pens, tearing out dandelions and thin grass that lived in those slender sanctuaries. A plank fence hid the vegetable garden, although a hand cultivator lay on its side by the gate and beyond was a small scorched pasture where a pair of brown milk cows stood under the shade of a black walnut tree. Between the pasture and the barns was the skidway from the woodlot where several dozen logs lay bruised with mud, pairs of saw-jacks and several whittled and chipped rounds used as chopping blocks with high heaps of split cordwood looming behind. There was a grim economy within the scene, each piece separate from the others not so different from his own workings but, taken together, lacking in harmony of order, as if the assemblage was arbitrary and not making any whole. August wondered if it had always been so or if there had been a slow falling-apart the past years from some original greater command. He could imagine it both ways.

When Iris returned with a pewter pitcher and tumblers on a tray, he saw a new set to her features and guessed she'd gathered herself while in the kitchen, much as he also had done. They sat again and passed time in light conversation of the summer weather, the heat of the long days, the race against fall coming sooner than any would guess but all knew. There were a couple of pauses, silences that might've been awkward but both waited them out until one or the other picked up some thread from the previous remarks and they went along so. They talked of everything except all of what was most pressing and August, while listening to her litany of garden problems, realized his appearance this morning had jarred her, one already deep in a whirling maelstrom of grief, guilt, anger, sorrow and confusion, strands not clear and separate but jumping one to the next when she was alone. He recalled how it was to be beset so. For his part, when she asked of his life he spoke in detail of Becca Davis with only a small prompt to remind her of the orphan's parents and did not hide Harlan from the conversation but allowed him entry as if it were only a natural occurrence, not altogether a misrepresentation, at which point Iris returned the conversation to the problem of corn-borers.

For an hour or more they spoke and as they progressed August understood he was offering what she so deeply needed: a respite from the grinding self-abrasion the loss of her daughter had brought upon her. For a short moment she might live as others did and he was more than happy to collude in offering her that. Doing so, he gained a bit of it as well.

The sun rose high over the roof beams and tree crowns and shadows were pooled tight about their sources when David Schofield appeared as a wavering heat ghosting from the far barn, then gained slow substance and form and came into the yard. The sow and piglets ran to him and he leaned to scratch the sow's ear as he studied the porch.

"Goodness, there's David now," Iris said.

August was already on his feet. "It's all right. I'll just walk out to greet him."

David Schofield's hands and trousers were speckled with drying blood and drips of black tar. "I've been cutting pigs," he said. "I need to watch em and see the daubs hold or they'll bleed out. Whatever your business is, you can pitch it to me there." Without waiting he turned and walked back toward the barn. August simply nodded, not bothering to protest he'd come visiting and not upon business—for surely it was business of a sort—and so followed along.

The barn was a long, low structure of a single story and loft tight against the rafters, but inside belied the derelict appearance of the exterior. The pens of rough-sawn boards were tight and square, the bedding not straw but marsh hay, ample and fresh. The walkway was packed earth swept clean and though the windows were few they were open to the light and air and the large door at the south end was also open, where a wheelbarrow and fork stood and outside rose a manure pile. Beside the manure pile a small fire was dying to a thin coil of smoke, the crossbar holding the kettle of scalding water and the smaller pot of warmed tar. The final pen before the door was larger than most of the others and it was here David led them. Wordless, he stepped to the wall and took down a pair of old milking stools, handed one to August and settled himself outside the pen. August sat a couple of feet away and surveyed the pen and young piglets within. Who minced gingerly on a thin bed of fresh hay, stopping to twist about and sniff best they could between their hind legs at the plaster of tar drying where their testicles had hung.

A strop lay over the top plank alongside a razor. The razor was washed clean and glistened in the light from the open door but David took a handkerchief from his trouser pocket and wiped it down, then let the blade rest upon his knee. He said, "The least drop of water missed will be a rust-bloom tomorrow."

When it was clear he'd say nothing more, August said, "The pigs look well cut and hardy."

David did not take his eyes from his pigs. "You're a young man yet. I can set here until dusk and leave thinking all's well but it takes only one to bite through the tar to get blood flowing. Then the others will swarm so by daybreak I'd be lucky to have any not chewed half to death."

"There's risk to everything, certainly. It's true: I'll get up more times of a night when I've got a first-calf heifer due than any time thereafter. I've also gone to the barn to find a fine cow trying to birth a posterior calf and exhausted by the effort. It was a job to dig that big a hole but it had to done." He stopped then, angry he'd reacted so easily to the comment about being a young man and wondering if he'd just proved it true.

But David only said, "It's a great burden lifted from me."

August waited and then said, "What would that be, David?"

The man perched up off his stool to peer into the pen, eyes tracking swiftly a young pig, perhaps two, then settled back and said, "Brother Stone has pierced the torment that wrapped me for so many years. It's a terrible thing, knowing your own flesh and blood is besmirched. For I saw it in the girl from a young age. Mother did not, but mothers will not see such a thing in their daughters. They will believe the best even when the worst possible is right before them. It's this blindness I faced, not only from Mother but my own trial as well. The girl never saw herself so but the unnatural is designed this way. Gathered it upon herself as a rightful pleasure. I don't know to what extent Brother Stone has informed you of this, but it will be in the public revelations of details that I'll finally shed this cloak of darkness. I know some will see it as a public shaming, but I care nothing for that; long since I ceased caring what others think of me. What lifts my heart in these dark hours is the humble truth that another man snared by her foulness may be exonerated, shall at least be understood as being not an instrument of destruction, but of his own salvation. For, you must know, his final helpless acts were born of the desperation of sudden comprehension. And those actions will be seen truthfully as the grace of the Lord and how His Spirit may infuse not only a man but a community of souls, as well as those who witness such compassion. Comfort for me, finally, yes, but small against the greater good. Yes, I shall lift up mine eyes unto the hills from whence cometh my help. You have heard the accounts, Brother Swartout, I know. And so must understand a measure of how this is for me. Nothing more than a measure; no man save myself can fully know the torments of the years behind me, and the release awaiting me. But it will be seen, for those who look. And who will not?"

August was silent but digging in his trouser pocket for the match safe and a cheroot. He struck fire and plumed smoke and pretended to study the young pigs. Finally he said, "It's only the last couple of weeks I've known anything about all of this, and then only bits. I never knew Bethany, beyond her name and face. The rest remains much of a mystery to me."

"There's no great mystery to it. The girl was born lacking, and inhabited."

August smoked. For no obvious reason the numeral eight came to mind, as if he were traversing at once both the inner and outer edges of those double rings that looped back upon themselves. "Lacking?" he asked. "What is a child born lacking?"

David Schofield was quick. "She had no sense of the world beyond her physical being. It's not that Mother and I did not strive to lift her into the fullness of life, but that she refused it. I'll tell you. As a little girl in her bath she'd employ her fingers for sensual effect. I only glimpsed that once; Mother was quick to gather her up and wrap her in sacking, making as if to dry her. She'd crawl from her cradle middle of the night to come to my marriage bed where she'd insert herself between Mother and myself but favoring Mother, as if she'd take her from me. And look at me without love. Yet she'd chase behind me around the barns and I thought it was myself she was learning from but came to understand it was the beasts she was watching. The boar mounting the sows. Roosters in their flurry topping hens. One wet afternoon I sent her to fetch the milk cows from the pasture and the time passed when they should've made the barn, so I set out looking for them. The rain was drumming down with fog all around and I spied the three cows ambling slow, pausing and looking behind, then moving on. I pulled my hat low to keep the rain from my eyes and walked wide around the cows through the high grass and came up behind from a distance and there she was: Her dress pulled up as she writhed belly-down in the mud of the cow path, pressing herself up and down against the wet earth. When I saw this I sat down flat on the ground, shocked dumb by the sight. I was frighted by it, soaked through with rain, and commenced shaking, a great roaring in my ears and my vision gone all red. I'd seen pure evil and Satan was close by, nigh upon me. Perhaps seeking to enter me as well. I clenched my eyes and prayed and felt the wrath of the Lord wash over me. I rose up then and walked straight to where she and the cows was upon the barn. She was upright walking then, her dress smeared with mud, her

161

hair and arms and legs also. I sent her to the house and Mother, and milked cold shivering. Even as I felt the heat of rage fill me and seep out again. She was an unnatural child but she was mine and I had a duty to her. That night I told Mother what I'd seen in as few words as I could and took the child to the shed. I told her, The flesh is the source of all great pain and you shall know that. And I strapped her until she did."

There was more. A great deal more and August sat, listening, offering no comment. None was wanted. It was easier to watch the young pigs than the fevered man beside him. And a headache bloomed behind his temples.

Driving away after turning down an offer of dinner by saying he was expected home, he recalled what Iris had told him: Those years Bethany and her father were not speaking, a truce of sorts had been made, or David retreated into silence against what he could not change. Also dating from that time was her vehement and absolute refusal to attend Meeting, further proof to David that she was in the grip of Satan. Best August could determine from all Iris had said, the girl and her mother remained friendly, Iris forcefully making clear to her husband a line she would not pass, a point she would not meet with him upon. Iris had said, "I would not turn her out." Then spoke of cabbages and brine. Nothing more was said about Malcolm Hopeton and the business Enoch Stone and David were concocting until at the very end, still in the hog barn, when David finally ran out of words and both men sat silent, August struggling to find a way to take his leave, David intent upon some far-distant vision beyond the open door and the heat of the gathering day.

David said, his voice one of great fatigue, the slip of sorrow encasing his words, "You see, then, why I welcome the proceedings ahead of me."

Driving not toward home but taking lanes and roads east toward the valley, but also north and dropping down toward the crossroads of

162

Friend and the Public Friend's manse, and in particular the burying ground there, August turned his mind upon the second question prompted by the conversations. For as David described his daughter's sensual engagement with the world, with herself, August was of two minds, the first being to what extent did David only see his daughter in these episodes and not else-wise. The second and most pressing was one of memory: Except that she was alone, how different was Bethany from himself as a child? And Narcissa? She of the black raspberry brake's hidden first kiss, on through all their exploits and efforts from the time they were children until finally old enough to declare themselves and join their community. All of the ways they had found with each other, the yearning swift pleasure of their young bodies, then and still justified by their spoken love, by their minds enjoined and bent upon the shared intent of ultimate and eternal union, all those years and all the years since that love seen as sacred and sanctified by intent. But now, the cart and horse down upon the valley floor jogging fleet the last mile, he turned over and again the question: If each of them had not had the other, what might they have done, alone?

Beside the manse there was a pump and trough as well as a tin cup on a string from the pump handle. He brought fresh water up into the trough for the horse and drank several cups himself, the first only against the heat of the day but that cup prompted a severe thirst and so he drank again and again. His headache grown larger, the pulsing putting him in mind of a steaming liver brought out of a slaughtered beef in November, as if the color and texture of the pain behind his eyes.

He walked back into the burying ground. No fence separated this land from any other, only the stones inscribed with the name and dates showed the place to be what it was and even this was almost obliterated, the grass grown high and spotted with daisies, butterfly-weed, Queen Anne's lace. The place needed mowing. But settled down in the grass with his legs stretched before him, his head propped

163

on a hand as he looked upon Narcissa's stone, he welcomed the tall growth. He was hidden and as alone in this place as he wanted to be.

Then he slept and dreamed. When he settled upon the ground he had no sense of pending sleep and when he woke the dream was vividly strong, then drained, falling away in moments. His head still ached, subsided to a dull ceaseless thrum that would not quit. When he stood he saw the long shadows cast by the cedars uphill of the manse and returned to the horse, where he pumped more water and drank again, then made his way home.

August had given Becca Davis no instructions for the day. As she washed up the breakfast dishes and then swept the kitchen she realized he'd never given her directions. There had been times, those first few months almost five years earlier, when he'd tell her where to find a certain thing, or that she might want to look to this or that; but these had not been instructions so much as suggestions offered when he noticed her uncertainty or hesitation. Otherwise she'd entered the house and easily known most all that needed to be done, from keeping house for Harlan and Albert Ruddle after her mother had died. Tasks or jobs particular to the farm had become obvious. She believed, though she'd never have voiced the thought, that she had a keen eye and intuitive nature that married together into an easy efficiency. Certainly this: August had not once in those years had reason to make complaint. If she'd misstepped upon occasion, most times she'd caught the error herself before it was noticed, and otherwise had realized it not by anything August said but from her own sense that something was off, and then her seeking eye had found and rectified the lapse.

And so she'd found herself this morning, with her brother and August gone off on their separate missions, with no purpose directly before her. She'd baked bread the night before, the laundry was done, the garden mostly stripped clear for the moment after the two days of pickling and canning. There was not even noon dinner to prepare, though it was in her mind to have something ready should either of them return in the afternoon hours. So she pulled the crane with the kettle from the dying fire and made a pot of tea and sat at the table and sipped slow the cup of dark smoky leaf that August had long ago suggested she seek out from the Italian merchant in town. It had been Narcissa's tea of choice and had taken Becca a bit to get used to, but now she could imagine nothing finer.

And sitting there, the work of the day came to her. The fire was dying and she'd let it go out, for a cold hearth was what she needed; but the weeping hard heat of the day would make the usual winter task all the easier.

When the fire was down to ash she got the scuttle and shovel and carried the ash to the new pile beside the garden, where it would grow over the months until next spring when it would be a grand porous conical pile that would then be spread and turned in as the garden was dug for the new season. She carried the empty scuttle to the pump in the yard and poured a slow drizzle over the pile against live coals and was rewarded with quick sizzles and jets of steam and then back to the house. She swept clean the hearth and fireplace of fine ash, then used a stiff brush and the last of the warm water from the kettle to scrub the grease and dirt free of the bricks, these bricks not the usual red building bricks but wider oblongs of a dark yellow, almost brown, shade. Letting the bristles of the brush work not only the surface of the bricks but also shifting the angle of the brush against the channels of mortar.

Her arm ached and her hands were rubbed raw where they struck against the bricks as she brushed; also strands of hair had worked free and fell downward and ran wet with the same sweat that beaded and dropped from her nose, but she scoured on, knowing she was only just begun. Finally she was satisfied and splashed a bit of fresh water over the hearth and sopped it with sacking rags and then went out to sit on the stoop and allow the bricks to fully dry.

She stood blinking, blinded by the light of day after the dim of the kitchen, the sweat in her eyes. Specks floated over her vision and for a moment she did not know the world before her.

There had never been a daguerreotype made of her, or her mother, father, or brother, but she'd seen others in the window of the narrow storefront in town that held the studio of the man: Twice she'd glimpsed him with his wagon and set-up shrouded device that people stood before wavering. She'd studied the images in the window and hadn't known a one of them but had recognized souls. As if this business were conducted in the partial dark between this life and another.

Which summed her mind: Her brother and herself both together now under August's roof—temporary, perhaps, but she savored it ever more greatly for the tentative nature of the arrangement. And thought August did as well, some part of his mind at least, one he did not even realize. The house was not empty save for himself and his ghosts but filled up with life. Nightimes she lay under a single sheet in her summer nightgown, aware of the both of them just up and down the hall from her room. Seemed she could hear August this past night as he tossed and coughed and then slept with deep, rasping, uneven snoring as if his very soul were troubled but she took comfort thinking this was not due to her presence but instead perhaps to somewhat of what had brought Harlan here. But August was a fair and tender man, she told herself, and so could make division between what worried him and Harlan's small role in that worry. Even if Harlan had made that worry more vivid by being brought here. And she reminded herself that that had been August's doing also—his insistence, in fact. He well might've left Harlan in the care of the doctor or for the authorities to deal with. And he'd chosen not to.

But his house was no longer empty and she no longer sweltered in the cheap thin-plastered walls in the room above Malin's store. She knew it was nothing more than this, and knew this was a mighty and wondrous thing for them all. With the faint tinge of fearsomeness to it, a taint she was determined to keep tamped down. There was no need of it. Idle thoughts. Though she would seek hard to hold this harmony best she could. If it was to fall apart it would not be her lack, not of her doing. Or of her not paying attention. She made this a solemn vow and offered up a soundless heartfelt prayer. All of it, for now, the best she could do.

She rose and went inside and paused in the kitchen and passed on through and up the stairs to her room, where she swiftly changed out of her clothes to her summer nightgown, pausing naked to let what air came through her open windows pass over her, and her skin prickled. Then pulled the thin cloth over her head and tied the hem up on one side so it rode above her knees and went back down the stairs. Certain if any person happened to turn into the farm they'd do so not on foot and so she'd hear the warning of hooves and wheels.

In the pantry she took down the black and red tin and pried off the top. A crusted balled rag lay atop the contours of the hard wax. And so she went to the hearth and began to wax the bricks—a matter of spreading the stiff paste upon small sections and then using the friction and heat of her hand with the weight of her body applying upon the rag to soften the wax and work it deep into the bricks and then buff over and over to bring the wax to a coating with a high and hard sheen. And then on to the adjoining section. As she slowly built the first new coat of wax. Long ago in a different house an old man had taught her how to do this job and told her, "Three coats will look nice once you got em down, but it's five, even six you need to make it worth doing, to have it hold as long as you'd want it to." She'd learned this was true, more ways than waxing a hearth.

Finally she was done, the wax buffed as hard and shining. It would be several hours before the summer heat hardened the wax all the way. She could build a fire to speed the job but saw no reason to. She sank back on her heels and felt the muscles of her back and thighs and arms pull hard and sore. Her nightgown was soaked through and stuck clammy, rubbing harsh in the heat against her skin. She thought of walking to the woodlot and the ravine there, where a stream ran, and finding the pool August had spoken of in passing but the tramp across the hot fields and dressed so was more than she could consider.

Without letting herself think greatly, she grabbed up a couple of pieces of clean sacking from the shelves and ran out to the yard, where she used a foot to turn over the wooden washtub that lay beside the yard pump and worked the handle until the tub was overflowing and mud was forming downhill from where she stood. Then filled the bucket that hung on the backside of the pump, glanced quickly around, and pulled the nightgown over her head. Still sodden, it caught about her neck and arms and she wrenched it free and balled it and threw it upon the ground. Then leaned and pumped water over her head and down through her thick long brown hair and stood upright to lift bucket after bucket and poured them over herself, finally standing in the washtub and cleaning her legs up to her thighs. She pumped more water into the tub as she stood there and looked down at herself, skin prickled and pink, cool and clean even as she felt the sun drying her shoulders. She was gasping and turned her face up to the sun and as she did saw the sway of her up-tilted breasts and stopped mid-motion.

She fled to the house. Up to her room, where she hugged herself and then tiptoed quiet as a thief to her window, where she looked out upon the yard, onward to where the road made a thin slice in its passing. She saw no one, had no reason to expect anyone. And fell then back upon her bed, the drawn-up sheet and light coverlet warm against her still-cool body. And she began to laugh, aloud and strong, her belly rising and falling, her eyes turned upward to the plaster ceiling, the whorls of horsehair thin curls of faint darkness within the dense cream above her.

A bit of breeze passed through the open windows, played upon her.

★   ★   ★

She woke with a sheen of sweat over her some hours later and lay languorous for some time until she heard the eight-day clock downstairs chime the half-hour between four and five and jerked upright. She quickly dressed in clean clothes, braided her tousled hair and on fleet barefeet went down the stairs. She laid a new fire in the hearth but didn't light it yet and prepared a cold supper of smoked hard sausage, radishes, scallions, sliced cucumbers, bread and cheese and then went out into the yard, thinking perhaps one of the men had returned home and not bothered to come to the house, or at least not beyond the kitchen where they saw it empty. And her face ran hot at that thought. But there was nothing to be seen beyond the cows bunched at the gate of the day pasture, ready for milking.

She crossed to the barn and heard the rustle of the penned calves, snorts far down the length of the barn from the hog-pen, also from the lofts high overhead the alarm of the pigeons nesting in the eaves above the haymows, then the flurry of wings as they beat out the slatted vents just below the pitch of the eaves, and she wondered if they'd heard the door or if the stirring of the calves and swine alerted them. Or some other sense she couldn't penetrate. Most all of her life Becca had known to take nothing for granted, because there's nothing that can't be stripped away in a single beat of an urgent and otherwise oblivious heart, but also if that is so, there must also be the unexpected, what sweeps in as you're looking another way.

The workings of the barn this time of evening were nearly as unknown to her as the boats under sail upon the lake she'd watched for stolen moments all of her life. This was the place of August, recently also, of her brother. Whatever the work of the day had been, she'd now be in the kitchen setting up supper; but that didn't mean she hadn't paid attention these five years. She'd listened and she'd watched. Mostly listened as, over supper, August was often in the habit of talking about the events transpiring in the barn, the changing course as

169

the year turned and in time she'd caught a sense of the rhythms in play for each season.

She walked the length of the barn and went through a door, where she tossed a day-old bucket of scraps to the hogs, and from the bin a handful of last year's dried cob-corn, on into the chicken shed, low and musty with old hay and hens already on the roosts, where she lowered the ropes that closed the doors to the outside fenced runs. A few hens stood about the wooden hopper of shell corn but as she shut the doors, they, too, flapped up toward their roosts, save for a couple of broody hens snugged tight in the nesting boxes.

Back into the big barn and evening light streaming through the windows, the wooden stanchions along the tie-up worn smooth by the tough necks of cows, heads rising and falling as they ate from the troughs before them, the troughs swabbed smooth from thick tongues. Old wood made older by the creatures that jostled, moved, pressed and scrubbed, lived against it each day. The warm still air held the deep stamp of life, of sweat and milk, of manure and hay, of shed hair and urine, of bright straw bedding, the sour and sweet ferment of chewed oats and corn. A place of deep and ancient habitation, bright and ongoing as the ending day.

She thought, I'll get the cows in. It was only the five summer milkers and the dry cows and bred heifers. She'd watched countless times as they'd filed up the lane and into the barn. She knew to spread forkfuls of fresh hay, to gather the washed buckets from the buttery. She knew how to milk; Albert Ruddle had kept a cow.

She slid open the tie-up door and walked down the short lane to the pasture, paused and pushed back the gate rails and, standing in the opening, called the words she'd heard many afternoons.

"Come boss. Come boss."

And they came. Three or four, the first ones, streamed around her and made their way into the barn and then she was surrounded by a milling bunch of the red and white cows, some balking at her in the opening, others pressing through and then wandering off one way or another, outside the fence but not barnward. Three snorted and trotted with the ungainly gait of pregnant cows back into the pasture. Several were headed toward the house, the flower gardens. It was a great mess, a chaos of milling, uncertain, half-wild cows. Eating the bright clover alongside the barn, the geraniums and nasturtiums in the flowerbeds alongside the house, one knee-deep in the kitchen-herb garden, tearing thyme and lovage, sage and dill, elderberry. Trampling and squirting shit.

The lonely work horse stood at the gate of his own pasture, alert and patient.

The left-behind mule, forgotten in the mayhem by Becca, also heard the gate open and trotted down toward the newly accustomed pen in the stable and his evening ration of oats. Busy with the cows, she didn't even see it coming until it flared with the uncertainty and fear spilling from the cattle and circled back into the pasture where it stood trembling, then its head came up and ears blinked forward and it brayed. The sound seemed to trumpet the last few of the cows to a panic but they'd not come past where Becca stood, their way clogged when they expected it to be open—no matter, as the mule proved he could fly by rising high, leaping clear over the back of a cow, an imagined fence or somesuch shadow, rushing not through so much as over and on into the yard beyond. Becca Davis didn't see a mule—just a sudden blot of red darkness against an evening already gone wrong. Quicker than he'd come he was gone and she was still contending with loose cattle.

But behind her she did hear the clatter of hooves in the gravel and then the loud greeting squalls of mules. She glanced over her shoulder and saw Harlan striding toward her, leaving behind him the two mules in a mule communion, a reunion of a team greater than its parts.

His voice both tired and patient, Harlan said, "If we leave the gate down and go to the barn, the rest will follow us. It's where they want to be. There might be one or two we'll have to chase out of the flowers, but we'll see. August Swartout is not yet home?"

"Would it seem so?" She darted fire-eyes at him. "I expected his errand would take a goodly time. And you? Gallivanting the countryside from the dust on your trousers and lather on the mule."

Harlan shrugged. He said, "Let me get my mules in and I'll milk. Why don't you get supper ready. I'd guess August'll be here shortly, and hungry too. I know I am."

"Where'd you go? You couldn't have spent all day with Malcolm Hopeton. And supper's spread on the table, the time comes. I'll help with chores."

"Suit yourself," he said and swung away to catch up the trailing mules. Already the renegade cattle were ambling their ways to the waiting barn door. He called over his shoulder.

"You could fetch the buckets from the buttery."

"Aren't I the one that scalds them? I guess I know where they are. Harlan?"

He heard her tone and turned and waited. A mule, the one left behind, slobbered against the dust-caked shoulder of his shirt. He reached and rubbed the mule's distended affectionate lips.

"Where'd you go?"

He breathed in and out, deliberate, and his shoulder rose and fell. "Here and there," he said. And turned and went on to the barn.

When August rolled down the road toward the farm the long summer day was draining westward, throwing pale golden light down the hillside to wash over the fields and buildings, so all he saw was in softened delicate relief. The barns a dusty rose, the stones of the house like butter, the pastures and hay fields, the grain fields, all muted and dulled, the pools of shade from the orchard and other trees extending broad and wide, as if overall the slow dusk was making its way from out of the ground to meet that from the deepening dark blue of the eastern sky.

His mind was yet troubled by the events of his day but on the slow thoughtful ride home from the burying ground there had come to him a bit of the dream that had fallen upon him as he slept there: Narcissa older than ever in life in the orchard with the apples heavy in clusters pulling down the limbs, September air and two children, a boy and girl of nine or ten helping to fill baskets, the boy up in the crotch of a tree handing down higher fruit to his sister, their mother calling out to take care, to not bruise the apples. She spoke their names and now he could not recall what those names had been. The dream image in his mind remained vivid and he could hear her very voice within him. But not the names, as if sucked off on the mild chill of a September breeze, tugging the grass, spraying the boy's brown curls about his head. Then, peering within, all was lost but for an empty echo of voice and a single small hand holding down an apple. To be lifted up by someone waiting below.

It was but a dream, but the false memory it provoked was calming, enough so his mind returned to the coming Sunday and Meeting. When, word was, Enoch Stone would rise and face the community and voice his intention to beg clemency from the state for Malcolm Hopeton, in the name of Christ's Mercy. August mulled this, and easily decided against attending. He had no interest in whatever dissembling Stone would engage in, of hearing how he would present his argument. Dressed up and dusted in plumy rhetoric about Christ's compassion and how such actions would serve the church within the wider community—no, he was too clever for that. He'd make reference to David and Iris Schofield and their loss, not only their most recent and worst possible one but also the longer and in some ways greater loss as their daughter strayed. That would be about it. Whatever the full manner of revelations and blame he'd elicit from David would be done in court, most likely in chambers. It would be terrible and jarring and, however the word got about of what had been said, it would not be heard directly but passed mouth to ear and onward, both diminishing and growing as the story circulated. And almost as quickly would not be spoken of: There's little lasting satisfaction spreading stories about the dead who not only can't rebut but also can't further act to feed the stories anew. August almost admired the man, his skills, as problematic as they were. But this truth also: August had been good as gone from active life within the formal structure of Meeting and he'd continue on so, living in close faith with his immediate neighbors and family. To his mind, what The Friend had always intended. Meeting had served for The Friend to preach, to articulate the simple basic tenets of Christian life only as Christ had spoken, of holding the Light of Christ within. The Friend had made no formal church beyond the charter from the state and, as importantly, no provisions for succession, which was to say none were intended by that rare personage. Three and four generations had gained the insight of the light of life, the shortness of Time, the simple laws of His teachings; those generations and the ones to come would falter or endure solely by abiding by those teachings so basic a mother could impart them to a child, upheld by the living examples surrounding those children.

So it had been for August and Narcissa. So it was for many, he believed. Perhaps, he corrected himself, only some. For it was clear Stone was wanted, if not fully in the capacity he sought at least in a capacity others assigned to him from their own needs. Who among us knows, he wondered, but a hundred years hence there will either be no Meeting at all but only those of us quietly practicing, or there will be a Church but a shadow of The Friend's intention. There was nothing he could do about that, less so since he was childless, with no one to instruct, no one to carry down his own beliefs. All he owned was quiet example, to be witnessed and emulated or not.

Thus tempered he came off the road into the yard and was pulled up by the wagon shed, unhitching the horse from the gig, when Harlan Davis stepped out from the house, wiping his mouth with his hand before walking down toward him. Harlan came to the far side of the gig and loosened the tug from the evener and went along like that, as they worked together wordless to free the horse and lower the shaves to the ground. The horse stepped out, the lines looped up over a hame and the men trailed it toward the barn.

"How was your day?" August said.

"Long. I only got back for chores. Yours?"

"Long also. How did you find Malcolm Hopeton?"

"Not good."

August nodded. "You spent the day with him?"

"I did not. And the Schofields? How are they holding?"

"Not good," August echoed. "Did you have dinner?"

"Not to speak of. You?"

"I had sustenance but no food. You sister has supper ready?"

"Of a sort. Cold. But hot coffee. She waxed the hearth bricks."

August paused and looked at him. "She did?"

"Said she couldn't think of anything else and it needed doing."

The horse ducked into the stable-end of the barn and stood waiting. Its mate was in a straight stall, head turned back, watching. August and Harlan stripped the harness and hung it upon its pegs and August went to the bin and carried a wooden measure of oats to the empty stall and spread them in the manger, turned and clucked and the horse came up in and bent its head and neck to eat. August came alongside the horse and stood beside Harlan, waiting for the horse to finish his oats, a token ration against the rich summer pasture.

"Your sister, she's a wonder."

"She's pesky, is what she is."

August cracked the least grin. "After you to tell her about your day?"

"She pestered me on it."

"And you did not share with her?"

Harlan paused and glanced away. He said, "I'm still trying to work it all out in my head."

August held steady a moment and then said, "You don't have to tell anyone anything at all. But if and when you're of a mind to share, you might think of talking to me. I saw and heard things today that troubled me and it's come to me there's men in this on most all sides of the issue and I don't yet trust any of them. Which is the reason you might share with me. I'll not lie to you or allow you to think one thing when I think another, which some of those men might. Otherwise, you don't have to say a thing, to me or any of em, at least until the law compels you to. And, Harlan Davis, you know that day is coming. When it does, you share or be silent, I want you to know I'm standing strong right behind you. I want you to know it. That's all."

The horse had finished his oats and, halterless, began to back out of his stall, intent now on pasture and water, a good roll to rub the sweat-grime and road-dust from his hide. The other horse, haltered and tied, began to rock side to side and thump his hind feet. Harlan caught the loose horse by placing a hand under his jaw while August stepped forward and freed the mate and then together all four walked out into the glowing twilight toward the horse pasture. The men halted and the horses went through the pen gate and August stepped to lift the rails into place. Then he said, "Let's walk up and see what your sister has laid out. Of a sudden I'm famished."

A dozen yards on Harlan came to a stop. He said, "He don't want to fight it. He don't want Stone or none of that. He wants to die, wants the state to hang him for what he done. All he sees is what he done, that one day. Killed his wife. He wants to die."

August laid a hand on the boy's shoulder but peered off to the green sky above the black orchard trees, the swifts and swallows and

bats out cutting the evening air. Quietly he said, "I guess I can understand how he'd feel that way."

"But he's forgot all the rest!"

August waited so long that Harlan turned and was looking up at
him, the boy's face a torment of ravage. August breathed deep and said,
"Think on this, Harlan Davis: Perhaps there comes a time, such as this,
when all the rest doesn't matter. When a man sees all the rest truly is
only details and details don't change a thing about what was actually
done. How details only become empty excuses and nothing more.
And how a man would hate himself for standing behind such
falsehoods."

"But they weren't! False, I mean. They were real, real as anything I
ever witnessed."

"I know." August lifted his hand from shoulder and ruffed the boy's
hair. "I know. But there are times in the world where a stack of truth
can be undone by one shining nugget of harder truth. I'm not saying
it makes sense to us outside those holding that nugget, only that when
it's in your hand you hold it and know it for what it is. The hardest,
strongest truth ever in the world. Maybe if you're lucky, or unlucky, I
can't tell which, delivered to a man once in his life."

Harlan stood silent, looking down and toeing gravel.

"Now let's get onto the house. I don't care if it's blue-molded
cheese and a stale loaf but I'm hungry for food. And coffee, you said?
That too. I had a mighty headache this afternoon and feel it tipping
back round my mind, set to bloom. All I want is to eat and get some
sleep and wake to a new day. Truth is, boy, I'm about done in."

End of day, night creeping in. He sat on the floor. The crusted high
windows flooded crippled light ever so briefly, flies swarmed. A man
came down the steps and pushed through a plate of food, a tin can of
tepid water, and went away without speaking, without looking at him.
After the deputies had beaten him, his appetite had returned; with his

determination to die had come the knowledge that he must die as the state dictated and not by his own hand. Or inaction. He pulled the plate close and took up the spoon and ate the beans, all of them, then the piece of hard cornbread, all of it, then took up the boiled sections of oxtail and chewed the meat from them, sucked out the marrow. He drank half the water and wiped his mouth and cleaned his whiskers with his hands, sucked his fingers clean and dried them on his trousers. Then in the graying light he pushed the plate through the opening so he'd not step on it as he paced in the night hours ahead and slid the cup behind the front post of his bunk, where he could find it easily if he wanted but would not kick it over by accident. He did all these things slowly, with methodical and measured motions, almost ceremonial but of a ceremony empty of meaning beyond spare economy, thoughtless. As if it meant little to him.

Then he rose off the floor and sat upon his bunk. Darkness falls. He did not dread night; neither day nor the dreams of sleep or wakefulness for throughout all the ghost was present, an image, a flicker over his shoulder, a sudden glimpse or bold before him. No specter but that of his mind, the sight of her once again lifeless upon the ground, the blood from her mouth and nose. Life cast out of her by his own swift and certain hands.

Throughout the years of the war he'd feared his own death, perhaps even more so after he'd been wounded and then found his work as a teamster, work that by its nature placed him at a remove from the density of death; but he'd seen enough, known enough to know that death in war, in battle of all sorts, was often arbitrary and unpredictable: The Reb sharpshooter up a tree in the woods across an otherwise placid meadow while the train was wending down a valley track, that sharpshooter knowing one well-placed shot could gum the whole train for hours; the sudden ambuscade of a small cavalry unit boiling up out of a hidden ravine; the mortar or cannon batteries turned upon the wagons. He'd seen all these occur. And so knew that as a teamster he held a long straw against the infantryman he'd been, or the cavalry, the messengers, even the bulk of officers; he also knew a long straw was slender defense before the onslaught of daily deadly chaos, for such was the fashion and nature of the war.

But then also, this: He'd not feared death as such for he'd come to understand death as oblivion. He'd feared death for what it would steal from him, his return to the remainder of his life, his span of years and she who'd walk beside him. Who awaited him, as he, in the mud and cold and bake of southern long summer blood spoor, awaited her.

Blood black as night from her nose, her mouth. Eyes open never to light upon him or any of the glory of life ever again.

Now he sat in blackest night, only waiting oblivion. Patient as he knew he must be but yearning toward the dark maw. To be done with all of this. There came time and then a slight pang at the thought of stepping off the earth that he loved so deeply, the work of the land and the beasts that made that work but also the small daily beauties of life, a summer shower on a hot day, snow whirling over the land in a flail of wind, the long spreads of geese across equinox skies, the workings of his own mind within but also around all such things as he made sense of his own works and questions and doubts.

But such moments came and flittered off. Much the way he dismissed the fantastic premise of the lawyer Stone, the notion of begging clemency for him. Another wild fantasy of a God-besotted man perhaps but also this: Say it was to happen. Say the court would agree to whatever wild claims and terms Stone trotted forth. What then, a life in a cage such as this with his constant ghost? Or, even worse, a step farther, that he was someway freed, turned loose, expected to resume his old life? How to live such a life? Empty and bereft of all he truly held dear within his deepest heart and such emptiness the product of his own hands? No more dreadful torment was possible, imaginable. Endless days and nights of plodding one step after the other, stripped not only of joy and beauty but of hope, of any meaning whatsoever. Shorn of God and well glad of it, this outcome was the closest to hell he could imagine but hell for what purpose? None.

If no purging is possible, why struggle toward pointlessness? More wretched, far more so, than death. For all this would provide would be a death prolonged.

He yearned for the gallows. The sudden drop, perhaps some moments of pain but had he not earned those moments? He could see the gathered crowd but in truth those people, all people save the one lost, knew nothing of him and so let them watch, let them take joy or heave with disgust over him; for how might that touch him? Not one whit. Let him drop and twist. Let him piss himself and stain his trousers. Even, and he'd considered this, let him cry out. He'd cry her name if he could. If some other sound scrawled from his throat he could not help that; he'd seen and heard all manner of last-throes babbles and screams to know all was possible. But that drop. And then all would be gone. Not some peaceful rest, but simply gone. Oblivion. Not only that he knew he'd earned but that it came to all of life.

As his ghost surely knew. She who lived now only within his eyelids, his fluttered mind. Some few other minds as well but that was all, a small lamp growing dimmer until memory wicked the flame out forever.

But this also. He would be buried next to his grandfather in the small plot fenced with peeled rails in the higher ground under a pair of elms in the larger pasture where both lakes could be seen. Where his body would rot and his pine coffin would likewise and he'd turn back to soil and commingle and join the soil his grandfather had made and the two of them would become slow host to roots and then seeds to send forth new life: grasses, flowers, perhaps sprout an elm. Perhaps be hay for cattle in winter. Torn stems to line a bird's nest. Perhaps only a stem that rose and died and rotted back into the earth to one way rise again.

And that would be enough. That would be miracle enough. Indeed.

Yet there remained discontent. Bethany was not in that ground. Stone had told him she'd been buried in Jerusalem. Where, Stone had not said but was clear it was a hidden place, a place of shame. Perhaps such a place was in need of her but he wished her close, close upon him for eternity. As he would be with his grandfather. And he thought, I am making too much of this; it matters not where we return to the earth. We return, that is the only truth.

He reached down in the dark and slid his hand around the leg of his bunk and lifted the tin cup and swallowed. Once. The war had taught him to conserve everything since had taught him to not care. Still, he conserved.

Stone had made passing reference to Bethany's father. Speaking for mercy. Ask me, he thought. Grant me a single day to do as I please. To stalk that man down as the rabid fox he is and clear him from our midst. To eliminate his foul and wrong memory of his daughter forever. As she needed but could not speak as much. So she talked circles about and then lived those circles.

He bent his head down and held it in his hands. Once more he would sleep so. Most dawns would find him so and he'd rise up cramped and stiff and deserving nothing less. Some few he'd have fallen to the floor and been prodded awake by a nervous boot. Or scant hours onward he'd bolt upright to pace the dark known walls.

His eyes ached. He lifted his head and rubbed knuckles against his eyes. Hours later, roused from sleep. His face hurt and he lifted his hands and worked his fingers against the stiffened muscles over his cheekbones. Prying gently to free something held.

The boy troubled him. So eager for life, so certain. How he had once been.

The boy troubled him.

NINE

HE'D ARRIVED EARLY on a summer morning made foggy from the night's passing rain and found her waiting before the store, watching him and then greeting him.

He stepped down from the wagon, looked her boldly in the eye, and said, "The peach man, am I?"

Then turned and lifted the first basket out and set it on the board-walk before Harold Pinnieo's store, where the bins were otherwise full. He lifted another basket from the wagon bed but when he turned she'd stepped close, filling the space where he would place the basket. He held it against his chest. He could smell her, a fringe of lye soap, the bruised petals of roses, her breath of chewed licorice root.

She nodded and said, "What would it cost me? To eat a peach?"

He almost told her he sold by the bushel and Pinnieo by the each when she reached into the basket still clutched to his chest, lifted a peach and tore out a bite, chewing as juice dripped down her chin, her lips wet, teeth white and shining, the flesh of the fruit working yellow and red atop her bright pink tongue, her eyes never leaving his.

He lowered the basket from his chest, not to the planks but to cover his midsection, where he'd sprung tight against his trousers. He said, "I think it shall cost you dearly."

"Indeed? I'm breathless to learn how." She lifted the peach back to her mouth and tore free another chunk. Her eyes full and wide upon his, both gone into the other, both knowing this.

"You'll learn soon enough. Go eat your boughten peach while I conduct my business. Meanwhile I'll ponder the price."

She didn't move but to eat the peach down to the stone. Her chin moist with juice. Then she tossed the stone into the mire of the street and said, "What peach?"

"All right. That was clever."

She said, "I had one man over me all my life. I don't intend another." Then she reached and plucked up another peach. "Go to your business," she said. "I'll be about. Unless I change my mind."

He watched her walk away. Surely she knew he was watching; but did not look back, striding tightly forward, no sashay about her, no warble or tilt of hips, nothing of the tease. He'd seen plenty of that. But nothing, he knew, of someone like this, a woman like this. In short moments his entire idea of what a woman was changed even as a goodly part of his thinking urged toward her in the way there'd be no return from. For either of them.

At the same time he felt it would be enough to hear her voice again. Her last words rang their threat in his ears. Perhaps not even a threat but a bald fact: Whatever had caused her to seek him out had been ruptured in their first few moments of meeting. She'd looked and found him lacking. This seemed not only entirely possible but reasonable the more he considered his clumsy responses to her sharp wit, as if she were testing him even as she greeted him.

Harold Pinnieo was methodical, a quality Malcolm appreciated, but this day the merchant was maddeningly slow, each peach, it seemed, lifted and studied carefully.

Malcolm said, "I had most of a meadow of dry hay I couldn't get in before dark last evening and those showers passed through the night with no warning. I'd get home and turn the hay soon's I can to try and save it. Just put aside any that don't meet your eye and we'll settle accounts next time I come to town."

Harold was using both hands to move peaches basket to basket and didn't look up. "I've worked hard to earn trust in this town, the papist Eyetalian. Your good neighbors might like what I sell but that don't mean they like my being here. So I work over and above to make certain all is fair and square. Fifteen years, always someone wanting to catch me skinning them, my thumb on the scale. I'm about done here." At this he glanced up and smiled. "Counting your peaches. You must be a sound sleeper, anyway."

Malcolm was listening but kept turning his head toward the point where the girl had disappeared down a side alley. So he only responded by saying, "What do you talk about, sound sleep?"

Pinnieo had lifted down the last basket from the wagon bed and was working through it. He said, "A downpour for a solid hour, just after midnight. It's wet all over; look at you, your shirt and trousers are still damp from when you picked your peaches this morning." He looked up. "The peaches are good, as always. Wait a moment."

"I got to get going."

"I know you do. Wait."

Pinnieo ducked inside his store and shortly came back out with two parcels tied in paper. Malcolm was up on his wagon seat, peering one way, then another, not sure why he was waiting except for the idea he was afraid of what he might not find once he set out. Pinnieo reached and set the parcels behind the seat.

He said, "A morsel or two you can eat without having to cook. Might come in handy. Don't thank me yet. But try to remember I'll want more peaches day after tomorrow. You know what day that is?"

Malcolm looked at him. "You think there's something wrong with me? Today's Tuesday."

Pinnieo smiled. "But will you know Thursday when it comes?"

He had no idea where to look for her and was feeling foolish and drove off from Pinnieo's store toward the road out of town and home, stooped on the seat, faded, when she stepped out from the shade of a storefront and stood looking at him. Wordless he halted his team with the reins and waited. She reached a hand to the whip socket, her other hand lifted her skirts and swung up into the wagon and settled herself on the seat beside him.

"Did you doubt me?" she asked.

"You have me at a disadvantage."

"How so?"

"You seem to know me, at least something of me. I know nothing of you."

"My name's Bethany Schofield. I hail from Jerusalem, where my parents and theirs were adherents of the Public Friend. I, myself, don't declare such allegiance, at least not as commonly understood. I've been told your own family suffered by a prophet proved false."

He was a bit thunderstruck by this news—he'd thought his past forgotten even to the small extent it'd ever been known—but said nothing as she went on.

"That perked my ears, I thought perhaps a kindred soul might be found. Then, further I learned your reputation as a single-minded man not easily turned by a pretty form or easy farm girl, intent upon building your world according to your own design. I decided this might be a man I should meet."

Because it was true, he said, "Such remarkable candor rolling off your tongue. I suppose you know my name, then?"

She said, "I also know you arrived here with your grandfather and word is there was a true affection between the two of you until his passing. To one such as me, that means a great deal. May we address each other easily? Even should this come to naught, dropping formality will allow us clarity sooner, rather than later. Wouldn't you say that was a worthy goal?"

"You've come courting me?"

"If you choose such words, Malcolm Hopeton."

"And me in my democrat wagon with the bed full of empty peach baskets?"

"Drawn by a pair of mules. Those are mules, aren't they?"

"Indeed, they are."

"I like a fast buggy as much as the next girl but if that's all I was after I wouldn't be here, would I?" She then looked around her and back to him and said, "I don't mind, but is sitting in the middle of town what you want? Why not cluck up your team and go along?"

"You have a destination in mind?"

"I assumed that would be part of getting to know one another."

"I've a field of hay got wet in the storm last night." He tautened the reins and the mules stepped out and with the motion she came against him on the seat, then righted herself but only slightly.

"How much of a field?"

"A handful of windrows I couldn't get to before dark and thought would only suffer the dew overnight. I had no sense of the storm that struck and went."

"I'm a hand with a fork if turning that bit of hay is how you wish to spend the morning."

He almost said, Of course it is. The mules were trotting the light democrat up the grade leading from town to the broad long tongue of land between the Crooked Lake behind them and Seneca Lake four or five miles east, up toward his farm. The fog had burned to ragged thin clouds, wisps like fleece pulled from sheep. The land steamed as the heat of day came fully on.

186

Then he thought, Tonight or tomorrow I can roll that hay up and let it ferment, and either the hogs will love the steaming mass this winter or, if it rots, spread it on my winter wheat plowing this fall and turn it in.

"I'd rather show you my farm."

"You let something go to waste on account of me, once, you'll do it again. And not forgive me either time."

"Bethany," he tried out her name. He said it again. "Bethany, there's always two or three uses for anything once you put your mind to it. As I said, I'd rather show you my farm."

She toed the packages Harold Pinnieo had set down in the front of the wagon, against the dash. "What's this?"

"I don't know. The storekeep put em there. So, you're content to see my farm?"

She said, "I want you to start by showing me what you think is the very best part. After that I want you to show me the secret place that you love the most, Malcolm." Then she paused and added, "If that makes a lick of sense to you."

In hearing that waver he lost all worry that until he did he hadn't known was within him, hadn't known he was voicing. He'd thought he was only being cautious on an ordinary day that had burst open but was tilted to fool him. He heard his grandfather tell again how it was to find a wife and wondered what that man would say to the woman finding him. He guessed old Cyrus Hopeton would be delighted and almost laughed aloud at the thought, hearing much else the man might say as well about this bright and comely girl beside him.

Instead he said, "I know just the spot."

She said, "My, it's pretty up here, so wide and open, such a sky. Those mules trot sprightly, don't they?"

"I'd show you the house first. Then we can walk about a bit." He was unhitching the mules from the wagon in the shed. He felt like a man

187

on an April day where one moment the sun is hot and nigh upon summer, the next a cloud scuds over the sun, the wind is chill and spring still feels a distant dream—his mind chittering between keen delight in her presence, then sluggish, awkward with uncertainty about what to do or say or what she expected of him.

"I like that plan," she said. She plucked up the two bundles Harold Pinnieo had set in the wagon. "Perhaps we can find a few bites to add to these and carry along in a basket so we might settle wherever we wish and make a meal together?"

He'd stripped the harnesses from the mules and set them with a slap on a rump toward their own meadow, from which long since he'd removed the gate. The mules stayed where they were supposed to be until they weren't, and then they went on to the pen in the barn, and no gate either place would make a difference to them. He said, "I've eaten many a meal in the fields when the chance to eat came. I'm happy to do so today. But those packages?"

She smiled, then was quickly serious. "Yes?"

"Pinnieo knew you were awaiting me? Is he the one told you about me?"

"Some bits. Most what I know I gathered from others, only in passing that you sold peaches to Mr. Pinnieo every year in July. And since I already knew him, that seemed a way to find you, without too many questions."

"Somehow, your answer doesn't set me at the ease I'd hoped for." But he smiled as he said as much and then said, "So why should he slip these packages into my wagon?"

"Because he knows what I like and he's not a fool. You're nervous, Malcolm. Please. Imagine how I must feel."

They walked the lanes between his fields and he pointed out his crops, the hay fields and meadows, the grain fields, noting their degrees of ripeness, holding silent on praising their beauty. Most of the lanes were edged by hedgerows and here and again trees for clumps of shade, the lanes following the contours of the land and as they walked he relaxed, from his pride in showing her his land but also from her admission of her own nervousness, and he wondered what it had cost her to work up the spunk to seek him out as she had. She'd said enough to convey an unhappy home life, but also a grit in her not to endure some similar version of it, to strive beyond. And on little more than rumor and story she'd sought him out. The tingle of nerves remained within him, a smidgen of caution also, but largely delight in her easy presence. For once out upon the land she grew quiet but her eyes were active, flitting and settling all about her; also her ears, as she listened intently.

He carried a wooden bucket holding the last of the dropped biscuits he'd baked the day before, a slab of ham cut fresh from his smoke-house, boiled eggs, a sweating tin cream can of cold water, a handful of ripe peaches from his orchard. Along with the packages from Harold Pinnieo.

When they entered the first farm lane, his herd of Jerseys, dun as deer or the darker tannin of autumn-dried oak leaves, stood in their pasture to one side, a mowed and already greening meadow to the other. She paused, placed a hand on his arm, and said, "Will we pass back this way?"

"We certainly can."

She glanced about, then backed up to the rail fence and perched against it, crossed one foot over the other knee, pulled a button hook from her apron pocket and swiftly opened her boot, tugged it off along with her short woolen stocking, stuffed the socking into the boot, shifted her haunches, and repeated the effort with her other boot. She stood and set the boots beside the trunk of a small wild plum and said, "Always, since I was a child, much as I can I like to feel the earth under my feet."

"Summertime, into the early fall, I do most of my fieldwork bare-footed," he offered. "It does save on shoe leather." He'd already gained the sense that whatever farm she came off, was a poor one. He thought to set her at ease.

"It has nothing to do with saving anything," she said. "But setting my feet free."

She slapped one foot against the remnant of a puddle from the night's rain, sloughing her foot down into a skin of mud, then kicked it before her and planted the foot firmly in the dust at the edge of the lane and walked forward.

They paused at a rise where the land rolled gently toward the east, where the oat and wheat and barley fields ended against a ribbon of woodlot and beyond that a sliver of Seneca Lake and the smudge of the rise of land beyond the lake. After his commentary upon his passing fields and crops, they'd walked a quarter hour or more in silence. So they stood upon the rise, the pause lengthening. He was waiting, now.

After a bit she sighed and said, "This is a beautiful land. I can't help but wonder." She stopped.

He waited, then said, "What? What do you wonder?"

"Never mind," she said quickly. Then, "Tell me. How do you manage to work it all yourself?"

"The usual way. Dawn to dusk and often earlier and later as needs be. Share with my neighbors on the larger jobs. And I have a hired man, of sorts."

"Well," she said. "However, you do it well. What now?"

"Have you forgot so quick?"

She looked at him. And in her face he saw that whatever boldness had propelled her toward him this morning had been lost before the actual man, or his place, both, these last hours. Her face was flushed and he understood that for the moment at least she was younger than she wished to appear. And he was old enough to know this sudden surge of youth was born more of fear than of her earlier boldness.

He reached and took her hand and said, "This is passing strange for us both, Bethany Schofield. But I'd not be able to tell you a better way I'd wish to spend my day. As for right now, I'd take you to the place you asked about, the favorite one, although I fear it's no great spectacle but for how it lies within me. Also, seems to me we would be wise to eat soon. Strength through sustenance, yes?"

She kept hold of his hand but bent and lifted the hems of her skirt to dab her forehead, straightened up, and said, "I forget nothing. Ever. Remember that, if nothing else, Malcolm. And I'm not one of those wilting girls who only eat a smidgen. My appetite is real as the rest of me. So lead me on."

Hand in hand they went a short distance down the lane, came to the end of an oat field, and he lifted out the top rail for her to step over and walked downhill toward a small bowl of hidden meadow. At first all they saw was the crown of a willow, then the tree entire and the upward gentle sweep of the meadow, the grass tall and undulating to the rhythms of breezes. His young heifers had been here in early spring, after which the meadow was held in reserve, waiting until the scorch of August burned back the dry pastures. The willow gave away the secret, if one knew how to look.

They walked through the tall grass that swished about them, parting as if they walked through water in some solid form made by heat and light, a notion that came to Malcolm and that he knew was a true one. Orioles and red-wings rose from the grass around them, a pair of bluebirds above, the cloudless sky sharpened and vivid, air-washed from the passed rain.

The willow stood at the bottom of the bowl of grasses, an ancient tree with bark furrowed and wrinkled as if plowed by age, the high crown with the feathered fronds of branches swooping elegantly low next to a small pond of dark clear water, the surface broken by bubbles from the springs below. On the farthest side of the pond from the willow was a bed of cattails, otherwise the grass grew right to the water's edge. Under the willow the grass was short, choked by the shade; and it was here Malcolm Hopeton led Bethany Schofield. He freed her hand and set the bucket down, then turned and looked at her.

Close to the trunk the canopy was wide about them, as if within a curtain of greenery, and she lifted a hand and let her fingers slide down those fronds of leaves at the other edge, for a moment caught in pure delight of the place and forgetting him altogether. And again he felt the jolt within, that this woman had found him, that he'd somehow also found her, finally, for both of them. She was lovely where she stood, and also complicated and earnest and true.

She turned and said, "So different, what we expect and what comes. Don't you find that so, Malcolm?"

He knelt by the bucket and pulled free the sacking, spread it over the short grass and began to lay out the food. He said, "This morning when I left early in the fog all I thought I was doing was delivering peaches to the man who buys them. Less than a quarter of a day later, look where I am. And I don't pretend to know all or even much of why we're here, but so far I couldn't have asked for a finer day. Should we eat?"

"I suppose," she said but wandered out to the edge of the pond and looked upon the meadow and the sky.

He had the food out, all of it, the mystery packages unopened. He said, "When I came to buy the farm I walked it all and so saw this place and liked it, but then I liked the whole farm. No, it was a couple years before I discovered this place for what it truly is." He paused and said, "I had coffee early but not much of breakfast. I'm going to eat a slice of ham and a biscuit. You sure you don't want some?"

She turned back and settled herself across the spread cloth from him, heels tucked under her. She said, "I want to hear your story."

He left the ham but ate the biscuit, poured water from the cream can into both tin cups and handed one to her, took a swallow from the other and said, "It was my second autumn here. My cows had been calving, one every few days for several weeks, and I was busy with that. It's a fine time of year, buttoning down toward winter without being cold yet, everything but the last of the shell corn harvested, the days grown shorter and the barn filling up with new life. One evening I brought the cows in and realized there was a heifer about to freshen that hadn't come with the rest. But it was nigh dark and I had a barn full of cows to milk and young calves to get fed, all my other chores too. I figured she'd lagged behind and so left the gate down and the barn door open, thinking she'd lift her head from whatever she was up to and come in. It crossed my mind she might be calving but the pasture they were in was close to the barn and small; it's the pasture I always use that time of year, for the very reason. I wasn't too worried about her wasn't the first time a cow had failed to follow the rest in. When I finished my chores I took a lantern and tramped around the pasture, expecting to either scare the bejesus out of her or have her rise up out of the dark and do the same to me. But I never found her. What I did find was a rail down, a hole in the fence. The soil was churned up by hooves in the oat stubble the other side and I followed that trail until it turned back onto the headland and was lost, headed into the woods. There was no following that at night. And ticking along in the back of my mind was that rail out of the fence, thinking maybe the heifer was stole.

"I went back to the house and told my grandfather the whole business. Like always he listened without a word; we were eating supper but that was his way, to hear me out. He mopped his plate and told me where I'd gone wrong. Cows are herd creatures and so I was thinking about the heifer that way. But, he said, like all the rest of creation cows are individuals and just because most act one way doesn't mean all do. He told me most likely my heifer didn't understand what was happening to her, that she was giving birth, so she did what most creatures do in that sort of moment, which is to hightail it into the deepest, most hidden spot they can find. He said probably come morning she'd show up with her calf by her side, maybe at the barn or the pasture she'd left, maybe along one of the lanes. I knew he was probably right so I slept that night, got up expecting a clear easy day.

"But it didn't happen. She wasn't anywhere to be seen, no sign of her at all. I walked the pasture again, then the lanes and finally went into the woods trying to find a young cow seeking the most hidden spot she could find. The thing is, in the woods she could be behind a clump of cedar or up or downhill fifteen feet and if she was hunkered tight I'd walk right by her. I was also thinking if the birth was a hard one she could be dead and the calf, too. The day was getting on and I knew less the more I went looking."

He paused then and drank more water. She hadn't so much as touched her cup to her lips. He said, "I bet you know how this story's going to end."

"Tell me."

"A thought came into my mind: Where'd she been before I'd moved them all to the autumn calving pasture? What lush grass had I drove em out of just weeks before? So I walked those same lanes you and I came along down to here. It was such a pretty day and there she was, grazing away and a whippersnapper of a bull calf wobbling along after her. The pond was covered with the yellow willow leaves come down and as I walked in a pair of ducks beat off the pond, leaving an open trail through the leaves. The cow looked at me and went back to her feeding. The little calf would go after her and get down on his front knees to butt her udder and nurse. Then he'd rise up and scamper a few yards away, trying out his legs. I knew I had to get her to the barn and milk her out, most likely he was going after the same quarter each time, but there weren't a great hurry to it. Both of em were healthy and just fine.

"I laid down and propped on a elbow and just watched em. I told you it was my second autumn on the place, which means my grandfather and I'd been here eighteen months, maybe a bit less. And I'd been working flat out the whole time, which was nothing less than I expected or wanted. But right there it came to me as much as I'd fallen in love with the place from the start, and each day had grown that love with the work I put in, and what came out of that labor, I hadn't had such a moment of reflection of where I was, and what it meant to me. To my grandfather and me.

"And there it was right in front of me, a pretty autumn day, a fine heifer become a cow and her healthy calf, the yellow leaves on the water, this old tree, the last of the year's good grass dulled by frost but still hardy and lush. There was a vee of geese southbound high above, surely not the same ones I'd roused hours before from my oat stubble as I walked through, but cousins to them. There was orange and black butterflies working the late flowers, milkweeds burst open with their seed pods floating in the air. I'd worked up a thirst and so rose up slow and both cow and calf looked at me and then went on with their business as I walked down to the edge of the pond and skimmed back the leaves to cup up handfuls of water and drink. I hope to remember it on my dying day: the cow and calf, the cold water clear and dripping down my chin. I knew my life in that moment as all of a piece."

Bethany was looking off over the pond, the meadow. When she did not look back or speak, as the silence seemed to dribble out between them, he felt he'd failed her, that she'd expected more of him than this offering. And he felt a trickle of irritation toward this girl who'd imposed herself upon him, diverted his day with her demands and expectations, a stranger, and one perhaps that was dangerous to him in ways he hadn't grasped before. Best to conclude this morning as gently as possible but return her to town and be done with it; he'd lived well alone and would continue to do so. There remained the urgency of his wet hay.

She did not look at him but in a small clutched voice said, "I understand your cow."

Her tone thrust barbs through his chest and he winced with her pain, knowing this was no calculation, no act of entanglement but what she could not help, also that she was entrusting him, confused as much or more than he was.

He said, "How so?"

Now she looked at him. "I like to walk about the woods at night. I got away with it for years until I was old enough so my father figured it out. But he couldn't stop me. He makes no secret of what he thinks I'm up to, but he's wrong." She paused but Malcolm did not ask what her father might think and she went on. "I'd walked the same places in daylight, which is how I learned most of them, but I wasn't more than ten when I first slipped out on a summer night. The fields didn't draw me. It's scanty land up on the Italy Hills. It was warm and there was most of a moon and that night I only went to places close by that I knew well. It was those places but also the walking from one to another. As if I'd left the old everyday world and entered a new one made just for me. There was a prickle of fear to it, no telling what I might run into out there, though there never was a thing but the one time I got too close to a fox den and the vixen sat atop the knoll barking at me; that scared me pretty good. Then I seen the shadows come up out of the den and slip back in and realized all she wanted was me to get away, to leave her babies be. One other time, this was last summer and I was much farther off, walking through a scrappy rough area, juniper circles and locusts, thickets of blackberry canes, but nothing high about me, though there was a good stand of woods both before and behind, I was just crossing this bit of ground when something jumped out ahead of me and darted off. Took my breath away and I stopped and at the very moment a great bird passed silent and fast right over my head and slammed into the brush ahead of me. There was a scream and the bird lifted up and flew toward the trees. I could see it clear then, a big-bodied owl with a rabbit dangling

196

from its claws. So there were those frights and the usual ones where you stop and study an odd shadow in the night. But mostly it was purely a delight for me.

"Something about the night," she said. "The thoughts in my head were all my own."

"Different than daytimes."

"Yes." She placed a level gaze upon Malcolm and said, "Something about day, most days at least, the light is harsh upon me, upon who I am."

"I don't doubt it."

"Even on my worst day I never don't know who I am. But most always, I have to strike through layers of what others think of me. But at night there's nothing there except walking as my own self. Maybe that's freedom, only just within myself." She paused and then said, "I'm not making any sense, am I? Perhaps I do need a bite to eat, after all."

"Is the sunlight too bright upon you?" he asked. "Feeling light-headed?"

"You make fun of what I say?" She set down her cup and started to rise, her face quickly spreading blaze upward from her throat.

"I'm sorry." He caught her hand and said, "Please wait. I have a odd sense of humor that pops out when I'm not sure what to say. My grandfather had it and I guess I learned it from him or it's just always been within me. I meant no offense, though I'm afraid that odd humor is something you'll have to get used to, you spend much time with me. I've done my best but can't shed it."

She remained standing but made no effort to free her hand, and he went on. "I love the night myself, how we slip a bit from our day-lit selves to some other during those hours. More true, if only for that time. Yes, you're right. We should eat. There's a bounty here and I confess I'm filled with curiosity about the packages you made sure Harold Pinnieo set in my wagon. That was a bold stroke of yours, one

197

I admire almost as much as what else you've had to say. So, will you sit and let us eat? We can talk on, I can't imagine not."

She sank down upon the earth, pulling her skirt again beneath her, her bare feet turned now toward him and said, "There's a soft cheese with a rind, you don't want to smell before you eat it, because smell and taste are across wide divides in this case. The other holds pickled sea creatures, horrible to look upon but again, delicious to eat."

He was on his knees, spreading all the food upon the sacking, lifting out the two bundles and with his pocketknife cutting the twine, but not yet unfolding the paper. He looked at her and grinned and said, "A test then, is that it, Bethany?"

She tilted her head without a smile and said, "I suppose it is."

"I'll win it. I love food."

She did smile then and said, "We'll see, won't we?"

It was no contest. They ate slowly, in the manner of strangers, fingers fluttering over the mound of biscuits, waiting for the other. He sliced the ham with his pocketknife, then opened the paper and drew out the round of cheese, cut it into wedges. He was uncertain about the white rind, also the pungent rank aroma and so waited for her as he sliced the cucumbers and peeled shells from the boiled eggs. He'd thought to add salt in a twist of paper and opened that as well. She took up a wedge of cheese and ate it, rind and all. He ate an egg, poured more water for them both and finally lifted a slice of the cheese. Coming close to his nose he thought it smelled of barnyard, paused and took a large bite, thinking best to get it over with. To his surprise the cheese was lush, creamy, tangy but delicious, unlike any cheese he'd ever eaten. Neither of them had opened the other package, the sea creatures she'd warned of. He lifted a slice of ham and chewed. It was most lovely, following the cheese.

Throughout, he'd been thinking of all she'd said. Most made fair sense to him, yet she clearly felt otherwise, as if she were a creature of some strange sea, herself.

He reached and slit the string and opened the second package, unfolding the paper to reveal a heap of oily brown glistening ovals. The smell of an old fire rose from them and he leaned close, then sat back up and split open another biscuit. It had been some years but he'd eaten oysters shucked raw from their shells and these were nothing more than the same creatures smoked and preserved in oil. He ate one with half the biscuit as the smoky salty flavors brined over his tongue, popped another into his mouth and the last of the biscuit.

She was watching this, a smile clinging to the corners of her mouth.

He said, "I had no idea Pinnieo had oysters this way. Thought it was only Christmas when he has barrels of them fresh on ice. I'd almost say these are better."

Her smile broke wide. "They are good, aren't they?"

"Yes, they are." His glance went down as he placed another oyster on a biscuit and lifted a wedge of cheese. He said, "Do you have brothers, sisters?" He ate the cheese.

"No. I'm alone with it all. And you?"

"Yes and no," he said. "They're lost to me. Not of my doing."

"Their own folly?"

"You could say so. Or a greater one. It' a sadness I've done my best to leave behind. My grandfather always said if any of them ever showed up we'd take them in but none of them will. A great dupe, is what they suffered. But after that, their folly was their own."

"Was it?" she asked. "Or was it cast upon them?"

"You take up the harness, you draw the cart."

"But William Miller was a false prophet. Not once but twice. If your voice of God fails once, it's because he's only a man. So you'll trust the second time, even more so. But to fail twice, he's nothing but a false prophet."

"Anyone other than a preacher who brought ruination upon so many would suffer greater consequences than scorn and contempt.

Allowed to scurry off like a rat to a hole, he was, and nothing more. While dozens who believed him live in poverty or upon charity, the rest of their days."

"Yet they made the choice."

"To believe the end of the world was upon them? Yes, they did. But only from the fire and conviction with which he preached. Ah, I can't change any of it."

She was quiet a moment, then said, "Have you thought to journey back there, seek out your family that remains and how they fare?"

"No," he said. "It was a great rift when we refused to join in following that lunatic. Terrible words were spoken, curses of hellfire laid upon both his head and mine. Yet before we departed, Grandfather left an envelope in the care of our family attorney, with enough cash money for any who wished to make the trip to join us. A couple of years after Grandfather died, almost ten years since we'd come together into the country, a letter arrived from that good man. There was a bank draft for the full amount of the funds left behind, as well as an account of how my one sister brought suit to have the money awarded to her, claiming Grandfather cast the entire family adrift. Nothing was farther from the truth, as the attorney was easily able to demonstrate to a court that knew well the foolish practices of Miller's followers. He—the attorney—added a note explaining he'd deducted nothing from the entrusted sum to defend against the charges, expressing his outrage that Grandfather's intentions would be so subverted by his own family."

Malcolm paused, then said, "Nothing remains to me of those people. They made their bed, as Grandfather would say, and did so twice or thrice." He reached and lifted a peach and neatly sliced it around the stone and split the halves apart. He held one out to her and said, "So I'm the peach man. Alone in the eyes of the world but not so alone as most think."

She'd moved while he spoke to sitting cross-legged, hands in the lap of her skirts, dirty bare feet poking out, her face bright and flushed, intent upon him, the sunlight breaking down through the high branches and thin leaves of the willow, a many-louvered shutter of light and shadow upon her. She reached for the half of peach but held it in her hand, looking at him.

She said, "Do you consider what happened a blessing upon you or making the best of things?" She bit the peach.

He laughed. "I've not looked back, there's little to be gained doing that. But you could say I count my blessings I arrived where I did." He paused. Then said, "Mostly I've worked. I'm not comfortable believing I was delivered from misfortune because of the actions of those around me, or my refusal to take part. I believe I was lucky, that I fell upon good fortune and worked hard to keep it so."

"You delight in that."

"And why not?"

She twisted an escaped long curl about her finger, looked toward the surface of the pond, and said, "Perhaps having your family grow so slender, at such a distance, emboldened you toward that work. The gift of enterprise as well as freedom."

He almost flared with anger, then understood what she was actually saying. He set down his half-peach and knife, wiped his hands, and took a drink of water. Then as gently as he could he said, "You've known your own false prophet, haven't you? And lack any means of escape or even the hope of doing so. Is that it?"

The look she turned upon him was not what he expected but the blazing eyes of one confronting a clumsy child. She said, "You're wrong most all ways and where you're right is only a bit."

She brushed crumbs he couldn't see from the lap of her skirts and stood. "I imposed myself upon you and was wrong to do so. I hope you can forgive me. None of it's your fault."

Then she walked off, through the grass up the meadow toward where they'd come. Again, from behind, striding hard and sure. But her outer skirt was caught behind in the garter high on her calf from where she'd stripped free her short stockings and she tramped through the grass heedless of the white flash of her leg. He stood looking after her, then down at the mess of food spread upon the sacking-cloths, and back to where she was gaining the ridge, growing into a silhouette against the heat of midday, not yet close to the fence but about to disappear from sight. The back of that one leg white against the darkening depth of grass.

He looked a final time at the strewn foodstuffs. There was much left and never once in his life had he abandoned food to waste. An oriole beside the pond trilled irritation or alarm at his presence, breaking his glance. The bird balanced on the tip of a cattail reed, plump but upright on the bent stalk. Bobbing gently.

Malcolm looked up the hill. Bethany was gone.

He ran after her. Up through the grass, up the hill to the lane. Vaulted the rail and came down in the dust of the lane and she was nowhere in sight. Trills of darker dust showed her track.

He caught up with her not far beyond the plum where she'd left her boots. He'd slowed to a lope before making the turn where the plum would come into sight and when he saw her he let himself walk. She heard him and glanced back but kept going. He jogged briefly again and came up beside her.

She'd taken off her cap and unpinned her hair, letting it fall about her face and shoulders in long dark curls. She didn't look at him but said, "I'll walk. It's not so far. I made a mistake is all and I'm sorry for wasting your time. You forget, or maybe weren't listening: I'm a woman that walks."

He lengthened his stride, went ahead and turned to face her. She glanced aside as if to pass him, then stopped and folded her arms over her breast. Her face without humor, a darkling cast.

He said, "Bethany Schofield, one thing you should know about me, even if there's nothing more you'll wish to learn. Unlike some men, I can admit when I made a mistake. You'd grant me that?"

"Are you toying with me?"

"I'm befuddled is what I am."

"You'd swear to it?" Now a glimmer of curiosity about her eyes. She let her arms fall loose to her sides.

He said, "Bethany. It was you came seeking me this morning. Ever since, it seems I'm chasing after you, turned one way and then another and yet there's something about you that makes me doubt any of those turnings were intentional or malicious. Rather, a person trying to explain themselves and cautious at once. Much as I am, standing before you and doing my best to comprehend you."

"Go on," she said.

"Perhaps to have you comprehend me also?"

"Why? Assume I might have erred this morning, seeking you. So, then. Why?"

He made a step closer and reached to place both hands upon her shoulders. She shivered under his touch, then rose to meet it. He went on, "It was many years ago I concluded I'd likely go through life alone. And the prospect was not unpleasant; in fact it seemed to me how I'd best live. There was no event, no girl scorning me that brought me to feel this was so. Rather it seemed part and parcel of my nature. I'd come to doubt I'd ever meet another soul might understand me, my past and present both with such a great gulf between them. I'm not unhappy alone, far from it."

She said, "A good thing for you, I think."

"I'm speaking my mind, is all. So, where is it you plan to walk to, now?" He'd spied that she had her stockings balled in her apron pocket. Her feet might be summer-tough but her leather boots would raise blisters on her heels, ankles.

"Home, I suppose." She looked away to the west, where that destination lay, more miles than he cared to think of, unsure of where exactly that home might be. He also realized when she'd first hailed him this morning there'd been no mud on her boots, the hem of her dress. Certainly she hadn't walked to town. She might walk about at night, but not the dozen or fifteen miles to town. He waited.

She looked back and said, "Well, I've made a fair mess of this, haven't I? My father claims I'm heedless and headstrong, willful and thoughtless. Perhaps there's a grain of truth there I'd rather not believe. I came seeking you to discover something of who you are, and also what regard you might hold me in. Now I tremble against what that regard might be: I wouldn't want to know."

All this said with his hands still on her shoulders, both very close, their breath upon one another. As if a separate conversation was passing between their bodies as their tongues and minds tangled.

"I won't presume to argue against your father, though I think he might be wrong most ways. Myself, I find you bold and brave, perhaps a bit fractious but I wonder if you'd interest me so, if you weren't."

"You're being kind." She waited, the turmoil of thought clear in her eyes.

"I think we have a choice here. I can hitch my gig up and drive you home, or to town or wherever you might wish. Or we can take this in stride as the to and fro of a fascinating and curious first meeting, walk back and finish our luncheon left for the birds and resume our conversation. Myself, I'm hoping for the second: I'm mighty curious about some things you've said, questions you've asked. I'm saying I'd rather not lose you so easy, this day—"

Interrupted as she lifted both hands to cup his jaw, leaned up and kissed him.

He'd caught his share of kisses over the years, hasty pecks upon his cheek, fleet lips pressed dry against his own, more than a couple of times in the dark of the loft of threshing or shelling, a wet warm mouth mingled upon his own.

He'd never been kissed by a woman with all body and soul and heart within the kiss. After the first moment he stepped into the kiss and she responded. He closed his eyes against the vertigo

204

overcoming him and lived then in her flesh against his, also the red and black spackling light against his eyelids. Once he opened his eyes and saw hers were shut also and closed his again and pulled her even harder against him and she came pliable and flowing, now both the all of them.

Some moments later he opened his eyes again and was looking into her own open eyes. And her hands that had been roving his back dropped and came upon his chest and she stepped back from the kiss. Both still and knowing that always they lived in a sun-drenched hot world.

"There," she said. "There we are."

"Nowhere else," he said.

"The first thing we do is save the food from the birds. I'm all appetite."

"Yes, you are. I'm half-starved myself."

"More than half, I think."

"Is it you," he said. "Is it you?"

"I don't know. Is it you?"

"It's me."

"Me," she echoed.

They lay back in the meadow by the pond, the food consumed and destroyed, much else also, lying back in the grass with the birds overhead or trilling from their hidden places, the steady midday trumpets of frogs, a lilting cloud toward the sun, then gone with the cool plaster over their dimpled flesh. A pair of crows chased a hawk high above, the hunter flapping slow, careless, as the two stragglers darted and cried outrage against some trespass. Likely known to all three parties, uncertain to those prone upon the earth. Grasshoppers popped stem to stem, passing over the bodies, small machineries of sunlight and heat.

Otherwise not stirring, her first words, "How many rows?"

Thick-tongued he said, "How what?"

205

"I'm a fair hand with a fork, if you've got two of em. It's early yet and I was thinking we could save your hay and, well, that would be a good thing. Maybe talk a bit as we went along?"

They had been ardent, passionate, near violent with each other and also innocent, striving, small fumblings. Her pained gasp when after groping attempts, he found entry and thoughtless of her pressed deep. That gasp ended soon enough and they'd rocked together, his first discharge only inflaming both onward. Finally uncoupled and separate, both upon their backs side by side, yet still joined, her blood upon him, matting and drying with the other fluids commingled upon him, within her, she had been the one to find voice and without losing what had just been made between them returned them to the larger earth.

The sodden windrows were already starting to dry along the tops and sides beneath the midday sun. They worked across from each other, using the forks to pull apart and spread the windrows to open them, the wet twined centers fluffed and lifted to the air and sun. Both barefoot, much clothing left by the pond—his go-to-town vest and jacket, socks and boots, her apron and shawl and underskirts, also those stockings and boots. Few words at first, less uncomfortable than both stunned to a simple silence.

Finally, still working, they spoke fragments that held worlds. She would punctuate by grunts or bursts of expelled air when a knot of hay proved tough to break apart. Or wanted emphasis. He worked on, steady and thorough, his words also, best he could.

She said, "Rich hay. Dense."

"Is it fatiguing you?"

"I'm a bit atremble."

"If you'd sit in the shade, I can finish this up quick."

"I'd stand across from you. I'm strong enough."

"That you are."

"Are you shamed?"

He paused, stuck tines in the earth and placed his palms over the end of the handle. "No," he said. "You?"

"It was not what I expected when I set out this morning."

"I did not think so. Nor what I expected when I brought you here. But."

"But what?"

He couldn't help his grin. "It's a fine day."

"Pleased with yourself?"

"I can't say what I am except I can't imagine changing a thing if I had a choice to do so. How's that strike you?"

"The way I feel also. Come, let's attack this hay, get the work done."

They went back to it.

She said, "You are not snared, any way. I want you to know that."

"I'm not? Well, my arms may swing free and my feet tramp the stubble but otherwise I'm hog-tied hand and foot and thrown upon the ground."

"No. You are not."

"I didn't say I was unhappy in that condition. Also, there may be consequences yet unknown to us."

"You'll not be snared so. If I think for the first minute you feel you are I'll rob my father's pig money, walk through the night and ride the trains into the western prairies of Dakota Territory. Or some such a place. Regardless of the consequence you speak of."

"Aw, Bethany. Since you stepped out of the fog this morning nothing that happened was expected, but none of it was anything but inevitable. That I know. So set your mind at ease on that point. I was present throughout, remember?"

"But you understand my caution."

"I honor your caution."

They'd come to the end of a windrow. One remained. Almost side by side they walked to the next but just as she was about to step to the far side, to resume work, he dropped his fork and reached for her elbow and pulled her close and kissed her.

When they stepped apart she said, "Well!" and then dug with her fork. They now traveled west.

She said, "So, honoring my caution, how do you propose we move forward? What is your idea of all this, Malcolm Hopeton?"

"That we finish this row. It will be late afternoon before we could get the hay up. While waiting we should retrieve the rest of our clothing from my pond pasture. Also, delicious as it was, our picnic was no dinner and after all this exertion I think we might want a proper meal. Easily enough found in my kitchen. That should give us time to consider this idea of moving forward. Unless you'd have me drop the fork and hitch my fast mule and drive you home now?"

"There's a bit of devil to you, isn't there?"

He lofted a forkful of hay high, where it wheeled, broke apart, and settled again. He laughed and said, "No, Bethany. Only a man lit all ways he never thought he would be."

Then a silence fell as they worked on down the row, her face turned to the job, his upon her, the spread of land so deeply known and loved yet all shimmering, new-made as the first day. The work was opening the muscles of his legs and back, also the pleasant ache of his loins. He watched her, her body swinging with the work of digging, lifting, turning. Her hips and thighs, her sturdy calves naked below her single skirt, the sway of her breasts, the ripple of muscle in her arms, the back of her neck.

Without looking up she said, "Never laid eyes upon you until this day and that only because of words caught in passing. The lusty man who'd not court girls, the one severed harshly from the Lord, who raised peaches to make you swoon, the farmer intent upon the life of himself. And somehow I heard myself in that."

He worked on a bit and finally said, "Mystery abounds in the world, might even make the world. Look—we've finished the row."

★   ★   ★

Easy together walking back down to the pond, swinging along with the newfound pleasure of each other, the hour of work adding to their physical ease, neither were prepared for the sudden awkwardness that came over them once back at the pond: the strewn food, the sacking blown by the breeze, the matted grass away from the shade where earlier they'd rolled together.

Malcolm was quick. "Ah, was it crows smelled those oysters and made off with them or some other creature? The rest I don't mind, but I was looking forward to the remains of those. I'll gather all this up, just be a minute with it." He was already doing this as he spoke. Over his shoulder he said, "Next I go to Pinnieo's, I'll have an extra reason for the trip. I'd guess he stocks them often, made as they are not to spoil. Would you have a sip of water? It's still cool." Saying this as he stood and turned.

Her eyes were moist and red, and a hand flew to cover her mouth as she tried to speak, then choked, which she turned into a cough and bent her head as if into the cough, then rubbed her eyes and reached for the can. "There's dust in my throat."

"Drink a bit. It'll help."

She allowed her eyes upon him, hiding nothing, and took the can and drank. Water dribbled through the hay-dust on her chin. She said, "I'm fairly parched. A mighty thirst." She drank more, then handed the can to him.

He swallowed long quaffs, pleasure filling him again as the water in his belly. He wiped his mouth and said, "My grandfather once said we think we're deep in life, until we truly find ourselves to be so and realize up till then we've just been skimming."

"That's a fearful thought."

"Or a joyous one. Let's walk up to the house, get out of the sun for a bit." He reached for her hand and after a pause she took it and they made their way up the hillside, the bucket bouncing rhythmic against his outside thigh.

"You were lucky to have him."

"I know it." They were out on the lane through the fields now, shuffling up afternoon dust. He said, "He'd been broken and busted most all ways a man can be but he loved life tenacious as a dog holding a bone right down to the very end."

She said, "I regret not knowing him. I suspect I'd have liked him."

Malcolm said, "He'd have enjoyed you. After all, he spent the best part of ten years preparing me to meet you."

She didn't say anything after that.

He'd been waking at night, mulling the purchase of a folding-top buggy and a fast driving horse, as well. He even had a horse in mind, a fine-boned bay he'd seen at Avery's livery, the same day in early September when he'd prowled through the shop floor of Burketts' buggy works, running his hands upon glossy lacquered sides, dashboards, shafts, over the finely grained and supple leather of the tops, testing the strength and flexibility of the iron mechanisms that raised or folded down the leather tops. Although when the fellow upon the floor with a brimless cap and spectacles had approached, he'd waved him away with the gesture of one only browsing, passing time. Finally, at a solitary breakfast eaten far too early as sleep had evaded him since just past midnight worrying the issue, he set it aside. She'd proven more than content with the mules and the democrat wagon, the single Clown mule hitched to his open gig. A farmer with mules was what he was and a farmer with mules was clearly what she wanted.

Still, he had the presence of mind to make arrangements at Avery's for that Tuesday morning in the third week of September to leave his mule and gig and drive to the courthouse in a buggy drawn by a comfortable if not flashy horse. And a good thing of that, also, the day having dawned raining steady. He'd stuffed his folded suit into a tin box, pulled his wide-brimmed straw low and driven to his marriage in everyday clothes, soaked through before he was a quarter of the distance to town. Though his blood was hot and fine, no chill upon him that day.

He'd changed in a stall of the livery, rubbing his raw chin where he'd shaved with cold water, too impatient to wait for the kettle; pressed his summer-hard wide feet into his boots and then snapped the whip over the horse to drive the buggy to where she waited under the portico of the courthouse with Merry Struther, the young married woman from the Jerusalem community who'd agreed to be both transport and witness and was clearly more nervous than either Bethany or Malcolm, once all met before entering to stand before the justice of the peace. Both women were splashed with mud and Merry clutched a drenched spray of purple asters.

Those flowers passed into Bethany's hands and afterward, back at the farm, Malcolm had taken them and set them in a lard bucket upon the table. Where, wondrously, they remained through the winter, long after the water was gone from the bucket, the dense florets slowly drying over months, the stalks and few leaves turning brown, the leaves rolling and dropping away but the florets only growing muted, holding their color until the February day when he noticed the phenomenon and carefully broke a sprig free and pressed it between the pages of his grandfather's crackled leather-bound volume of Bunyan's *Pilgrim's Progress*. Where he would forget it for many years.

Bethany was kind. Once outside the courthouse she thanked Merry Struther, kissed her upon both cheeks, told her not to worry and thanked her again. The rain still streaming down. Then she and Malcolm looked at each other and she grabbed his hand and together they ran laughing through the rain to the waiting buggy, careless of their laughter, careless of the rain, careless of all things. They'd made the great hurdle.

★   ★   ★

Malcolm had taken great care about the day. His shuck mattress on the cherrywood sleigh bed had been replaced with a new one stuffed with steamed and dried goose feathers plucked from the breasts of geese—or so the placard promised. Beyond that, he'd noted a remark of hers made in passing one day in July when they'd met in town and spent the afternoon strolling the shops and emporiums before dining at the Lakewood Hotel and attending a performance at the modest opera house by a traveling troupe of theatrical performers. In the small section of Brigg's Home Furnishings devoted to kitchens, she'd paused before an iron range made to stand before the existing home hearth, the stovepiping shown to be easily entered into the chimney above the hearth.

She'd only said, "The advertisement in *Godey's Lady's Book* claims these end the drudgery of squatting before a hearth to turn out burnt bread. Really now—I've baked good loaves all my life from the hearth oven. How we're teased to an easier life, as if such is better. Now, look here, a tool that makes sense: It shaves nutmegs by turning the handle, the same as a grinder renders peppercorns to flakes. How many times have I sliced my finger trying to scrape a few twists of nutmeg to flavor an apple pie?

He'd returned to Brigg's twice over the next few weeks. The first time to learn how such stoves worked, then going home and making careful measurements of his hearth and chimney. The second time he placed an order through to the manufacturer in Oswego. Her stove would have double ovens, a vast cooking surface, twin fireboxes either side for greater or lesser heat as needed, a water tank attached to the back with a spigot on the front for hot water, and a raised shelf above for keeping foods warm. What had been a plain iron box also gained ornamental scrollwork on the legs and sides, even medallions of ornate roses centered on the oven doors. It was a grand device almost beyond his imagination but then he was in love.

The range arrived by rail at the Dresden station, in a heavy crate of green lumber, disassembled, the parts all wrapped in felted wool and packed in sawdust. He met the train with Amos Wheeler and together they wrestled the crate into the bed of the democrat wagon. It barely fit, after much heaving and scraping and the mules broke a hard sweat hauling it home, where it sat in a corner of the barn loft until one evening Malcolm unpacked the pieces and laid them out and studied the smudged diagram. After a time of moving pieces here and there and back again it began to form a picture in his mind.

He wheelbarrowed it all to the kitchen the evening in September the week before his marriage, knowing she'd not see it until after the simple ceremony they'd agreed upon. That day he and Amos had got in the last of his scant but rich third cutting of hay and the day fell swiftly toward night, summer rolling up, the dense golden light spreading over the land as the night gathered, puffed cool, a shudder of coming cold. Maybe a light frost by daybreak.

Amos asked, "You want a hand with that?"

"I got it. You go on. Enjoy your night. That girl still hanging around?"

"What girl?"

"That's right. I never laid eyes on her."

"Then what makes you think there's a girl?"

"It's a fair palace you've built in my woods. Get on, Amos. I got a bit of work ahead of me. And I'd do it alone."

"No need to be grumpy."

Malcolm heaved up and looked the young man in the eye and said, "Things are changing, here. For the best. You get used to it."

"You say."

"I do. And don't forget it."

"No sir. I won't."

Over the course of the summer he'd become familiar with what appeared to be her three sets of clothing. He presumed a couple of rougher skirts and shirtwaists and such that she wore at home. At the courthouse there'd been a small grip passed from Merry Struther up into the buggy, which Bethany had tucked wordless between her feet. Well before that day, he'd thought to himself, She's a farm wife but I'll dress her better than she's had, she deserves such. Two weeks before the ceremony at the courthouse he'd come from the fields late for his cold noon dinner to find a cedar chest upon his porch, recalled then the trail of dust upon the road glimpsed midmorning. Someone had taken pains to avoid him and he easily guessed who that might be once he laid eyes upon the chest. Opened, he glimpsed stacks of crisp bed-linens and a folded snowflake quilt. Atop all were a pair of silver candlesticks wrapped in flannel and another flannel packet holding six silver teaspoons. He closed the lid, heard the solid thump of good cedar and moved the chest into his dining room. Her dowry chest. His own chest thumped a frantic tender heart for her.

So then, both wet from the rain, the damp grip dropped just inside the door, she'd halted, drawn up by the bulk of the stove in a room she thought she knew. She walked about it, touching it here and there as if touching a strange beast suddenly loomed but before this day only heard rumors of.

She looked at him and said, "My goodness." Then her hand flew to cover her mouth, her eyes wide. She said, "Land sakes, Malcolm, I've already failed you."

Mildly he said, "How so?"

"I wouldn't know where to start, cooking upon such a thing. And worse, I gave no thought to a proper meal to celebrate this day."

"Rest easy, Bethany. With the rain it's enough today to kindle a fire for a bit of warmth and I can show you how the thing works."

He stepped and kissed her, wanting to lift and carry her up the stairs to the new mattress and find again that moment three months past beside his pond. She met his kiss fully, and hungry for it but only with her mouth, her body a slip of distance away. He ran his hands through her hair and buried his nose there and felt her relax, though she came no closer.

He spoke into her hair. "I failed also. I had no thought for a grand feast, that sort of celebration. All I wanted was to reach this day and all that will come after. But Bethany, we're not as alone as we might think. Yesterday afternoon as I was trying to heat pressing irons on the stovetop to smooth wrinkles from my shirt and coat, fearing I'd scorch em, yelling at my hired man to tend to the chores, someone drove up and hailed me. I was befuddled with the irons and stepped out the door with ill humor only to find Harold Pinnieo. So in the cool of my buttery waits an array of food and more. A bottle of wine all the way from Italy. Much else also but including, I'm sure, stinking cheeses and strange sea creatures."

As he finished he stepped back so she had no choice but to look up at him. Over her tremble her face broke light and bright, a twisted smile that turned down again, furrows plowing her brow.

"It's a terrible distress," she said. "You're so kind, so thoughtful. And what do I bring you? Nothing."

Gentle and simple he said, "You bring me everything."

TEN

AUGUST'S BACK PORCH looked out upon the orchard pasture, also the vegetable gardens, but between those gardens and the base of the porch were flower gardens. Some few plants had long been there—blue iris in the spring, tiger lilies, daisies. Narcissa had added more—forsythia to bloom early, lily of the valley, poppies, a handful of precious Dutch tulips, peonies and hollyhocks in a mass against the south-facing side of the vegetable garden fence. A purple lilac marked the western edge of the porch, large and old, twisted stems thick as a man's upper arm, lofting outward to cast a spot of welcome shade, heavy with scent-drenched blossoms the end of May. A pleasant boundary between porch and vegetables, a spot of ever-changing color spring through fall that demanded little upkeep beyond a morning or afternoon and in November stripping out died-back growth, or, missing that, the same work could be done the next March.

In the newer section of the garden stood a stone plinth protruding some three feet above the ground with irregular sides blotched with orange, yellow and pale green lichen and near the top a rusted rod extended from the stone, ending in an eye that held an iron ring. A post to tie a horse up to, once upon a time.

Once upon a time it stood before a different house, though built upon the same spot, the house sited so this was the front and not back yard. Becca Davis had almost no memory of that house, where she'd been born and four years later her brother, and where her father had died months after Harlan was born. She remembered eating hasty pudding with the single kitchen window layered either in frost or drifts outside, while small ridges of snow formed along the cold floorboards from cracks of the ill-fitting door. She remembered the black smoke fighting the small flame from the tallow candle alone on the table. She didn't remember anyone else in the room, although there must certainly have been. The pudding was steaming in her bowl; she remembered eating quickly as the pudding cooled, the spoon handle large in her hand.

She did not remember the night her father died but only her mother's story of how she'd left the house in the wet autumn night to walk to the closest neighbor for help, holding her infant son wrapped against her breast, leaving the little girl sleeping and unknowing all of life had just changed. It was only after returning to work for August Swartout did she realize that the neighbor had been August's father, and a boy in his young teens had come back to the house to carry the little girl out of the house, or of her father's burial, the quiet ceremony marking his passing out of Time. Her memories of these events and her mother's subsequent retellings, the images these conjured, had commingled over the years so she no longer knew what was memory and what imagined and did not care: They all were real as the day before her.

She'd never once made reference to that lost world once she was employed by August: There was no reason, all of that was gone and she was grateful for the job. He'd never mentioned it, either. He'd had his own dreams built and lost here, new ones formed—or at least he persevered. And she, in her lesser but vital way alongside him. She expected nothing more but, in the moments she thought about it, only prayed it might continue.

It had been a quiet few days since Harlan had returned although Monday afternoon Enoch Stone arrived and held a brief conference with August in the barn before driving out again in his fast buggy. August sat tight-lipped at meals, speaking mostly to her brother about the work ahead of them. Though never failing to offer compliments, to thank her for the food. Then he'd press back his chair and stand, Harlan following him. Even at supper, late in these days of long work, at best he'd rise and pluck one of his black-wrapped small cigars, strike a match and walk out to look over his barns, his livestock, to be alone. When he came in it would often be by the back porch that led to the back stairs and up quiet to his bed.

This morning she was wringing washing and spreading it to drape on the garden fence to dry. With herself and Harlan now at the house she no longer washed linens on the same day as clothing: It all added up to too much for a single morning or she hadn't got the hang of it yet. Time would tell about that. She knew most women washed everything once a week and maybe she'd gain that knack or not; most women also baked once a week and Becca turned out new loaves every couple of days, always had and saw no reason to quit that just because there was one more hungry man able to eat half a loaf, a round of butter with his dinner, then a wedge of pie with his supper. It was summer, easy to launder twice a week for those extra linens for now. Come winter, if all remained the same, she'd face that. And gladly, she thought.

She walked back and forth between the basket of heaped wet-wrung clothes and the garden fence, her skirts damp from the work, her arms pleasantly sore as she shook free the wrinkles, then draped the garments upon the fence. It was a job she could just about do in her sleep and so her eyes drifted, watching the honeybees among the flowers, following their trails off best she could, knowing they were headed for the woods along the gorge and so intent on direction: flying northeast or northwest? So she might suggest to August where to look for the bee tree come late October. When her eyes fell upon the old stone hitching post.

Came a day long ago over her mind: The stone post loomed above to one side of her, overhead a sky of fleet spring clouds moving fast, the sky aching blue between the white, she on her back with legs and arms kicking up, a blanket the gray softness of a dove's breast spreading out to meet the high deep-green grass spotted with the suns of dandelions, the lilac within her sight, dripping with heavy blossoms, the dense scent over her and somewhere, she could not see but *knew*, her mother was close by. Or even her father, that man lost out of Time, not even his voice or the sense of his hands but no reason to think it was not him, there, then on that day when her forgotten self lay in this same yard but an altogether other yard also. This a memory surfaced like a fish from deep water, never before glimpsed and she knew it was true, not some union of memory and her mother's telling. The lost world suddenly drawn close upon her and the pang in her breast greater than she'd ever felt, or perhaps only once upon a time.

She glanced about the yard quickly, laid down the snapped-free blouse upon the fence and darted among the flowers, crouched and looked upon the back porch, then closed her eyes tight, willing that other older house to appear in her mind, her hand upon the post for balance, a talisman, calling in what it also once witnessed. Behind her clamped lids passed bands of red upon the black field, also freckles of pin-bright light. But nothing more. Nothing at all. She ran her hand upon the stone to no avail. No surging image, no pathway stamped in the dirt of the yard to lead from this post to that vanished door. Where long ago the snow had blown through during a storm as a small child sat eating a rough meal made by hands of love.

She opened her eyes and stood. Lifted the front of her skirts and stepped from the flowers and made her way back to the laundry basket. She reached and lifted up a pair of trousers and shook them as she looked about her. She thought it only moments but had no clear sense how long she'd been squatting and walked to the fence to spread them to dry, having spied no one. August and Harlan were ditching. The shadows of the sun hadn't moved more than a quarter hour. Her skirts were nearly dry, as they would quickly on such a summer day.

She continued spreading the laundry upon the garden fence and then over the lower branches of the lilac, shirts tossed up like wings upon the forsythia long since shed of blossoms, the array of tight small branches catching the shirts as if darted. Over and again she glanced down the lanes but did not see the men coming yet. They'd be along soon.

Her brother had taken to drinking coffee but had yet to determine when he'd want it. August, always in the morn, now and again after supper but never midday in summer: Then he only wanted cool water suffused with cider vinegar, grated nutmeg, gingerroot and a touch of cane or maple molasses. She'd tasted it once and hadn't liked the bite, though an hour later had been struck by a restlessness to finish every-day tasks before her.

The wind had mostly died, the air coming off the barley, oat and wheat fields sank about her, smelt of bread and porridge, of winter cow breath, of yeast and heat. It was very hot and the days were long but soon would be longer.

What she did remember clearly was the day she'd left: the bitter winter day of high pale sky, wind whipping snow devils off the drifts as she huddled between her mother and the man driving a bobsled, her brother wrapped in blankets and held within her mother's coat and shawl—Becca's own coat thin against the wind, her scarf over her head and tied tight about her throat. The squeal of the runners against the brittle snow, the slap and thump of the heavy harness on the horses, plumes of breath freezing above the big heads nodding up and down with their work. The sled held the frame of the bed her father had died upon, two shuck mattresses, the table and two chairs and a wooden box holding her mother's kitchen goods. Three flour sacks held what little clothing they were not wearing.

Her glance back revealed the house, a single story with a loft under the peaked roof, sides of rough-riven shingles, all of it surrounded and covered with the same hard wind-packed snow they were driving through. And beyond the house, stark in its hugeness as a strange vessel beached on an unknown shore, rose the large, neat and tight barn. It had never held more than a milk cow, hens, a single pig bought in the spring to fatten upon the land for fall butchering, empty now but also, as her mother would tell her, never but a ghost of promise, as good as empty always.

"Your father," Phoebe Davis had told her some years later, "was a good man, a loving and tender man who counted to six and thought he'd reached ten. I loved him dear, but when his heart quit upon him it seemed only one more misstep in his planning." This said gently and free of knowledge of her own death already brewing in the swamp downstream from Albert Ruddle's house that would settle upon her the next summer.

When the bobsled came to a stop, Albert Ruddle refused to open his door but stood in the snow and argued with the driver: Becca had searched her mind but had no idea who that driver had been beyond a member of their community who'd taken on this task. Albert had a buffalo robe wrapped over his winter clothes, his woolen winter cap with the earflaps turned down and tied under his chin, and what showed of his face was small and tipped up, sharp-snouted and red with the cold. Becca thought him to be some creature come out of the woods, a large muskrat or fat mink that would chew her up to be rid of her. She thought a mistake had been made—that this man wanted nothing of her and what remained of her family.

221

Then her mother spoke up. "Arriving as I have, Mr. Ruddle, I know better than you how cold it is. But I won't leave my possessions, few as they are, standing out in your yard in hopes of a warmer day. Look how quickly we can move them inside and be done with it. And I'll poke the fires up straight away. Cold? Yes it is."

She stepped down from the sled to stand before Albert Ruddle and opened her shawl and handed the bundle of her infant out and Albert took the bundle without knowing what it was, pure response to being offered something.

Phoebe Davis said, "That's my chap, there. More froze than the rest of us because he can't dance about and worry over a moment of cold that'll be set right in a heartbeat, you stop carrying on. I know you're used to life alone; it was never my plan to live so either but we need each other and soon enough we'll come to terms with it. Meantime, sir, wrap that boy under your robe and step aside, for I'm coming through."

The summer her mother died of malarial fever, Becca Davis was fourteen and for two years had been working summers and after school as a clerk and helper in Malin's store at the Four Corners. Harlan was attending the same dame school that she did, run by two older celibates. Marcus Malin and wife, Judith, were not followers of The Friend but understood many of their customers adhered to that simple faith and held both sympathy and respect for Becca Davis—facts she knew when she sat down two weeks after her mother died and outlined her plans with them.

"I can do my sums, account entry work also, and read and write a fair hand. I know geography and the scripture well. I'm on my own now but not alone. I'd work all the hours you'd want and be grateful for it; I know you prefer to board your help to save cash money but I need to watch over my brother and Mr. Ruddle at least a year or two more. Harlan ain't but ten and I'd not set him loose to his own fortune so soon. But I'd work all hours you needed—as long as there was food the two of them could warm when they needed. I'd rise before dawn to cook it. Earlier, the dark winter months, to serve you well."

Marcus began to speak but Judith Malin interrupted him. "You're an earnest girl, Becca Davis. But your brother and Albert Ruddle both need you evenings and I dare say you need them as well. We'll arrange your hours to suit."

Marcus said, "That can't last forever, though."

"Yes, sir. I imagine a year will suffice. Harlan will speak again soon enough; his silence is as much worry over what comes as what has gone. And once he does, he and I'll work out a plan. He's a smart boy."

"The two of you have had a hard row to hoe."

"Not so much as some. The negroes you shelter in the basement, awaiting their night passage onward." She stood and said, "I'm also not living scant miles up the road at the Poor Farm. I'll be here in the morning, first light."

Albert Ruddle's parents had followed The Friend out of Philadelphia and up the Susquehanna through the narrows and over the gaps to the valley of the Chemung and then northward along the eastern shore of Seneca Lake, from there west the twenty miles to the new Jerusalem tract. The settlement was not a dozen years old when he was born; and following that event his mother had forsworn the bounds of marriage and moved into The Friend's new-built manse to live out her days as a celibate acolyte, leaving Albert and his father to eke out as they would, which among other results left Albert's father an involuntary but resigned celibate himself; no great surprise that Albert chose to follow the same course. Their one stroke of luck had been the random award of their holding, eighty acres of prime bottomland in the valley through which flowed the Kedron Brook to where it spread into the small marshy delta and then into the west branch of the Crooked Lake at the Four Corners. His father had sold all but ten acres to the

223

farmers north and south of him and raised beans. Ten-foot-high corn, thick swales of barley and wheat stretched either side of their fields but his father chose beans, and beans it was. Speckled, pea, navy, cranberry, soldier, bird's-egg, all the varieties that Albert's father had carried out of western Connecticut down the seaboard and then north and west into this fabled new land. He was a true believer, a man of faith and an old-time Yankee: Rumors of great bounty would not tide a man through a long winter but honest beans would stew with only water and time, a bit of salt pork, maple or dark cane molasses, if you had them but even without, the covered clay pot set in the banked coals of a hearth would turn out food against starvation. A loaf of bread, corn dodgers, a slab of pan-fried ham—all those things and more would make the beans a feast. And all but the beans, come winter, were extra.

The Ruddle men grew beans. The plants pulled when the pods were drying, late summer through the fall depending upon the variety, hung to finish in the long, low barn that was more shed than barn, then the pods cracked and the dried beans gathered, winnowed free of dust and sacked true to type. And their neighbors who did not waste ground to plant beans but had their own bean pots, receipts handed down, larders of ingredients, each fall felt the stirring toward winter and made their inventory against the worst possible winter and so trekked to Ruddle's for their sack of beans—also knowing the elder and then the younger as years passed, knew what might be best offered in trade. Hard coin was not refused but more welcome was a crock of brined cabbage, combs of honey tied tight in waxed sailcloth, sacks of cornmeal or wheat flour, stone-milled oats, potatoes, apples, head cheese, sides of bacon or hard beef sausage. Parsnips, carrots, turnips, any such thing come October that would last.

The Ruddles, even after all those years, lived to survive lean times.

Albert sat across the table from Becca. A spring evening two years on. They'd supped on cornbread baked in a hot spider, boiled young nettle leaves, bacon sliced thick and buttermilk, and Harlan was now in the small room he and Becca shared, bent close over *McGuffey's Third Reader* to memorize Washington's Farewell Address. They were drinking tea made from the previous year's dried wild spearmint: Albert did not hold with coffee or tea, believing their stimulating effect to be deleterious to thought and violently purgative.

"Missy," Albert said. "You're lingering. The Malins have been gracious in their patience but if you're to make a go of it with them you need to give them your full attention. You do it well but you split yourself twixt them and us two, here. The boy and I get on just fine. He's a hand to hoe and come autumn knows his beans and what needs to be done with em. He's weary of the school and has learned most all he needs of it. Truth be, all you try to do for him and me mostly gets in the way of our doing it ourselves. He won't let me lift a hand to supper if he thinks you're aiming to make it back in time to cook it for us: We set hours sometimes waiting but he won't let me speak of it. So there it is. I'd think your mother would agree I'd done my part by you, but it's time for you to go."

She wasn't so surprised but said, "And you'll set to the wash kettle and paddle yourself? Or will you have Harlan do that work?"

He tipped his fingers together as prayer, touching his chin with the tips and said, "The Widow Gould at the Corners has agreed to pick up the clothing and linens as needed Monday morn and have them back clean, dried and folded neat before end of day for pennies a week."

"You're ahead of me," she said.

"It's the benefit of age," he said. "Also, you seem to forget it's little over a mile from here to Malin's. My guess is you'd see your brother as often, and easier for the both of you if he was to step before your counter and buy a peppermint stick or a cone of salt for the house when the need or urge came than if you stayed on here."

Quiet a moment, she then said, "I'm not ready to leave him."

Albert Ruddle nodded, paused, and then said, "I'm not either. But I will, sooner than I'd wish. And we'd welcome your visits, as long as they were of free will and carried no efforts to provide meals, tucker, the like. Likewise, Malins are happy with it and the weather suits, no reason why we all shouldn't continue walking to Meeting together. So you see, the world need not change so much as you think, but rather direct both you and your brother onward into life. As I said, the day will not be so far off when I've done all I can."

She looked at him. "Are you ill?"

He smiled at her, with most of his teeth the color of corn. What hair remained on his head could be counted by strands but for how wispy they flew about, the liver spots on his skull as visible as those on his hands. Like many of the older farmers, Albert dressed each day in black wool trousers and jacket over a white shirt, though his shirts were yellowed with age. His dress and comportment were equal parts antique and of his self-imposed withdrawal from the world that whirled in Time.

He said, "Nothing is hidden from you, but the earth pulls me downward, the spirit urges me home. Truth is, Becca Davis, when I was asked about taking in your mother and you two children I was greatly troubled by the prospect—such a change in how I'd always lived, how I'd thought I'd live all my days. But we are not asked what we cannot bear and so I said Yes. Odd thing, that: These years have been among the best of my life, though the loss of your mother was a blow. Yet you and Harlan are part of my household as much as the floorboards and walls. I watched you rise up as a young woman, those months the chap would not speak so struck he was by her death.

"You're already looking forward, and our dear Harlan knows loss but sees one day following after another. You move to Malin's, he'll gain a freshened sense of the loneliness central to life—and so cast his eyes a bit tighter upon me. And when I drop or grow feeble it will not be his place to step in and take upon himself the beans but rather the certainty within that he's of value to other men. That he's of stout heart and disposition that will serve him well for some greater farmer."

"You'll make of him a hired man."

Albert Ruddle said, "Don't discount it. A good one can become nigh a partner, more so if there happens to be a daughter and no son. No, I can't foresee the future for any of us but I do know the sort of man your brother's growing into, and whatever may come his way he'll rise up and meet boldly face-on."

She paused, thinking herself only a shopgirl, after all. Then, dipping her voice low but also full of wonderment, she said, "You love him, don't you?"

Without pause Albert said, "Dear as a son. You as well. But upon Father's death these acres' value reverted to The Friend; I'm but a life tenant and not unhappy, it's how such things should be. Upon your mother's death my pang of regret that I could not bestow the land upon you and Harlan was momentary—not enough land to support one in these coming days, let alone two, and their families. The days of beans is about done."

She rose and walked around the table, stood before him, and then leaned and kissed his brow.

"There, now," he said, flushing under spring sunburn. "That's enough."

"Not hardly close," she told him.

August and Harlan were scything ditches, had been at it for two days now. The reaper sat ready on the barn floor, the cutting bar greased and knives sharpened, three worn ones replaced, the drive wheel and cogs, the wheel bushings spread with axle grease from the tub. The platform and wooden paddles checked for stoutness and suppleness and the belt from the drive wheel to turn the paddles tightened, checked for wear. The granaries and threshing floor had been swept

227

clean of dust, old chaff, mouse droppings. All was ready but for the ripeness of the grain and that was drawing close. Each afternoon August would wade to the edge of his oat field and strip two separate stalks, worrying the oblong oats free of their hulls and biting down on two from each stalk, one at a time. They were almost hard, almost dry-cured upon stalks the pale yellow of the stone his house was built from. But not quite: Each gave a bit in the middle, the last moisture holding in the germ of the grain. A matter of days.

So they scythed ditches. Around them the grain fields, the oats and the bright brass of the barley, the more dusky yellow of the wheat. Also pastures and meadows of hay growing toward the second cutting which would start as soon as the threshing was done. A month and a half of long, hot, dusty days lay ahead. It was hot work what they were doing but free of dust. The ditches ran along the farm lanes to draw excess water off the fields, with a fence running along the bank of the ditch on the field side. August walked with his feet in the bottom of the ditch, scything upward toward the fence, cutting not just the lush grass that grew there but also the burdock and thistles and young saplings of sprouted trees hidden in the grass. His feet feeling for any stones or clods that had rolled into the ditch to impede the flow of water. Now and again he'd find a place where water had caved the ditch bank and blocked the flow altogether. Those places he'd note to return to later with a spade to clear. Because of the moisture in the ditches there were plots of wild spearmint and peppermint and he left those so come September they'd remain as high, bright green stands, easy to find and gather to dry or boil with apples from the orchard to make a jelly whose tangy sweetness married well with darker meats in winter—beef or ham, venison if he had the occasion to shoot a deer between corn harvest and hog-killing time.

Harlan worked a dozen strides behind, his own feet upon the lane and so swinging his scythe downward and back to cut the near bank.

Like August's, an unnatural stroke made harder by repetition—the backstroke offered the chance to catch breath but no relaxation of muscles—lifting the scythe upward instead of feeling it loose its load and slide empty back across the fresh stubble as the man stepped forward to swing and cut again.

Beyond spare comments passed on the prospects of the weather or the heat of the day, creatures or conditions noted in passing, they'd said little to one another during this spate of work and the silence suited both. Until mid-morning of the second day, when August climbed out of the ditch onto the lane, rested the tip of the snath upon the ground and pulled his stone from his pocket, spat upon it and began putting a fresh edge to the chine. He heard Harlan stop behind him and soon heard the sing of Harlan's whetstone upon his blade. His own cutting edge began to glisten, silver in the sun. He squinted and studied the edge, looking for deeper nicks or pocks where he'd have to peen the chine but it looked good, a small nick in the toe but nothing that wouldn't hold an edge a day or more.

He dropped the long whetstone into his rear pocket, lifted the scythe by the snath and pivoted on one heel, planting the snath again upon the lane and crossed his arms over the beard of the blade and leaned, looking at Harlan. The boy tracked the movement but kept his eyes upon his job as he finished sharpening his own scythe, his head cocked as he studied the edge being drawn out, eyes squinting against the sun the better to see. Then he pocketed his stone and, too short to lean against his upright tool as August did—or possibly disinclined to mimic—turned it downward and held it by the grips across his body. Ready to swing it back and go to work.

"What?" he said.

August said, "I told you I'd respect your desire to hold your silence. But you've a troubled mind. These past couple days I've seen you studying me when you think I'd not notice. As if gauging if you could trust me, or perhaps just waiting a moment seems right to you. Last time was up the ditch, not a quarter hour ago."

"Of course my mind's troubled. Isn't yours?"

August considered the sky before answering. "Many are the things that may trouble us in this life. But there's that grand unknowable design behind it all, where we can't know what the Lord intends, how far His reach and understanding is. Which alone is the Glory of the Lord. But also, our questing is why He sent His Son unto us. So we might better grasp our place in His unknowable scheme, how we comprehend His Love and devotion to us weak and fallen vessels. And to know that and raise our hearts and souls and place our trust in that love of Our Heavenly Father. And you know this, you were raised so. Would you say otherwise?"

"I'd say the Lord don't want us to stand by with silent tongues when we see a wrong being done. What sort of a Lord would that be? Was that what Jesus did? Set back silent and wait for His Father to sort it all out?"

"There now," August said. "Are you ready to give voice to the question your eyes have been darting my way?"

Harlan paused, pushed a roughened foot in the dust of the lane and said, "Are you gaming me?"

"I don't know where you learned such talk, though I can guess. But the answer is no; you should know me well enough to not say or think such things. I'm offering you the chance to speak your mind and perhaps, by doing so, you'll find clarity. Has happened to me upon occasion."

Harlan eased the scythe from hand to hand, shifting the weight. Finally he said, "I know Stone doesn't want to hear what I have to say. He's set upon a course and all I'd say would muddy his waters. And Malcolm Hopeton, he doesn't want any of it, Stone or me. So I wondered if I should set back and let it go the way it will—guessing the judge could be well inclined to listen to Brother Stone and

Bethany's father, the two of them together. But even if they did, not only would they be wrong but wrong in a way Mr. Hopeton could not bear. So it comes back to me and what I seen and heard, what I know."

August interrupted: "You assume the judge would not be interested in what you have to say. It's his job to not only listen but to hear how a thing is told. Meaning he might hear in your version some elements missing from Brother Stone's account—also how the judge might view David Schofield's account, that man speaking of his own daughter."

"You're thinking I need to speak to the judge."

"I'm thinking you already know that. I'm thinking there's some other part to the matter you're wrestling with."

Harlan grinned, couldn't help himself, though the grin slipped off quickly. "I been talking in my sleep?"

"No." August smiled shortly himself, then said, "I think if it was only your concerns, you'd have answered that question by now."

Harlan nodded. "All right," he said. "There's another part."

"Share it or hold until you know."

"I'll share. But I'm not looking for answers, except from myself. As you said, airing a question aloud sometimes helps it come clear."

"Fair enough. Speak and I'll not say a word, unless you decide to ask my opinion. But before you speak, let me say this: If you decide to talk to the judge and you want me along, I'll be there with you."

Harlan reached out and snagged a long stalk of timothy and stuck the stem into one corner of his mouth as was his want when he was parsing hard upon a matter. August recognized the impulse, which he answered with cheroots, again marveling at this boy so much like himself in ways he'd never give voice to. Feeling as if he was performing those duties of a father that just days before had bothered him, doubting his ability.

"I'm not the only one living who saw what went on there at that farm those years. There's another was a close witness, who seen and

231

heard much, also heard and seen things I didn't. Who could, she wanted, stand and tell the judge much the same as I would. And if she did, the judge would have to listen much harder than if it was just me. But I got doubts she'd do it. I can't understand why; she was stung bad by that mess. But that's how it stands, just now."

There was a pause between them both and August patted both his trouser pockets, hoping to feel the stub of a cheroot, wanting that moment of distraction, the clarifying smoke in his lungs. But his pockets were empty, not even his match safe. Finally he said, "I told you I'd ask nothing less you asked my thoughts, but there's a question—"

"I think I already said too much. What is it?"

August halted in anxious pause and then jumped. "That day. When Enoch Stone come by the house and talked to you—"

"I know the day you speak of. What about it?"

"He mentioned a woman from Utica. Is that the one you're talking about?"

"She ain't much more than a girl." Then Harlan stopped. A ragged line of three low-swooping crows crossed over the lane and on into the pasture beyond, barking and agitated, and he turned and watched them go until they passed into the woodlot now a green smudge in the heat of the day. Yet he looked after them, as if to spy if they might reappear. Only when they did not after some moments did he look back at August.

"That's what's on my mind. I think I said enough about it for now. Let's get back to work." He turned toward the ditch.

August said, "You hold on, there."

Harlan stopped but held himself a moment before he slowly turned back from where he studied the dock and chamomile growing at the edge of the lane above the ditch and raised his face slow and dark-cast.

"What is it?"

232

"Not so much as you think," August said. "What I see now is a high sun. Your sister will have dinner ready about any time we walk to the house. Which is what we should do. You hungry?"

"I'm hungry enough."

"You're always hungry, Harlan Davis."

"You tuck right in, yourself."

"I wasn't making a complaint, only noting what should be expected. Shall we walk up?"

"We could cut a bit more ditch."

"I think we should walk up."

"All right." Harlan lifted the scythe by the grips and turned the blade backward, over his shoulder, rested the snath so the blade hung behind but didn't otherwise move.

August caught the snath by his hand at the balance point and walked with the tool gliding alongside, sweat-burnished wood and hard keen metal bobbing even with his stride. He passed Harlan and spoke and kept going.

"For what it's worth, my experience is a woman will do the right thing, given time to think upon it. More so than many a man."

Becca stood watching them come. She'd pulled a beef tongue from brine the previous morning and soaked it throughout the day, changing the water whenever she thought to. In the evening she'd set it to boil, then as the fire died left it in the pot overnight, the coals enough to keep a low simmer. This morning she'd lifted it from the still-warm water and placed it on a length of plank in the buttery to cool. After hanging the wash, she'd cut up tomatoes and cucumbers, stewed a pot of yellow wax beans with butter, dug horseradish and grated it into clotted cream, then fetched the cool tongue and sliced it onto the platter. Set out crabapple jelly. All of which now waited on the table.

They paused at the barn to rest their scythes against the stable door, then crossed the barnyard, feet kicking dust. Harlan looked tired, his clothing dark with sweat and grime, his face turned down. She looked at August. He walked loose-limbed but upright and alert, as if his body were tired but he gave it little mind, a man intent upon his day. Becca studied him and thought she'd never seen him before, which wasn't possible as she'd spent every day for the past four years in his household, working and moving around him, somewhat the way the Moon circles with the Earth around the Sun and the wonder came into her head if the Moon even knew the Earth was there. As quick as the thought came into her mind it was gone and she'd lost all sense of it but for an echo she couldn't quite recall. August Swartout walked on toward her, close enough now so she could see the movement of his eyes, over her, yes, but also about the place, the orchard with the attentive horses and disdainful mules, the pasture where the young heifers were in with the borrowed bull, even a toss of his chin over his shoulder toward the back of the house and the laundry there. His eyes upon her again. And like a jar smashed or a bell cracked, it came to her that she was home and always had been.

Giddy of nerves, she sang out, "There's my men."

Harlan looked at her as if about to weep.

August nodded and said, "Yes. Here we are." His mouth was full and moist within his beard, his eyes crinkled at the corners as if he might be understanding all she was saying. And again she had no idea what she was saying, what message was within her, let alone sent out toward him.

Then he echoed her. "Your men." His eyes full and deep with a concern she could not name. Her face grew hot and she looked down.

She looked back up as August said, "You might've wished for better but your brother and me seem to be what you get. At least for now." The snap and flutter about his eyes now seemed to be laughter, not at her but something shared. He said, "It's another long day of a summer. Shall we follow you in?"

Becca Davis was never so glad to turn her back, to lead the way into the kitchen and the plentiful board she'd laid.

During daytime, the windows revealed the hour, however dim. Not that he needed such; even in pitch dark his mind knew the quarter hour within minutes, seemed it had always been this way—though he guessed it had been learned or otherwise gained as a boy. So when the door opened above and boot soles began a solemn downward tread, he knew it was somewhere just past two in the afternoon and therefore too early for his supper to be delivered, which meant whoever might be descending was no one he wished to speak with and so turned sideways upon his bunk, facing the rear wall, the stone courses cut so true and plumb as to need no mortar. Guessing by simple deduction or subtraction of possibilities the visitor was not the sheriff or one of his deputies—certainly no neighbor finally arrived to wish him well or ask if some help might be offered up, nonesuch existed and he knew this with gratitude, not regret. So deduced it must be Enoch Stone, who twice had made such visits and twice had been rebuked with silence. As he would be again.

Boot steps light and quick across the floor: not a man he knew.

The voice when it came was gentle, almost sad but upticked with an unmistakable concern. Of a sort he'd not heard here—holding some shadow of the boy's anguished entreaties, although issued with a slender certainty of self.

"Malcolm Hopeton? Mr. Hopeton, sir."

Came a pause. The voice again:

"It's no easy task I'm upon this afternoon. But one duty demands of me. Duty, as you must know, can be a damnable thing and yet, once charged with it, we must fulfill it. Did you not learn that in the war? If your manhood did not know it before, which I suspect to be so. Given what I know of you, given what I've learned."

235

There was one line in the course of stones that held a small fissure. Beads of water rimmed the crack and ants time to time could be seen working along the fracture, some of them carrying great loads of crumbs or egg sacs, he did not know which. Perhaps both. The man speaking behind him seemed burdened likewise. He knew the voice but could not put a face to it, save it was not a lawyer, lawman or judge. Surely not the boy.

"Malcolm? Would you not turn and look upon my face? For I'd be a better man if I met you eye-to-eye for what I have to say."

He rose off the bunk and turned and stopped.

The doctor, Erasmus Ogden, stood in a finely tailored linen summer suit, his round-brimmed bowler held by both hands before him. As he spoke he slowly rotated the hat in his hands, an action metronomic to his words. His face held a sheen of sweat but he looked Malcolm Hopeton in the eye throughout.

"I don't believe I bring any comfort to you, only the truth. And I've wrestled with doing so but my conscience demands it of me. I've studied carefully upon the matter and for the life of me can't tell if by coming to you, I violate my oath or uphold it."

There came a pause then as it dawned over the doctor that Malcolm would remain silent. Perhaps he'd been so warned. He glanced off once, diverting his eyes from the man before him and firmed his grip on his hat, arresting the revolutions and spoke, his eyes wide and clear.

"Your silence is as famous as the remarkable, if wrong-headed, efforts being promulgated by the lawyer Enoch Stone and your father-in-law. But my purpose today is not legal but moral. Ethical and damned difficult. It brings me no ease to bear this news to you and I don't believe this news will bring you any measure of peace, in fact I expect otherwise. Still, I would have you know and so here I stand."

After a moment he went on: "You may or may not know that it was my job to examine your wife's body to ascertain cause of death. One determination I reached was that her death was likely the result of hard contusion caused by violent contact with her head upon the ground. There were bits of gravel embedded in her scalp and her neck was broken between the second and third vertebrae. My conclusion was this was the result of an accident: There was a small derringer pistol of the sort favored by women found upon the ground, both barrels discharged, and reasonable deduction would presume you grasped her and cast her roughly upon the ground for your own safety, perhaps hers as well."

Hopeton did not respond, did not move. Erasmus Ogden now looked down at his patent boots, the rough basement floor. He sighed and lifted his head and went on:

"Beyond that, in observing her body it was clear that sometime within the past year or at most two, her right clavicle had been broken and healed without proper setting, as indicated by an irregular knot of calcification raised upon the surface of the bone. And finally, upon her body, at the time of her death, prior to her death, there were numerous bruisings of some age upon her torso, front, and back. Upon her thighs, also. In short, the body I examined was one of a woman who had suffered degrees of physical abuse over a period of time and the inference must be drawn that she held little control over her actions. I am pained to deliver this news to you, I'd say again."

Again he paused and again Malcolm did not take his eyes from the now sweat-drenched face of the doctor.

Who nodded as if agreeing to something and said, "I thought it my duty to do so. Good evening, sir." And nodded again and placed his bowler hat upon his head as he turned and with the oddly firm steps of a man with too much to drink or uncertainty of soul, went up the stairs.

Malcolm Hopeton felt the air pull in the basement as the door was opened and closed.

Hollow he felt, hollow he was.

★　★　★

237

Seeing Bethany again and again in those few moments after so many years, vivid and living and all wild-eyed, then as a broken china doll upon the ground, the lines of blood from her nose and the corner of her mouth. He had no memory of feeling her against him as he'd grasped and then thrown her to the ground. And that damned little gun: Had she been so terrified of him? And the answer was, Of course she had been, regardless of Amos Wheeler, regardless of the truth of what Harlan had told him, of which, once told, Malcolm had known to be true. His head heavy with constant ache, his chest pained as if straining to contain what couldn't be contained, he understood she was a woman who feared every man in her life, had come to fear the one man she had no reason to fear. But had, for what she'd done—if done by her or done to her, she, he knew, was less capable of knowing than he might be. Or others. How he ached, how sore his own bruised heart.

A roaring blind idiot had destroyed the woman he loved. Had allowed her to be destroyed. Comes to the same thing, in the end. He had failed her, utterly, all ways. Had tossed off the trust she'd given him. And such a brave, terrible, and wonderful thing that gift had been. An idiot.

He'd known and loved and celebrated the strength of her. And allowed himself in some vulgar obscenity of vanity to believe he'd lifted from her that warble of doubt and fear she owned. Doubt in herself. In all humanity. Perhaps even, finally and rightfully, doubt of him.

For one long moment that could have been seconds or an hour, he saw himself locked in a room such as this, a room removed from time or sight or knowledge ever of anyone beyond the room, alone with Amos Wheeler, and there visited upon Wheeler every manner of horror the war had shown him and horrors also only out of his own mind, such tools that warfare can't even conjure.

Then he sat on the floor weeping with his face rubbed hard against the stones of the rear of the cell, rubbing as if to rid himself of the skin of his face, to remove his face, to abrade himself clear but never clean. He sat silent and unmoving upon his bunk for unknowable hours, gazing at nothing, his eyes and mind not able to own focus.

His memory was failing—her voice already gone, her face only almost caught as if in a quick sideways glance, then gone. Yet, and yet: As pain or balm—he could not say—she remained within him large as life and known all ways, known as no other had known her, known as no other had known him. Ever would. Until he too was gone, departed this earth. And then nothing. Neither of them truly known to anyone left upon this earth.

He wept again, soundless. Sitting on the bunk, throat raw but water running down his face, eyes burning. Salt upon his wet lips when his thickened tongue swabbed out. The hollow man. He did not weep for himself but only for her. For her alone.

Bethany. Alone. Done ill by all men. In death as in life.

Gray light of dawn paling the basement. The door above opened and the morning jailor came down carrying a tin plate and tin cup of coffee. As always he turned to face the rear wall, heard the cage door open and the grate of the plate pushed through upon the floor, the small thunk as the coffee was set down and then the harsh snap as the cage closed and locked again. The footsteps snapping and clacking as rough boots went away and up the stairs and again, the door. Again the suck as the air was pulled from the basement.

He stood from the bunk and turned and looked down. The plate held the usual heap of corn mush and thick tag-ends of burned bacon. He stood wavering back and forth as if overnight his knees had decided to abandon him, to quit the job of allowing him to stand. He regarded the coffee. A summer morn, yet the subterranean room cool enough so faint steam rose and swam into his nostrils.

All mornings he'd simply ignored both until they were collected when noon dinner was brought and his slop pail was also changed. He looked again at the dented tin plate and stepped back once without knowing he was doing so and swung his right foot hard against the plate, which lifted up and turned over as it spun forward and clanged hard against the bars of the cage and shivered downward, come to rest upon the floor, the food a spew upon the bars and beyond.

He ignored this but bent and took up the coffee with both hands wrapped around the tin and sat again on his bunk. Again he studied the tight-laid stones of the back wall of his cage. Some man, some crew of men, had done a good job.

He lifted the cup and drank. Thinking: He was the vessel that had held her.

He'd failed her.

The question was how best to not do that again.

ELEVEN

HE SAT AT the table with his cousin Marsh, nephews Daniel and Isaac, and Harlan Davis, drinking coffee, talking of which fields they'd cut this day of oats, which the next day and following. The talk was desultory, half-hearted. They were waiting for the heat to burn the dew off the grain so they could get to work. Mostly, they were taking a last pause, their bodies slack in the warm kitchen, before stepping out into the long days of harvest.

Finally August stood, stretched as he looked about him, and said, "Let's get to it, boys."

The reaper belonged to him and so he drove but only on his fields; when they moved to Marsh's fields, Marsh drove. Each man knew his own land best. Daniel, Isaac, and Harlan took turns, one raking the cut stalks as they folded automatically from the platform, one gathering the stalks into sheaves and tying them with a straw selected from each bundle, the last loading the sheaves upon the wagon following, driven by the other older man. No shocks were built as the sheaves were hauled directly to the barn and stacked alongside the threshing floor. The clatter of the cutting bar and the constant snick of the knives slicing oat stalks, the tramp of the horses' hooves, the rumble of the iron wheels of the reaper and following wagon made it hard to speak beyond a sudden shout; and if the noise weren't enough to quiet jabber, the work was. By the time the first swath around the field was cut all were soaked with sweat and by the time the first load was trundled off to the barn, the raker now replacing the loader to ride to the barn and unload, the loader now making sheaves and the sheave-maker now raking, all were black with chaff and dust. The first load made and the first field only a quarter cut and it not yet noon of the first day. This work would've taken two days, perhaps even three, without the reaper. And it allowed for far more grain to be planted. The work had not grown less, only the yield grown greater.

Noontime they all sat in the shade of a tall elm in the southwest corner of the field. Two loads along. So they looked out upon a wide swath of short stubble with a thick band of high oats in the center, awaiting them. The uncut oats seemed dense and dull in color, while the stubble almost sparkled. Shadows passed through the stubble, mice and moles and other small displaced creatures, darting for the still-standing oats or those farthest from that false refuge, daring the unknown toward the hedgerow. Overhead the pair of resident red-tail hawks drifted low, time to time sweeping down fast and up again. Feasting, harvesting.

Becca had walked out the hour before wearing the milk-house yoke with heavy wooden buckets each side, her free hands holding tin buckets of cold water doctored as August liked, the wooden buckets filled with fresh-baked steaming loaves wrapped in sacking, a whole ham cut in slices, a wedge of hard cheese, and a crock of ten-day cucumber and pepper pickles. A tin of molasses cookies.

The men sprawled and ate and drank dippers of the harvest water. Midday, the shade was pleasant enough, but the air had died and the heat drove down upon them. Sweating where they lay. The

242

afternoon and on into the long evening would only grow more heat. Not a cloud in the sky, which was good. The great fear, once harvest started, were thunderstorms creeping in late afternoon or even in the night.

August was in ill humor. Early on, partway around the first swath as he perched high on the seat and watched the oats coming sweeping against the cutting bar, he'd spied a meadowlark flare up then drop back down and seen the frantic fledglings trying to fly, fluttering helpless off into the oats that, until this moment, had been their entire safe world. And the horses walking forward, the work to be done, his traveling eyes striking back and down at the very moment the cutting bar bloomed red and wet with blood. Moments later, when he again glanced down, the bar was clean, oats falling backward under the swirling, relentless paddles. Every field offered tragedy. Yet it stayed in his mind as he ate, half-listening to the comments, small complaints offered up around him. Burning eyes, a pulled muscle in a back, a wicked chestnut. Work.

It was then he saw the spout of dust coming down the lane toward the field. From the dust-mirage he made out a leaping team and carriage. No one else had seen it yet, so he eased up from his elbow and watched it come. He'd seen that carriage before.

Judge Ansel Gordon wore a trim black suit furred with road dust, a white shirt with a string tie, and a square-crowned bowler hat of best quality, his long white hair spilling onto his shoulders as he wheeled up before the group, brought his team to a frothing stop, and raised one finger to touch the brim of his hat and by greeting said, "Gents."

August and Marsh stood, the three young men remained prone. August did not look at Harlan.

The judge looked at August. "I'd thought to catch you at the house but your girl sent me along."

Marsh said, "We're cutting oats. You passed no other crews at such

243

work, all the way from town?" An edge of challenge in his voice: He knew as much of Harlan's ordeal as most others in the community.

August overlaid, "It's a hot day for a buggy ride."

"Hot for any labor but my efforts don't stop any more than yours." He redirected to Marsh and said, "I observed some other men at work in their oats. Are you in a competition?"

"Only to get the work done, nothing more."

"Ah, yes. And I wish you the best of it. But I'm afraid I'm going to relieve you of a laborer." He looked then at the younger men and said, "Harlan Davis, come along with me."

"Now, wait," August said. Already feeling he was failing Harlan as he'd promised he would not. "Are you arresting him?"

Harlan had stood when the judge spoke his name. The judge glanced at him, then to August.

"No, I'm not arresting him, but he'll come with me. Or shall you gentle farmers form a mob against me?" His voice sparked and acid, the lace of laughter within.

August said, "He was released to my care, and I'd know what your business is. Such was my understanding."

The judge said, "Get up in here, boy. I don't have all day to sit here jabbering, and neither do you." To August he said, "My business is mine own. I intend to confer with the boy, as is my duty."

"It's all right, Mr. Swartout. I been expecting something like this." Harlan walked forward toward the carriage, then stopped. Unsure what to do, where to sit, perhaps waiting one last direction from August.

Who did not truly have one but did his best. "You'll return him before the end of day?"

"I did not say that." The judge waved his free hand in a broad gesture. He said, "Climb up beside me, boy. And brace yourself; this is a hot-blooded team." He turned his eyes upon August and that dark lace of humor was altogether gone. He said, "See to your work, while I attend mine."

Harlan looked back at August and said, "Get your oats in. You done good by me." And he stepped up into the buggy and settled himself, looking off away from all of them.

August stepped forward and said, "Shall I take this matter up with Enoch Stone?"

Ansel Gordon smiled and said, "If you truly so wish, by all means."

He swatted the lines against the backs of his team and as quick, seemed to August quicker, as he'd come in, he was gone. For moments the bulk of the buggy visible, then lost as dust rose from the spinning wheels and fast-plunging hooves.

August walked a short distance down the lane after them, stopped, and pulled a cheroot from a pocket and clipped fire from his thumbnail, smoked a bit. Marsh started to walk toward him, his feet crunching in the stubble, and saw his cousin's shoulders arch and stiffen, so stopped and waited.

Finally August turned and said, "What're you gaping at? There's oats to bind."

Harlan looked away off his side of the buggy until they passed through the Four Corners and the judge remained silent also. Despite the heat, the horses were fast and air passed cool about them. The judge took the longer but more level route along the base of the Bluff and Harlan wondered was it to save the team the climb out of the valley or to slow his arrival, wherever that might be. So he turned to face the judge.

"I never did a wrong thing."

The judge had been driving with rapt attention upon his team. Both hands working the lines, taking pleasure in his horses. He glanced at Harlan and back, flexed both wrists to slow the trot a bit but not break it and said, "How old are you?"

"Sixteen come November."

"Fifteen years old and never done a wrong thing? That would make you a first by my experience."

"I seen plenty of wrongs, I'd say. But I never broke no laws, least that I know of. And I've pondered that question hard."

"No doubt. Given where you were the last four years. Now, though, you must feel washed clean, rescued by that community of simple saints."

"Those are the people I come out of."

Ansel Gordon was quiet for a bit and then said, "Forgive my last remark; it was uncalled for. While this business before me is not entirely to my liking, the truth is, I've seen none of your people come before the bench until now. Esquire Stone is a curious man, wiser than many believe. Beyond his great reach for what can only be termed Christian mercy lies a wider comprehension that most might miss. He understands that this terrible war just now ended has not only preserved our federal union and unleashed vast machineries of death, but in those machineries has glimpsed a future where the yeoman's life will be hard pressed by the very means of greater facility. The men engaged in manufacturing arms and goods of such great quantities will certainly now turn their eyes to peaceable but similar gains from such industry. Those of your ilk will need a man such as Enoch Stone to stand as both guard and translator against the press of such industry upon you. We are witness to a changing world. I tell you this to illustrate the prudence and fairness I attempt to bring to the bench. That said, I will not be trifled with. Do you comprehend me?"

Harlan looked off away. South of them the great bulk of the Bluff rose, splitting the upper branches of the Crooked Lake, neither of which could be glimpsed from this vantage. He turned back to find the judge waiting.

He said, "I told the few who asked, I'd answer any questions needed answering, anytime."

The judge took pause and reached up to tug his bowler down tightly upon his forehead and said, "I'm heartened to hear that."

246

Harlan drew a breath and said, "You know Mr. Hopeton won't allow his wife to be dragged in the mud of another's making to save his own skin."

The judge said, "Ah, that. In fact, this morning before I drove out after you I explained to Hopeton he had no choice in the matter. That deal is done, signed and ready for the seal of the state. There remains only a simple hearing of sworn testimony that doesn't involve your Mr. Hopeton and the matter is finished, closed. The particulars of the law are such that Malcolm Hopeton can't make formal objection to clemency offered under those proceedings. And despite his utter silence these past weeks, I'd hazard that he'll welcome the gift of his life more quickly than he may believe at the moment, once it stretches before him."

"He don't have a say in it? At all?"

"The law is a curious and wondrous creation. The presumption of innocence being the foundation. Almost as important, in some cases overriding the necessity of proving innocence, is the principle of extenuating circumstances. Meaning that which first appears to have been the result of one set of actions is determined to actually be the result of other, greater, actions. Such is the case of Malcolm Hopeton. But to speak directly to your question: For the time being Malcolm Hopeton has not deigned to speak his mind to me. He stood unblinking as I delivered this news."

The judge went on: "Wherever he might be a year from now, he'll think back and thank his lucky stars, his God if he's got one or not, and perhaps even me, for how this all went. It was not a easy job. I felt like I was nudging three lunatics all into place, all the while needing to let at least two think they were guiding me against my wishes. Men are fools when they see a wink of power within their grasp and my job is to figure out what that power truly is and then dribble it out to them so they think they gained it themselves."

Harlan listened, also thinking if the judge would talk, Harlan was not yet compelled to. Perhaps after they arrived at the courthouse, the jail cell or whatever it would be, that would change. But for the moment simply struggling to comprehend all the judge was saying. Also trying to place where Hopeton stood with all of these doings, though it seemed clear he'd not changed his determination to die, even with the efforts of others to save him. Perhaps more so, because of them. The judge grew silent and they rode along and Harlan again looked off away. They'd gained ground on the swelling ridge above the lake before they'd drop down into town, a cluster of roofs, tree-tops, glimpses of streets and a pair of higher steeples visible below.

Finally Harlan said, "There's a whole ugly pile to this story no one seems interested in hearing."

After a moment the judge replied. "If I had the time I'd be half interested to hear more about how you and Amos Wheeler got along. But I don't have time or interest enough. I can imagine and that's part of my job as well. What seems shocking or outrageous, what most any two people can get up to, after enough time and enough stories all the surprise has gone out of it. I say this: You count yourself lucky, and like all others that made this sordid episode, quit looking over your shoulder and march forward. It seems you have a good job, one that, what with your sister long ensconced, almost certainly assures you a good home. That's where you need to dig in and make your place now. Is that clear?"

They went along without speaking further downhill into the town streets and turned off Main to Elm and onward toward the courthouse. Harlan was now as confused as possible. The judge's last words had upset all his expectations: It seemed there was to be no cell for him, no great interrogation. But if not, then for what purpose this ride? To inform him he was to play no role, that the job was as good as done? Seemed a mighty effort on the part of the judge for such small return, an informing that could've been done seated under a shade tree at August Swartout's. The judge is lulling me, he thought, and will reveal himself once we arrive. Perhaps nothing more than locking him up under some pretense or another until the clemency hearing was over. Perhaps something more sinister. The judge seemed a fair man but also one used to the smooth speech of authority vested upon him: He could so easily be speaking half his mind, holding half back. And Harlan saw that the workings of the law were a mystery to him: The more he learned of those workings, seemed the less he knew.

They wheeled up the drive past the small cluster of buggies and waiting horses on this quiet day when no court was in session, around the back side of the building where a small carriage shed stood separate from the longer public shed. The judge pulled up and let his team come to a stop as a boy darted out of the cool, dim shed and caught up the bridle of the near horse.

The judge stepped down from his rig and motioned to Harlan. "Get down, boy. Step lively, now."

Harlan stood and dropped down onto the packed gravel as the boy walked the team and carriage into the shed. He glanced at the rear of the building where a single plain door let in, with the legend No Entry in black block letters painted on the white door. He stood waiting, suddenly aware and self-conscious of his bare feet and rough clothes.

The judge blocked a nostril with a finger and blew a slug of road dust into the gravel and looked back at Harlan. He said, "I'll admit you're a curious young man, Harlan Davis. Should I live long enough and you don't hie off for the western territories or such but remain in the area, I'll keep my eye upon you, to see what sort of man you become. One such as you, that can produce enough steam to send me off to gather you in at the bidding of a man I'd otherwise pay little attention to. And mark me well, it was not his feeble excuse but my own curiosity that sent me on my way. Perhaps, though, this ride into town, I'm beginning to understand a bit more."

Harlan said nothing.

The judge said, "I made you a compliment. Does that count for nothing to you?"

"I don't understand a word you're telling me."

"Ah. Of course not. This business, by damn, it is a thing, isn't it? Upon all of us. No. Wait. I've done my bit for this day. You, you walk down to the end of the long shed and you'll find the man asked me to bring you. Which I have done."

"Who is it? Do I have to? "

"Do you have to? Would you stand in contempt of my court?"

"I might. Who is it?"

The judge looked off at the sky and reached to his trouser pocket and pulled forth a silver flask the size of his hand and thin as a deck of cards, pulled the cork, and tipped it up to swallow once, and once again. He replaced the cork and then the flask in his trousers, looked at the boy and said, "There's no reason to lock you up. Yet. And you don't want there to be one. Just walk down and talk to the man. I'd say there's an even chance you're a match for him."

"Hold there, Harlan Davis."

Harlan stood, blinking. In the depths of the shed Enoch Stone sat in his sleek buggy, the horse a blood bay. Sunlight on the afternoon's angle striking the polished brass of the harness fittings.

Stone said, "Climb up. I'd have a word with you." He lifted his broad-brimmed hat from where it rested upon the seat next to him and held it in one hand over his lap, keeping his head bare and face open to the day while using his other hand to indicate the space free on the upholstered seat, quilted by buttons in a pattern of diamonds. He said, "Come now. I won't take a minute or two. I know you've been talking with the judge and would know what passed between the two of you."

Harlan said, "It weren't much. I need to get on back, there's work waiting."

"Perfect. I'll drive you to Swartout's and we can talk along the way."

"No, sir. I'll walk myself."

Stone placed his hat on his head and stepped down from his buggy before Harlan. He gripped the boy by the elbow with one hand and ruffled his hair with the other and said, "All right then. I'll walk along with you a bit and we can talk and then you can find your own way home. I was thinking to assist you but if you don't want my help, so be it. But talk we will."

Harlan twisted to free himself and could not. He said, "I got nothing to say to you. Nothing you want to hear. Let me go."

Stone tightened his grip and stepped off into the shade, deeper onto the lawn away from the street and Harlan had no choice but to go with him. Stone set a good pace and it came to Harlan that the judge might well be watching and so, determined to grasp a measure of control of the situation, he stepped along brightly and said, "You think you know something about me. You don't know nothing at all."

Stone was striding hard and made no response. They came to a bench placed upon a small rise of the courthouse lawn, flanked by a pair of young oaks, and behind the bench was a small copse of tall cabbage roses all abloom in white and red, some few with pink centers and with the effect of a shaded hidden place—perhaps an accident, perhaps placed there by civic women of the town who considered there might be a need for such a spot of solace and privacy for the families encumbered or daunted by the proceedings of the court. And Stone pressured Harlan's arm and so side by side they settled into the bower of shade, making a tensely odd company.

Harlan did not wait but spilled out. "All of you have got it wrong. Backward. You are blaming the wrong person."

"We are blaming no one. Simply making clear a truth and saving the life of a decent man, a war hero, a trusting soul, who cannot be blamed for not wishing the truth of his wife's duplicity to be known. But, Harlan Davis, all knew of her actions long before this recent unfortunate incident occurred. You must know that comprehension was widespread and so also there's a great and earned sympathy for Malcolm Hopeton. You're a loyal young man and it's understandable you are swayed by Hopeton's distress over learning the truth. He would deny it? Why, what man would not? Truth is, as we proceed these next few days there's every intention of letting it be known publicly of Hopeton's objections. He's a good man, Harlan. Who loved his wife. And it will not serve him well should his objections be buried—why, then there would be those wags who'd claim he'd not killed her by accident, as he surely did, but murdered her in a jealous rage, as he very well could've if he was other than who he is, but is now claiming otherwise, to secure the clemency being offered, the mercy he surely deserves. Do you not see that?"

"I see you talk a fine streak. But you are aiming at the wrong target. Which you must know if you've talked with Mr. Hopeton."

"You're speaking of Amos Wheeler."

"I am. And, begging your pardon, but you should be too. Not Bethany Hopeton."

"Ah, boy, I know you were there those past four years and saw and heard the Lord knows all manner of things. How well you understood what you were seeing is not to be debated. But Amos Wheeler—why, if the whole wide world does not know what scoundrels he and his family were, then certainly the whole county does. First-hand, many people. No—there is no surprise in Amos Wheeler. Do you comprehend that?"

"Missus Hopeton was terrified of him. For good reason. That's what I know."

"Which explains why she went gallivanting about the state with him? Why she helped strip bare the fortune of Mr. Hopeton's farm once he was off with his life in jeopardy every day in this terrible bloody conflict? Why she donned finery and flaunted it about the town? There are a great many who can and have spoken of her as being full of life those years. And you'd have me believe this was all Wheeler's doing? Has it occurred to you she was merely making a show before you to conceal her true nature?"

Stone had released his grip upon Harlan and the boy used the moment to move down the bench, turning as he did to not only face Stone but make it harder for the man to grab him again. Harlan's face was hot with anger and also the blush of fear and self-hatred, but he drew a breath and spoke.

"All what you're saying makes sense and it's all wrong. You did not see what I did and you don't want to hear it. It strikes me as mighty strange neither you or the judge want to hear me. All what I have to say takes the blame from where you're trying to lay it and set it where it squarely and truly belongs."

Stone studied him a moment, a dark clutch of anger passed over his face, then it cleared and he crossed a leg over a knee and leaned back. "Tell me, then, Harlan Davis."

And Harlan was struck dumb a moment, the memory swarm of Amos upon him in a jumbled cascade but the urgency of the opportunity also swelled and he would not lose this chance and so tumbled words.

"It's so much, so much over those years—you understand that? It's a pile of a mess and hard to sort. But throughout I never doubted it was Amos because once word come Mr. Hopeton had been wounded, everything changed and it was all Amos after that. Before it was mostly life as it had been but without Mr. Hopeton: We worked the farm and things was normal enough even though I could tell Amos didn't like my being there, but he hadn't any argument against me. I was sleeping in the old bedroom that had long ago been Mr. Hopeton's grandfather's room—where Mr. Hopeton put me when he hired me—and that room hadn't been changed so much all those years, but it suited me. What I'm trying to say is things much of that first year ran the way they should've and although

I knew Amos didn't care for me, Missus Hopeton was kind and saw I was well fed and kept up the house as if her husband would walk back in any moment. Which was what we all thought that first year. When word come Mister Hopeton had been wounded, we thought he'd be home soon and so kept right at it. But it wasn't so long after that when things changed. She got a letter from him; it was me brought it back when I drove the butter and cream cans in one morning. There came a strange time after that when Amos wasn't around at all, off in his cabin in the woods, we both, Missus Hopeton and me, both knew that's where he was but we didn't speak of it. I just held to my chores and she helped best she could: She was more handy than most might think. Then Amos came back.

"It was a late February day and I recall it well since he walked in and slammed the door while she and me were sitting to dinner and he sent me to the barns and I asked him what for. Since there wasn't nothing needed doing just then but to hitch the sledge and go to the woodlot, which I couldn't do alone; and he pulled me up by the hair and told me things had changed and I best pay attention and then booted me toward the door. Well sir, I went fast enough but was angry over it all and set in the barn tinkering with this and that, passing time until it was time to milk, which I done and then finished up and walked back up to the house in the dark, the windows lit up in the kitchen and walked in and seen em. Missus Hopeton setting by the stove all pinched down and Wheeler leaning over her with one hand laid up against her cheek, his face down almost against hers, and when I walked in he reared up and I seen how her cheek was red and also wet. Then she stood and left the room and Wheeler stood looking at me and then he left too. Followed her and I stood there listening to her steps and then his going up the stairs and a door slamming shut and a moment after that the sound of a boot crashing against a door. I set down my milk and went back to the barn and slept in the hay that night, which was the first time but not the last.

"It went on from there. I can't tell you all. One time I walked in and seen him holding her with both hands one around her neck and the other twisted in her hair and she was lifted right up against the wall, her feet kicking and he was spewing vile words at her. But when he heard me he turned and dropped her and she ran off upstairs coughing and he came to me and folded his arms over his chest and asked me was I ready to get the hay in. Other times, most other times it wasn't so harsh unless you was there—you know what I'm saying—it could look like one thing but I known it was another, her voice pitched up a bit high even as she was nodding and even chiming in as Amos told me what to do while they were going off to talk to a man about the wheat . . . but even the way he said that I knew he weren't about any such thing but something else. Or when he'd have his family members come to help with something, getting in the corn or making hay or even just slaughtering the fall beeves how he'd send me off on some other job that often as not did not make sense for the time, but I couldn't tell him so: He had it timed so it was all just close enough. You know what I mean? How a fellow can do that?

"It's what I'm trying to tell you. I seen her one time with a eye bruised the color of rotted meat. She told me she'd walked into a door the middle of the night. Maybe she did. Another time they'd been gone a few days and come back and she was all alone and so after I did my best to get everything right I walked out to the woods where Wheeler had a cabin made years ago and I called out just to see if he was there and he come out of there in his trousers and beat me so bad I couldn't breathe a couple of weeks without my side hurting and he never said a word the whole time. Or any word at all the day later when he come back to the farm and settled in, except the time he asked if I'd got the butter down to Dresden and laughed at me when I was only able to nod since it hurt too much to talk. And Amos Wheeler grinning at me. He knew I knew. You understand that? He knew."

Enoch Stone waited, let his silence dribble out until it hung between them. Waited until Harlan felt the pause flow over himself and doubted not what he'd said but how he'd said it, doubted his words made any sense to anyone save himself.

Finally Stone uncrossed his legs and leaned forward and quietly, almost kindly, said, "It distresses me of course to hear how Amos Wheeler would brutalize a woman. Even in such a situation as the both of them clearly were in. But, Harlan, lad, you must consider two things: the first being why Malcolm Hopeton would've hired such a man in the first place. And the second, the most difficult one, is irregardless of Wheeler's behavior, of what you saw of it, there exists a history of Bethany Hopeton prior to her marriage that most strongly suggests she, also, was not the person Malcolm believed her to be. And while it's a terrible thing for a hired man to abuse his master in the countless ways Wheeler undoubtedly did, it's by far a greater transgression for a wife to befoul her husband in the varied and wide array that Bethany undertook. As your account not only suggests but corroborates what is known of her character. By those who know better than any others. It does pain me to tell you of these things: You're a trusting, loyal young man and I'd not want that larger trust in humanity to be ruined by these experiences of yours these past years. But you must understand, Harlan, whatever Wheeler's wrongs, and they were many and fully evil—though his history suggests he had no education of the meaning of evil beyond petty and momentary gain— Bethany Hopeton was raised in the grace of the Lord and so turned away from that with a comprehension fully otherwise than Wheeler's limited and rank notions of life. And so she stood above him, all ways. But she did not rise but yielded. Not only willingly but willfully. As she had all of her life and as her father will attest. For no man can know a woman better."

Harlan said, "Mr. Hopeton has said otherwise and my own eyes told me he was right even before he was back to say it to me. I think you chase words around like horses on a track, wanting to see your horse win. But you ain't following the right horse. I keep trying to tell you that."

Stone said, "You insult me from your own passion and I forgive you that."

Harlan said, "I don't want your forgiveness. I want you to see the truth."

"I see it most clearly. I saw it two weeks ago when I first came and talked to you and asked you questions. And I asked a certain question and you fled. So I ask again: Did Bethany Hopeton not come to you? Naked in the night? Rose-pink from her bath? Did she not prevail upon you, Harlan Davis? You've already answered that question by fleeing once. How will you answer it again?"

Harlan sat stunned a moment and then was rising from the bench and turned upon Stone, for those short moments towering over the man, his face a red heat, the same heat poisoning his body to where he felt he was ripping and jumping as he said, "You don't know a thing, you don't understand at all. Not a bit of it."

Stone smiled and said, "I don't? Do tell. And will you tell the same to the judge?"

But Harlan was off and running.

Stone called after him. "I'll find you as I need to."

He didn't look back until he'd run a block from the courthouse, then glanced around as he was coming upon the merchant blocks, saw nothing of Stone but did catch the curious glances of passersby and so cut down an alley and slowed to a walk, near an amble, with his hands in his pockets, his chest thumping with a wild heart and his mind awhirl. Of course, he thought, he ain't chasing after me, he's gone upstairs to report all I said to the judge. Or maybe not even that, maybe he's just riding on home and will ponder what I said and what course of action he should take. He knows where to find me.

It was those last words kept rolling around his mind as he exited the alley and crossed before the opera house, again among the afternoon throng. He stopped to watch three heavy wagons loaded with shocked wheat making their way down to the mills—either farmers without their own threshing machines or those simply using the expedient of selling direct to the Burkett brothers, pennies less the bushel but less work on the farm. Market wheat. He stood then, smelling within the effluvia of town the bright sharp smack of fresh-cut grain, the smell mostly rising from the wheat straws all redolent of what he should be doing. Cutting oats. And it was then it came to him that he could not go back to August Swartout's. He had no notion of how he might help Malcolm Hopeton now, following all he'd been told this afternoon. But did know if any such a thing was possible he needed to be hidden and alone, to ponder, consider and, for the moment as important, not be found by anyone intent upon his not undertaking further action on that course.

His destination became clear. The only place he might go. He had a terrible thirst and recalled the trough built of soapstone slabs that stood before Burketts' to refresh the teams and so went along his way, catching up to the last of the loaded wagons rolling down to the cavernous doors where the teams entered and the loads were swept clear. He paused and worked the pump handle and then knelt as the water sluiced forth and turned his head to gulp down water. When he stood the front of his shirt was wet but he felt clear and of purpose and so walked through the town. His day, this day, once again seemed a new one, freshly started.

He was used to open horizons of stretching fields and folds of the land and wide skies but even here in the cluttered closeness of several-storied buildings he felt the freshened air, a breeze coming off the lake and his eye went up to spot the few high scudding clouds. And thought It ain't going to rain, it's only a spat of cooler air rolling down from the north, keep things fresh and dry for days to come, good to

258

make oats. But he turned east not west and felt lighter with the clari-
fied air and his own mind, striding along, the boardwalks less crowded,
his feet purposeful and rolling easily toward the street that turned
gently uphill as it became the Milo road. The thought came that the
judge might've had him followed—a foolish idea, the judge could not
care one whit if Harlan hurried around the courthouse to seek out
the basement cell or merely hightailed it back to Swartout's and his
work. He could see up the leafy avenue that led toward the table of
land stretching out into Milo, toward Hopeton's farm. Dogs lay in the
shade, the houses quiet, a few children playing listless late afternoon
games, overdressed town ladies taking the air on their porches. The
slow flutter of fans. The day gone gold, greens bright in the light or
darker in the shade. Wedges and bars of shade; golden light crosswise
upon the yards and houses.

And he paused then and let his mind drift off a bit, as if overhead,
riding the thermals of a hawk, or better, the air as a crow flies. And
saw then his route, not along the road, but among the fields and farm
lanes, the wooded ravines and gulleys that stitched together the land
as a rumpled quilt, and continued walking until he came to the next
to the last home on the rise of land, where as he passed he glanced
about and seeing no one, turned as he came upon the carriage barn
of that home and slipped quickly down the shadowed north side of
the barn and beyond, past the vegetable garden and then was among
trees and dense shade, moving downhill quickly over rough ground,
into the ravine where a stream cut down toward the eastern head of
the Crooked Lake, a ravine he'd cross and then work uphill and
onward crosslots toward Malcolm Hopeton's farm, his own home
these last years.

He came out of the woods and onto the road that opened up both
sides to the rich broad land of Milo, the skies wide and high as if falling off the earth and both sides now he saw men at work in their

fields, the clap of reaper paddles and the cries of hawks overhead. He turned forward again and found he was barely a mile from the farm, his feet tossing up a flimsy trail of dust. Where the land fell away to the west he saw the rise of the Fultons' barn and doglegged down a farm lane, now walking full into the afternoon sun but hidden between a corn field and a grown-over pasture thick with wild blackberries and burdock, thinking Benny Fulton lacks the backbone to make that lazy Calvin get out here and dig up the thistles. He turned when he came to the overflow ditch from Fulton's farm pond and followed it up and then cut around the pond, behind Fulton's barn, all the while unseen and certain of it, not sure what his detour had gained him but for the sense of stealth coming in.

He crossed the road again not a quarter mile from where he'd left it and paused, peering down the road; but it was broad and empty, fading into dust mirages of the distance. He crossed and was once again on the land he'd tended and left not a month before, entering into a hay field that was thick with high hay gone to seed and new undergrowth pushing up between the tough stalks and felt the quiver of anger over a job not done. He gazed across at the corn he and Hopeton had got into the ground, the young leaves paled with coffee-colored dust, the rows between grown up with dock and lamb's quarter, loosestrife and—brought a grim smile—young burdock. As he came up the field behind the house and barn he slowed and lowered himself to the ground and crawled along the row, the sharp rasping corn leaves scraping his face and bare arms, and he kept his head down, smelling the soil. Then he was a dozen feet from the end of the row and so sank down flat and waited and listened. He heard nothing but for a single crow over the field who'd spotted him and sawed back and forth harking alarm and bringing Harlan to a fury of rage until he recalled he'd seen crows do all sorts of such things and never paid a mind to it, even on any of his worst days. So he hugged against the hot earth and waited as the sun dropped more and lit the rows at a low soft angle and only then wormed forward until he could look out upon the buildings, his head lifted on his elbows yet still a yard or so back in the corn.

He knew at once the place was empty and was struck by how shabby the house appeared, as if it hadn't been painted in years, and realized it might've been bright all those years before when Malcolm Hopeton first brought him there but nothing had been touched in the time since. The barn reared high and strong but it was the smaller things he noted, the weeds growing up on the rear bank-entry to the barn's haylofts, the thicket of high grass about the back entry of the house, all of which had always been scythed down at least twice a summer; also the window lights of the house, dull and smeared and empty of life within, the blank squares where a pane had broken or been knocked out by a stone—Harlan thinking of Calvin Fulton and guessing he'd slipped up a time or two at dusk to fling a rock, half-hoping some form of Bloody Hopeton would issue from the house and terrified such might occur. Racing homeward in the thinning light or pale wash of moonrise without looking behind for the thrill of what he might see pursuing him down the road.

An hour later while there was still light enough to see he was inside the horse barn, the mule pens with their mounds of old manure like so many apples heaped in a fallen pyramid, sprouting pale white slender mushrooms already tipping over to show their dark gills, the ink-blot stains along the stems. Fresh and old cobwebs strewn between every post and rafter, some few flies droning their death songs where they were caught, the big summer spiders hunched in corners waiting, in no hurry to race and wrap the flies. Above the pens toward the north end of the barn the big trapdoor was open into the loft, where stale dribbles of flung-down hay were likewise caught in the webs, old hay, old webs. And he thought I can't stay here.

★   ★   ★

Another hour on he crouched in the woods among whirring, stinging skeeters, the pale orange dusk behind the canopy of big trees, the open sky dark blue where a swollen moon sifted behind the horizon clouds. Not yet dark, the slow pulse of summer dusk turning toward night. Fireflies danced their best to lead him astray, darting beacons here and then gone and spotted again. As he approached the woods an owl burst from a field-side tree and batted off along the woods-line, fluttering his heart before he turned and watched the thick body moments before it plunged into the mass of trees.

The shack was a low smudge within the big trees; if he hadn't known it was there he'd have thought it nothing more than a heap of land.

Harlan started when a mourning dove fluttered up from the brush beside him, trilling soft notes against the glooming night. Seeking only a higher branch. He waited where he was, watching, listening. He had the distinct sense of not being alone, wondering if he was merely spooked by the memory of Wheeler, thinking then of ghosts and surely if there was a ghost of Amos Wheeler, this is where it would be. Harlan did not believe in ghosts, or at least never had.

There came a sharp flare of light reflected through the window and then that was gone, shortly replaced by the lower muted glow of a fire catching within and the sweet roil of wood smoke lofting from the stick-and-daub chimney. He settled back against the earth. The thick acoustical night air carried the snap and crackle as the kindling caught, the crunch as larger sticks were added to the fire. Sticks, not logs, and the smoke cleared and rose thin straight up through the leaf-works of the chestnut trees. He saw no match flare but of a sudden the window and he could see the open door as there bloomed the wick turned high of a coal-oil lantern, then muted by degrees to a warm soft light, turned low as it would allow and yet make a steady flame. The form of a woman moved past the window.

He stood slowly and leaned to brush the twigs and woods-trash from his trousers, then stepped easy toward the door. Half a dozen paces from it and outside the cone of light thrown from within, he stopped. He smelled coffee and in an offhand voice he said, "Alice Ann Labidee. It's Harlan Davis standing outside here."

She stepped out into the light from the fire, facing him. In her left hand, down at her side but close to the light so he could see it, was a five-shot Colt's revolver. He'd seen that gun before. "Hello there, Harlan," she said. "First you scared a owl, then you snagged your pants back in the brush and last spooked a night bird right outside. If I hadn't guessed who it was I'd have blown a hole through you."

"What're you doing here?"

"What are you doing here," she echoed. Then she said, "I guess same as you. After you come to see me at the hotel I wondered who else might come looking for me. I know for a solid fact there wasn't many knew about this place Amos had made for himself. So I come here."

"Malcolm Hopeton surely knows it's here."

"Did he send you to try and find me? I told you, there's nothing I can do to help him. And if he's after me so bad why send you and not his lawyer or even the sheriff?"

"I never said he sent me. Or anyone at all. Truth is, I was figuring the place would be empty."

"So you're on the run."

He said nothing.

"You don't have to tell me anything," she said. "Long as there's no one after you. But then, if you're on the run there likely is someone after you. That's how it works."

"It ain't like that," he said. "There's a lawyer I'd as soon avoid. Though he just doesn't want to hear what I keep telling him. But see, he's got no way of knowing of this place and the only person could tell him about it, who might guess this is where I lit out to, is Malcolm

Hopeton himself and even if he was asked, he wouldn't tell that man."
Harlan had broke a sweat. Dark as it was, the air was still and hot yet.

"What is it about men? They ain't never in charge of what they
think they should be, but keep right on believing they are," Alice Ann
asked. Then said, "You might as well come on in, Harlan. Don't you
think? You're not going anywhere else tonight and neither am I."

She raised the gun with a smooth practiced gesture and had him
clear in the sights best he could tell, then dropped it and turned and
walked back into the shack but left the door ajar. A flicker of moths
beat about the opening, milk-white wings in dense flutter to stay aloft,
battering to and fro.

Harlan stood watching the open door and the spill of light into the
growing dark. There was nowhere else to go, nowhere he could
imagine the end of this long day. And was also led on by a curious tug
within, down low in his belly. A child of the Lord, he knew there were
no accidents and so wondered what had brought both of them here,
now. And knew it was upon him to learn this. And upon all of that, he
was staggered by his day, tired and hungry. And truth be told, now that
he was here, not unhappy to find her.

He thought, She's just a soul ill-used and not so different from me.
He followed her into the cabin and stopped. It was not the rough
place he'd thought from his glimpses of the outside. The table was of
well-joined planks, and along one wall a bed was built into place with
a thick mattress and blankets and pillows heaped at one end. The
opposite wall from the bed had neat shelves with crockery and tins
and jars of various sizes, a pie safe built into one shelf. Above the
mantle stone were pegs to dry wet garments or hang hats upon,
perhaps a spot for a rifle as well—though those pegs were empty. The
hearth was of wide stones set well before the fire and the fireplace
itself was larger than he'd expected.

Rugs covered most of the packed earthen floor and comfortable
wooden armchairs were on the fireplace side of the table. He'd seen

those before, also. And beside the coal-oil lantern there sat a pair of silver candlesticks with half-burned stubs, now cold. Alongside them on the table stood a rank of stoppered bottles of beer, two empty.

Alice Ann Labidee waited between the table and the hearth, back-lit, glowing, her face in shadow. A wrapper and other garments were piled over the back of one of the chairs and she wore only a simple tight-fitting long-sleeved white blouse and a billowing indigo skirt he recognized from magazines as a habit for riding horseback. The Colt's five rested against her hip as she watched him. He couldn't see her eyes.

He said, "Where's the horse?"

"Where there ain't none going to find him except me."

"How long you been here?"

"Most of ten years. Off and on a bit, you understand."

Without a thought he said, "Ten years? How old are you?"

"Harlan," she said. "Didn't anyone ever tell you not to ask a lady's age?"

"I'm sorry. It's just when you said ten years—"

"I said it for a reason. I'm twenty-three years old."

"So you was thirteen when Amos first brought you here?"

"It was March. I turned thirteen in May. The fourteenth, for what it's worth."

"That's pretty young."

She was quiet a pause but did not look away from him. Finally she said, "Yes. Young. And whatever happened then, it wasn't nothing like I expected. At all."

She turned and leaned to the hearth, her hips up in a fast jaunt as she reached for the handle of the coffeepot and sucked breath and reached upward for a rag to take up the hot handle of the pot and came back up and around and set the pot on the table, the rag wrapped around the handle as she took her burned hand to her mouth and sucked against the pain for a moment. Then she shook her hand and her head both and said, "You hungry? Coffee?" She cleared her outer garments from a chair back and eased into it.

"No," he lied.

"Come and set," she said. "You might as well be comfortable as you can, listening." From her seat she twisted and took up the coffee and poured a tin cup, and another. She moved the second one down the table before the other chair and then crossed a foot over a knee and unlaced the high riding boot and pulled it off with a struggle, then did the other. She looked up as he settled into the waiting chair.

She said, "I knew Amos Wheeler better than anyone. He was vicious as a man could be, although he never was to me, at least until the end and then I knew I weren't any different than any other soul to him, though I long believed it.

"You see, I was the least of five and the night the house burnt I was the only one still trying to live under that roof; the rest had fled out into the gutters and alleys of Utica—" she paused and asked, "You know Utica?"

"I heard more than I care to about that place—it was a favorite of Wheeler's. Horse races and the like?"

She inhaled a snort of ill mirth and said, "Some sleigh races in hard winter and plenty of horse races in the summer but not in March, not when Amos first found me. All right then. Let me tell you: My ma and pa kept a shop making cheap tinware; times she did as much of the work as him or more, since he liked to nip right along, though she wouldn't turn it down oncen't it was noon or round there. They got the lead sickness afore I even come along, although they'd set of a evening and fulminate about the lies set to put a honest body out a work. You get the idea?"

Harlan nodded, listening to what could've been tales from the South Seas, so strange the world he was hearing of and yet knew enough to simply be quiet.

"That night weren't so different than most cept for how it ended. He had me set up to hawk papers morning and night at the station and in between them hours I was going to school much as I could, though I had to skim pennies from the newspaper fellers to pay for my books and all. But it was a better way to spend the days than most. Also, after I done the evening papers, I had a job at one of the taverns on Bleucher Street, a foul place there ever was one but happy to have a young girl like me carrying pitchers of beer to the tables and swatting away the gropes of hands. That, you understand, was a good part of why I was hired and the German who run that place thought it was funny how I kept em all at bay. But my papa had been kicked outta every joint on Bleucher, so it was a way for me to make a little money and also not go home so quick each night. When I was a little girl and some of my brothers and sisters were still there it weren't so bad, but by that time it was just two old sots going at it with each other, outta their heads and me just a quick place to swat or kick. How it was.

"So there come a cold March night and I'd just got to sleep and they were going at it the next room. I'd got so I could sleep through most anything, even screams and cries of murder. Anyways I was full asleep when I woke to fire burning through the wall: One of em either kicked over a lantern or fell someway. I was up quick as quick but when I opened the door it wasn't anything but roaring, like looking into a stove with a open flue. I mighta heard somebody screaming or it mighta been me but I turned back and picked up a big pitcher that didn't have any water or basin to go with it either and heaved it through the window. That was a part a town where fires were common and us kids talked amongst ourselves about what to do, usually standing in the wet cinders of a house where some other kids we all known had perished. I went out that window and slipped on the shingles and landed face first on the shed roof and rolled off that and down another drop to the street. Which, being March, was a trough of mud, so I landed rough but not dead. I turned around and looked and the house was like a big pine knot burning, one big flame twisting up into the night. Some people was rushing around but I was back in the shadow of the shed and the house alongside and no one seen me. It was raining a cold rain and there weren't the first sound of bells; there weren't no engines rushing down to that fire. They never did bother with Bleucher, easier to let it burn itself out, knowing one sorry soul or another would throw up some cheap house soon as the embers cooled.

"The only reason I was up on Water Street the next morning was to try and cadge some pennies from the feller who I bought my news sheets from. He was worked up I'd missed the dawn trains, but when he seen me with my singed nightdress and the wallop I'd took to my eye going off the shed, he took pity and give me a nickel, then told me I was all done I failed to get the evening sheets and kicked my butt to get me away from him. So I had a nickel and was thinking about a loaf of sweet bread and coffee, treading along through the mire of Water Street, when yet one more horse sloshed by, spattering me with mud—but that horse turned and come to a stop before me. I thought to walk around it but the man atop it reached down with his crop and prodded me in the chest and said, "You got a world of trouble heaped down upon you, don't you little sister?" And I looked up and there sat the most handsome man the whole world could produce. Like I said, I weren't but twelve years old but I knew what I was seeing. Setting easy on that frothing horse and not taking his eyes from me, a sharp little hat tucked down on his brow and that devil-may-care hair slicked down the back of his neck. He was smiling as if the day was brand new and he owned it. And he reached down a hand and asked me if I didn't want to get up and ride with him. I didn't think twice because I knew I did. And so he brought me here. Time we finally lit I'd a shot anyone I thought posed the least threat to him."

She paused then and took a sip of coffee. It had grown cold on her and she rose and tossed the dregs out the door and prized the stopper out of a bottle of beer and paused, looked at Harlan and said, "You want a bottle of beer, Harlan?"

"No thank you."

"You never tried it, have you?"

"I tried it once."

"Uh-huh. Some things take getting used to, then you learn to like em, time to time." She took a drink of her bottle, then lifted another and pulled the stopper from that also. Set it on the table before Harlan and took her seat again.

"Amos Wheeler treated me like I'd never even imagined—like I was a treasure, like I was a fine lady. After Utica this was grand, and it was all mine—least it felt that way. And we wasn't here all the time, either. Not just going back to his home place in the Outlet Gorge, which was pleasant enough also; his mother thought the sun rose and set on him, same as me, and we hit if off good enough. I believe she liked having another woman about, her surrounded by all those men. And Amos and me had our little side trips also: We'd take the steamer to Watkins and spend the day on a frolic, or Geneva to do the same. Once he took me all the way to Elmira to see a circus and there was a actual live elephant there and for a nickel you could buy toffee and let the elephant eat it out a your hand. That long trunk swinging down gentle as you please and lifting it out of your palm, then curling backward to pop it into its mouth. That delighted me and Amos paid a dollar to let me do it as many times as I wanted. And he taught me about horses—oh, Amos was a fool for a good horse. That black I got tied down in the woods was one he gave me not two years ago. 'A horse'll get you through times you got no money,' he'd say, 'better than all the money in the world, will help when you need a good horse and quick.' I thought I knew what he was saying but I studied on it lately and wondered was he warning me about what was to come? I'll never know now. Amos talked outta both sides of his mouth, I say he was expert at it cept it was nothing studied or practiced with him, it just come natural. One time I was down at the Wheeler camp setting and waiting, some winter night, now this was years ago, even before Hopeton went and married that fool. Anyways, I was down there setting with Missus Wheeler while the boys was off somewheres on one of their schemes and she and I got to working on cups of coffee mixed with red whiskey and I said what a sweet-tongued man Amos was and she laughed and said even as a swaddling babe he'd cry for titty one side of his mouth and chortle the other, since he was getting what he wanted. Yes sir, there was that part a Amos and I never once doubted it. When he come upon me I was ready for him and he knew it, too. And it took him ten years to figure out how to show me how wrong I was. And that right there is the key to Amos Wheeler."

The fire had fallen to coals and the remnant ends of sticks and the lantern light wavered brighter against the dark, shadows more dense but liquid, flowing as the wick guttered and gained. Her bare feet on the hearthstones were flushed pink. An oily slow flow of air pressed for entry through the open door, sucked by the hearth rise.

Her eyes upon the small hot mound, she said, "Drink your beer, Harlan."

He was slung low in his chair, stuporous, weighty and numbed. "I never cared for it," he said.

"You might want it. I got more to tell."

"You told me what I already know. Amos Wheeler suckered you and stung you bad like he did every other soul he came across."

"You don't know as much as you think." She paused, sipped and eyed him across the top of her bottle. "Say," she said. "Why does a lawyer not wanting to hear what you have to say, make you hide out from him? Seems like it should be the other way around."

Harlan looked away toward the fire, which was settling low. He got up and crossed over to hunker and add some sticks. His back to her, he said, "It ain't his not wanting to hear what I have to say, makes me want to avoid him. He got other things wrong too."

He pushed up and took his seat again. This time he lifted the beer and took a swallow. It surprised him, the dense taste of grains, of yeast. He swallowed again and then set the bottle back on the table. He'd seen Amos Wheeler with too much beer in him and didn't want to get that way himself.

"What things has he got wrong?" she asked.

Harlan studied the fire, now leaping and cracking in its swift burn of the sticks. Without looking he reached back and took up the bottle of beer and drank once more. He turned to where her face was again delineated by the firelight and said, "Most everything about Bethany Hopeton." He looked away, drank some of the beer, and said, "I don't care to talk about it." He looked back and said, "So Amos was telling you his plans, all along?"

She nodded. "A course he was. Telling me once he'd wiped Hopeton out best he could he was going to cast off that bitch and come for me and we was going to head out on a new life together. He'd laugh about it, saying how he'd leave her nothing but ruined for her husband, and him lost everything but her. If he ever did return—and Amos doubted he would. I weren't so sure but kept my mouth shut."

"So you didn't trust Amos either."

"Do I strike you as a fool? Then the war ended and word come that Malcolm Hopeton was on his way home. And Amos and that bitch run. I was some stung, I can tell you."

"I can't say how you strike me."

"Can't or won't?"

"That don't matter, does it?'

She was quiet then a time. She reached and finished the beer and pondered on. The fire was a cooling heap of small spits of red and black, the lantern throwing a wider circle of light, night air now wafting in through the open door and a small cyclone of moths and night insects swirling about the chimney of the lamp.

Finally she spoke again. "There's more you don't know."

"How so?"

"That caught your ear, didn't it? See, Amos come down here often as he could all those years, even when he had Hopeton's wife

271

in a lather, but there was also times we both knew he couldn't get away and I'd drift on up to the barn and wait in the loft above the horse barn; he'd most always come even if I had to wait a hour or more into the evening. You know it: A man can always make a excuse to get out of the house to the barn for a spell. And he'd come to meet me there. Because even when he had her wrapped like a present he still wanted me. And most times found me waiting. I was good at waiting; it was that grand plan of his. Me only wrapped in a old blanket, my clothes piled in a heap atop the hay. Say, the night's cooling pleasant but you're looking mighty hot, Harlan. You ought to take a swallow of that beer."

He took up the bottle, studied it, and set it back on the table. He said, "I do believe you're crazy."

"Let me tell you a couple things, Harlan Davis. I was the one lured Amos and Bethany back here and got em killed, which was one more thing went a way I didn't intend. But also, one night in March a year ago, it was a warm night, raining, I was up in the hayloft waiting for Amos when the both of you come in and I seen what Amos done to you, what he made you do—"

Harlan erupted from his chair as a cry blew out of his mouth and he was caught, thickened motion trying to make for the door as she thrust out of her chair and tackled him down to the ground, he already undone and she, quickly expert, pummeling his shoulders and chest as she sat upon him, pressing him hard against the rugs over the dirt floor. His escape ruptured, his charge of agency against harming a woman, his drain of all this day and week and the years spreading back endless, brought him to a slow moaning roll beneath her, his eyes refusing to meet hers, that final cessation that left him helpless and defeated as the beaten dust of the rug rose and filled his nose and eyes and tears broke in small beads to track trails down his face. His eyes pressed tight to shut the world and then open again as his brain churned a bright red black and orange lace behind those lids.

A SLANT OF LIGHT

As Alice Ann Labidee leaned close and in urgent voice deep from her throat whispered, "It ain't good, Harlan. None of it's good. You come here to hide out and what did you find? Me. You interrupted my plans but that don't matter. Not for the moment. But you ain't going nowhere. Not just yet."

Then her hands came up and turned his jaw upright and she leaned close, her eyes wide, strands of hair brushing his face and her lips came against his.

Malcolm Hopeton stood that very moment in full darkness, his hands lightly placed on the crossbars of his cell. He looked out, however, not upon darkness but upon the curious darkness of an otherwise light day lodged in his mind.

Married only weeks and all but the shell corn dried on the stalks for winter feed had been harvested—that work to be done in the cool or cold of November. It was a bright day of clear skies and no wind so the weakening sun held soft warmth and the trees about still held patches of bright color, even those leaves turned brown or copper but still holding to their limbs—the oaks, the beeches—in that light seemed to glow. He'd declared a holiday over breakfast and suggested that while he finished his morning chores, she pack a noon dinner that they might carry out and eat beside the pond.

Those hours later lying on the frost-stung grass beside the pond where no air moved to break the dark surface of the water, reflecting the few high round clouds that drifted with a seeming purpose across the sky above, also the southward beating vees of geese, high at midday, none yet seeking fields for their nightly rest and he was lying back, sated all ways and wondering how it was that some of those geese came to earth each night while others remained aloft, as any given night he might wake and hear the faint cries as they beat on overhead in the dark. Did each flock operate by some schedule peculiar to themselves and so some might rest while others worked on to make

273

their time? He did not know: there was no one to ask and in his present mood he felt a great peace with the notion that the world contained mysteries uncountable and that it was good and right that it should be this way.

From where he lay he could just see her seated upon the same quilt that was under him, a strange skewed image almost behind his line of sight and covered over her shoulders with a second quilt. Their dinner basket out of sight but the faint smell of oat bread, the tang of pickled cabbage and the slabs of fried pork. The sweet rise from apples cooked with sugar not two days ago, larded with raisins, nutmeg, cinnamon. His belly rumbled and his mind turned to what he guessed to be many pleasures held suspended and waiting in the afternoon just come upon them.

"You've told me," she said, "of your grandfather. How you came to leave the rest of your family, to make new lives together, just the two of you."

"I have."

"But don't you ever miss them? Don't you sometimes wish it could've been different?"

He rolled over on his stomach to face her, to also cover his own nakedness, which of a sudden felt wrong for the direction of her query.

"Miss them? No. I have to say I don't. Maybe once I did but I've come to accept that they made a choice and it was not a choice I could live with. Sometimes, families are not what you'd like or think them to be."

Both quiet then a long pause. Other than his grandfather, she'd asked him little of his family and he considered this opening, aware of her distance not measurable by miles from her own parents and he waited.

"Your father," she said. "Was he a just man?"

He propped himself on his elbows and smiled.

"Until the fervor of William Miller overcame him, I'd say he was a just man."

"And when you were bad, got up to mischief, did he punish you?"

"Oh, but I was a good boy." And got the smile he'd hoped for even as he plumbed his mind to seek what she was after.

Then the smile was gone. "Delightful as I find you, no child is always good, at least as parents determine the meaning. Surely there's some incident you recall when you misbehaved and he punished you."

"Of course."

"There." And she braved another smile upon him. "And," she added, "knowing you even this short time, I'd hazard there was more than once you were caught out one way or another. So tell me: Surely, as a godly man, he did not spare the rod. Yes?"

He rose to crab upright and sat facing her, also cross-legged and reached both hands behind him to tug the quilt not over her shoulders as she had but around his lap. He looked off toward the pond, a pair of swallows there darting over the water after insects no man could see and watched them a time moving back and forth in sudden swift streaks.

Finally he looked back to her and reached a hand to brush a damp swath of curls from the center of her forehead and then ran a finger down her cheek to her chin, which he lifted and held a beat before he took his hand away and spoke.

"Once, I was but a boy of six or seven, I stole a cone of sugar from the mercantile at Poultney Market and ate it all as I walked home. I'd been sent to trade eggs for flour and stole the sugar when I thought no one could see me. The next day my father found me working my sums at the school and waited until I left my desk and joined him outside. He did not speak to me but walked off toward home and I followed him, no choice but to do so. And I'd not forgot the sugar, of course, and halfway home he stopped and did not speak but pulled the crumpled paper of the cone from his pocket and handed it to me. Then he resumed walking and, miserable as I could ever hope to be, I followed. When we arrived at the farm my mother was standing on

275

the porch watching until she saw both of us and then went into the house, closing the door. Oh! When I saw her I'd felt great hope she'd intervene and that closed door was a slap to my heart. Father looked down at me and shook his head and walked on to the woodshed attached to the house.

"He shut the door but I can still see him clearly as he sat upon the chopping block, then reached and stripped the belt from his trousers and folded it in half, passed it back and forth in his hands. He asked me if I understood why we were there. I was crying but I told him, 'Yes sir.' Then he looked away from me, still working the belt, until suddenly he stood and passed the belt back through his loops and told me to come along with him. I followed him out of the woodshed and then out of the yard and we walked on up the road toward the village. Halfway there he stopped and told me I was the issue of God's love between my mother and himself and he would not bruise me any way he could help, any way given to him to not do so.

"Of a sudden I realized we were making direct way to Harrington's Mercantile, where the day before I'd stolen the sugar. And I began to hang back, which was when he turned and squatted down and told me how it would be. That I was to go in with him and it was my job to sit alone with the storekeep and explain again why I was there and apologize for what I'd done and also to tell Mr. Harrington he was to determine what my punishment would be.

"I tell you, I froze solid as January. I couldn't imagine a worse thing. And Father was patient with me but only just. He explained it once more and when I still hung back he took me up in his arms and carried me inside. He set me down in a chair beside the block held a wheel of cheese and the bin of crackers and stepped to the counter and told Mr. Harrington I had something to tell him and that he'd be waiting outside and out he went. Left me there with the awfulness of what I'd done plumped down in my lap and nothing but the eyes of the storekeep upon me.

276

"I wouldn't talk. Couldn't talk. Most of an hour passed and Harrington kept up with his trade but time to time came to ask me was I ready to talk to him but I only shook my head. I was crying most all through this.

"Then Harrington had a slow spell again and came and knelt down by where I sat and told me it wasn't the sugar. He'd seen me swipe it. It was he'd always seen me as a boy he could trust and wanted to be able to do that again. That most all people do wrong things in their lives but it was the ones had the strength to admit to doing so that others would trust. There wasn't a perfect person ever born and never would be. That the whole business of life depended on each of us not only knowing that but being able to speak so about our own selves, when we did wrong. He told me he'd done such mischief himself when he was a boy and was still here today to say so. Then asked me again if I had anything I wanted to tell him.

"He was barely up and moving away when I choked out his name and he turned back and I broke out crying and talking all at once and he knelt again and held my shoulders and let me blubber and talk until he saw it was enough and then he pulled me in close and told me it was all right. That I was a good boy and had done the right thing. He raised me up and shook my hand, said my father was waiting outside and did I want him to tell Father all was good and I looked up at that kind face and told him there wasn't a need. He clapped a hand to my shoulder and together we walked toward the door and then he told me, 'You do the right thing, however hard. Otherwise, it turns back upon you. Always.'

"I went out that door and down onto the street and caught up with Father and he took my hand and we walked on toward home."

And Malcolm saw that she was crying, silent but tears tracking down her cheeks, and he sat silent a moment and then leaned and held her. As she cried hard against him, freed from silence.

★   ★   ★

277

He'd forgotten this. Or perhaps he'd come to believe he'd lifted her, allowed her to lift herself—that together their life had informed her of another way. So much so that when she'd begged him not to leave her for the war he'd seen only any worried wife. And now wondered if she'd seen in Amos what he'd missed, even then, in those now long-ago days.

What the doctor had told him. He stood silent. A man filled with question.

For, after all, there was only one.

He was the vessel that held her. He'd failed her. How best to not do that again?

Other words: What to do? To do and be true? For was that not his job?

His last job. The work of life.

TWELVE

It was evening of the day following the judge's going to the farm to take Harlan away; two days remained until the hearing in the judge's chambers to determine Malcolm Hopeton's fate and unless Harlan reappeared before that time, August had every intention of being within those chambers with his own questions. Questions he understood might slow down if not derail the entire affair; but he was of a rare mind—the boy had been used in a way August couldn't clearly determine and if disturbing the proceedings was the only way to gain a clear answer, then disturb he would.

Marsh and his sons had gone home, leaving August to his evening chores, heat-stunned, grimed with chaff and field dust, muscle-weary right down to sore bones, moving slowly as he milked, settled the cattle back to pasture, fed the hogs, watered the draft team a second time just before retiring in the gathering dusk to the house and supper.

Late the previous afternoon he'd entered the barns to milk, tired and out of sorts, worried about the boy, angry he hadn't been stronger with the judge, though search his mind through he couldn't see what he might've said or done; and there, waiting inside the tie-up of the barn with her arms crossed over her breast, her face all grim determination, stood Becca Davis.

"Was that Harlan arrested and you kept on working?

"It's my understanding the judge only wanted to talk with him. I'd expect him back soon."

"And if he's not? What do you intend to do about it?"

"I think he'd find a way to send word, he needs to."

"You do, do you? That's it? Perhaps you should alert Brother Stone—"

He interrupted, "Becca Davis, have you forgot I've been cutting oats all day and have cattle and other livestock to attend to? Perhaps you also forget that Brother Stone, as you so grandly term him, greatly upset your brother the last time he was here? I told Harlan I'd look after him and I intend to do so. On my terms and by my best judgment. Now I suggest you see to your work and allow me to see to mine."

Heat rose in her face, her hazel eyes flared then hooded as the bow of her mouth clamped tight. Then each word sharp as if cut from tin by shears said, "That's right. I forgot I'm only the hired girl." And turned in a swirl of skirts and fled the barn, stumbling up the wide door sill worn smooth as soap from years of weather and cattle passing over. He stood blinking before her onslaught and felt a tender lurch within him match her own. Then she was off across the yard. Out of sight. He balled his fists into the small of his back and pressed himself into a stretching arch. Heard the half-door slap shut as she entered the kitchen and felt the slump of fatigue come even greater over him. He was close to believing what he'd told her but saw no other course forward. He went on to his waiting cows and hogs. The tired team and just-now useless mules.

Now, twenty-four hours later, he'd led the fractious bored mules out to the night pasture and stood within the canopies of apple trees, drops rolling under his boots, tired not only from the long day of work but also the conversation with Becca the night before that left him uncertain. He was standing in the still air drained of any taint of breeze and holding the heat as a caul down over him when he heard the faint footfalls of a failing beast and the asymmetric squeal and grind of an axle within greaseless hubs, the spokes rattling dry and with each turn of the wheels almost falling free before refitting themselves within the felloes. He walked out from under the apples into the taller grass and passed among his cattle spotted with flies to where he could see past the house and what was coming down the road, knowing someway it was bound for his driveway. And felt a surge of anger born of fatigue, thinking such an ill rig could only be a tinker or peddler disturbing honest folks late on a day of endless days. He strode toward the intrusion, stepping through the rails of the orchard fence, then realized it could be no peddler, their seasons invariably spring and fall when people were lean-pressed from the winter for new goods or laying in stores before the snows came.

At the same time Becca came out on the stoop and also stood peering toward the road and heard him, glanced and looked away, unsettled from the night but her curiosity high. So he crossed the yard and looked her way and nodded a greeting, knowing she was yet uncertain of her future. Then went on toward the road.

Where came a small cart with high canted wheels and an ancient pony between the shaves, clambering best he could along the road with his feet not only free of shoes but untrimmed, his hooves grown out and curling upward before him so he walked with a mincing hurtful pace, head lowered, ropes of green mucus billowing from his nose, his body lathered soapy about the straps of his dry-cracked harness, the bony escarpments of his ribcage either side of him heaving as driven by a frayed but determined bellows. His head was tilted sideways, one blinder missing from his bridle, so his near shoulder over and again rubbed against the end of the near shaft.

281

Perched on the high seat with the reins slackly clumped in one hand, the other holding a sun-shade parasol aloft, an old bonnet clamped about her ruined face and her skirts and blouse mudded with loops of sweat, road dust and darker blots of rust, rode Iris Schofield, eyes white and rolling as those of the pony.

August stepped forward as the turn was made off the road but neither pony nor woman seemed to register any presence but their own, as if they would drive onward until a fence or gorge or some other blockade halted them. As they passed he pressed swiftly forward and caught up the near rein and stopped the pony, which turned its head against him, rubbing his belly and August slid a hand down the beast's head and stroked its jowl in comfort as he looked up at the woman.

"Iris. What burden brings you out so late in the day?"

She tipped her head to clear the bonnet brim from her face. "Why, it's August Swartout, isn't it?"

"Surely it is. Did you intend another destination? Iris, is there trouble upon you?"

She made a clip downward with her chin that might have been a nod but only said, "I told Napoleon we'd go see August Swartout and he'd know what to do but I might only been thinking it. And here we are." This last spoken as in wonder of the miraculous.

He studied her face, the brightness of her voice belied by the bruised fatigue and dark cast of her features. In a careful even tone he said, "Surely you guided him, your hands upon the reins."

"Perhaps," she said. "No, I don't recall a bit of it. It's a terrible fatigue over me, these long days and nights."

"I can but imagine. And so hot. Wait—" he caught himself and turned.

Becca Davis hadn't left the stoop but otherwise stood watching. He called to her to bring water. She stood a long beat as if she hadn't heard him but just as he was about to raise his voice and repeat his call

282

she turned for the house. He heard the pump working, the chuffing of the handle and then the rush of water.

He turned back. "There now, water coming for your proud beast. Would you step down? We've been cutting oats but are about to set for supper. You'd be most welcome."

"Water Napoleon. There's nothing left in this world I want for myself, nothing at all. There's nothing left."

He heard the door slap behind him, bare feet hard upon the stoop. He said, "Iris, wait just a moment while I fetch the water for your pony."

"Can't your girl bring it? She looks spry."

"I've another task for her. Only a moment."

Without waiting he turned and walked quickly to the stoop and spoke to Becca. "Give me the bucket. Then go to the barn and get the Pete horse from his stall and harness him for the cart. You seen me do it a hundred times."

"What's this all about?"

"I don't know yet."

She let go of the bucket handle and he hoisted it. She said, "I'm most ways a fool." Then pushed past him toward the barn. He watched her go, the jerk of her head and hips in counterpoint that struck within him. He turned and went back to the waiting exhausted pony. He stepped up beside the cart and swirled the dipper and lifted it neatly to where Iris could easily lean and take it up.

She said, "I told you I want nothing. But reward Napoleon for his labors. A trusty beast who carried Bet back and to school all these years since."

August halfway turned and held the bucket and let the pony drink. He reached his free hand and rubbed between the ears and turned back to Iris and said, "Tell me, Iris. What brings you out on this hot day?"

She turned then to look off away at the ridge behind her, the sun huge and red within the trees there, the long shafts of light upward against the sky, high clouds red-lit and blue-bellied.

"Recall The Friend," he said. "We all stand shoulder to shoulder; your burden I lift gladly."

In the pause he could hear his horse led to the shed, Becca's low voice as she fitted him between the shaves, her audible suck as she worked to hook the tugs to the singletree.

Iris Schofield turned back and said, "David is dead by his own hand. I found him so this morning."

August stood silent. Later, as through a pale veil, he'd recall the first thought through his mind was, Why in the world did I have the girl hitch the horse? As if there were somewhere to go, aid to be found. Otherwise his mind a thickened clot: He'd never known a suicide, self-murder the worst of all possible acts against the gift of Christ; the brevity of the human span against the entirety of the eternal soul.

Iris, as if answering a question he'd asked, said, "Last evening Enoch Stone come and talked with him and David wouldn't take his supper after. He went out to the barn and spent most of the night. When he came in the house I don't know, but afore first light he eased from the bed and, curious for him, told me he was off to the woodlot. That was the last I saw of him until mid-morning I was hanging warsh and heard the shot like a snapped stick. I walked out there and found him. And here I am now. It seemed the only place to come."

This admission, drained of emotion, restored August to himself. He stepped forward and lifted both hands.

"Iris. Step down now and I'll attend to all the best I can, the Lord be my guide." He felt he was speaking nonsense but found no other words and none were needed as she rose and delivered herself over to him. She reached for his hands but he slipped them beneath and caught her under her arms and lifted and swung her free of the cart, settled her upon the ground. How insubstantial she was, a slip of an old woman, as if spirit had fled her body and left not much behind but the bare mechanism short of death itself. For a moment she came against him and he patted her back even as his mind formed forward.

He said, "Come. Let me settle you inside and then I'll fetch my girl." Turning as he spoke and slipping a hand to the crook of her elbow and she stepped off with him as by habit unbreakable. They crossed the yard to the stoop slowly, her feet in their high-buttoned shoes tentative, which she fought against, trying to hide this from him. As they went she spoke, her voice a bouncing vaulted thing, capricious and nigh beyond control.

"What shall you do with me then?"

"Get my girl to tend you, some tea, perhaps a bite of food. Whatever you wish."

"And you?"

"I have a larger duty. You understand?"

She twisted to peer up at him from her ancient bonnet and spoke with a bright rancor. "Don't you be going to Enoch Stone."

He had no idea what he was about to undertake but said, "I hadn't even considered doing so. Rest easy, Iris. Here we go with the steps now."

"You'll take care of Napoleon before you're off? Such a grand heart, he is. He was Bet's, you know. And sorely ignored these years: David wouldn't touch the creature but to fork him hay time to time. Oh my heart, so sore, so sore!"

They were within the kitchen and he settled her into the chair beside the fire, the room in twilight glow, the table arrayed with a cold supper. He poured water from a sweating pitcher and set it beside her and said, "I'll take care of all best can be done. The girl will be along in a moment."

Iris looked up at him, the ash shuttle of bonnet with the face far within. "Do I know her?"

"She's Phoebe Davis's orphan daughter. Worked for years at Malin's before I hired her on to keep house. She's a good girl." Not

285

mentioning Harlan and hoping Iris might not know that part of her daughter's life.

"I recall Phoebe. Hard luck and fate for her."

"Perhaps for us all," he offered, a sudden fool. Then said, "She'll be here directly."

And was out of the house quick as he could while holding his pace, wondering if her ears would even make note of such a thing.

He reached Becca and lifted a hand against her questions and gave a blunt account. Then said, "She'll want little or much. Do as you can."

"And you?"

"I'll do what has to be done."

She looked down, then up. The horse was sidestepping in the gig beside her, the light leaching upward, dark rising from the ground. She said, "It's late, and a long day already."

He nodded. "Longer before I'm done. Don't put her pony out with the others, but in one of the empty calf pens. I don't believe he has the habit of other creatures. If she sleeps, you do the same; don't wait up for me. I don't even know where I'm off to yet—it's a wretched business all the way around."

He walked around her, gathered the coiled reins, and stepped up into the gig. The horse jogged forward then stopped, awaiting his word. He said, "Becca."

"Yes?"

"Last night."

"There's nothing to speak of. I'm the one was amiss. I own a weakness is all. You'll never see it again, I swear to that."

"No," he said. "We'll talk again. Tend to the woman, I'll do my best for us all."

He started out and then stopped. Becca had called his name and ran after, alongside the gig. Again he looked down, this time held himself silent and waited.

"Are you going to Enoch Stone?"

"No." He paused. "He's not the right man for this job. Truth is, I'm not sure who is."

She gazed up at him, reached and stayed him with her hand upon his wrist, then said, "The one you need to see is that doctor. The one who helped Harlan. He'll know what needs doing and all the rest. Don't you think?"

August patted his shirt pocket and found it empty, a gesture beyond control, and so was at once both dismayed and relieved and so only said, "Might be, Becca Davis. Might be."

He snapped the lines and the horse forged ahead, flared around the apparition of the pony and cart, and was up on the road, turning into a green and blue twilight.

He halloed the dark house and the doctor's wife poked her head from a second-story window open to the night and called down to know the urgency and nature of the crisis. When August first entered the outskirts of the town a lean hound had followed him soundless, a floating liquid shape degrees darker than the starstruck dried churn of the streets, steady beside the off wheel of the gig. The horse had snorted, then accepted the dog as harmless, a traveler curious of them, following along to see what would be.

The woman was in a white nightdress and dame's cap, the night so still August could hear the groans of mattress ropes as the doctor pulled himself from the bed behind her, out of sight.

"Like all others," August said. "I'd not be here if the choice was otherwise." His voice almost conversational, lowered against restless neighbors. He added, "My name's August Swartout. Doctor Ogden assisted my hired boy not so many weeks ago. The matter is related."

He heard the mutter of the doctor and then his wife said, "Pull into the side entry, next to the office, if you know where that is."

Once under the porte cochere, he stood down out of the gig and waited. The hound drifted up and he leaned and roughed gently the

287

base of the dog's ears, and the hound leaned against him and rubbed his head against August's trousers, then the bright light of an oil lamp filled the windows and the dog slipped away. The office door opened and August stepped within. The room was close with heat redolent of a sulfurous wash that did not conceal the taint of blood, viscera, vomit, the high reek of anxious sweat.

"What is it, Swartout?" Erasmus Ogden wore a burgundy dressing robe with black and indigo paisley trim. Under that were trousers and a collarless shirt, fine patent-leather boots. He retrieved a briar pipe from a pocket of the robe and struck a match, pulled smoke and waited, wafting sharp bursts of dense blue smoke that coiled and lifted above the heat of the lamp chimney.

"You've been following the Hopeton affair?"

The doctor shrugged. "I read the newspapers."

August noted the plural. Then went on: "Hopeton's wife's father shot himself this morning and his wife, a troubled soul for all obvious reasons, rode into my yard at sunset this evening with that news. She needs care beyond what I can provide and those in our community she'd otherwise seek out, she'll have no part of." He paused. Ogden was very still, his pipe cupped in both hands before his chest, eyes snapping wide upon August. Who took his chance and finished. "So I came here."

Ogden tipped his head a bit and lifted his pipe, smoked and said, "What would you have me do?"

"Come attend the woman. That's your charge, is it not?"

"You could've brought her."

"I could not ask her to travel farther."

"Chances are I'll end up carrying her back here anyway."

"That would be all right. If she agrees."

"It's quite late."

"It is. But someone needs to inform the authorities. The sheriff or whoever?"

The doctor turned and walked to his glass-fronted cabinet, turned the key resting in the keyhole, opened the cabinet and selected a handful of stoppered phials, wreathing smoke as he did so. Without turning he said, "We could stop at Ansel Gordon's on our way out of town."

"We could. But Iris, Iris Schofield is her name—"

"—And husband David, now deceased as you or she maintain. Their names have also been in the papers. Go on."

"Iris is quite undone by all of this. I fear for her mind. And so was thinking perhaps—"

Again Ogden interrupted him. "Despite what you might believe, I took to heart my Hippocratic oath. The fine line of the law can be attended to but the woman comes first. My wife has already harnessed my horse to carriage; she's quite expert in these midnight incursions. I'll follow you out and help the Schofield woman however is best, though I nod my head to you—most likely bringing her back here for observation, some sedating medicinals as well, will prove the best course. And I can exert some control over whatever authorities wish to question her about this sad development. Though I can't see how to alert them until morning: My wife is no midnight messenger and will be attending to needs here. David Schofield will have to wait, but then there's nothing to be done for him, is there? The one who'll suffer for that delay is myself, as I'm also the coroner and in this heat, well . . ." He went silent and rubbed his temples. "I've seen it before. I wonder if that satisfies you; you don't care for me much, do you, Swartout? Blamed me for your wife's death, didn't you?"

"I seem to recall the blame came from you, for my waiting so long to summon you. But fact is, she died, despite best efforts made by all around her. Including you and there's no blame there."

The doctor came close and said, "To the matter at hand, then." He leaned and said, "Good God, man. You're wall-eyed and all atremble. Fatigue?"

289

"I had a long day and it's not ended yet. Does your wife need a hand with your horse?"

Ogden had shed his robe and pulled on a light overcoat hung from a peg beside the door, tucking the phials into a pocket. He said, "We step outside, you'll find all is ready. I'd offer you anything you like but there isn't even cold coffee the back of the stove." He tucked his cooled pipe into a pocket of the overcoat.

August said, "I hate to be a bother."

"What is it man? A brandy? I can do that."

"No. I was wondering if you might have a cheroot. I rode out in haste tonight."

"Of course you did. Cheroots? No, none of those, I'm afraid." He turned and went back to his cabinet and lifted down a wooden box, opened it, and turned. He said, "This is a good Havana. Perhaps better for a night as this: will last longer than your cheroot, at the least. Here, tuck it in your pocket. Have you a match?"

The big horse jogged easily along the night roads, through the pressing shadows of tree shade, then out again past silver meadows and moon-washed milky fields of grain. The star field hung near as close as winter, the old moon high overhead, haloed as if for rain, the world lit: even in passing woodlots the crowns of trees rose distinct, a hillside dappled with diverse trees, the dark defile of a ravine and for one short moment the silver cascade of the nestled stream. The doctor in his handsome buggy with the raised top followed at a short distance, far enough behind to escape the dust from August's gig, close enough to not lose sight. Soon enough August forgot he was back there; lodged in the center of his mind was the idea the doctor had been fetched and would be there when needed, when they rounded the yard of home, but for now lost to thought.

The cigar was pungent, rich and without the sweetness of his usual smoke and he quickly found to clamp it between his teeth in the corner of his mouth. The faint glow as he pulled upon it only a beacon toward home, the smoke released from his mouth a pale trail of his progress, the threads of calm clarity rising upward to filter his trench-ant mind.

And cast him back to the night before, not forgotten so much as overwhelmed by work throughout the long day since.

After August left the barn and made slow way toward the house, stopping at the yard pump to strip off his chaff-caked shirt and wash himself, arms and head and chest, thick handfuls of sweet cold water, finally bending his head to pump directly over it, runnels of water flushing the crust and blear from his eyes, hopefully his mind as well. Turned the shirt inside out to escape the worst of the grime and dried himself best he could and went into the kitchen. Becca was not there. He took down a folded square of clean sacking and dried his torso and head as he went up the stairs to pull out a clean shirt, stopping for a moment before the tall glass first to look upon himself: His hair and beard wanted trimming and he lifted a hand and squeezed the damp beard tight against his face and wondered if he should take up shaving, a daily job he'd abandoned less than a year after he began at fourteen. He pulled on the shirt and sat on the edge of his bed and removed the hard brogans he wore when driving the threshing machine, the clatter of the knives back and forth only inches from his propped feet too great a danger to be barefoot as most otherwise he was summers. When he first bought the thresher he'd not even thought about this until one morning after harvest he'd been in town and come across a man mostly unknown to him from up toward Potter, who, along with himself, had been one of the first to buy the new reaping machines and there he was hitching along with crutches under each arm, one foot in a hard boot, the other stretched before him to not hit the ground, the foot bare and bare of toes, the cauterized stubs still flaring the color of old ham. August wore boots or heavy shoes ever after, threshing, mowing hay. He held nothing but delight and respect for his new machines but did wonder if the time might come a man would have to work shod year-round as more jobs were made mechanical. He guessed he wouldn't mind that bother so much.

Barefoot, he went down to the kitchen. The room was hot from the day, the cold supper laid out: roast chicken cut to quarters, a loaf of bread, wax beans doused with vinegar and chopped dill, new pickles, a bowl of blackberries and cream. Becca stood across the table now, hands resting on the uprights of her usual chair. Her face yet stern upon him.

He sat in his place and said, "Harlan's off on an errand of some sort, I do believe. For Mr. Hopeton is my guess. Now, why don't you sit and eat also." He took up three of the beans and ate them, their crunch almost meaty, liquored with the cider-bite, the sweet smack of the dill.

She remained rooted where she stood. "What did the judge say when he got him?"

"Becca, sit and eat. Harlan's not locked up; there'd be no sense in that. He's on some bit of work that needs doing. That's all, I'm certain of it."

"What makes you so sure? A hour ago at the barn you told me you could only guess at what was happening. You're not being square with me. My stomach's sick with worry. None of this makes sense to me."

He sighed, propped his elbows on the table, and rested his hands before him. "Becca," he said. "Of course you're worried. I'm trying to tell you to let me shoulder that care. I needed that hour in the barn to ponder all this. And I realized Harlan's safe as can be and the rest, we just need to be patient a day, maybe two. Now, please eat and I'll tell you what I can."

She took a step forward but kept her arms crossed as if clutching her worry close. She said, "He's truly safe? You swear?"

Holding calm he said, "I've never painted a lie in my life. You should know that."

She regarded him a beat longer, then pulled out her chair and sat. She poured herself a cup of buttermilk from the pitcher and filled his cup as well. She said, "Busy as we been I forgot to tell you we're most out of sugar. Those blackberries might have wanted a good pinch more but I guess they'll do. So then, what would you have me know, all this mystery?" She commenced to reach from platter to bowl and filled her plate but then sat, bright-eyed upon him, her face lit with heat sheen, strands of her hair loose from the knot behind her head and tangling down about the sides of her face. Her mouth parted, waiting, the sleeves of her blouse pushed up so her summer-brown forearms lay either side of her plate. Likewise the waist of her skirts had been rolled and her bare feet and calves were naked as the heat of the day.

He drank buttermilk, wiped his mouth and as he did she tore a hank of bread and slathered butter, ate it and nibbled at a thick chicken wing, neat workings of her teeth as she held her eyes, waiting.

He ate a handful of the beans and tore his own bread, careless of the butter and ate that and then said, "I don't know everything, Becca, but what I do know makes me not care much for it. It's not Harlan and not even Malcolm Hopeton I'm speaking of, here. It's others, mostly the judge and Enoch Stone—now wait. You asked, I'll tell you what I can. They have this deal cooking, with David Schofield as the central part of it. To ask clemency for Malcolm Hopeton. I don't believe they care much about Harlan."

She spooned pickles onto her plate, tore more bread, slathered butter and said, "Why not?"

"Because they might believe they've got their play sewed up tight and think he's harmless."

"You don't think he's harmless though, do you?"

"All I know, the only truly important thing to him these past years, has been Malcolm Hopeton. Who has done a terrible thing, by accident or design it comes to the same end. Word has it Hopeton is not happy with the mercy being offered him, less so the way it's constructed. I wouldn't hope to know what Hopeton does want, but if your brother can help him, I'm sure he will. We'll see, is what I say." He picked up a drumstick and ate the dense meat off the bone.

"You know a pile more than you're saying."

He nodded, his mouth full and grateful of it. And, his own deep belly hunger shared, she reached and ate a handful of wax beans, then speared a breast from the platter. Again she hefted the earthenware pitcher and poured buttermilk for them both.

"He's my brother. You don't have the right to keep anything from me."

August swallowed, drank and swallowed again. Wiped his mouth with the flour-sack square folded neat beside his plate. He said, "It's simple and wrong as this. Tell me, anyone, anyone at all, drives in here this time of year looking for me. Saying they're looking for me. But I'm way out in the fields cutting oats. Who is the first person they're going to see?"

"Well, me. What's wrong with that?"

"Mostly, nothing. But say it was a man seeking Harlan—"

"The judge, you mean? Like yesterday?"

"Sure, say him. Or the sheriff or even Enoch Stone. Or someone you nor me ever laid eyes upon. Whoever it might be. They come in and you're the first one they talk to. Those men, most all of em, maybe each and every one, they've spent their lives learning to say a thing that sounds like one thing when it really means another. What I'm saying is they could trick you to telling them something they wanted to know and you not even knowing you're telling it to them, thinking you were only helping your brother. And so, what I don't tell you, you can't tell anyone else. Can you now?"

"You think I'm stupid?"

"You're clever as can be. But I also know I've maybe been stupid a time or two so far with all this and don't intend to be that way again.

294

For the sake of your brother." He paused and then said, "I guess Malcolm Hopeton as well."

She was quiet, mopping bean and pickle juice with more bread. A slaughter-spread of chicken bones upon her plate. His also. Talking, the end of day hunger had taken them. Finally, tentative, she said, "Brother Stone?"

August stood. "I have nothing to say about that man, this night. I'm going out to the porch. I'm in desperate need of peace."

She looked up in the now full dark, the lamp quavering on the table. She said, "The blackberries and cream?"

He walked to the shelf and lifted down a new cheroot and said, "Leave me a bowl. I'd eat them before I sleep."

He sat in the gloam, one knee crossed over the other, smoking and watching the red-and-white forms of his cattle work their slow way across the night pasture, milling more than grazing, aiming for the spots where they liked to bed. The tip of his cheroot an orange glow extended from his fingers, flaring red light against his face when he inhaled, the smooth smoky ropes of pleasure drifting outward, upward, quickly gone in the falling night. From the door open behind him he heard the rush of water from the kitchen pipe into the deep soapstone sink, the rattle and swish of crockery being washed, a pale oblong of lamplight now extending down the hall and fading on the porch from where she worked. Hot as it was, high summer, yet dark earlier than a month ago. He listened to Becca cleaning up and considered how quickly he'd grown comfortable with her presence: Only weeks earlier she'd already have left for her walk down to Malin's, a year ago during this same season of long days she might've been hurrying to finish the job, the walk still stretching before her. And now she washed up, then was done, all done for the night. He smoked, unsettled, unsure why.

She stepped soundless from the hall onto the porch, hauled a chair a bit closer to his and also to the rail, settled into it and propped her feet upon the rail. There was a waxing moon up now, caught by its lower edge by the barn cupola. Not for long.

"I don't know how you smoke those things. They smell like a chimney fire." Her voice light despite the commentary.

"If they offend so badly there's other places to take the evening air."

"No. I like it here. I love watching how those cows buckle themselves down upon the ground, almost like they do it in sections at a time."

"Maybe if you had four legs you'd find the same problem. Or maybe it's not a problem at all, for the cow. It's just how they get the job done."

A host of bats came out of the barn cupola backlit by the moon, then were gone as they spilled down within the orchard after food.

Becca said, "You really think what Bro—what Enoch Stone is trying to do is wrong? To save Malcolm Hopeton?"

August smoked on for a bit. Then said, "It's not what Enoch is trying to do, so much as how he's doing it. And his reasons. I mistrust all of that."

"You think he should not stand as a guide for the community? He spins a clever homily."

"The Friend made no such provisions. I believe she showed uncommon wisdom in that failure. We shall stand or we shall fall. But it's up to us. Recall, Becca, The Friend never made any such claims for herself, the only gift she had was to preach well and that was bestowed by Christ and the Father, not a choice she made. So no, to answer your question. Enoch Stone should not proclaim himself as a successor to that rare being, and there are no reasons he can offer that will change my mind on the matter. Clever homilies aside."

"But The Friend left Time almost forty years ago; surely the world today is not one she could have imagined."

"I'll offend you, but such thinking is the province of youth, who believe the world is made anew for them. But The Friend knew that while the decorations might change, the elements of life do not."

"There's sadness in thinking so."

"Time to time. Then the day turns and glory is before you once again. Nothing could be finer on this earth. Nothing at all."

She was quiet then. He smoked, studied his cheroot in the dark and saw it was less than half gone. No hurry with that; the shroud of fatigue had lifted with supper in his stomach and now the cooler night air, a desire to not end the day so quick as he'd wanted only an hour before.

"August?" She queried, unable to hide the tremor in her voice. He noted the tremor and felt a pang unbidden and surprising.

"What is it, Becca?"

"I've been a steady worker for you, these years? Enough to please?"

"I couldn't imagine what I'd do without you."

"Truly?"

"Very much truly." He paused and blew smoke and said, "I know your concern."

"You do?"

"If the scheme works, we might lose Harlan back to Malcolm Hopeton. I confess I've grown fond of Harlan and would hate to see him go, though would be happy for Hopeton. Also," he paused and smoked again and the pause extended, drifted outward as a smoke of its own toward the night, the orchard, the now-bedded cows. The moon lifted above the barn by a three-hand span as seen from where he sat. From where they sat. The lamplight from the kitchen having gained with the dark and joined the moonlight to show his crossed legs, the lap of his belly within the clean shirt; as well as her skirts spread with the dark shanks of her calves and her feet pressed against the porch rail, her knees up, arms resting upon the arms of her chair as she rocked gently, steady on the tipped-back chair. The lights of coal oil and moon struck opposing sides of her face, making a luminescent glow, her steady-ahead gaze sharpening her profile against the night, her forehead near-hidden by her hair, her nose, the dark flare of her

297

nostrils, the open purse of her lips, jut of chin. He could hear her breathing, knew she was waiting for him to speak more.

He delivered himself simply. "Also, I'd not be happy to see you return to that stark room above Malin's."

"If I may?"

"Yes."

But she did not speak. From the orchard came a last movement as the final hidden cow settled herself. There came also the delicate scent of cut onion and he was distracted, wondering if wild onions were growing in the pasture, tainting the milk and butter with that hot scent, thinking come morning he'd need to walk out and see what he could find. Then Becca spoke, a small voice in the still night, "You were content with that arrangement for years. Why be unhappy with it now?"

Just like that he said, "Why Becca Davis, surprised you should ask. I've gotten easy having you around. You fill my house, in a way I never expected to have it filled."

Her response was to stop rocking back and forth and drop her feet from the rail and then rise and walk down the porch to the end, where she stood looking out toward the barn and the night sky now salted with stars, her back to him, the solidity of her in the porous warm night almost a surprise. He uncrossed his legs and eased straight upright in his chair, smoked and waited.

She turned and walked back halfway, just enough so he could make out her face.

She drew herself up, almost lifting on tiptoe, and said, "That's all right. I done it before, I done it for years. It's not such a bad thing. It's not a bad thing at all. And, and these weeks here 'round the clock, well, I learned better how things work. That would help me do even a better job, coming and going. Don't you fret about me. Just now we best be putting our hopes toward Harlan and whatever he's up to. And having that all work for the best."

He sat silent a pause. He'd forgotten the strength of women. And in that reckoning he'd also forgotten his own strength and the idea came and bloomed in his mind. He smoked and sat watching now back out over the night, the dark misshapen clumps of the apple and cherry trees, each one known to him clear as if by daylight or of a full winter moon off snow. He looked back to her and saw what he guessed she could not know he might; her face torn and awkward as if her mouth was skewed sideways with the effort of her words.

"Becca," he said. "Come sit. I have a thought." When she did not move he leaned and patted the rush seat of her chair and again looked away. This time to give her the moment to compose herself, to take the step forward. Meanwhile the idea gained upon him. He was smoking with great energy, jets of smoke and the red end of the cheroot grown long and pointed, a hot tip arcing as he jabbed it toward the night darkness. She stepped and settled in the chair.

"Sometimes," he said, "I fail to comprehend the range of my own convictions. I suppose that's a good thing, as it means the world may surprise me over and again. And also that my own mind, my faith and heart, reveal themselves at a pace undetermined by myself but by a greater force. Which is a grand thing." He flicked the stub of cheroot into the grass where the dew was already down to make a sizzle as it landed.

She said, "I'm not understanding you."

"I strive for clarity." He paused, considered again the moon and dropped his gaze to her half-lit face, now leaning toward him slightly, lips just parted. He said, "Be patient, Becca. It's a fraught time for us all but more so than needs be. Now then. We have no idea of the outcome of events for Mister Hopeton. All these rumors don't make a conclusion. This effort put forth by Enoch Stone and, I presume, also for his own reasons by Judge Gordon, may well come to naught. That web appears cleverly strung but the thing about webs, is even the best constructed creation may be destroyed by some clumsy beast wandering through. Such a person, hardly conceivable to the spider. Do you see my meaning?"

"That Malcolm Hopeton might still hang for his crimes and Harlan will have no choice but to return here?"

"I doubt he'd hang, even if their scheme falls apart. And that is not my point, not what I wish to address. Becca Davis, should circumstances fall in Malcolm Hopeton's favor and Harlan return to assist that tortured soul, as he would, there's no reason for you to return to Malin's, to that daily tramp back and forth that we've learned deprived both of us so greatly. There's no reason for you to do a thing but remain here. As you are now."

She twisted her hands in her lap, twisting them as she worried a corner of her lower lip with her teeth, and finally said, "You're saying the two of us? Without Harlan? Alone together under your roof?"

"I am."

She lifted her feet to the bottom rung and smoothed her skirts over her knees. Her ankles and bare feet showing. She looked down at her twisting hands and said, "But August. What would people say? What might they think?"

He nodded and said, "For those that matter, those that know us, nothing at all. For those inclined to titter and cast idle rumors, why I'd guess they've worn themselves out of that habit by the years we already spent together. The two of us stand together, unimpeachable in the eyes of all that know us. The true wonder is that it took your brother being brought to us in his hour of need, to understand the essential truth. Years ago I should've stepped up and put a stop to your tramping back and forth to Malin's. Your duties here should fairly include hearth and home, a bed and a roof. And the pleasure such leisure time would allow, the greater ease with which you'd undertake the job of work, that while I may rarely voice it, I fully understand to be a heavy yoke upon your shoulders. Put simply: Why should you trudge an hour both ends of the day for no good purpose?"

Her voice low but heated, she replied. "In the years I was at Malin's you were never there when I went to the market or those times you carried me to town with my list and set me free to obtain the goods we needed. Or not even, most of the time, when peddlers or the meat wagon come by and it was me out in the yard to dicker with those men. Men, all of em, wherever. Not to mention whoever was gandering about while I done my trades and heard the sly comments or the eyes of em running over me, all asking ever so polite how you was. You were not there for any of that. And I never said the first word to you about em. Any of it. For what purpose? You say it so easy and clear but you don't know what you're asking of me. And how could you?"

"Do you take me for a fool? In a way you've given an answer to your objection. It's not what others think, be you under my roof or wasting time walking those miles each end of the day. It's what makes life best for both of us, Becca. Whatever effort we extend in this life, and toward whatever ends, there will always be those who misunderstand, who see only what they wish, what their own hidden fears or desires allow to be placed upon you. Or myself. The only thing that matters is how we construct our lives under the eyes and within the heart of the Lord. He is our sole witness, come the end of Time."

"Seems to me there are a host of witnesses quick and free with their tongues. Perhaps you was a woman you'd understand it not quite so lofty as you do." She was looking off into the darkness as if those voices drifted even now among the scud of breeze filled of wild onion, the flare of fireflies stippling the grass of the orchard pasture, the slight scrape of apple limbs, the thud of a loosed fruit striking the ground. Watching her, he caught the faint echo of those selfsame murmurs.

"It's true I'm only a man. A woman stands against another lot. But I'd offer if we stand together, we stand stronger." He paused and sighed, then said, "No need to answer now, I only wanted the thought in your mind. It's a good household we have, here. No one can accuse us otherwise."

She jumped from her chair, said, "Oh, you don't know," then darted for the door before she stopped and turned. Her voice aboil she said, "You don't know, you don't understand. Women, women, some have outright said to me, others with only a glance or a smirk. They think I've set my cap for you. They do. With Harlan and all I felt all right being here, the emergency of it. But you just don't see, do you?"

He stood and stepped toward her, hands open before him as if toward a skittish creature. "Why, Becca Davis, what are you saying? What are you telling me?"

"I'm telling you it can't be one way, can't be another. I don't blame you. I only just seen it myself."

Then she fled through the door and up the stairs, a frightened creature escaping. Only the scamper of her feet and then they too were gone. The soft sigh of a door carefully closed.

Now, riding home in the liquid warmth of night some hours after midnight, the big horse in ceaseless trot as if he might take the gig to the ends of the earth and off if August asked him to. August, tired as a man could be and yet joltingly awake, his mind a turmoil of thought, struck by the suicide of David Schofield and beginning to see that David had cast a pivot among the workings, the energies of his fellow men. Wondering if the act had been meant so, or simply a ravaged mind unable to endure what he might've seen as a greater, further and final mortification burdened upon him by his daughter. August could not imagine the madman he'd spoken with the week before as a being of such subtlety; but from his own brush with a mind set adrift, reasoned he had little experience to make a judgment of motive. But guessed it likely David, whatever the final impulse, had owned such fury: the burden splitting to clarity too great to bear and so jerked abrupt the door of Time. To step off the earth. Christ in His fathomless compassion enfolding the wretched soul, caring little for the rules man laid at the feet of the Lord. There

302

remained Iris, living so many years within the fold of her husband's bilious anger and loathing, if she might find freedom finally or be so swamped as to sink farther, and August, recalling her nigh-giddy reaches toward normalcy, wondered how Iris might fare once the worst of the summer was behind her. He knew the women up and down the valley of Jerusalem would do their own quiet work however was needed.

It came to him that the horse might not only be jogging homeward by memory but sleeping as he moved, the horse also caught out, missing rest between long days of work. He chirped once and the horse lifted stride, then he reined him back to the steady trot. Let the horse set the pace.

August rode along, the red nugget of the cigar a lodestone either cocked below his right eye or held time to time out over the offside high wheel of the gig. He'd come down the valley to the crossroad of Friend, half a dozen miles north of the Four Corners, and the horse made the turn without the least effort by August. Half an hour, no more, until home. They passed by the first farmhouse with a lamp lit in a kitchen window and the light thrown into the yard dimmed the star field overhead and the black shadow of a dog came out to watch him pass, standing there without giving voice of alarm. Then back out into the full night on a road narrowed by the corn growing either side, the stalks and broad leaves starkly dark against the moonlight as if so many scarecrows had been erected, the slight breeze here coming up the valley from the lake enough to scrape those rough-edged leaves one against another. He held the reins in one hand and rode down the valley holding the cigar and lifting it to smoke, then down again by his side. It was good tobacco, small constant triggers of thought spilling upward into his mind. For a moment he wondered if he should give up his cheroots and then knew the cigar was not only expensive but a gift given that fitted alone to this night.

He rode on. And then of a sudden knew his work for Becca Davis. Brought forth from her words the night before but also from the deep nudge of his own shared life.

He'd not so much forgotten this moment as his memory had set it aside some long time ago: Narcissa sitting cross-legged in the barley straw, a golden trampling hidden from anything but the noontime sun overhead. He on his back looking up toward that sun, three crows wheeling the fathomless sky. Both naked as the hour they first entered this world sixteen years before, an ancient passage of time. She held a straw between her teeth, both sweat-smote and languid. Grasshoppers leaped and scraped into the standing stalks.

She said, "I expect I'll die before you. I don't have it in me to stay, I wish I did. My soul yearns onward. You listen: I'm serious as death. When I'm gone I'll haunt you all your life. There's not another for you but me." She leaned down then and kissed him. Every word she'd spoken was true. Her eyes so close upon his he'd seen three of them. She said, "God made us a package, didn't he?"

And now he thought Of course the women speak or hint such things to Becca. It's their nature to do so. Perhaps she feels somewhat that way also, would be natural as well, a young woman herself. There's none to blame except perhaps myself for not grasping it sooner. But the answer to such is simple and the right thing to do, all ways. I stand up as a father would for her.

He saw it then unfolding as if it were already under way: Quietly he would seek out and speak with some of the older men, the ones with sons of an age to marry but not yet with prospects. Those men in turn would mention this to their wives and the women would understand the task better than the men informing them and, in the way of women, would look at Becca anew, not only for the comely and diligent girl that she was but one who, courtesy of August, would bring to such a union not only the experience of running a household and the general

304

labor about the farm as needed, but also backed with the dowry of money and seed livestock that August would provide. It might well take some time because he knew Becca Davis would not undertake such actions lightly or of simple mind; he'd only have to speak quietly to her and assure her he'd rather she look long to make certain the match was the right one, to entertain a prospect and then reject, and wait to see who else might step forward, rather than rush into a marriage that would prove unhappy. Unless it was the passion of two souls smacked up against each other and he guessed he'd understand that. And take up his own reins and do the best he could to help such a thing thrive. Truly, now, the sky a wash of stars, the lacy-feather leaves of roadside elms batting by overhead between heaven and earth, such a match was what he wished and hoped for her.

And there it was: Harlan.

Young but a stalwart boy, a steady hand and what he didn't know of farming he didn't announce but watched and learned. And certainly of a large heart and uncommon soul. One who most surely would be returning to assist August through the remainder of the harvest year. For however it went with Malcolm Hopeton, the gift of freedom dreamed by Enoch Stone as a gesture of grace and forgiveness would be denied by even the most sympathetic of juries. The man was prison bound and there, then, August saw it also, the judge would claim Hopeton's farm in forfeit for damages to the court, perhaps an award of some sort to Iris Schofield—August determined to put that idea forth if no other did at the hearing, assuming there still would be one. Not today. He shook his head to clear it. No—not the day soon to lighten in the east but the one following. Unless the death of David stalled it all; seemed it might but there was still the need to press Stone about a judgment considering Iris.

He was put to mind how after a rainstorm the otherwise dull pebbles in the yard revealed themselves in a bright sparkling pattern— the works hidden by dust washed clean to light of day.

He could not align the future from this one spot of nightfall, this spring and summer of calamity and disaster but he could spot opportunity and walk forward toward that goal, long as the goal could shift shape and re-form as time passed. As all goals and hopes did in this life under the sun and stars, under the heavens.

Becca Davis might meet love with a man settled upon his own inheritance. She might also meet love with a landless younger son of a younger son. She might leave August and Harlan to fend for themselves as she built her new life a dozen miles, three miles, away. He might hire a new housekeeper, this time a widow woman, to clean and launder and keep food on the table for those years as he and Harlan labored upon the farm and Harlan grew and learned this land. And as young women placed eyes upon him and he did the same until that one caught his eye.

August aware that the peculiar circumstances of Harlan's life, these past months especially, would bring him into a certain vantage of interest among young women.

Details. Worthy of thought, of holding in mind but only details. Not a one of which he knew he could guess correct. Only vague and general forms as the looping shadows of the trees passed this night, glimpsed ahead, then changing upon approach, the short passage underneath where the tree was most and least substantial all at once, then receding behind. Then another farther down the road.

But most large was a single wondrous thought:

Life has brought these children back to me and I'll do my best right down to the hard ground to honor that gift. Because they are not my children, they are not substitutes for my children. They are of a larger cycle, of a greater charge upon not only me but themselves as well. And so I see myself more clearly in this vale of Time, so short in passage. But a caretaker, only a steward, is what I am. As they are, also. Of this spot of earth we inhabit.

For, truly, hadn't Becca and Harlan Davis come home?

★   ★   ★

Crossing the bridge over Kedron Brook and pulling uphill toward home, gliding along now in the dark broken by the few stars glimpsed above the tree canopy, the ripples of fireflies off in the meadows making siren trails, the small sparks thrown as the iron bands on the wheels glanced against stones of the roadbed. Then swift hoofbeats and Ogden's rig came alongside him. The doctor calling over to him, "Have you fallen asleep, man? Your horse is plodding."

A lamp burned low on the kitchen table. Becca and August sat across from each other, talking.

Not half an hour had passed since the doctor and August had entered the house to find Becca at the very spot she now sat, with Iris Schofield bent over in the old rocker set back fireside in the corner, keening, her chin upon her breastbone but her hands in furious counterpoint upon her thighs, her voice lost but for the wracking wet sobs coming from her, short intervals when she'd arrest her moans and cry her daughter's name before slumping again. Becca had not looked at August but addressed Doctor Ogden, her own voice calm and matter-of-fact, low as if she'd not have the stricken woman hear her account.

"This is how it's been," she said. "When first I got to her here she was almost sensible but while I was making tea as my mother showed me—chamomile, lemon balm, geranium leaves—to ease her—"

"None of that does a thing," Ogden said. "Old wives' nonsense."

She'd nodded and gone on. "They helped my mother and she had reason to know. But as I was making the tea, Sister Schofield commenced wailing and crying and calling out, to her daughter mostly as I could make out, also her husband time to time. Raising her head up to the roof beams then dropping it into her lap, pummeling her legs or breastbone as if she'd drive out the pain from those spots, but only seemed to make it worse. I don't know if she heard a word I spoke but I done my best, moving about and getting her honey for her tea, fetching a shawl to drape over her shoulders which she balled up

307

and buried her face in as she cried out most terrible. Then she went silent and gazed off, at the fire, the lamp, all about as if trying to place where she was, but was quieted. I took that as a good sign and got the long fork, cut a slice from a loaf and toasted it over the fire just so. I guessed she hadn't had a bite to eat in I don't know how long and thought that might help, but time it was done and I got the crock of butter down she was wailing again. Then after a bit it seemed to take the starch out of her and she slumped down much as she is now and I didn't dare try a thing but pray you two would roll in soon."

"And here I am," Ogden said. He'd approached where Iris sat and knelt down and took her hand and turned it over to count the pulse of her veins. The woman keened on, bent over upon herself, an exhausted grief that could not allow cessation as if to cease would bring dishonor upon what she grieved. Ogden dug in the pocket of his coat and lifted out a phial and undid the stopper, ran out a white paste upon his index finger, and then slipped the finger into her mouth, between her cheek and jaw. As if administering chewing tobacco. He withdrew the finger and wiped it clean upon his britches and stood, turning to August.

"That will give her peace in a few short minutes. Then I'd ask your help loading her into my buggy. I have a strap to hold her in place and a lap robe against any chill but she's best with me, as we discussed. Tell me, did you enjoy the cigar?"

"About our conversation last evening," August said. "I've had some fresh thoughts." Both with cups of the tea before them.

"Not now, please," Becca said. Bent over her cup as if to read the swirl of leaves. "That will wait. Tell me, is the hearing today?"

"No," he said. "The next."

"Then you cut oats today?"

"Barley," he said. "We start on the barley." Then, needless, he said, "We finished the oats."

"Drink that tea and get on to bed. You need what sleep you can get."

"I don't know that I can." He was painfully tired and the headache was back.

"Try. Drink that tea."

He did. It was both sharp and sweet going down. He said, "I've found a solution that you'll likely resist at first but makes all the sense in the world. Iris Schofield opened my eyes." Becca stood and looked at him.

He said, "Let's get through these hard days ahead—then we can talk as you need. But I'm tougher than whatever people may say or think. At the least I'll be happy to hear you out."

She tipped the crane with the kettle over the low heap of coals the faster to boil water come dawn, then turned and walked out the hall to the stairs. He watched her go and then walked out the door to the stoop and down into the yard, where he stood and made water, head tilted back to look upon the stars. What could be seen of heaven.

He then went in and up to his own bed. Where he lay on his back under the linen made soft by use, certain he'd not sleep this morning, his mind in turmoil, his head throbbing.

Then he rolled onto his side and drew his legs up, pushed the linen down about his waist for the cool air floating through the windows lifted by their sash-weights. His breathing fallen slow.

When he woke the sun was hard upon him.

THIRTEEN

Mid-morning and the heat had not yet penetrated the chestnut grove.

The door and glassless windows stood open, though no air moved through them or the woods either but the faint cool of night and dew, of ever-shaded earth held tight as the moss on the cedar shakes of the roof. It would not be until late afternoon and the evening stretching toward and beyond dark that the heat would beat through the grove, pressing down and holding until the early hours. But for the time at hand the room was pleasant, easy to lie idle in. Only the morning of his second full day there and already he knew this much.

He knew also the heat of late afternoon and dusk was not unpleasant if free of the dust and grime of labor but made instead a slippery grease for skin upon skin of a newfound labor where sweat might burn his eyes but was easy blinked away.

He lay spraddle-legged on his back, the thick feather-stuffed mattress and blankets an uncommon daytime luxury beneath him that he'd grown used to, as much else. The woman on her side beside him, head propped on an elbow as she looked off, her eyes lazed and sleepy, as he'd first noticed the afternoon before. Careless of his looking, allowing him to study her. A wonderment laid bare before him and not only her wondrous body, which she'd made available to him over and again and not even all the rest of the sweet labor both performed when he lay joined with her, but also the long hours before and after their couplings. Times one or the other slept, times both slept. She moved about the cabin wearing a shift that informed him further of her, which was what he was studying, not only in this morning moment while the air was still cool but ongoing.

The night of his arrival she held him pinned to the floor and kissed him slow while without thought he began to kiss her back as the world collapsed to nothing beyond where he was, engaged rapturous and thoughtless. She helped him from the floor and guided him toward the bed, peeling away her clothes and gently his own as he'd stood mute and motionless, and then pressing him down into the mattress and lifting herself above to straddle him again. Her hands on his shoulders as she worked, her eyes intent upon him throughout and then his sudden oblivion and abrupt descent into sleep. The enormity of the day rolling over him and taking him down as if to allow his mind escape, not from her, not only from her, but all of that long and strangely twisting day.

When he woke that first night she was beside him and had left a lamp guttering on the table so he could find his way outside to pass water and stand with his head tilted back, searching for the few stars and moon visible beyond the giant tree crowns. He stood a longer moment but there was nowhere to go but back inside, back to the bed beside her. And nowhere else he wanted to go. She lay awaiting him, covered only by the sheet, which she lifted against any hesitation he might own. Once beside her she pushed him gently onto his back, the lamp still low as she raised on an elbow and spoke to him.

"I did that because I wanted to," she said.

When he struggled for words she laid a finger over his lips and shushed him. Then she said, "Like most things there was a host of reasons, but mostly because I wanted to. But Harlan? Also I couldn't let you go. Like I said, I'm hid out too. And I didn't want you telling anyone I was here."

And she took her finger away and waited.

"All right," Harlan said, as old as he was, which was much older than he'd known himself to be, all ways. "Tell me what you're hid out from. You already made clear you wasn't about to speak up for Bethany Hopeton. I didn't come here expecting you, or looking for you. So what could it be you're hiding from?"

She pressed over him and stood out of the bed and walked to the table and prized the cork on a bottle of beer and swallowed and came back to the bed carrying the bottle. She again stepped over him but settled down with her back against the wall, cross-legged, the sheet tugged over just her lap as she sat facing him, one knee nudging his ribcage. Her breasts high and pink in the light, her face swaddled by her tangled hair. She reached her free hand and traced a line from his belly button up to the hollow of his throat and took the finger away, wrapping both hands around the bottle upright atop the sheet.

He watched her as she did all this and watched also as she sat worrying her lower lip with her teeth and he said, "It's what you said at the hotel, ain't it?"

"Oh," she said. "I been sick with worry you'd recall that and tell someone. Have you done that?"

"That it was on account of you that Amos and Bethany rode in that day? That's what you were getting at?"

"Don't torment me. You don't have to torment me. I never expected it would turn out how it did! Can't you see that?"

312

"Hey, now." He reached and placed a hand on her knee, letting it rest and then working the hand upon her knee. "I think it's fair to say that was a day where nothing turned out how anyone thought it would, any one of us. And no, I have not told a soul. But their coming in like they did? You play a part in that?"

She looked level out into someplace on the far dark wall, beyond the lamplight and said, "After Malcolm Hopeton come home, after Amos and Bethany run off once they got word he was coming home, I sat down here in the woods and got worried Hopeton would come looking for me and so went to my friend Bertha Pinckney and she took me in and put me up and never once asked why. I set up there in that hot attic room and knew Amos wasn't coming back—that he'd throwed me over once and for all. All he'd said, all he'd promised didn't mean a thing cept to keep me on the string for his own amusement, his own use when he wanted me. You know Amos and you know he'd take what he wanted when he wanted it. And I set up there thinking about all he'd told me, all he'd said about Mr. Hopeton over the years and it come to my mind that Amos was due a lesson, one he'd maybe never had. Slick? How Amos seen himself as if there was a magic butter run over him that made him a tad smarter than any around him could see and that kept trouble from pouring upon him, if he'd earned it or not. Maybe especially if he'd earned it. And I seen that all those years it had worked for him. He'd fooled us all. Hopeton and me, most. The longest. Bethany Hopeton also, though it ain't fair to strictly say he'd fooled her: I think he made sure she had no choice but to take what he offered. Amos was a mean creature, no doubt there."

She drank off the rest of the bottle and tossed it toward the open door, where it clattered and then went soft against the night. Now she looked at Harlan. He was waiting, had been waiting, her eyes.

She said, "So I thought to myself, Two can play that game. What could draw Amos back? What could make him think he hadn't shook that tree yet for all it was worth? All I wanted was the chance for him to get caught in his own dirt, to think things was such a way that he could squeeze it all for the last bit. It came to me, just like that. I sat down and wrote him a letter. And I sent it to the Huntsman Hotel in Utica, where, even if he was only to pass by now and again, he had an arrangement for such things to be held for him. I wasn't even sure they was in Utica. Amos was always cagey with money and God knows he could've had enough to take him and that bitch most anywhere on earth they might decide to go. But while I knew it was possible, I had a good strong gut telling me if he weren't in Utica he weren't far off. A fox, if it thinks the hounds is after it, won't hightail ridge after ridge but will circle around and around, trying to see if the way back to its den is clear or not, when it might be safe to slip back in. So I sent that letter. And he got it and sure enough come back not a week later."

"You lured him back."

"I did."

"How so? What did you write him?"

She stood off the bed again and walked to stand in the doorway, looking upon the darkness beyond. She wrapped her arms about the front of her and he saw her skin was up in gooseflesh, Harlan still stunned with the sight, still trying to understand the vast strangeness of a woman, how similar to himself, how very different. And how she shook in the doorway against a cold that was not within the cabin nor coming from without but some far greater distance. He thought to go to her, rising up from the mattress when she turned back.

She stood looking at him. Now all upright and free of any tremor. Her eyes locked upon him and she strode forward and was talking before she perched upon the side of the bed, this time blocking the lamplight so she was a medium of dark form, the lamplight a corona behind her.

314

"I wrote that Hopeton was ruined from the war. That he was useless as a man. That after he got home he run you off or you took it upon yourself but you were surely gone and he wasn't making the first attempt to farm or do anything at all. Told how I snuck up there in the evening and peered through a window and saw him setting in that half-bare house muttering and talking to himself, sometimes getting up to walk back and forth talking out loud and gesturing with his hands like he was in conversation with someone but wasn't anybody there but him. How he done that all hours of the day and night. How I'd seen him sleeping middle of the day out in one of his grown-over hay fields and other times he wandered about the farm ragged and dirty as a tramp, his hair and beard grown out and his clothes a mess. I didn't mention Missus Hopeton; truth is I figured it most likely Amos would come back alone to scout it out, learn what he could make of it."

"When you mailed that, what did you want to happen?"

She looked off a time and then said, "I guess I was hoping Malcolm Hopeton would give him a beating. Remember, what I wrote and what I saw was two very different things. And Amos, like many men of his nature, was at heart a coward. It was easy for him to hurt and scare folks weaker or less able than him and he knew it, which was why he done it. But a able-bodied man, a man lived hard and rough as Hopeton had through the war—why Amos wouldn't a been a match for him. Maybe I was thinking Hopeton would have Amos arrested; Lord knows there was a bounty of charges could've been brought. Maybe I was hoping for that, too. Have him locked up a time, was my thinking."

"That's what you were after? Truly?"

She was quiet a bit and then said, "Regardless how he explains it, or how it comes to be, when your man is fucking another woman there comes a time you tell yourself, 'Quit this.' For me it was more complicated. I thought, How far will he take me for a fool and how will I let him know he's done that? And that was my plan to let him figure it out. I thought he'd have a good long time to ponder upon it."

"I guess he's got eternity now. To ponder upon it."

"I guess you could say that."

He gazed pensively a moment and said, "I don't think there's a thing for you to worry over. If he'd carried that letter with him, someone would've found you, the hotel or here, by now. There ain't anyone knows but me."

"And you're here. Hid out, as you say. I aim to keep you that way a day or so." She leaned and kissed him. He kissed her back, reached for her shoulders, and she came into the bed.

He said, "I'd be in town for the hearing, though. To see what happens."

"That could work," she said, leading him up as she moved under.

He woke from dreamless sleep, aching beside her, and she lay waiting for his eyes to flutter open and then reached to hold him and then guide him. He was clumsy and swift and she purred soft sounds almost words into his ear as if to console him or mark her own pleasure with the moment—he did not know and somehow until the moment knew not to ask. She was patient and allowed him to discover his own strength and this time he was more certain, beginning to discover not only himself but what measures of motion seemed to please her. To stop and start. He was a gentle boy and if there were times she wished for less gentleness she gave no signal, no urging whisper. As if knowing he needed to learn his gentleness in this way, to prove it upon himself and demonstrate it for her.

An ill-used boy who confused force with strength and she knew this of him. More so than he did, yet.

She made coffee and fed him and went out, taking care to tell him she was going to the stream for water, obvious enough as she held the empty bucket in her hand but he understood why she told him such and lay back upon the blankets and watched a small rill of dust work free of the shake roof where some wood-boring insect drilled, the dust falling fine as captured trickling ancient sunlight. When she returned her hair was wet and the shift she'd left with was over one arm, her skin beaded and prickled from the water. She stood beside the bed and handed a dipper to him and said, "Later we'll go together. It's a nice pool."

He'd started to ask "Why not now?" when she touched the cool dipper to his upward prodding and came back into the bed. The dipper thumped and bounced upon the rugs.

That afternoon he woke alone and was alarmed to note the absence of her riding clothes, was seated upon the bed wondering if she'd left, if she'd someway found him lacking. Then saw the spider over the coals holding a diced hash of bacon, potatoes and onions, smelling this across the room as a dart to his stomach. Squatting before the fire and spooning up food, he decided they weren't so unlike, perhaps more alike than he could know.

He was back on the bed, drifting in and out of sleep in a daze of restlessness, the full heat of late afternoon now descending through the canopy, the cabin close and moist and sotted with the scent of her rising all around him from the blankets when she walked back in. She set a basket of wild plums on the table and looked him up and down and said, "Maybe someone's been working you too hard, you sleeping so much as all this."

He sat up blinking and rubbed his hands against his eyes, the backs of his palms against the bone sockets, and said, "It's high summer. Until I fetched up here I was cutting oats from first light to full dark."

She was removing her clothes, then slipped into her gown but did not come to the bed. "Put your trousers on," she said. "It's all you need the off chance we run into someone."

"Where we going?"

"Where you wanted to go, earlier."

317

"You think we might come across someone?"

She looked at him, let her shoulders rise and fall. "No. There's no reason to think so. Let's go. You ready?"

They left the cabin, Harlan wearing his trousers, Alice Ann carrying the plums. Once they threaded the path through the chestnuts and emerged into the open woods the heat poured on them, sunlight refracting from lesser leaves, shafts like drills breaking through, deer-flies swarming around them. Alice Ann walked through it all as if there was nothing there but her destination. Harlan following on the narrow path, batting against the swift darts of the droning flies, his eyes swinging between the basket of plums and Alice Ann's backside clearly visible beneath the cloth.

He thought he might follow her all of his days, thus, and happily so.

Once while walking he thought he heard a horse whicker and turned toward the sound but only saw a running clump of hickories and oaks and when he thought to look back Alice Ann's head was straight forward, forging on.

They went down a steep path with small outcroppings of shale in thin layers, some broken free and sharp underfoot. In his four years upon this land he'd never been here, not even known it existed. He bent to pick free a sliver of shale from his foot, the color of oil and half the size of his hand, lifted it and saw in the rock the spiral of some ancient snail shell and stood, wondering over that. A perfection of detail cast in stone, coils and scrolls. Then looked up and saw she was far below him and tossed it aside and went on.

The pool was only a bend in a small stream beneath oaks and syca-mores, the water deepest where the bank had eroded under the roots of a looming oak, clear but copper colored from the pea-stone gravel in the outer shallow edge, the drift of sand under the deeper water. Alice Ann pulled off her gown and laid it on the dry pebbles and waded across and hung the basket over a low-slung stub of root emerging from the bank so the plums were washed and cooled in the flow, then settled down and stretched out on her back in that same flowing deep water, digging her heels into the gravel of the bend to hold her in place, her hair flowing wet around her shoulders, her face tilted toward the sunlight coming at an angle from the western slope of the ravine. She'd closed her eyes.

There was a scattering of browned oak leaves caught in the jewelweed growing beside the stream. Harlan stood on the small pebbled beach to unbutton his flies, let his trousers drop, and stepped out of them and waded in, aligning himself alongside Alice Ann on his back, his own heels dug next to hers to hold against the slow current. The water was cool as a new sheath of skin and quickly his body was no longer hot nor cold, as if the water had made him neutral and bound to the earth from which the water rose. As Alice Ann did, he kept his gaze upward, all but his toes and face submerged, and he could not turn to look at her without his mouth going under the water and so witnessed her from a place both close by and distant.

She lolled in the water toward the tree root and back against him and one of her heels lost its anchor and she drifted, then caught and pushed herself back. Once settled she lay quiet a moment, then said, "Mostly life makes promises it can't keep. But every now and again it surprises us, isn't that right, Harlan?"

He held silence close then.

After a moment she lifted her arm from the water and took a wild plum from the basket and reached it across to him. It was near-black, stippled with purple along the seams of the fruit, dripping. She said, "You want a plum?"

He took it from her and bit into it, tearing the thick skin and then a gobbet of the fruit came free, his teeth raking against the stone, his mouth lit sweet and sour as he chewed. And bit again, the hunger sudden and deep upon him. And also saw her cocked elbow as she ate a plum, the sound of his clicking jaws filling his under-water ears like heartbeats, the wash of water over it all until he tossed the stripped stone downstream and lifted to watch it float away. Turned on his elbow and she was also up, sitting in the water low about her waist. A shred of plum skin stuck upon her lower lip.

"I never understood it," he said.

"That would cover a mile of country all around and some beyond," she said. "But you're gaining."

He grinned at her and she smiled back, reached and did something with his wet hair upon his forehead, then dropped her hand back into the stream.

He looked back down between his knees at the turmoil of gravel and said, "That second winter when he cut all the peach trees down and split em up. That filled a shed of wood. He done a lot of things didn't make sense but that's one sticks in my mind. I was out there watching not that he'd of known it. He went at those trees like a fury. He was a hand with a ax, although that was the only time I seen it. The rest of those years wood was my job."

"You ever seen him eat a peach?"

He thought back and said, "It was only the one summer when Missus Hopeton was cutting em and drying em and there was always a heap on the table and she and I both ate em. He never once did." He paused and went on. "Then the trees were gone."

She said, "I never knew what it was about peaches: I used to beg him to bring me some and more than once I snuck up after dark to grab some but I knew better than to let Amos know about it. Those first few years I thought it was all how Amos told me; he didn't trust to tell me what his real thoughts was for a good while, even though he knew from the first day he had me heart, body and soul. It wasn't even when Hopeton married that woman—Yes, I hate her, but I feel sorry for her also. She never had a chance against Amos Wheeler once her man went off to the war. And it was only then that Amos made clear he'd known that somehow he was going to ruin Malcolm Hopeton from the first moment they met. He never would tell me why, or even when that was. I almost thought it was all high talk cept you got to recall I'd seen Amos in action all sorts of ways, other places. Truth is, you get down to it, the only person he ever truly didn't take full account of was me. That's not a brag; I been thinking about it and I see when he plucked me up he didn't know a thing about me cept he saw something in me and then he forgot about that a little bit—not a whole lot because that was not his way but just enough so he told me and showed me a bit more of hisself than he thought he was doing as he spun out his plan for how we'd get rich off Hopeton's farm and hightail it out a here. Thinking I'd believe that. And I did. For a while."

As she spoke her face was ripped hard in a wild anger and Harlan knew this was also the woman being revealed to him. The water flowing cool and soothing around him, her eyes a hard-glanced green as high dusk.

He said, "Just when did you figure that out?"

She took a deep breath, his eyes falling helpless to her heaved breasts and she said, "I asked myself that. The truth is I knew it before I'd allow myself to allow that I did. The way you can know a thing is wrong but you want so bad for it not to be that you pretend it's something else altogether. Or that it's not even there at all."

She was quiet for a moment and then said, "I'm not talking about you and me."

"I know that."

She said, "It's more like about what Amos made you do. You understand that?"

Even in the cool of the water he felt his face go hot and his eyes swam and he looked away from her. But after a moment he said, "I know that, too."

★   ★   ★

321

That night, heat lightning stippled the sky through the chestnut leaves and far-distant thunder sounded in rolling tattoos, but there was no wind and the air hung dense and heavy about him as Harlan hunkered out in the clearing watching what he could of the storm that was passing far to the south of them. Lacking wind, the storm seemed unlikely to make rain, at least nowhere close by; and his thoughts returned to August Swartout and Malcolm Hopeton and he worried he was not doing the job he should be doing. Even if now it truly seemed the best hope for Malcolm Hopeton was for Harlan to stay distant and hidden from Enoch Stone. All ways. She left him be, as if she knew his thoughts or even only the need to break away a time. Which he'd only discovered himself.

Later in the night the air freshened and drew cool about them, enough so they roused from slumber and pulled blankets from under them to coil together beneath, the heat of their bodies now a different pleasure and he had a moment when he thought of how a winter night might be, lying so. Then cast it from his mind, knowing without once venturing beyond thought, approaching words at all, that this time was in all ways short and so a gift and let it be so. He slept and when he woke the day about them was thin and clear as water in a jar, the leaves on the canopy above the cabin no longer a blur of heat shimmer but each distinct as a paper cut and placed against the sky. No rain had fallen, none would soon. He rose up vigored and renewed and she was as well, the fire pokered up and coffee boiling as they coupled, then ate as if neither could last recall when a crust of blue-molded bread had passed their mouths.

He wanted to ask her the plan for the following day but did not. If there were questions or discussions needed they'd have time come that dawn. Knowing this was the final day of nothing but lost within each other.

Come the afternoon they lay fallen back head to foot of each other, both propped on pillows, a linen sheet twisted in a rope over their midsections, the air hot again but yet clear, draughts pulsed through the door and window-chunks. A cottontail she'd brought in earlier from a snare, then skinned and quartered, was in a spider over the coals, stewing with potatoes and bright new onions he guessed had come from the bit of garden he and Malcolm Hopeton had got in, steam lifting rich and dense against the brightened air.

She moved about the bed so she lay beside him and reached a finger to stroke along his jaw, the prickle of stubble there. If Amos Wheeler had left a razor in the cabin Harlan had not gone seeking it, even as stubble bruised his jaw and cheeks.

"Why'd you never leave?" she asked. "With all he done, not just to you but Bethany Hopeton also? Why'd you stay and stay?"

To mild surprise he found the question did not bother him. He propped one ankle over the other and let his eyes drift toward the low dark rafters and considered his response.

After a time he said, "Mr. Hopeton hired me some months before he went off in that fall of sixty-one. So I thought I had a pretty good idea how things worked before he ever went. A couple days before he left he found me one day in the mule pens and told me he hadn't any notion how long he'd be gone but reckoned it would be a good while and told me also he was counting on me to stick to it, however long it was. I hadn't a thought of doing otherwise and told him so and he grinned and shook my hand and told me we was agreed, then. During those months I never got a sense he didn't harbor a thing but trust for Amos Wheeler and why would I? If he'd known a hint of what Amos had in mind he'd either not of gone or hired a able man and not a scrap of a boy. When I finally saw how things was turning I didn't know why, or how bad it would get. All I knew was he'd asked me to keep an eye on things. So even when it got bad I reckoned I could do that. And I did."

"That's uncommon thinking," she said.

323

"Maybe so. And I been studying it and know it was more than been hired on, given a job and a trust too. It was how I was raised." He paused and said, "You ever heard of the Public Friend?"

"You talking about that maphrodite preacher?"

"What's a maphrodite?"

"It's a person has both male and female parts."

He considered the possibility of such configuration, intrigued. Then he said, "I don't know anything about that. The Friend was a mighty preacher and it's true she was a celibate and some of those that followed her preaching was also. Not many but some. That gets me back to how I was raised, and likely why I done what I done for Mr. Hopeton."

"A celibate? Someone who don't have any relations, is that right?"

"Well, they have relations all right. Just all behind em, most gone out of Time. No little chaps or such, no husbands or wives."

"Relations is what you and I been getting up to. Fucking."

He rubbed a finger along his chin and then said, "All right. It amounts to the same thing, I guess. But you asked and I was trying to explain why I hung in there with all that trash Amos Wheeler put on me. And Bethany Hopeton."

"Yes. How was it you was raised so as to hold steady through it?"

"It's a story," he said. "From long before I was born. There was a old man who mostly raised me and he told me this story happened when he himself was a chap but he recalled it clear as a bell ever after. And I was of a doubtful mind, a orphan child myself and my sister mostly gone into the world even it was but a couple miles away and I seen her every few days. But it was what was to come had me worried, truth being I had no idea what was to come and just old enough to know that, which caused me to be doubtful."

"Are you going to tell me the story or only all about your worried mind?" She softened the jest of her voice by running a palm over his chest.

324

"This he told me," he said. "The Public Friend and the couple hundred people that come with her, families and odd ones, were the first to settle this country but of course it wasn't so long after them that others got wind of it and at first trickled in and then a flood of em. So what started as the New Jerusalem was turned into a redoubt for them folks and there was a plenty of em that were made uncomfortable by The Friend and the people about her. Now we're talking ten, fifteen years along. First thing was some of those newcomers tried to get the court to get her up on charges of heresy but the court wouldn't touch it: The community had a charter from the state that allowed em to be as a church. Still, them new settlers wouldn't let it rest and some fool started a story about how The Friend claimed she could walk on water like our Lord did after the miracle of the loaves and fishes, if I got that right. Now, The Friend didn't care a spit what any man said about her; she'd learned that lesson over and again. But she was a strong soul, no way around that for all she done. So she had a broadside printed up about how she'd hold a meeting with all welcome on the first Sunday of October down below the Four Corners where there was a nice lay of open land that led right down to the lakeshore and invited all doubters to come witness her walk on water, if such was what was required to bring them to the Lord. She spat mud in their eye, right there—suggesting those newcomers were lacking in their own faith.

"So come that first Sunday in October and by nine in the morning there was five hundred people gathered, maybe a third of em followers of The Friend, and that was the appointed hour printed in the bills. And The Friend was not there. But buggies and wagons kept rolling in to see the show and by ten there was over a thousand people all milling and some angry talk, some folks commencing to eat the dinners they'd brung in baskets for after the show and kids splashing in the lake and calling out how they was walking on water the way kids will do. But mostly it was a solemn crowd that kept on swelling and those followers of her were getting nervous: A good many of em had spoke up against her making such a show anyways but she'd just told em to hush and wait and see. Then at half past ten The Friend's chay rolled in and she stood down out of it with her broad-brimmed hat on her head and her long, brown, plain smock dress and she walked up to the highest point of land there where she could look down around the entire crowd—not above em but right in the middle where she could see all of em and they all could see and hear her. And she began to preach. She wasn't no fire and brimstone preacher but spoke only of Christ and his teachings and how to live a life in the shadow of that gentle Lord who walks side by side with each and every one of us each and every hour of the day, who carries our travails and guides us on our way if we only but ask. She went on like that until sometime in the early afternoon.

"I never heard her, a course, and there was never any of her words written down: She wouldn't have it, saying all any of us needed was to listen to our hearts close enough and Jesus would enter upon us and speak Himself. And I guess maybe that's true because every time I wondered was I doing the right thing, or was I doing the wrong thing, I always felt like that answer was already inside me. All my life I heard about The Friend who had a gift to preach in such a simple way that people heard her and then heard themselves in her."

He paused and took a breath and let it ripple slow out of him and said, "Which is how it works, is what I been learning, over and again." He fell silent and brushed a fly off his hip and watched it rise and swirl and settle upon her thigh and he brushed it away again.

"Wait," she said. "That's it? That's the story?"

"Isn't it enough?"

"It's something all right. But I got to know—"

"What? What do you need to know?"

"Well. Did she walk on water?"

He smiled and lifted himself and kissed her, settled back. He looked off toward the low roof again and said, "When she got done preaching there was nothing but silence. Imagine that. A whole thousand or more people, most of them doubters a couple hours before and not a word from any of em. So she just stood and waited. Then, whatever it was broke the spell of her words, maybe a dog barking or a hungry baby squalling, whatever it was she spoke again. She thanked all of them for coming and wished them all to welcome Christ into their hearts. The old man told me it was silent again so much you could hear a watch tick in a man's pocket a dozen feet away. Like they was all holding their breath against what she might say next, as if most all of em was ashamed of calling her out in such a way. Which was when she spoke once more: She told em she'd welcome them to watch her walk on water. Said she was fearless about that as all other things. And those who required that of her would only have to meet back in that selfsame spot the second Sunday come January and she'd happy oblige them. Then she walked to her chay through the newfound silence and mounted up in and rode off."

"You ask me, she reminds me of Amos."

"How ever so?"

"He had that silver tongue. Could convince anyone of anything, leastways until they caught on to him. The few that did."

"I see what you're getting at. But it wasn't so. I guess you could say The Friend was the direct opposite of him. Never uttered a word, let alone a sentence or even a thought, that wasn't heartfelt and true. And that's the way I was raised."

She didn't say a word but pulled her hands behind her head and with her elbows lifted high she cracked her neck.

He said, "It's the only way I know how to live."

After a time she said, "These last days. You learned any other possible ways?"

327

He looked off where the light beat crippled through the chestnut leaves against the log-chinks and threw tattered beams on the faded and dirt-obscured patterns of the rugs. Then he said, "It's adding much to what I know."

She heaved a sigh and her ribcage rode her breasts up and down and she remained silent.

After a time more he said, "You reckon we should eat that rabbit?"

She rose out of the bed and stood looking down at him. A jet of air blew through the cabin and her skin prickled and she said, "I'm hungry always. More than I could count. I guess I always been that way. Eating rabbit seems a good idea."

FOURTEEN

FOR MOMENTS AUGUST struggled against the day, hazy gauze upon him, feeling he might press himself back into the dream seemingly yet there, awaiting his return. His wanting to return. She there also waiting, her long limbs, naked body, face and buttocks in the way of dreams both ably and strongly pressed against his own face. Her hair spread about her face, eyes laughing and full mouth meeting his. The rest of her also.

Then the day upon him, hot and late and he rose from his bed and pulled on clothes, almost trotting on his way downstairs, his urgency now for the work before him and came into the kitchen where she knelt before the hearth making fire, also late to rise and still in her nightgown of summer wash-faded gingham. Stretched down against her back and over her hips, her hair not yet braided and pinned up but flowing down along her bare arms and her own hot, caught-out face turned up to him. He went on roughly, his feet off-kilter, out into the yard and the waiting barns.

Where he milked and worked his other chores and carried his pails to the cooling well in the buttery and glanced up toward the road

where his cousin and his boys would be coming soon and throughout, bits and fleets of the dream came back over him, the ache also in
his loins and he stopped finally and looked back at the house where
Becca waited breakfast for him, dressed for the day now he was sure.
And so paused there in the buttery door, unable to walk those paces
to his own roof, his kitchen, and the girl from the dream waiting
inside. And it came to him that he'd grown old so young.

FIFTEEN

HE WOKE FROM a dreamless sleep, the basement already pale-lit with daylight, and he lay on the bunk blinking up at the ceiling, placing himself and then trying to recall when he'd last slept so deeply and untroubled and could not. Some months before the war, so long past he could not place a single one but rather the vague and general sense that such nights had once been his. He stretched and stood. Pushed through the opening at the bottom of the bars was a tin plate of food and a tin cup of coffee; he'd always been awake and pacing often for hours before the meal was brought.

He knelt and lifted the coffee first. It was still warm and he sipped and wondered if perhaps it had been the jailor entering and leaving that had stirred him from his sleep. The peace that had infused his sleep, that had made possible that sleep, returned and fell over him and he squatted and drank all but an inch of the coffee and for the first time in weeks enjoyed the warmth and vitality spreading through him. He set the remaining coffee on the floor and took up the plate, steadying it with one hand, and took up the fork and ate the two fried eggs with unbroken yolks atop a mound of cornmeal mush, pressing the fork sideways to spill the yolks and cut apart the whites to bits and stirring the cool eggs into the still-warm mush. It was good. Enough so he wished for salt but was grateful all the same. When the food was gone he finished the coffee and placed the cup upon the plate along with the fork and bent to slide them through the opening and walked to the corner and passed water into the slop bucket and then sat on the bunk, facing the cell front, the basement, the stairs. And waited.

As always when the jailor came down after the plate he came alone. When noon-dinner was delivered there were always two of them for it was then that his cell door was opened and his slop bucket exchanged for one intended to be clean—a crusted, foul wooden bucket, some few times sprinkled with a dust of lime and those times the one man held a short double-barrel shotgun while the other man did this job. The first time or so they'd asked Malcolm to bring the full bucket from the corner to the door of the cell so no man would have to enter, but he'd sat on his bunk or as often stood with his back to them at the rear of the cage, staring at the blocks of the basement wall. And so after, he guessed, a consultation with the sheriff, the one man had stood back leveling the gun at such a range that discharging a single round of buckshot would take his head off while the other came and went and never once even in his worst days had he so much as twitched for even then he was intent on his end and they soon enough came to realize he offered no threat but there was no dropping of the vigilance, nor did he expect any. Or care.

But now he rose from the bunk and walked to where the man was bent, picking up the empty plate and cup.

"Good morning."

The jailor tried to hide his surprise but the tin cup rattled on the plate. He did not respond but stepped back to place distance between them.

332

Malcolm said, "When Judge Gordon arrives, would you pass the message that I'd wish to speak with him? I'd be grateful if you would. Or do I have to speak with the sheriff first?"

The fellow cocked his head and a slight frown passed over his face before he composed himself. "The judge is already in his chambers."

"So early as this?"

The man said nothing but was intently studying Malcolm. He shrugged and said, "I'll tell the sheriff what you asked and he'll decide what to do. It might be a while before anyone can get down to you."

During the war he'd seen many men who held news or at least rumors of news and would speak in such a way as to convey that they did so, or to test if the bearer was not alone with that news, and so Malcolm understood this man. But all he said was, "I'm not going anywhere."

The man regarded him a long pause as if coming to a decision and then spoke. "I'll pass the message." He turned and crossed toward the stairs.

"I thank you."

The man glanced back, hesitated, and then turned again and went up the stairs. When the door opened it seemed there was a brief loud babble of voices but Malcolm could not say if it was different from any other day or if he was only noticing it for the first time. He went to the remainder of the bucket of fresh water that was brought in evenings and knelt to cup his hands and drink, then washed his hands and face best he could and combed out his hair and beard with his fingers.

He went back to the bunk and sat, his hands on his knees, as he watched the faint light grow slowly brighter in the high western windows.

He stood at the sound of the door and boot falls upon the stairs and watched as the judge was followed down by Enoch Stone. He kept his eyes on the judge, only once glancing at Stone as they came to a stop

333

now side by side some feet from the bars. Stone's clothing was dusty as if he'd been traveling for days and his face sagged, eyes circled dark with fatigue. Malcolm looked swiftly back at the judge, who was neat in his suit, his hair brushed down upon his shoulders and his face freshly shaven, eyes bright and alert.

The judge said, "You asked for me?"

"I did."

"Go ahead, then."

"May I ask a question before I get to my matter?"

"You may."

"This man." Without taking his eyes from the judge, he tilted his head to indicate Stone. "I never hired him."

"He's working in your interest."

"I'm sure he believes as much," Malcolm said. "But let me speak plainly. My understanding is that a man accused, such as I am, has a right to hire an attorney of his choice. Is that correct?"

"It is. Of course. Unless you can't afford one and then the court will appoint one for you."

"I may also act as my own attorney, is that not so?"

"Generally speaking, as judge, I try to discourage such a course. Few laymen have such knowledge of the law to undertake their own defense in a reasonable fashion. And as I said, he's working in your interest."

Malcolm nodded. "I can fire him?"

"I would not recommend it."

Malcolm paused and then said, "I've just fought a war over the idea of one man having full and total control over another. Without that other man's consent."

The judge paused and considered this. Enoch Stone remained silent. Malcolm waited, not taking his eyes from the judge.

Finally Judge Gordon said, "I take your point. Is that why you asked to see me? This morning?"

"It is not. But I'd not expected him to be with you."

"You wish to speak in confidence?"

"I do."

The judge turned to the man beside him and said, "Esquire, I ask you to leave. We can discuss this later."

Stone looked from the judge to Malcolm and back to the judge.

The judge said, "I have my own obligations and duties. And I'd dare say you need rest. I'll send word when I'm ready to speak with you." He turned back to Malcolm.

Stone paused, his face of a sudden deeply flushed. He said, "My intentions are only the best. Regardless of these sad events. Malcolm Hopeton—"

The judge interrupted: "Sir. There's been no shortage of foolery and I'd have it stop now. As should be apparent to you as well."

Enoch Stone regained himself, squared his shoulders and raised his chin to glance down his nose upon the caged man and lifted his eyebrows. He said, "You'll need me yet." Then turned on his heel away from the judge and made for the stairs.

Both the judge and Malcolm Hopeton listened to him go, listened for the door to open and shut above.

Malcolm stood silent.

The judge said, "You asked to speak with me and here I am. What would you say?"

"It's simple in my mind but grows complicated as I try to put voice to it."

The judge nodded. "Recall, I'm familiar with many of the details. Perhaps more than you're aware. So speak simply and I'll question as I need to."

"My wife," Malcolm said and stopped. Then went on. "I take full responsibility for my actions. I shall plead guilty to the murders."

"We can discuss your plea and the charges presently. I believe you were about to speak of your wife."

"She is—she was not the woman so many make her out to be."

The judge stroked his mustache with thumb and index finger of one hand. In a deferential tone he said, "Oft times there are aspects of a person we do not know. No mother's son is ever guilty being the most obvious example."

"Exactly. Almost."

"Go on."

"I gravely miscalculated Amos Wheeler. I'd never have left her had I an inkling of his true nature. This was my first mistake."

"You can assert that of him yet not allow the same possibility of your wife?"

"Yes. Yes, I most certainly can." He paused and went on. "I knew her true nature. She shared all of herself with me. It's difficult to speak of."

"Say what you will. There is nothing formal to this conversation. I'm listening and I'll advise. All of which falls within my purview. It's the difference between a judge and an attorney: I not only offer judgment according to the law, but I'm charged with making the points of the law clear to all who come before me. What they do with that knowledge is their business. Unless, in my view, they're going astray and then I reserve the right to counsel again. Is that clear to you, Malcolm Hopeton?"

"It seems generous of you."

"The law is generous. It is lawyers with their angles, hopes, dreams, wild expectations that make the law seem a rigid thing."

"We are gone afield from what I wished to say."

"You summoned me intending to right a wrong. You may be correct in wishing to do so, but it's my job to ensure you do so knowing the range of your options to achieve what you would. Let us return to the subject of your wife."

"Thank you. I wish only my chance to stand in a courtroom and speak of her, of all she carried into my life, what we made together that apart neither of us truly had—also of the ways I failed her, countless and horrible. Right up to that final wretched morning these few short weeks past. And why I ask for no pity, save for her. There are a multitude of stories and events that must be told, in order to correct the prevailing judgment of Bethany Hopeton. That is my only wish, to do so best I can. If I fail, the failure will be my lack of eloquence. But I'll not fail for lack of trying."

"And so you rebuke the efforts of Enoch Stone?"

"I do not know Stone. But his effort is rooted with her father, David Schofield. A man who never knew his daughter. To that statement I can fully swear and with great certainty."

The judge pulled his watch from his vest pocket and studied it. He replaced the watch and said, "You may be right. But let's speak of that man later. Let me understand fully: Your sole goal is to exonerate your wife, Bethany Schofield Hopeton, from the role most all people have determined heartily belongs to her?"

"I do. I shall. I care not what it costs me. She was not that woman."

"It might cost you your life, as you plan it now."

Malcolm paused and waited. He felt his heart beat strong in his chest. He answered, "I believe it should."

The judge held up a hand. "Allow me to explain. What you seek, correct me if I'm wrong, is an open venue to address the prevailing view of your wife's activities these past years, to bring your own account public, to make clear that you believe her to be a victim, rather than a collaborator, of Amos Wheeler. Am I correct so far?"

"I wish to make clear that my inaction, what I see now as a somewhat willful blindness, allowed me to pursue a course I was bent upon. Regardless, my inaction placed her in a great and terrible jeopardy. It's of vital importance that this truth be allowed to come out."

"Let me ask you again, because I seek to be certain of your intent: You will do this with the full understanding that it would mean your death."

Hopeton paused. Then said, "No man seeks his own death. In fact I welcomed it after my brutal attack upon her. But it came to me that in order to have the truth be told, I must face life, to not walk mutely to the gallows but to stand alive as I might and speak for her."

The judge nodded.

Malcolm said, "And you have allowed me to fire Enoch Stone. Who, perhaps well-meaning, was acting against the truth, in concert with Bethany's father."

The judge nodded again. Then said, "I know little of your relations with Mr. Schofield. But why would you suppose he'd do such a thing, if there was not truth to it?"

"I do not know him. He as much as cast her out once she found me. By her account he'd cast her out long ago. My understanding is these actions of his were a madness of another kind, one twisted by fear, some version of God, of the Lord, that blinded him to the most natural business of life. That is all I can fairly say about him; I could speak at greater length of my own experience but my only care is to shed clear light upon Bethany."

"I do believe you speak your true convictions. Now, if you will allow me to outline the steps you must take."

"If they don't suit my intentions, am I bound to them?"

"You're bound to nothing."

Malcolm waited, silent.

The judge said, "You need an attorney. You fired Enoch Stone and for reasons I'll disclose, that was the correct choice. You do not have acquaintance with a lawyer?"

"When I first returned from the war I'd thought of finding one. But I was attempting to set things right and I yet hoped Bethany would return to me. I already had an understanding of the truth of the matter; there was a young hired man—"

"Harlan Davis."

"He'd informed me of most all that had happened. But to answer your question, I have no attorney. My grandfather passed the farm to me by simple quit-claim deed before his death."

The judge nodded. "I can recommend a couple of lawyers who would stand well beside you. You will be charged with two counts of manslaughter and you will plead not guilty."

"No."

"Sir. Please allow me. As I said, you're bound to nothing. If you determine to not take my advice, that's your right."

The judge waited then and Malcolm stood in deep frown. Finally he said, "Go on."

"The first and most important consideration is this will allow you the venue you desire. You will be allowed to speak at any and all length. The county prosecutor will object; that's his job. But there are other factors to be considered as well. If you plead guilty to that or any greater charge, the jury will think you insane, for, as you yourself said, no man wishes to die. And that will cloud how they hear everything you have to say. Listen to the mad fool rant, would, in my experience, sum up what most will think. You'd find sympathy, but more for you than for your wife. Do you understand that?"

Malcolm held his frown, his lips pressed tight.

The judge went on. "Juries are strange things, made of individuals but tending to flow together in a current. But there's more to support the plea I suggest."

"I truly only care for the truth of my wife to be known, to counter the rumors and ill talk that have circulated about her, that her father would perpetuate."

"Well." The judge cleared his throat and again stroked his mustache, studying briefly one well-polished boot tip, then looked again upon Malcolm. "Allow me to conclude in my own fashion. The hired boy, Harlan Davis. He also would testify to the events that transpired while you were at the war. Correct?"

"Yes."

"And he's already told me what he saw that unfortunate morning."

"I was insane then."

"Not a term you should use. Tell me. Did Amos Wheeler employ that derringer pistol upon you?"

"No. I'm sure Bethany was terribly frightened just by riding in. I can't imagine what they were thinking but Amos Wheeler believed he could talk himself out of anything."

"I'm too well familiar with the Wheeler family and their particular belief that whatever the world held, was theirs by simple right of existence. So she fired the gun."

"I can't see how such action, even undertaken in fear of the moment, would encourage people to believe my account of her. I fear you are going afield with this notion of yours."

The judge sighed and said, "After he came and spoke with you, Dr. Ogden came to my chambers."

Malcolm gazed blank upon the judge, then dropped his chin to his chest and covered his face with his hands.

"It is a terrible business," the judge said softly, kindly. "But, you see, in order for people to believe you, they need to understand all of it. As much as you can stand and perhaps a good bit more. But, as you imply, you cannot save her from all that, now. You can only save how you understand her, and how people judge her. Which is your intent, is it not?"

Malcolm raised his head and gazed silent upon the man before him. Then made the smallest of nods.

The judge said, "Unraveling the truth, to find justice, is seldom anything but a messy and hurtful business. But it is a fight worth fighting. An ordeal worth undertaking. Don't you agree?"

Malcolm waited silent. The only answer he could give.

The judge said, "This afternoon, after you've had an opportunity to mull all this, I'll send down a lawyer to speak with you. Peter Marks is his name and he's a good man. If you agree to have him represent you, he'll not attempt to turn you into a monkey to his organ grinder as some lawyers do, but listen carefully to you at every turn. You could not ask for more."

"I have to think about all this."

"You do. And now, I regret to inform you, two days ago your father-in-law, David Schofield, took his own life."

Malcolm paused, then closed his eyes, rubbed his forehead and cheeks with both hands, his breath sharp and shallow.

"He'd spoken with Enoch Stone the evening before," the judge said. "He'd voiced doubt about his testimony against his own daughter's character. Stone says he could not determine if Schofield was speaking from shame or self-blame. He also claims he had no idea David was so untethered."

Malcolm was quiet a time, studying those high windows beyond the judge's left shoulder, then looked at the judge and said, "I hated him for the self-doubt he bestowed upon his daughter. And now, I only pity him, for all he lost."

The judge took a respectful pause and then said, "And so my final words to you this morning. I leave you where I began. How you plead? The choice is yours."

He went and sat on the bunk. After a time, aloud, he cursed God. Then he thought, It's nothing to do with God, it's what men do in the name of God, in their craze of wanting to be known and loved by God.

Of what they fear.

SIXTEEN

THEY WERE AWAKE in the pale pearl light of dawn and she stepped from the bed and crouched by the hearth to stir ashes to find coals, adding a handful of sticks to set the coffeepot to boil. He watched her squatted thus, studying the knobs of her shoulders and shoulder blades protruding as if wings might break through her skin, the slender waist and spread of her hips, the knots of her spine down her back, her long bunched crouching thighs, the muscles of her calves and her dirty bare feet. Aware he was etching her to memory.

She came back to the bed to wait the coffee. From the woods came the mewls of doves, the staccato drill of a woodpecker, a plaintive phoebe and the harsh snarls of a crow threading through the trees. He reached for her and she came against him to kiss his mouth and fondle his hair and then rolled away and said, "No, sweet boy, we're done with that. This is the new day before us, now."

He flopped back and a hiss of air escaped his lungs, pent up and irksome and he knew it wasn't fair but couldn't help himself.

She heard something of this and followed after him, pushing the one blanket free and moving down along him as she placed one finger gently upon his lips to still his words and then did the one thing she hadn't these past days, the one thing he'd someway feared and knew she knew the reason why; and so after a few minutes he relaxed against the bed and took her hand in his and lifted it free of his mouth and held it and rested his other hand within her hair.

They drank coffee and then walked in the broken sunlight to the pool, where they washed with a slip of hard soap, small bubbles of froth spewing away, the smell of flowers rising from their skin. They sat a short time on the pebble beach that caught the early sun and so dried and neither spoke. Returning to the cabin, she stopped and told him to wait and walked off into a grove of young woods down a slight ravine and came back leading a black horse with a saddle thrown loose upon his back.

She cut the last of the bacon into thick slabs and fried it in its own grease, and they ate that with the last of the bread and several cups of bitter coffee each. When they were done eating she took the tin cups and plates, the spider, and the coffeepot and tossed them off into the brush beyond the chestnut trees. Now he was only watching and she went about her work without explanation or comment.

She had a set of saddlebags of good size that she placed upon the table and opened one side. She laced herself into a corset, pulled on stockings and bloomers, and then dressed in the riding habit she'd been wearing when he first came upon her. A couple of times during this she glanced at Harlan but said nothing.

She opened the other side of the saddlebags and lifted out a wide belt of fine leather and a folded document sealed with a blood-crimson blot of wax. She opened the buttons of her habit and worked the belt around her waist, snugged it tight and rebuttoned the habit, then fitted the vest and buttoned it. With her fingers at work she glanced at him and said, "That's a money belt I got hid there, Mr. Dying of Curiosity."

A sudden fool, he said, "It looks good on you."

She looked at him and arched an eyebrow and said, "Can you saddle a horse?"

"A course I can." His face was hot and he guessed some shade of red.

"Not just tightening the girths. There's a scrap of burlap behind the door he's familiar with and I want you to rub him down all over and talk to him while you do it. He's not been ridden in days and needs a gentle hand."

"I can do that just fine—"

"His name's Pepper. Once he knows you, he'll eat outta your hand without the least nip and carry you to Kingdom Come, you ask."

He said, "A horse knows its name and how it's treated, also. I'm happy to gear him up for you. But I'm wondering—what's the plan, we get to town? I know what I have to do but I don't have the first idea what you're thinking."

"All the better that way, Harlan," she said, her tone but not voice raised a bit. "We got time to talk on the road but for now I've got some more work here. Could you just see to the horse, please?"

He stood looking at her a moment and then found the wadded burlap smelling of horse sweat and dust and went out the door to where the horse edged about among the chestnut trunks, the saddle and pad on the ground, the horse watching him come, eyes rolling and a bit of froth at its mouth. He stood and spoke to it and spoke again and the horse turned to face him and he opened the burlap and scrunched it together again and kept talking as he moved a step at a time toward the horse. Once the horse bunched low to bolt and Harlan only kept talking and the horse shivered and settled upright, then jerked its head against a deerfly. And then Harlan had the burlap against the horse's withers, the other hand rubbing about the halter and his mouth close to the near ear and was still talking to him.

As they went along, both Harlan and the horse watched as Alice Ann came from the cabin, carrying a bridle headstall and reins. She said, "I knew you was a hand with horses."

344

"Me and Pepper been coming to understand each other."

"I guessed you would." She handed him the bridle and he held it against his side a moment as the horse cupped its ears forward and nosed the bridle. Harlan fitted the bridle to the horse's head and slid a finger into the side of the horse's mouth where the gap of teeth was and Pepper slipped the bit in easy as if eating an apple from his hand. Then the horse turned its head as if appraising the upended saddle and thick felted pad.

Alice Ann said, "You drop his reins on the ground he'll stand like a statue while you finish him up."

"I heard about that trick with a riding horse," Harlan said. But Alice Ann was off at the woodpile the far edge of the clearing, pulling forth small dried branches and looking at the lesser splits of kindling wood, selecting as she went until she had a considerable pile all of fine small wood that would not make a fire, even all put together at once, of any consequence. But she gathered it up and carried it inside.

Harlan rubbed over the horse once more with the sacking, taking the easy pleasure of working with a good, smart horse. He stepped away and untangled the pad from the straps of the saddle and brushed both sides clean and set it up high on the horse's withers. He lifted the saddle and studied it a moment until he knew how all the gear worked and placed it gentle as could be upon the pad, let the stirrups slide down either side and then eased both saddle and pad downward a scant inch or two, making sure the hair of the horse's hide lay flat beneath the saddle and pad. No telling, he thought, how far this feller will have to run later this day.

Alice Ann came from the cabin and looked at him but went on back to the woodpile, which she studied, and then walked on off out of the clearing. Soon she returned laboring under a load of a dozen long snapped-off branches of deadwood, each a couple or more stout inches around and six or seven feet long. She glanced at him as she passed but went on without words within the cabin.

345

He walked the horse in a circle and waited.

After a time she came out again, this time carrying her saddlebags and the document in her other hand. She set down the saddlebags on the woods floor at the edge of the grove and slipped the document within one side.

She turned and studied the cabin, casting her eyes not only over it but all around—at the big trees, the fire ring of blackened stones, the woodpile, back to the cabin again. She stared long upon that building and Harlan watched her and was silent, waiting.

Finally she looked to him. "Why don't you come in, one last time?" Without waiting she walked inside.

He spoke to the horse and then walked to the low, wide door framed with old peeled log uprights, the bark also long since fallen from the log walls. He stepped in and stopped.

A fire burned in the hearth and then about a foot away there was laid a small windrow of heaped kindling wood that stretched across the floor to underneath the table, where the row met a larger pile of wood. Likewise the tabletop held an even higher stack of wood, layered neatly and made so as to fall inward as it burned. Rising from within that stack were the long poles that spread outward up among the timbers of the rafters like an Indian tepee frame turned upside down. The chairs were leaned in against the table also.

Alice Ann squatted next to the hearth sipping the last bottle of beer. Beside her was the final stack of kindling, enough to breach the gap between the fire and the beginning of the row of wood.

She lifted the bottle and squinted over the top of it toward Harlan. "What do you think?" she said. "Should I take away the chairs?"

He studied the setup and said, "You're worried the table will burn too fast before the roof catches."

"I don't think it will. But I'd hate to make the effort and just end up with some ruined furniture and scorched rugs."

He shook his head. "That tabletop will take some effort to burn through and you want a hot fire: Those chairs might just do the trick. Taking em away, you risk the poles not catching, or the roof."

"Good," she said. "That's what I thought." She took a swallow of beer and motioned him closer. He remained where he was.

"What is it?" she said.

"You want to burn the place down, it's easy enough to do. Why set it up so slow and risk not having it take? A gust through the door or a handful of sticks falling the wrong way could end the whole thing, the fire not even getting to the table."

"Because I want it gone. But I don't want to make a quick alarm out here. We laid a fire sure to burn fast and we'd not even make the road before there was smoke billowing up from the woods—all these blankets and rugs and such, even the roof has enough moss on it to make a dark smoke. I want it gone but I want us gone also. So we leave a little fire that becomes a mite larger and then burns on and gets the roof frame going from underneath and it could be as much as a hour before it burns through. That's what I want. And I got my sticks laid right."

"You do," Harlan said. "We shut the door as we go, that'll keep a stray breeze from mucking about. But you want the fireplace burned down a bit first, so there's not too much draw, there."

"You'd ever of been here on a winter night you'd know that chimney don't draw so good: nights where there was more smoke inside than going up the chimney. Amos Wheeler was a wizard at many things but not a hand to build. Besides, you look close, this little fire is going quick, just enough to light the kindling when I add it. Which I'm about to do and then we walk out."

"All right."

She paused then and looked about her and spat in the dead ash spread on the hearth. She lifted the bottle again and said, "You want to have a swallow of this before we go?"

"I don't believe so. I want my head clear as it can be."

She laughed and chucked the bottle underhand at the wall of open cupboards, where it landed and caused a rattle of collapse among the tinware and pots. She said, "Let's go then."

She rose up and turned and lifted handfuls of the wood from the trail upon the floor toward the burning fire, stopping a couple of times to adjust the new stacking, then, with both hands full of the last of the kindling and a six-inch gap between the fire and the waiting wood, paused and looked up at the roof and all around, seeing there what she would or had no choice but to see one last time. Then she turned to Harlan and said, "Wait for me outside."

He was holding the horse when, faster then he'd expected, she stepped through the door and pulled it shut behind her. He could hear a faint popping and hiss but nothing more than a fire burning in the hearth would make. A pale plume came from the top of the chimney but was lost in the air and shadows as it rose into the chestnut grove. She walked to her saddlebags and lifted them and tied them in place. She came and took the reins from him and kissed the horse upon the nose and began walking, leading the horse and not looking back. Harlan right beside her.

They came out upon the road and stopped. He held her stirrup as she stepped up into the saddle, the horse dancing a bit sideways until she curbed the bit back and settled her seat against the horse and he felt it and came to a full stop. Both she and Harlan looked first up and down the road and Harlan realized they were closer to town than he'd guessed, less than a half hour at a man's pace walking, then also back toward where they'd come but all he saw was the track between two high stands of corn and then the distant crown of trees that marked the ravine and woodlot around it where the cabin stood. The heat stood shimmering over the fields and the tree crowns were murky under white sunlight, and if any smoke rose there it was pale and diffused into the day.

He turned back to study the road again, fearful of coming across anyone, unsure what waited him this day and steeled to do his best, when she spoke.

"There it is."

He looked to where she sat on the horse and followed her turned head and saw the least coil of inky smoke rising from the woods. And it came to him that Amos Wheeler was dead, truly dead and gone.

He said, "We best walk on. It would help, one of us had a watch." And turned and started down the road toward town.

She caught up fast and then held the horse back alongside him and she said, "Have you ever owned a watch?"

"No. I have not."

"You ever been late? Anywhere?"

"No. Not that, either."

"I didn't think so. Besides. I have a watch. Do you want to know what o'clock it is?"

"It's about half-past nine."

"I believe you're about right." She made no effort to produce a watch but rode along.

He said, "I'm going to be most of a hour early."

She glanced down at him. "What's your plan?"

He did not look at her but kept walking. He said, "I'm going to tell em exactly the sort of man Amos was. I'd tell em everything I seen, everything I heard, everything that happened. They'd at least have to listen to it, in court like that. Wouldn't they?"

"I guess so. But you know, they do that, they're also going to be able to ask any questions of you they want. Isn't that what made you run off in the first place?"

He was quiet but did glance at her and she was waiting for his eyes and nodded at him. He wasn't sure what she was saying yes to, then did know.

He said, "Enoch Stone has it in his head that Bethany Hopeton did something to me, or some such a thing. But *she* never did. And I can look him or anyone else in the eye and swear that's the truth."

Quiet a moment but for the creak of saddle leather and the chip of the bit in the horse's mouth. The soft pad of Harlan's feet in the dust. Quiet enough so he looked up at her. She said, "I know you can."

He nodded and looked again upon the road and they went on for a bit. Finally he looked up at her and said, "I'd be lying I said I wasn't nervous."

"You'll be fine. You'll be grand."

"I hope so."

"You will. You are."

With that they went on along the road that was dropping on the slight grade toward the canopied village below. The upper branch of the lake lay to the west in a long expanse with small white-capped waves, the breeze moving up the lake. One of the steamers was beating south toward the end of the Bluff that rose from the water and on the Bluff the farm fields and woodlots and gorges were outlined clear as a stencil in the morning air, the fields varying greens and golds as they held hay or pasture or ripe grains one sort or another. The thin-burnt look of grain stubble where the oats or barley had been cut. A pair of hawks rode the air rising off the Bluff and from the village below a bell tolled twice and then was silent. The spotty rise of dogs answering the bell rose and trailed away.

Harlan looked back up the road, worried that by burning down Amos Wheeler's shack they'd set the woods on fire, hot and dry as the days had been. But they'd crested down and could no longer see that place to the east of the crown of land and no pulse of dark smoke rose from over the edge of the eastern earth. At most a thin smudge against the white pale thrown down by an engorged and desolate sun. Something, perhaps. Or nothing but vapors rising.

Offhand best he could, speaking to the dust about his feet, he said, "So what are you going to do?"

"I thought I'd go to Saratoga. It's barely high season there and I know a couple of people. It would be a good start. Nobody that matters has ever laid eyes upon me but I know those sorts and how it works. I think I could make a go of things there. I suspect I could make a go of things most anywhere. Don't you think?"

Of a sudden he was miserable and shuffled the dust up with his feet. He said, "I guess so."

She rode along beside him and didn't say a word.

They'd started down the residential street toward the village when she stopped the horse. They were beside the house where Harlan had darted down the side of the carriage barn and into the woods after fleeing Enoch Stone and so after Alice Ann halted the horse, Harlan looked around, half expecting that man to materialize, and when he did not, looked up at Alice Ann.

"Now, then." The horse stood easily, glancing around as a horse will but steady and patient as Alice Ann twisted around and opened the near saddlebag and lifted out the waxed document. She straightened forward and held it and studied it a moment.

Then she looked down at Harlan. "Do you have a dollar?"

He almost asked why when he caught himself and only said, "I'm sorry. I don't have a thin dime. I was working afore I was started on this that ended me up here and I'm not in the habit of carrying cash money about me in the field. Are you short of money?"

She smiled and it was a smile closer to sadness than mirth but also a kind smile and she said, "I shouldn't have asked that; I knew better." She dug in a pocket of her habit and pried free a Liberty dollar and handed it down to him.

"What's this?" he said.

"Call it a loan. Now hand it back to me."

"Why?"

"Just do it."

He did. She pushed the coin back in her habit and swung down from the horse and held out the document and waited until he took it from her. She said, "Break the seal and read that."

He did and then looked up at her. "I don't understand this."

"There's nothing to understand. You just bought a horse. A damn good one, too. If you don't mind my saying so."

She'd dipped her head away as she said this but not quick enough to keep him from hearing the break of her voice or seeing her eyes in sudden liquid flitting blinks.

He looked at the paper again, a bill of sale, simple as any could be but solid nonetheless and there below the jagged rough scrawl of her own name was his own, in tight up-and-down loops that were not close to what he'd drilled over and over in school or home at Albert Ruddle's table with that man or his own sister leaning over him, but instead a making of his name done only as differently as possible from her own style; and Harlan felt the soft blow of tenderness as he realized the work this woman had undertaken for him, likely furtive while he'd slept, day or night, these past days.

He said, "Why are you giving me your horse?"

"Let's walk on down," she said. And stepped off, both arms swinging free. The black horse followed her, then paused, the reins still looped upon its withers. Harlan stepped up and pulled the reins over the horse's head and caught up to Alice Ann, the horse happy now to trail his people.

She said, "I thought you might need him, however things work out. One way or another."

"But how are you going to get to Saratoga?"

They were striding at a good pace. She shot her chin toward him and said, "You don't like him?"

"He's the best I ever seen."

352

"That's right. He'll do you well—whatever you need."

They walked on a bit more. They passed a house where an old man sat out on a porch in a rocking chair, wearing a rusted black Sunday suit but bare-headed. He was reading a newspaper but lowered it so his eyes dipped above and followed them a moment. Then he lifted it and was hidden again.

They were most at the end of the residential street and could see the bulk of Burketts' mill rising, the sharp angle into the mercantile blocks, when quiet and easy Harlan said, "You ain't going to Saratoga, are you?"

"Whatever makes you say such a thing as that?"

"Because you sold me your horse."

Alice Ann glanced at him and made a snorted laugh and said, "One day, you're married, remember this: You out-think your wife, it's not always the best thing to let her know it."

"You ain't answered my question."

She walked on a bit, ahead of him now.

He stopped. Because he was holding the horse's reins, the horse stopped as well. She walked on a couple of paces before she felt the silence behind her and turned, looked at him, and shook her head. But she was smiling.

She said, "I'm going to catch the first boat I can down the Outlet Canal and stop in Dresden to get my trunk from the hotel and say good-bye to Bertha Pinckney. Then the noon boat to Geneva and the train from there overnight to New York City. I got no interest in going to Saratoga. It's too close to Utica for me and neither place is one I want to be. I'm not looking to run into a single living soul that knows the first thing about me cept what I choose to tell em. I'm not exactly sure what comes next for me, but for a long list of Will Nots. Which I think is a pretty good place to start from and I think New York City might be a good place to do that. Still, anybody here asks, I'd appreciate it you said Saratoga. And I know you will. But I'm happy having you know otherwise. Is that enough for you?"

He nodded and said, "That sounds sensible. Shall we walk on down and see what we shall see?" And he walked off, toward her, the Pepper horse following. But she'd heard the quaver in his voice and as he stepped to move around her she also turned and fell into step beside him and reached and for a half-dozen steps squeezed tight his hand and then let it go. But not before he'd squeezed back.

They passed the steamboat landing and went along toward the canal. Behind them rose the three stories of the mill, the buggy works and tannery sprawling alongside in the shade of the high banks from the Outlet gorge. Three barges were tied up and being loaded with sacks of grain from heavy dray wagons, stevedores pushing hand trucks up the narrow gangways where crew members stacked the sacks chest-high front to rear. Teams of mules in harness stood along the towpath, flicking rattails against flies. A light buggy passed them and pulled up, the driver climbing out to hand sacks of mail up to the captain of the lead barge. This gave them a purpose to stop.

He turned to her but she walked to the horse and unhitched her saddlebags and hoisted them over her shoulder. She walked back and kissed him before he knew she was going to. She said, "I ain't never said good-bye and won't start now."

"Alice Ann."

She shook her head. "Go on. Get up on him. Don't even think of kissing me again. Last thing you'd need is someone seeing that."

He said her name again.

"Harlan," she said. "Think of me time to time." Then she turned and began walking down the landing.

He stepped into the saddle and nudged the horse with his heels and caught up alongside her and looked down and said, "You be careful, you hear?"

She smiled at him and said, "I think I done all right so far. You get on now. Go. Put your mind where it needs to be."

She walked off and passed around a full wagon and out of sight. Then she reappeared the other side and wended through the press of the loading and made for the first boat.

He turned the horse and rode back beyond the steamboat landing toward the reed bed that ran across the head of the lake, where he turned the horse and sat, waiting and watching. Even this short a distance the figures moving around the barges now seemed small and he peered toward the first boat as a team of mules was brought up and hitched to the towline, men working to loosen the heavy hawsers and set the barge free upon the still water. Then he saw her, a faint figure snug between the load and the rail, looking away, downstream toward Dresden, and he sat the horse and knew she would not look back, and knew also however his life came to pass it would not be the same, this emptiness falling within atop the lovely fullness that was Alice Ann Labidee, how she would be within him there, then, forever.

When the barge was gone from sight he turned the horse again and a pinwheel of grackles burst from the reeds and spun outward toward the lake and he watched them, the slant of the sun on the water bright as the blade of a knife.

He kneed the horse and they went up the hill toward town, on toward the courthouse.

Acknowledgments

For their friendship, support, and encouragement beyond all reasonable expectations, I'd like to thank Sally Hostetler, Dan and Karen Morgan, Jean and Wendy Palthy, Henry Lyman & Noële Sandoz, Rob and Petra McCarron, and Michaela Findeis. My mother, Patricia Adams Lent, continues to offer her deepest faith on all levels.

For Sally Davis, an old and dear friend. By birthright, and by how she leads her life, she gives proof to August's prediction for the endurance of the legacy of The Public Friend.

Anton Mueller understood the vision and with grace and wisdom helped me to distill it toward the novel it became.

Howard Frank Mosher and Henry Lyman read early drafts and provided keen insights and enthusiasm. In addition, I'm indebted to Howard for providing the inspiration for Amos Wheeler.

For more than a quarter century of friendship and quiet advocacy, I bow to Jim Harrison.

My English Setter, Bella, offered solace and joy when I needed it and when I didn't.

My daughters, Esther and Clara, are the greatest pleasures of my life. As often as I'm the rock around which their waters swirl, they keep me tethered to this earth.

Finally, and always, my great love and fellow adventurer on this journey, Marion Walton Lent.

357

A Note on the Author

Jeffrey Lent was born in Vermont and grew up there and in western New York State, on dairy farms. His first novel, *In the Fall,* was an international bestseller and a *New York Times Book Review* Notable Book for 2000. His other novels are *Lost Nation, A Peculiar Grace* and *After You've Gone.* Lent lives with his wife and two daughters in central Vermont.

jeffreylent.com